Also by Ambrose Parry

The Way of All Flesh

THE ART OF DYING

AMBROSE PARRY

BLACKTHORN

This paperback edition published in 2021 by Black Thorn,
an imprint of Canongate Books

First published in Great Britain and the USA in 2019 by Canongate Books Ltd,
14 High Street, Edinburgh EH1 1TE

Distributed in the USA by Publishers Group West

blackthornbooks.com

1

British Library Cataloguing-in-Publication Data
A catalogue record for this book is available on
request from the British Library

ISBN 978 1 78689 673 5

Typeset in Van Dijck by Palimpsest Book Production Ltd,
Falkirk, Stirlingshire

Printed and bound in Great Britain by Clays Ltd, Elcograf S.p.A.

MIX
Paper from
responsible sources
FSC® C018072

PROLOGUE

here is not a woman in this realm who does not understand what it is to be afraid. No, not even she who reigns over us, for she was not born sovereign. She was born a girl, and that is why I can be sure that even she has known the fear and the helplessness of being subject to man's dominion. Every woman has felt the fear that derives from her own weakness before men whose greater power derives from a stature that is not merely physical.

Many men have held power over me. They were not great men. Oftentimes they were not even strong men. For in this world, you need be neither of those things to exercise your will upon the weak and helpless. Or at least upon those who have come to believe that they are weak and helpless.

In my life I have learned much about treachery and deceit, but surely the cowardliest trick of all is that of persuading someone that they have no power when you know the opposite to be true.

In order to survive, it is thus vital that a woman should learn to assuage her fear; she must recognise and harness her power. But this must be done with subtlety. Without intimidation. Without overt threat. It is the lot of remarkable women that the world will not know our names: that we might not take the true plaudits for our achievements, though they outstrip the deeds of men.

We must exercise our power unseen. As women we may not venture forth alone beyond the dusk, but I do not speak of time when I suggest that we must operate in the twilight. I speak of the interstices, the places in between darkness and light, the blind spots in men's vision.

You wish to know how I could have done what I did, how I could have taken so many lives without arousing the merest suspicion. The answer lies within yourselves. It is easy to hide in the plain sight of those who do not consider your presence worthy of notice.

1849

BERLIN

ONE

e could feel warm blood upon his face. He could see blood upon steel, upon cloth, upon the walls and upon the ground. But what mattered was that blood still pumped beneath his breast.

Will Raven caught his breath and steadied himself. He heard footsteps slapping the flagstones as his assailants disappeared into the darkness of the winding passage, the sound slightly muffled by the shot still ringing in his ears. There were sweet smells on the breeze, a bakery preparing its pastries for the morning's sale. Such warmth in the night air had seduced him into dropping his guard. He would not have walked so freely under darkness in Edinburgh, where even on the most drunken night he remained soberly alert to what might lie around every corner. Here in Prussia that vigilance had become distracted by how different the place felt.

They had been attacked as they walked down Konigstrasse, a broad avenue leading from the expanse of Alexanderplatz across the Spree to the Konigliche Schloss. A castle in the centre of the city was at once a reminder of where he had come from and a stark illustration of his distance from it. With its striking green cupola and rigid geometry, it was hard to imagine a more vivid contrast to the grim barracks atop the old volcano at the end of the High Street back home. But even here, the widest avenues were still transected by dark and narrow passageways, and it appeared that what lurked there was the same the world over.

Three masked men had set upon them, emerging from the shadows where they had lain in wait. One of them demanded money. His German had been strangely accented but the instruction was clear enough. However, one of his comrades had evidently decided it would be easier to raid the pockets of the dead. A pistol was drawn and everything thereafter was a blur.

Fate had turned upon a single stroke of a knife. Few surgeons could boast of such an outcome. This thought passed in a fleeting moment of relief before he was overtaken by a terrifying new fear: that there would be yet a greater price to pay for cheating his destiny.

Raven was a man haunted by the premonition that he would die by violent hands in just such a dark and squalid alley. It was a vision born in Edinburgh on a cold, wet night in 1847, two years before, when he believed he was about to meet his end. He had survived, but the vision had haunted him ever since; not so much out of a fear of death, but of not having made something of his life. He worried that it was a path he was fitted for: that his high aspirations were mere delusion, and that in his essence he was the kind of man who *would* end up dead in an alley.

He turned and looked to the mouth of the passage. He could see Henry slumped against the wall, half visible beneath the light of a street lamp. It felt like the report was still bouncing back and forth between the walls, but really it was just bouncing around inside his skull. His memory of the last few moments was a blur. He recalled the familiar crunch of fist upon bone, Henry being spun by a punch and his head striking the wall. The raising of a pistol; Raven lunging to deflect the arm that held it. A gunshot. Then they had run, and Raven had chased.

Raven hurried to his fallen friend and crouched before him. He lifted his chin to look at his face, upon which blood was running in streams. Happily, his eyes were open, though not exhibiting their usual focused scrutiny.

'Where are they?' Henry asked.

'Fled. Are you hurt? Your face is bloody.'

'I could say the same. This is just a scalp wound. They bleed out of all proportion. Think I struck my leg on something on the way down, though. That hurts more. What about the ladies?'

Raven looked down the street, where he saw Liselotte and Gabriela by a fountain on Schlossplatz. He had yelled at them to run when the attack started, but they hadn't got far. These things were always over far quicker than one realised. Events that seem an hour's battle pass in the blink of an eye to those merely observing. They had stopped and were looking back towards where Henry had fallen.

Raven attempted to help him to his feet, at which point Henry howled.

'Gods!'

They both looked down, seeing a glistening darkness on Henry's thigh. Instinctively Raven put a hand to it, whereupon Henry howled twice as loud.

'I think you've been shot.'

Henry's expression was a mixture of pain and confusion.

'How did he manage to shoot me in the front of the thigh? I had my back to him and was in the process of bouncing face-first off the wall when he pulled the trigger.'

'An unfortunate ricochet,' Raven replied, conscious that it could have been so much worse. He was sure the coward holding the pistol had been aiming for Gabriela when Raven grabbed his arm.

Liselotte and Gabriela had hurried back to assist, concern on both their faces.

'We heard the shot,' Gabriela said. 'Which of you was hit?'

Raven looked at her quizzically, thinking the answer obvious: the one who is bleeding. Then he put a hand to his face. There was blood spattered upon it, and all over the sleeve of his right arm.

'This is Henry's,' he told her. Not entirely the truth, nor entirely a lie. 'He was struck in the leg.'

'We must get him to a surgeon,' Liselotte said, urgency in her tone.

'I *am* a surgeon,' Henry reminded her. 'Just get me back to Schloss Wolfburg and I can assess the damage.'

Raven ripped off the bloodied sleeve of his shirt and tied it tight around Henry's thigh to staunch the flow. With support on either side he was able to hobble on one leg. They were not far from the apartments they shared on Jagerstrasse.

They had been on their way back there when they were set upon. Perhaps they had been assumed to be rich travellers from overseas. If so, Raven would accept it as a compliment that someone thought he looked sufficiently respectable, but though they were travellers from overseas, he and Henry were anything but rich. They were studying at the Charité Hospital and had been there for two months, following a stay in Leipzig. Before that they had been in London, Paris and Vienna.

Raven opened the door to the apartments and began lighting the lamps as Liselotte and Gabriela helped Henry inside.

'Get him to the bedroom,' Liselotte urged.

'Words spoken with a familiar insistence,' Raven said with measured impropriety.

Liselotte tutted. She had been around them long enough not to expect better.

In truth, after what had just happened, Raven wasn't feeling inclined to give rein to his impish nature, but he wished to keep his friend's spirits up.

'No,' Henry objected. 'The light is better here. And I need to sit up.'

They helped him to a couch by the fireplace in the central room.

'Bring in all the lamps.'

Henry let out an agonised moan as Raven pulled off his trousers, the pain starting to overwhelm him. Shock and urgency had muffled the worst of it at first, but now he was being spared nothing.

Henry examined the wound, probing with delicate fingers. He looked at Raven, who was holding a lamp over his thigh.

'The ball did not go through. It's not deep but it's stuck in there.'

He was wincing with every word. Sweating. Raven knew what was coming; had known since they discovered the wound.

'I'm afraid I'm going to have to ask you to oblige me, old friend.'

'Ah, but what is it your esteemed Professor Syme maintains? Obstetricians ought not to be carrying out surgery.'

'And how does your esteemed Professor Simpson counter? We are all licentiates of the Royal College of Surgeons, are we not?'

'Very well. It would appear that I have little choice in the matter.'

Henry lay back upon the couch, resting his head, then let out another groan.

'What? I haven't even started yet.'

'I just remembered I left my instruments at the hospital. Do you have your own?'

Raven masked his feelings with a smile as he patted the pocket of his coat, inside which sat his knife.

'And more importantly, do you have chloroform?'

'No. You'll just have to tolerate it.'

Raven was echoing the words Henry once used when he had been called upon to stitch Raven's cheek. His hand went to the scar as he spoke, by way of reminding him. Henry looked despondent.

'I jest,' Raven said. 'Gabriela, would you fetch my bag from the bedroom?'

'Thank you,' said Henry. 'It's not so much for the pain, as to spare me the greater agony of witnessing your ham-fisted butchery upon my leg.'

'Oh, don't be so precious. You have another.'

Raven pulled the knife from his pocket. Henry's eyes were immediately drawn to the blade, noticing that it was blood-smeared. Raven hoped that in his delirium he did not think to wonder how.

'I hope you're going to wash that thing first. Remember Semmelweis.'

Henry was referring to a doctor he had spoken to in Vienna. Semmelweis had published a paper examining the far higher death rate of maternity patients on a ward staffed by medical students compared to one staffed by midwives. He maintained that this was because the students were coming directly from the dissection room without washing their hands, postulating that morbid material was being transferred from the students to the patients. When he made the students wash their hands in chlorinated water, the death rate went down. Despite this, Semmelweis was having difficulty convincing his colleagues that he was right and was venting his frustrations at anyone who would listen. Henry had proven a sympathetic ear.

Raven did not need to be lectured on this subject. For years Simpson had been teaching his students that puerperal fever was a disease transmitted from one patient to another via the attending doctor or midwife.

He bade Liselotte fill some jugs with water and tear up some sheets to make bandages. While she obliged, Raven prepared the chloroform, asking Gabriela to pay close attention in case he required her to administer more while he worked on Henry's leg.

Raven shaped a small piece of muslin into a cone and proceeded to carefully angle the bottle so that the liquid fell onto the cloth in small drips. He could not help but think of how Dr Simpson's discovery had preceded him on all his travels. Chloroform was transforming surgery, its use spreading fast. In London he had heard John Snow lecture on the importance of precision and control in the dosage. Raven had then witnessed him demonstrate his vaporiser device, invented for the purpose of administering a quantifiable amount of chloroform. Tonight in Berlin he would be relying on an untrained assistant dropping the liquid from a bottle in poor light, and all of them half drunk.

'The drops must be small,' he stressed to Gabriela. 'So that he does not inhale too much.'

'Right now I'm concerned with inhaling too little.'

Raven held the cone above Henry's face.

'And take care not to let it touch his skin. It is an irritant and apt to leave a mark.'

'Much like yourself,' Henry added pointedly. He was of the belief that Raven had a gift for attracting trouble.

'I had no role in bringing down those men upon us.'

'And once again, here I am, in your company in the bloody aftermath of a fight.'

'Maybe you are the one who courts mayhem and you are merely fortunate to have me on hand to assist. Have you thought of it that way?'

'Not once. But often have I said you'd be the death of me.'

Raven searched his memory.

'You have never once said that.'

'No,' he admitted, 'but I must have thought it. So please prove me wrong. And don't forget to wash the knife.'

Raven dripped more chloroform into the cone and bade Gabriela hold the muslin while he poured water over the blade. He watched the blood dilute and run from the steel, trickling into the dish he had placed below.

He thought of something Gabriela had told him about her former home in Madrid. She had grown up in a place called Lavapies. It was at the foot of a hill, where the rainwater from the city had flowed down its carefully maintained gutters for centuries. People would wash their feet there, hence the name.

Unfortunately, there was only so much that mere water could wash away.

Raven cleared his mind, hoping the wine he had imbibed served to steady his nerve rather than tremble his hand. He tentatively touched the area around the wound. Then with the lack of a response from Henry confirming that he was unconscious, he was able to feel for the hard lump where the ball was lodged.

Upon his instruction, Liselotte drizzled water from a cloth to gently wash the blood away as Raven made a small incision. Mercifully, the shot had not struck any of the major blood vessels, though it had been perilously close to the femoral artery. The difference between life and death on this occasion was less than half an inch.

Raven tugged the ball free with a pair of tongs. He was about to discard it but decided that Henry might like it as a memento.

Liselotte drizzled more water to clean out the wound, her face intent upon the task.

The blood and water were soaking into the fabric beneath Henry as Raven commenced his suturing. He tried not to think what their terrifying landlord, Herr Wolfburg, would make of the staining to his couch.

Henry came to a short while later, blinking and groaning. Gabriela looked to Raven, ready with more chloroform, but Henry was awake enough to refuse her.

'Thank you, my dear, but I am impatient to survey Raven's handiwork.' He grimaced. 'Gods, it looks like a pigskin football.'

Then he offered Raven a smile.

'I jest. Neatly done, old friend. You have my gratitude. Now, if you don't consider it rude after your considerable endeavours, it is my firm intention to lapse into unconsciousness, which will not require the assistance of your chloroform. If it turns out I am not dead in the morning, please do make sure I am roused by eight. Langenbeck is giving a lecture on battlefield amputations at nine and I do not wish to miss it.'

TWO

'hat was very courageous, what you did,' said Gabriela. It was the first either had spoken since they fell upon each other.

They lay upon Raven's bed, tired, languorous, yet far from sleep. Liselotte had stayed with Henry, ministering to him overnight, although not in the way she had perhaps intended some hours ago. For Raven and Gabriela, however, the proximity to danger had produced an unexpected amorousness; morbid fear transmuted into passion.

Raven had known her for several weeks, having been introduced at a dinner hosted by the Charité's prosector, Dr Virchow. Although he was head of the pathology department at the hospital, Virchow had an interest in obstetrics and therefore an interest in Raven, who, despite his lowly status, had worked as an apprentice to the famous Professor Simpson. Everyone was keen to know more about the great man and his remarkable discovery. Gabriela was a friend of Rose Mayer, soon to be Virchow's wife. She had shown little interest in what Raven had to say about chloroform but became considerably more attentive when he mentioned his experience with the Edinburgh photography pioneers David Octavius Hill and the late Robert Adamson.

Gabriela was a slight woman with dark eyes and dark hair,

curls loosely swept up, always at imminent risk of unfurling. He was constantly struck by the contrast with the women at home, their hair pulled rigidly into place, their skin so pale. It was not merely their appearance that seemed constrained by comparison. Fifteen years Raven's senior, Gabriela was a writer, artist and sometime artist's model who had some years ago outraged her wealthy family by leaving her aristocratic husband. She was not a woman prepared to be bound by convention, which both excited Raven and yet made him wary of her. They both knew their relationship was not something that could last: its very transience, no doubt, was part of the allure. Neither would have sought the other out as a suitable partner otherwise.

Raven looked at her in the light of the candles she had placed around the bed, jammed into the necks of wax-encrusted bottles.

'I have performed surgical procedures before. Surgery, however, is not my primary area of interest. The courage was Henry's in entrusting me with the task.'

'No, I mean how you fought off those men who tried to rob us. There were three of them and you faced them alone, knowing one of them had a pistol.'

Could he detect an edge to what she was saying? One of the things that made him wary of Gabriela was the fear that she had the wisdom and experience to see through him to the truth of what he might conceal.

'I wagered he would not have time to reload it.'

'Something of a high-stakes wager.'

Raven looked away, fearing what more his expression might involuntarily disclose, specifically that his wager had been wrong. He opted for a playful response instead, as though making light of it.

'I would have given them money had we any to offer. Having drunk it all, there seemed little option but to fight them off. I think it unlikely they would have accepted our apologies in the absence of payment.'

'Nonetheless, three on one is not a fair contest, yet you did not shrink from it.'

'It was not my first brawl, if that is what you are implying. I have the experience to know that those who prey upon the weak and unsuspecting do not always rise to the challenge when faced with a real fight.'

'You placed a high-stakes wager on that too.'

Raven said nothing. His gaze was drawn to the letter that lay by his bed, to which he still had not replied. Dr George Keith was leaving 52 Queen Street to set up practice with his brother Thomas, and Professor Simpson was offering Raven the position of his new assistant. He was fully qualified now, an apprentice no more, and in his year abroad he had expanded his medical knowledge more than he would have thought possible in such a short space of time.

And yet.

He thought of what Henry had often intimated regarding his 'perverse appetite for mayhem', as he put it. Moreover, he had his mother's words echoing in his head, spoken sometimes in jest, sometimes in earnest.

You have the devil in you.

Raven had come to hope that was no longer true. He had not been involved in any such chaos for a long time, certainly not since leaving Edinburgh, and thought it was because he had tamed his nature. He wondered now whether it was merely that the opportunity had not arisen. When bidden tonight, the devil had roused itself, proving it was not dead but merely sleeping. And back in that alley a man had paid for disturbing its slumber.

Gabriela placed a hand upon his shoulder.

'Remember me?' she said.

'I'm sorry. My mind strayed. Thinking about Henry.'

She laughed. 'Your mind strayed much further than the next room. Do not take me for a fool, Raven. I have been with you many times, remember? Whenever we lie together, afterwards you are not here.'

It would be folly to deny it. Certainly not to her.

'You are somewhere distant, in the company of someone else. I have always wondered who she is.'

He wanted to say that it was a more complex matter than that, but he did not wish to encourage further scrutiny. She was older than him, wiser than him, and he feared there was little he could hide from her. He wondered, then, why he wished to.

Raven thought about the men Gabriela must have had before him. He did not contemplate it in a way that was jealous or disapproving. Rather, he wondered what version of herself she had presented to each of them. He wondered at the lives with which she had intersected, the many people she had been.

'Gabriela, you have lived in several different places, uprooted yourself and started again. Is it possible to become someone else, to create yourself anew? Or do you always bring with you the person you truly are?'

Gabriela traced a finger across Raven's chest.

'I think the question you must ask is who it is you wish to become. Do you even know?'

'I wish to be a successful medical practitioner. Respected by my peers and sought after by patients.'

'Why would you need to change yourself in order to do that? It is everything you have been educating yourself for.'

'Yes, but in Edinburgh the standards and expectations are so high, and I fear I will betray myself somehow. It is a place where reputation is everything.'

Gabriela raised an eyebrow and stared intently at him.

'You would speak to a woman such as myself about reputation? If you had any notion of the disdain to which I have been subject . . .'

'But that is why I ask. Can you truly become the person society expects? Or is it always a matter of wearing a mask to hide your flawed nature?'

Gabriela considered this a while before answering.

'If you wear it long enough, a mask will become a comfortable fit. But you risk losing the man behind it.'

Raven thought it sounded a price worth paying.

'I have been to London, Paris, Vienna, Leipzig, and now Berlin. I have studied at great institutions, learned at the hands of great men. I should feel transformed, and yet in many respects I fear I have not changed at all. I thought that the more I learned, the more I experienced of the world, the more of a man I would become. I thought that I would feel certain of myself. But instead I feel as though the world just keeps getting larger and I am not growing to meet it.'

Gabriela nodded, giving him a sympathetic look that was at once comforting and yet made him feel like a child.

'I suspect that you have journeyed long enough, Will Raven. If you have become lost, there is only one place you can be sure to find yourself.'

EDINBURGH

THREE

he waiting room was crowded, as usual, the patients jostling for a position on the chairs closest to the fire. It was early yet, and Sarah suspected that the throng would soon be spilling out into the hallway and onto the stairs. Despite the chaotic nature of the domestic arrangements, Sarah still loved 52 Queen Street and was determined that her change of circumstances would not alter what she saw as her role here. She felt embedded in the place, bound to it.

It was so much more than a house or a family home. It was a place of learning. It provided an opportunity to acquire knowledge of medicine but also how best to apply that knowledge and look after those who were suffering. Here were rich and poor together, although only the former were expected to pay. Irrespective of financial means, or lack thereof, the treatment was the same: need alone was deemed just qualification. The variety of conditions which presented here also meant that the clinics were the best classrooms and every day was a chance to learn more. She sometimes liked to believe that the opportunities afforded her by working here were better than those of many a medical student at the university.

She was no longer a housemaid, but there were days when she still felt like a servant. Dr Simpson had a habit, when the weather was cold, and as he had done that morning, of shouting for tea and a dish of oatmeal for the patients in the waiting room. Many had travelled long distances to be there and were cold and hungry when they arrived. This would have been harder to bear were it not for the fact that Mrs Simpson was usually serving the patients alongside her.

There were other days when she felt more like a nurse or assistant, and days when she felt almost as if she was a member of the family. She often helped with the children and had become particularly fond of Jamie. He was prone to eczema; the itchy eruptions were a constant torment to him and she was often tasked with bathing him and rubbing his inflamed skin with olive oil. Despite this he was a sweet child; calm where his older brothers were boisterous.

Sarah heard a clapping of hands.

'Come away now. Let's have another.'

She led an older lady down the corridor to Dr Simpson's consulting room. He was standing at the door waiting as they approached, unsuccessfully trying to stifle a yawn. 'I had a hard drive last night in a carriage without springs,' he said by way of explanation. 'I changed it but was no better off and today I feel well pounded.'

Sarah returned to the waiting room to collect the empty cups and bowls from the morning's repast. She carried her loaded tray down the hallway, negotiating a route past David and Walter, who were using umbrellas as Arabian tents, and Glen the dog, who was as usual stationed beside the coat-stand, hoping to accompany his master should he choose to go out. She entered the kitchen to find Lizzie scrubbing at the porridge pot and Mrs Lyndsay chopping vegetables at the kitchen table.

'Has he finished feeding the five thousand then?' Mrs Lyndsay asked. Sarah was never sure whether the cook was a supporter of Dr Simpson's largesse or not. She was a religious woman in the conventional sense – a supporter of the Free Church and regular attender at Sunday services – but whether this extended to opening your house and your kitchen to the poor of Edinburgh was not apparent.

'I think that's all for now.'

Sarah took her tray over to the sink. Lizzie looked up from her scrubbing and gave her a thin smile. Lizzie had been rescued from the Lock hospital, one of Dr Simpson's waifs and strays – as Sarah had once been herself, although mercifully not under the same circumstances. Lizzie had been a fallen girl – Mrs Lyndsay's words – and though her venereal disease had been cured, the canker on her soul had yet to be expunged. Hard work had been deemed the remedy for that, and as a result the poor girl was given the work of two.

'The good doctor should have more care for the contents of his pocketbook,' Mrs Lyndsay said. Sarah was about to reply that funds did not seem to be in short supply when Mrs Lyndsay gestured to her to come closer. In a conspiratorial whisper she said: 'There is money gone missing. A discrepancy in the household accounts. It has Mrs Simpson worried.'

'A simple mistake, perhaps?' Sarah suggested, but she could tell from Mrs Lyndsay's tone that the cook thought something more sinister was afoot.

'Has anyone checked the windows?' Sarah added, referring to the time when Dr Simpson had used a ten-pound note to stop a rattling sash.

Mrs Lyndsay did not smile but looked over at Lizzie, still up to her elbows in hot water. 'I have my own suspicions,' she muttered.

On her way back to the waiting area, Sarah was called into Dr Simpson's consulting room, where he had finished examining the older lady, a widow by the name of Mrs Combe. He helped her into a chair, then sat himself down on a stool beside her, preferring to be at eye level when discussing a patient's condition. He disliked standing over people, particularly when imparting bad news.

'Dr Simpson, don't sit on such a lowly seat,' Mrs Combe said, evidently unimpressed by his solicitude. 'It's not fitting for a man such as yourself.'

'It's more than I merit, for your condition has baffled me,' the doctor replied, shaking his head.

'You look tired,' Mrs Combe told him, seemingly unperturbed by the lack of a diagnosis; concerned more for her physician than for herself.

'Well, I was six flights up in a room on the Cowgate last night, trying to save a poor woman who had been badly mauled by her husband. I happened to meet the police and they asked me to look at her. I think she'll live.'

Dr Simpson ran a hand through his tousled hair and then roused himself, standing up with some effort and rubbing his lower back. 'Forgive me,' he said. 'A touch of sciatica.'

He walked to the desk and wrote down a prescription while Sarah dressed a sore on the patient's shin. 'Though the diagnosis eludes me, I hope this might provide some relief from your symptoms,' he said.

The lady began to rummage about in the little bag she carried. Dr Simpson placed a hand on her arm.

'Put your money away. I will take no fee,' he said. 'I have done nothing. I deserve nothing.'

Sarah wondered if he had been made aware of the hole in the household finances and, more importantly, whether he knew who was responsible for it. The old lady rose from her chair and made her way to the door.

'Do see that you take some rest, Dr Simpson,' she said. 'So many in this town rely upon you – we cannot have you becoming ill.'

'I thank you for your concern,' he replied. 'Ordinarily your good counsel would have to be disregarded but I am happy to say that I have found a replacement for Dr Keith. I have appointed a new assistant.'

Sarah stopped what she was doing. This was news to her too.

'And who is this new assistant?' the lady asked. 'Do we know him?'

'You might have met him before. He was my apprentice not so long ago.'

Sarah dropped the length of bandage she had just finished winding into a neat roll and it slowly unspooled as it wheeled across the floor.

'His name is Will Raven.'

FOUR

here was a bite in the breeze as Raven climbed from the carriage and hefted his bags down to the pavement. Late autumn in Edinburgh. He permitted himself a wry smile at its chilly embrace, like a welcome home from a relative with a grudge. Its teeth were not so sharp as they once felt, however. He used to think that the wind off the Forth was a cruel presence. That was before he had felt the gusts that whipped along the Danube.

The familiarity of the city's sights and smells was heartening. He had only come to appreciate how much he missed Edinburgh once he had committed to return, and if he had doubts as to the wisdom of his decision, they were blown away like steam as his eyes lit upon the door to 52 Queen Street.

How vividly he recalled the first time he came here. He had been unconscionably late, dishevelled in his worn and grubby clothes, and sporting a recently sutured wound upon his face. He raised his hand to his left cheek in a semi-reflexive action, his index finger tracing the length of the scar. He thought of the individual responsible for it but quickly put that ugly visage from his mind. It was said the best revenge is living well, and he was certain their respective fortunes would have been satisfyingly divergent in the time that had passed. Raven had left that world behind, while his assailant was no doubt utterly mired there, if he still lived at all.

His facial disfigurement aside, he felt his appearance to be considerably improved since he first presented himself here. His wardrobe, like his travels, had been financed largely by the involuntary contribution of another gentleman, late of this parish, who had no need of luxuries where he had ended up. His clothes were new, tailored to fit, and his boots were polished to a high shine. He wondered if he would be recognised, so complete was his transformation.

When Raven had first seen it, 52 Queen Street had represented a route to wealth and renown, his aspirations filled with aristocratic patients and their hefty fees. Professor Simpson had shown him what it truly meant to be a doctor. This house and those who lived there had been the making of him, had saved him from himself. Now that he had returned, he wanted to show them all how he had flourished.

He paused on the front step, trying to anticipate the changes he would find inside, conscious that things were unlikely to be as he had left them. He remembered with a mixture of fondness and exasperation the gallimaufry of messy humanity which was often to be found behind this door. The personality of its owner was stamped upon the place from the attic to the basement. It was warm, cheerful, bustling, challenging and inspiring; but it could also be chaotic, confounding, fraught, thrawn and downright overwhelming. There were animals running loose, children running looser, patients spilling out of doorways, staff scrambling to accommodate the guests invited upon a whim of the professor, and somehow amidst it all had been made a discovery that changed the world.

As he rang the bell, he thought about who might answer, the faces he was about to see. He thought about Jarvis, Simpson's redoubtable butler, whose very politeness towards Raven was itself a means of conveying how much he would like to turn him out onto the street for a wretch. He thought about Mrs Simpson, perpetually in mourning for the young children she had lost and vigilantly dedicated to the care of those who survived. He thought of her unmarried sister, Mina, left heartbroken after she mistakenly believed her search for a husband had finally come to a happy end. Foremost in his thoughts, however, was Simpson's housemaid, Sarah Fisher.

Hers was the image he had most tried to conjure throughout his travels: her pale complexion, her honey-coloured hair, the soft touch of her hand as she administered ointment of her own making to salve his wound. He remembered the smell of her – lavender and fresh linen – the way she carried herself, her smile. He remembered also her withering disdain, her sharp intelligence and her tendency to let her frustrations talk her into trouble. Most of all he remembered the kisses they had shared, the swell of feelings he had not known around a woman before – or since.

He shook his head in an attempt to clear his mind. Such reminiscences had been in equal parts a comfort and a torment over the past year. They had been thrown together by circumstance, but propriety dictated that to pursue any kind of relationship would have been damaging to both of them. There had been no contact between them since he left. Deliberately so. He had written letters to her during his time in Paris, and again in Vienna, but they had never been sent. He was a doctor, a physician. She was a housemaid. Anything other than a professional relationship was surely out of the question. What possible future could there have been for them? None that he could see. He had tried to explain as much to her before he left, but she had been reluctant to accept the intractable realities before them; strong-willed and argumentative to the last.

He had been sure that a period of separation would cool his ardour for her, and there had been interludes during his travels when she seemed far distant in time as well as space; a treasured step on his journey, but one he had been ever progressing away from. However, as he stood on the doorstep, he was conscious of an increase in his heart rate, an excitement of the body in defiance of anything his mind might wish to deny.

It was more than an excitement: it was a longing. And the closer he drew to seeing her again, the more imperative that longing became.

He was therefore quite unprepared when it was not Sarah but another young woman who answered the door.

'Can I help you, sir?' she asked, peering up at him from beneath her cap.

'Yes. I am Dr Will Raven, the professor's new assistant.'

Raven's pride in being able to announce himself this way helped conceal how crestfallen he was suddenly feeling. The girl stood aside to allow him to enter. He handed her his hat and gloves.

'Very good, sir. I was told to expect you.'

'You are new here, are you not?' he asked, peering past her down the hall in a search for more familiar faces.

'Been here almost a month now, sir.'

'Is the professor at home?'

'No, sir.'

'Mrs Simpson?'

'Mrs Simpson and the children are out visiting.'

'And Miss Grindlay?'

'She is at her father's house in Liverpool.'

Raven thought again about Mina and her marital disappointment. He had hoped she would by now have found a suitable partner, but some things, as he well knew, were not meant to be. He looked up the length of the hallway again. Everything was preternaturally calm, causing him to feel uneasy. He decided he could stand it no longer.

'Where is Miss Fisher?' he asked.

'Miss Fisher, sir?'

'Yes, she is a housemaid here. Or was,' he added. Sarah had

received a promotion of sorts before he left, and he was unsure how he ought to refer to her now.

'There is another housemaid here besides me, sir, but none called Fisher.'

She stared blankly and Raven suppressed a sigh. The girl had evidently replaced Sarah but was by no means a substitute for her.

He smiled benignly at her.

'Perhaps you know her simply as Sarah.'

A realisation passed across her face like a shadow.

'Oh. You must mean Miss Fisher as was, sir.'

As was? Raven was gripped by panic, his disappointed heart thumping again and his guts churning. What had happened to Sarah? Was she dead? He would surely have been told if something catastrophic had befallen her. Then he remembered all of his unsent letters. Perhaps no one would have thought to inform him. After all, they had endeavoured to keep their connection concealed.

His palms were suddenly moist. In that instant it all came flooding back and he understood that far from fading, his feelings for her had merely been suppressed by time and distance. Then he noticed that the girl was smiling.

'She is no longer Miss Fisher, sir. She is now Mrs Banks.'

FIVE

arah had got to her feet and begun placing teacups and saucers on a tray when a hand reached out to stop her.

'Sarah. There is no need for you to do that. Ring for Mrs Sullivan.'

'Of course. Force of habit,' she added, offering him an apologetic smile.

It was the second time this morning that she had forgotten her recently elevated status. The first instance, at least, had gone unwitnessed. She had caught herself making up their bed, and as she was already halfway through the process, she had seen no reason not to complete it.

She still tended to wake early and could not get used to the fact that she did not have to rise immediately and commence a slew of tasks.

Sarah sat down again and gazed out of the window. She was distracted, and she knew why.

'Is all well, darling?' Archie asked.

'Yes, quite well,' she told him, though she knew that she could not hide her unease. Archie was a close reader of her mood, one of the many things she liked about him.

'It's just, you seem a little restive. Could it be your mind is already at Queen Street?'

Sarah felt exposed by the suggestion, then realised what he meant. Although they had taken rooms in Albany Street, Sarah was still attending Queen Street every day. She had rendered herself indispensable, having become adept in the administration of chloroform. Dr Simpson was assessing its usefulness in all manner of complaints, from dysmenorrhoea to biliary colic. Working with the professor was something she had not been prepared to give up, and that had, as a result, formed part of their agreement.

'Yes. I am thinking of the patient we have coming in today. Dr Simpson warned me that it might be a trying consultation.'

Sarah's words sounded hollow emerging from her own mouth. What she said was true, but that didn't alter the fact that she was concealing the real reason her mind was already at Queen Street.

Raven.

He was due back today and would most probably be there by the time she arrived for work that afternoon.

She had not given him much thought in such a long time. Why would she, with all that her life had become? But since finding out that he would be taking up the position vacated by Dr Keith, his return had loomed ever larger in her thoughts.

She didn't see quite why it should. Perhaps it was not so much Raven himself as what he represented that seemed so vivid in her memory: the time not only of Dr Simpson's great discovery, but of all that had attended it. She had taken great risks in joining Raven to unmask the most murderous villainy and deception. When people are thrown together in fraught circumstances, it is possible for them to confuse the heightened emotions they are experiencing as feelings for one another.

Although it had been less than two years ago, it felt like a different time. So much had changed. She had been but a girl then. Now she was a woman. Now she was married. Now she had Archie. Though it was Raven who had drawn her into danger and had forced her to appreciate what she might be capable of, Archie was the man who had truly transformed her life.

She looked over at her husband, Dr Archibald Banks, who was sitting in an armchair by the window, squinting at the front page of the *Scotsman*. He owned a pair of reading glasses but rarely wore them. He said they made him look like an old man, something he was sensitive about given the age difference between them. He was thirty-six years old but could pass for a man several years younger. Sarah hoped that his youthfulness would work in his favour.

She had met him when he came to Queen Street on his quest to consult with the great medical minds of Edinburgh. He had encountered Dr Simpson back when they were both students, and they had remained friends since. He was handsome, lively, articulate, well read, and, as a medical man, fascinated by the role Sarah had, the fact that there was no title that encompassed all that she did. He was not in any way bemused by her scientific curiosity and her determination to better educate herself. When they first spoke at any length, he had listened as though he might learn from her. She could not think of another man who had ever done that.

He was a wealthy man from a good family and yet had no qualms about associating with her. They often walked together in Queen Street Gardens when the weather permitted, discussing matters as diverse as current affairs and the contents of medical journals. They attended public lectures at the Assembly Rooms, listening to speakers discussing everything from philosophy to phrenology. They traded novels and eagerly compared their impressions.

She could not help but compare his attitude to that of Will Raven. When their relationship deepened, he had sought to put distance between them. He became too busy to spend time with her; the work for his MD thesis had to come first. And as the end of his medical studies drew near, he seemed to become increasingly uncomfortable with what he perceived as the gulf in social standing that lay between them. He had left her in no doubt that he thought their relationship to be impractical, impossible and ill-advised.

Then he left for Europe and she had not heard from him since.

In contrast Archie seemed to care little for how their attachment might be perceived. Idle gossip held no fear for a man with his perspective. 'Life is too short to be held back from pursuing one's wishes by something as vapid as what other people might think,' he said. 'True opportunity is by its nature fleeting and must be seized before it evades one's grasp.'

Life is too short. Words to live by, indeed.

Nonetheless, it had come as a surprise to Sarah when Archie proposed marriage. Though it constituted an ever-decreasing share of her duties, it was still as a household servant that she was perceived. It was one thing to have a friendship with such a woman, but quite another to marry her.

Archie had made his feelings clear: 'I no longer need to care about whether someone's patronage is jeopardised by my conduct, or contingent upon acceptable behaviour and opinions. I know what it is to truly live in a way most men never will.'

Most significantly, he had made it clear that he did not expect her to give up her cherished work at Queen Street. Unlike some, he did not regard it as pointless for her to expand her knowledge in an area from which she was effectively barred. In the circumstances, she had found it difficult to refuse his generous offer.

Sarah not having any surviving parents, Dr Simpson had taken the role of giving her away, and any residual feelings she had for his one-time apprentice were soon forgotten as Archie took her hand at the altar.

It was easy not to think about Raven when he wasn't there, but she was about to discover the truth of the corollary.

The rustling of newspaper brought her attention back to the room, the breakfast things still littering the table. Sarah stopped herself stooping to clear them once again and this time reached for the bell.

'My goodness,' said Archie, smoothing down the page in front of him. 'Four members of the same family fell ill and died over a period of two weeks. Dreadful. There is always some poor soul worse off than yourself.'

'Were they very old?' Sarah asked, still fighting the urge to take the tea tray down to the kitchen herself.

'The oldest was in her sixtieth year, but her son, his wife and their daughter perished too, all of them previously healthy.'

Sarah looked up, suddenly concerned.

'What was the cause? Not cholera again?'

Everyone was terrified of its return after the last outbreak.

'There is no mention of cholera. All natural causes.'

'Where was this? The Old Town?'

Sarah thought of the squalor she had witnessed there, how easily disease could ravage the unfortunates forced to inhabit the cramped and unsanitary tenements.

'No, Trinity. A fine house with a view of the Forth, apparently.' Archie looked over at her and smiled. 'I wonder who's to inherit? Whoever it is, I'd be checking their pockets for arsenic.'

Sarah laughed, though she still felt an instinctive wariness of inviting disapproval in doing so. She could not have said whose: it was a legacy of her years as a housemaid. Archie was aware of it, and thus relished her response to his remark.

Archie laughed all the time, despite everything. It was one of the reasons he and Simpson got on so well.

He folded up the newspaper, put it down on the table and picked up the *Monthly Journal of Medical Science*. Sarah had noticed that, since he had started taking small doses of morphine for the pain in his throat, he could seldom concentrate on any one thing for long.

He turned the pages and sighed. 'Oh dear. Another letter.'

'Not the mattress dispute again?'

'I'm afraid so.'

'Who is it this time?'

'Professor Miller. It really is unconscionable. Such spats do the profession no good at all. And I don't believe the pages of the medical journals are the place to air such petty and personal grievances. They really should know better.'

'It is little more than gossip. What evidence do they have to support such accusations?'

'The upholsterer, Mr Hardie, has seemingly confirmed that the patient's mattress was stained with blood.'

'That is hardly conclusive. If they are claiming that she died of haemorrhage, the quantity of blood is more pertinent than its mere presence. The most apposite organ in this matter would appear to be the spleen, and I do not mean that of the late patient.'

Archie smiled and nodded his agreement, a sight that warmed her. She liked to make him happy. They liked to make each other happy. But as always, when she thought of that happiness, it prompted a corresponding sorrow.

She wondered how long they would have together. Perhaps all married couples did that, from time to time. But not every day.

SIX

f I made a mistake, it was in killing four members of the same family.

I can appreciate in retrospect how that might have seemed conspicuous. Perhaps I was blinded by my desires, but in mitigation, such a tragedy would not necessarily be deemed worthy of note. People in the same household die all the time. Whole families died when the last epidemic swept the city.

I suppose complacency becomes inevitable when one's actions go so long undetected. For years my deeds were shielded by people's incredulity that a woman could be capable of such things. She is the angel of the house, entrusted with the care of those around her. People would not believe that I was killing their loved ones because they simply could not afford to. Where would our society be were women to resist our given roles, to slough off what we are told is our gentle nature?

But do not make the mistake of thinking me uncaring, incapable of feeling, incapable of love. No, I am not a mother. But I know what it is to care for a child, for I have been charged with the care of many, most recently little Eleanor. I understood how her fragility and vulnerability made her all the more precious. I understood the hope that she represented to her parents, the essence of themselves they saw reflected in her features. I had a profound appreciation of just how much she meant to them. Otherwise how could I have derived such a sense of power and accomplishment by taking it away?

Nobody knows the value of a life who has not ended one. And there is nothing so precious as snuffing out the life of someone so young, someone uncomprehending of the enormity of what is happening to them, or of how much they are about to lose.

I loved little Eleanor. Who could not? She was such a darling. I still picture the sparkle in her eyes, the energy she had, the joy her curiosity and mischievousness brought to her parents. She was a clever girl, strong-willed and with good instincts. She fought me, in her own unknowing way. But her parents were recruited as my allies, not hers, as they urged her to do as I bid.

'You have to take the medicine,' they would insist.

'I don't like it,' Eleanor would say. 'And I don't like her.'

'She just wants to make you better.'

But I did not.

To me, other people's grief is like fine wine, and I do not mean merely that I savour it; I appreciate the many different flavours and textures, the subtle notes that distinguish one variety from another. When Eleanor died, her parents' grief was a powerful thing to witness. You might well have found it intolerable to behold, in which case you might say it was a mercy then, on my part, that I would soon bring it to an end.

I killed her mother, and shortly after that her father. Last of all, I killed the matriarch of the household, her grandmother. I wanted her to witness this devastation before she was taken too. She deserved to suffer. I had encountered her sort before. But we will get to that, in time.

I do not fear anyone's judgment. You might endeavour to understand me, and I do wish to be understood. But first you must grasp that if you think me some abomination, some kind of monster, you will understand nothing.

No doubt you have seen paintings depicting Hell, and recoiled at the snarling, twisted features of the demons torturing the forsaken. How much more frightening it is to understand that a true demon has a kindly face.

When I look at such paintings, I see only representations of evil and cruelty as though they were entities in their own right. They say nothing of where such evil and cruelty comes from. For this I know: every true demon was once a child, one that knew fear and suffering.

Every true demon learned cruelty and evil at the hands of another.

SEVEN

he ticking of the clock was the only sound as Raven sat in an armchair beside the fire in Dr Simpson's study, feeling uncomfortably alone. He could not remember the house ever being this quiet. It felt bereft, shorn not only of familiar presences, but of much more besides. Nothing here was as he had imagined it would be, but it was not mere absence that was accentuating his feeling of isolation.

Sarah was married.

He heard the housemaid's words over and over in his head: *She is no longer Miss Fisher, sir. She is now Mrs Banks.* What she had conveyed was instantly understood and yet somehow incomprehensible.

Jarvis had shown him to his new quarters, helping him heft his trunk up the stairs. The butler had observed that Raven looked 'less like a vagrant than when you first darkened our door'. It was hardly the most generous of compliments, but it was as warm a welcome as he had received, the place seeming comparatively deserted.

Raven's new accommodations were larger and finer than the room he had been given as the doctor's apprentice. However, part of him wished for the reassurance of its familiarity, or perhaps he merely wished for other things to be the same.

Raven had busied himself by unpacking his things, though he had halted each time he heard the front door open downstairs, waiting for the accompanying boom of Dr Simpson's voice. Thus far it had not been forthcoming. His new window offered a view of Queen Street Gardens, and he had gazed out each time he heard hooves, hoping to spy the approach of the professor's brougham.

Eventually he had come down the stairs and asked Jarvis when the professor might be due home.

'Any minute,' the butler assured him, ushering Raven into Dr Simpson's study. Raven recognised the tone. It was the same one Jarvis used in addressing patients and other visitors when they made a similar enquiry. 'Any minute' turned into almost an hour, and Raven was beginning to feel sleepy, lulled into somnolence by the ticking clock, when the sound of a carriage pulling up outside roused him. He got to his feet as he heard the front door open, and moments later Dr Simpson burst in, instantly filling the house with his presence.

'Will Raven! What a pleasure it is to see you again. And just in time too. We have an interesting patient to see. A young woman with troublesome abdominal distension.'

Raven stood and smiled, relieved that some things had not changed. He was reminded of his first day at Queen Street, when not so much as a cup of tea had been offered before he was hurried into a carriage and driven off with the professor to see a pressing maternity case.

Dr Simpson appeared to be much as Raven remembered him. There was some more grey in his hair perhaps, and a little thickening around the waist, but otherwise the same: the permanent sense of urgency, an air of perpetual motion.

'How are you? How is Henry?'

Raven's mind suddenly ambushed him by conjuring images of blood upon his hands and spilling in rivulets around the course of his knife. He first saw Henry's leg, cut open that he might remove the ball fired by the masked assailant, but, more unsettlingly, that image gave way to the incision he had made not an hour before.

He had not lied to Gabriela. He had chased the men into the alley believing them cowards who would run when confronted with the prospect of a real fight. In that regard his judgment had been sound, but a coward will still fight if he believes he has the advantage. In the dark of the alley Raven saw the man with the pistol raise his weapon a second time. He had indeed reloaded quickly, or perhaps he had a second pistol. Either way, he had straightened his arm and aimed point-blank at Raven's head.

Raven had reacted without a thought, his blade an extension of his hand, of his mind. The Liston knife opened the man's throat like it was opening a letter, but it was a letter from which devastating news poured forth.

At the very mention of Henry's name, he instantly felt shame and regret. Why otherwise would he have concealed what happened from him, and from Gabriela? He knew his actions had been driven by sheer instinct, near-involuntary reflex, and that the only choice had been to take a life or surrender his own. But none of that made it easier to live with the memory of what he had seen, what he had wrought.

And what of that instinct? The thought of that troubled him as much as the guilt: what it said about his nature. What he feared he had inherited from his father.

You have the devil in you, his mother had often said, and though she spoke with humour and affection, he could not help but wonder if it was a way for her to express her own fears for what he had been born with.

Perhaps the hardest thing was that there was nobody he could talk to about it. Standing here now in the professor's study, he donned a neutral expression and concealed his feelings.

'My travelling companion decided to extend his stay in Berlin.'

'A city I have yet to see. Chance would be a fine thing. Always so much to be done.' The professor looked around for somewhere free of clutter to place his bag. He moved a pile of papers from his desk to a chair and seemed sad for a moment. 'I hunger for a book and thirst for the time to read it,' he said.

Raven had so much he wished to tell the professor. There were names to conjure with, institutions of vast renown, techniques and procedures that he was sure would fascinate his ever-curious mind, but there was to be no such opportunity, as almost immediately the doctor began discussing the details of the patient they were about to see. It was frustrating and yet oddly reassuring. This part, at least, was like coming home.

'A widow of more than a year. Her husband was an army surgeon who succumbed to an infectious fever within days of their arrival in India, leaving the poor woman to make her own way home. She now looks as if she is in the advanced stages of pregnancy and, with the husband having been dead for longer than the period of a normal gestation, a certain amount of embarrassment has resulted from her condition. What do you think of that, Dr Raven?'

Raven felt a slight inward glow at being addressed by his hard-won title, but this quickly left him as he sought to make an intelligent reply to the professor's query. He thought for a moment. Her apparent condition was bound to prove highly injurious to the widow's good name, but her reputation might well prove the least of this woman's worries.

'She might actually be with child,' he suggested. This answer directly questioned the woman's virtue but there was no room for drawing-room decorum when discussing medical matters.

'Sometimes the most straightforward explanation is the correct one,' the professor agreed. 'It may, of course, be a phantom pregnancy – I have encountered one before – but on that occasion the patient fervently believed she was carrying a child, whereas this lady insists that pregnancy is not a possibility, in spite of her appearance.'

There was a knock at the study door; at the threshold stood two women, both of whom presented a disconcerting sight in their different ways. One was the patient, introduced as Mrs Elizabeth Glassford, but Raven found his eye drawn to the other.

Sarah escorted Mrs Glassford through the study door, a supportive hand upon her arm. A cursory visual assessment revealed only that she looked well. Her hair was swept upwards into a loose bun and she wore no cap. She was wearing a plain gown, neat and well fitted – a far remove from the servants' garb he had become accustomed to seeing her in.

Was he imagining it, or did she carry herself differently? He could not stop thinking of the implications, of knowing what she had now experienced. So often he had thought back to the small intimacies they had shared, and the nights he had lain in this house, troubled by the attendant dangers should they share more. Now she had shared all, with someone he knew not, a face he could not even picture. He was not sure if this was a consolation or a further torment.

His staring, he was sure, would have become prolonged and awkward had his professional attention not been drawn to the patient. Mrs Glassford walked with the gait of one far advanced in years, although she could not have been much more than thirty. As she moved slowly across the room, she supported the sides of her protuberant abdomen with her hands. In contrast to the swelling of her belly, the rest of her seemed excessively thin, as if whatever was growing in her abdomen was leeching all nourishment from every other part of her. The effort of her short walk had rendered her profoundly breathless. Raven knew immediately that this was not a pregnancy, real or imagined.

Sarah helped the woman onto the examination couch, as Raven had seen her do with countless patients before. She then pulled across the screen that shielded the couch from the rest of the room and assisted in loosening the patient's clothing. Raven could hear her making encouraging remarks to the woman, though he doubted she would have any misapprehensions about the likely prognosis. He remembered that she always had a good diagnostic eye despite her lack of formal training.

Raven went behind the screen, with its incongruous embroidered panels depicting chrysanthemums and peacocks, and proceeded with his examination. He was unsurprised by what he found. The skin of the abdomen was stretched tight, the umbilicus protuberant. Fluctuation was easily discernible, suggesting a large volume of fluid contained within. There was also gross swelling of both legs and of the lower abdominal wall. Where he had pressed on the abdomen, an imprint of his hand remained. The diagnosis was obvious.

'Well?' asked Simpson as Raven emerged, his eyebrows raised. Sarah had gone behind the screen again and grunts of effort could be heard as the two women attempted to squeeze the patient's misshapen body back into her clothes.

'I think this is a case of ovarian dropsy.'

'I agree,' the professor replied. 'How should we proceed?'

'Abdominal binding, mercurials and diuretics,' Raven said, confident of his answer and yet despairing of its likely effectiveness.

'That is certainly what many would advocate,' said the professor. 'However, given the degree of distension and her breathlessness, I think we must remove some of the abdominal fluid directly. We will ask her to return tomorrow for tapping.'

Raven felt a familiar thrill at the prospect of performing such a procedure, an excitement tempered only slightly by the inevitable discomfort that the patient would have to endure – to say nothing of the fact that this was likely palliation rather than cure. Yet doing something was so much more appealing than doing nothing. To Raven's mind, in desperate circumstances, action trumped passivity.

This train of thought prompted the resurgence of an unpleasant memory, a case he had seen while in Paris of a young woman felled in her prime. She had collapsed suddenly, without warning, and an examination revealed evidence of concealed bleeding. There was some debate about the likely diagnosis and possible interventions, whether anything could or should be done. Wise old heads had counselled caution, holding back their younger counterparts. Prevarication had proven fatal and the post-mortem had confirmed what had been suspected: a belly full of blood as a result of a ruptured tubal pregnancy.

In the aftermath there were voices raised in recrimination, a wringing of hands by some, a shrugging of shoulders by others. Vague promises were made about lessons being learned, which was of small comfort to the young man left bereft by the loss of his wife.

Raven was still undecided as to whether it had been prudence or cowardice that had held them back from attempting some form of surgical treatment, although frequently he felt that the scales of his judgment were tipping towards the latter. Surely a heroic failure was better than sitting idly by letting nature take its course. A slim chance of success still represented the possibility of survival.

It was always better to do something rather than nothing.

Always.

EIGHT

arah escorted Mrs Glassford to the waiting room to allow her to catch her breath, though in truth she was as much in need of relief as the patient. The moment she became aware of Raven's presence in the room, she had felt a tension in the air that reminded her of those rare clammy summer nights just before a thunderstorm broke.

They had been at close quarters and yet unable to communicate. Sarah had felt at once both a powerful need to talk to Raven and a profound gratitude that the circumstances precluded it. In her time here, she had observed that there was much human congress that could be avoided through protocol, decorum and the practical demands of duty. Sometimes it was a frustration, sometimes a relief, and occasionally both at once.

'Would you like some tea?' she asked, thinking that in her current state Mrs Glassford was unlikely to be able to make the short trip home.

'Tea would be most welcome.'

Sarah returned a short time later to find Mrs Glassford already significantly improved. She watched as Sarah poured the tea, a frown creasing her brow.

'What is your position here? If you don't mind my asking.'

Sarah smiled. 'My role is rather unconventional. I help with the patients and administer chloroform on occasion.'

'And do the patients find this arrangement acceptable?'

Sarah stopped smiling. 'I'm unaware of any complaints.'

'That is refreshing. Some would have us believe that making ourselves useful will bring about the end of civilisation as we know it.'

Mrs Glassford leaned forward and placed a bony hand on top of Sarah's.

'I have long thought that there should be more to life for a woman than being a wife and mother.'

'But you were married,' Sarah observed.

'Yes. I had thought that it would be an adventure. He was in the army and we were going to live in India. I wished to see the world and experience other cultures. But it wasn't to be. He died shortly after we arrived, and I was forced to return. If you want to make God laugh, tell him your plans. Though I suppose it could have been worse.'

'Worse? How so.'

'In India there is a tradition that the widow throws herself onto her husband's funeral pyre.'

Sarah made no reply as she struggled to take in what Mrs Glassford had just said. It brought to mind the burning of witches and martyrs and she decided she must have misheard or misunderstood.

'The widow is immolated alongside her dead husband?' she asked.

'Yes. It is known as suttee.'

'And would I be right in assuming there is no tradition of the reciprocal?'

Mrs Glassford managed a smile, despite her obvious discomfort. 'A curious oversight.'

She drained her cup and with some effort got up from her chair. 'Thank you for the tea. I shall return to my home and rest in preparation for tomorrow.' As she reached the door she turned. 'Perhaps we can talk more when I return.'

Sarah hoped that would be the case.

NINE

inner that evening was initially a quiet affair: just Raven, the doctor and Mrs Simpson. Raven hoped that now he would be able to discuss his recent experiences and impress upon the professor how much he had progressed. During the afternoon's consultation, he had become conscious of their adopting familiar roles, of the master and his apprentice. He knew he still had much to learn from Dr Simpson, but nonetheless felt a need to establish his credentials as a medical practitioner in his own right.

He would have to wait, however. As soon as they were seated, discussion immediately turned to household matters. The nursery nurse had sought advice on how best to treat young Jamie's skin complaint, which had flared up again. Jamie was almost three years old. When last Raven saw him, he was barely weaned.

'I have asked that his bed be stripped, the sheets boiled, and the mattress aired,' Mrs Simpson said.

'Is she still rubbing the skin with olive oil? That should help,' Dr Simpson suggested. Raven imagined this would primarily make the child more difficult to apprehend if he was wont to run about the house as his older brothers did.

Jarvis entered bearing a decanter and two glasses on a silver tray. Raven, who had been hoping for a drop of the doctor's claret, was disappointed to see that the liquid in the decanter was translucent.

'Ah,' said Dr Simpson, rubbing his hands as Jarvis poured. 'My special champagne.'

Raven was now intrigued as he accepted a glass of the effervescent beverage. He noticed that Mrs Simpson was not partaking and briefly wondered why.

'What is special about it?' Raven asked as he took a sip.

'It is carbonated water with some chloroform added to it,' Simpson said.

If Raven had not already swallowed his mouthful of 'special champagne' it would have been sprayed across the table. He put his glass down and looked at Simpson hoping this was some kind of joke.

'Chloroform?' he asked.

'Yes. It livens up the dreariest of dinner parties – not that this should be interpreted as a comment on present company.'

Raven dabbed his mouth with a napkin and pushed his glass further from him. 'If it's all the same, I think I'll stick to wine. I have learned altogether too much respect for your special champagne's active ingredient.'

Simpson put his own glass on the tray and indicated to Jarvis that he would like it removed just as the dining-room door opened and dinner arrived. As the various dishes were placed on the table, Raven felt a pang of disappointment over who was serving them, or more specifically who was not. He watched the young girl who had answered the door as she made her way round the table, and it brought home to him once again what had so dramatically and irrevocably changed in his time away. He tried to imagine Sarah sitting at her own table with her husband, but he could not bring the image to mind. Even the attempt caused him to feel a distinct ache in his chest.

He found that he was disproportionately pleased by the things in the household that had remained the same: the irascible Jarvis,

Mrs Lyndsay's cooking, even Glen the Dalmatian, who was sitting by Simpson's right hand waiting for scraps.

'Tell me, Will, how fares chloroform on the Continent?' the doctor asked, interrupting his ruminations.

'Almost universally used in surgery in preference to ether.'

'And in midwifery?'

'It tends to be reserved for difficult cases. There are concerns about its safety.'

'I am entirely convinced that it is safe,' Simpson said emphatically. 'Problems only arise when there is a want of caution in its administration. If improperly given, chloroform may well prove injurious or even fatal – as will opium, calomel or every other powerful remedy or strong drug.'

'When in London, I heard John Snow speak at a meeting of the Westminster Medical Society,' Raven said. 'He advocates the use of an inhaler to determine and control the precise amount of chloroform the patient receives.'

'I find a handkerchief serves well enough.'

Raven felt that the professor was being a little dismissive.

'Snow maintains it was an excessive amount of chloroform that was responsible for Hannah Greener's death.'

Hannah Greener was a fifteen-year-old girl who had perished within minutes of receiving chloroform for the removal of a toenail. The case had provoked a prolonged debate about why she had died.

'As I understand it, in that case the girl fell into a state of syncope which I have occasionally seen myself,' Simpson replied. 'But then cold water was poured into her mouth followed by brandy, which of course she was unable to swallow. She was no more able to breathe than if her whole head had been submersed. The girl died of asphyxia. She died not of the chloroform but of the attempts made to revive her.'

Raven was beginning to feel discomfited, as though his contributions were not being given due weight. He decided to change tack.

'In London, concern is still expressed about anaesthetic midwifery being anti-scriptural.'

Raven sat back, expecting an entertaining eruption of some kind. There was none.

'I am pleased to say that religious opposition has almost entirely ceased here, if we except the occasional remark from some caustic old maid whose prospects of using chloroform are forever passed.'

Mrs Simpson frowned a little at this remark, but the professor continued without pause.

'An Irish lady said to me recently how unnatural it was for the doctors of Edinburgh to be taking away the pains of labour. Painless labour, she said, was both unnatural and improper. How unnatural it is for you, I replied, to have swum over from Ireland to Scotland against wind and tide in a steamboat.'

The professor laughed at his own story, a laugh that became infectious the longer it went on, until Mrs Simpson and Raven joined in.

Raven thought that, on this point, the professor was probably right. There was always a certain prejudice in some minds against anything new, a resistance to breaking with tradition and custom. He remembered the concerns expressed about the speed of the new railway carriages, how such unaccustomed forces applied to the human frame would induce apoplexy. He was about to say as much but was prevented from doing so by a knock at the door. A man entered carrying a sheaf of papers.

'Mr Quinton, I thought you had already left,' Dr Simpson said. 'Your wife will be wondering what has become of you.'

The newcomer looked curiously towards Raven, whereupon the professor made introductions.

'Dr Will Raven, this is Mr James Quinton, who I have hired as my secretary. Mrs Simpson finally prevailed upon me that I ought to engage help in organising my papers.'

He said this as though talking about some trivial undertaking over which his wife had made an undue fuss. Mrs Simpson's expression betrayed nothing, but Raven knew the truth of it. The professor was quite chaotic in his organisation, often forgetting appointments. And his lackadaisical attitude to certain practical matters was best summed up by the fact that it was one of Jarvis's tasks to go through his pockets at the end of the day and collect the payments he had secreted there, as he was liable to forget about them altogether. Jarvis had also complained that Dr Simpson's keen interest in archaeology led to him wrapping arrowheads and old coins he had found in banknotes of high denomination, lest the butler be tempted to throw them away.

Quinton was a thin man with a long face. He had a sombre look about him, as though heavily burdened by something. Raven could well imagine that organising the professor's affairs was the cause.

'Quinton is currently assisting me with a most vital project,' the professor said. 'I am in the process of collating the results of my enquiry into the mortality attendant on surgical operations and whether anaesthesia makes any difference.'

'As well as the papers on the suction tractor, galvanism and hospital fever. Not to mention the professor's voluminous correspondence,' Quinton added. Still the severe face; not even a hint of a smile. 'I have left some papers on your desk that require your signature,' he stated. 'I bid you good evening.'

'He is a graduate of Oxford University,' Simpson said as the dining-room door closed, as though this explained everything.

'What is a suction tractor?' Raven asked.

'Something that I have devised as a substitute for forceps in tedious labour, a rubber cup attached by suction to the infant's head.'

'Mrs Quinton has kindly agreed to take one of our babies,' Mrs Simpson added, deftly changing the subject.

Raven wondered what she meant. He thought about the Simpsons' children – David, Wattie, James and Jessie, who had been born just before he left on his travels – and wondered which one Mrs Simpson was planning to give away; trying and failing not to form a preference. Surely not the infant, he thought. Mrs Simpson noticed his confusion.

'From time to time it is necessary to find foster homes for babies; orphans and those who cannot be looked after by their own parents.'

'Yes, of course,' Raven said, thinking she had described the matter with admirable delicacy. The unwanted, inconvenient progeny of upper-class indiscretion would perhaps be a more accurate description. He had not appreciated that the Simpsons were involved in such a project.

His thoughts returned to an odd sight he had once witnessed, despite the efforts of Simpson's coachman to conceal it. The professor had visited a house on Doune Terrace, where through the window Raven saw him embrace a woman and then delightedly hug her child, an infant dressed in pink. The sight had troubled Raven ever since, unavoidably speculating as to Simpson's role. Now, however, there appeared to be an alternative explanation, one that could account for the coachman's discretion.

It might be a mystery solved, though it was not the prime question Raven sought an answer to. He desperately wanted to ask about Sarah but remained unsure how to broach the subject. He opted for an oblique approach and decided to enquire about the professor's former assistants first.

'I imagine that Mr Quinton is an extremely useful addition to the household,' he said. 'Of course, there have been a number of changes since I left on my travels. I believe Dr Keith has set up a practice of his own.'

'Indeed. With his brother Thomas, who was once my apprentice, like yourself. They have premises on Great Stuart Street.'

'And Dr Matthews Duncan?'

If there had been a thermometer in the room, Raven was convinced it would have indicated a sudden drop in temperature.

He noticed an involuntary stiffening on the part of Mrs Simpson, her eyes darting towards her husband. He frowned before replying.

'He too has set up his own practice.'

Raven decided not to pursue this, although he sensed that there was more to be said. He would find out soon enough, no doubt.

'And Sarah,' Raven continued, swallowing to clear his throat. 'I understand that she has married.'

'Yes,' said Mrs Simpson. 'To a doctor, would you believe.'

'A doctor?'

Raven struggled to keep the incredulity from his voice.

'Yes. Dr Archibald Banks. A truly charming man. From a very good family.'

Raven did not know how to respond. His recently consumed dinner suddenly felt heavy in his stomach. How could she have married a doctor? Given his own history with Sarah this added a new and perplexing dimension to the whole thing. He noticed Dr Simpson was still frowning, his mind on undisclosed matters.

'They have taken some rooms on Albany Street,' Mrs Simpson continued. 'They wanted to remain close by.'

'Sarah is indispensable,' Dr Simpson said, brightening a little. 'She has become quite skilful in administering chloroform.'

Presumably with a handkerchief, thought Raven.

At that moment there was the sound of running feet and the dining-room door burst open. Jarvis entered looking as rattled as Raven had ever seen him.

'Come down, Dr Simpson. For God's sake, come down. I think I've killed the cook.'

TEN

 am the equal of any man, as you will come to know, though it took me a long time to understand the truth of this. For there were those who drove it into me that I was a lesser being. Who beat it into me that I was worthless.

Worth less.

My mother seldom had time or money, but my most treasured memory is of her taking me to the theatre when I was a child. It was a realm of artifice and illusion, a respite from reality. Perhaps that is why, when I look back upon certain times in my life, it is as though I remember watching those events played out upon the stage, rather than happening to me. It appears my mind will not permit me to recreate the view from behind my own eyes, and instead places me without, watching: sometimes staring up from the stalls, other times gazing down from the grand circle.

Look, there I am now, see? Emerging between the painted flats. Emerging from the interstices between what everyone else notices.

The set is small, requiring only a fraction of the stage to recreate the cramped room in Cumberland Street in the Gorbals, where Murdo MacDonald and his family lived in a tenement single-end.

We moved there from Ayrshire, where my father worked as a farm labourer in places where his reputation did not precede him. He was known as the angry bantam, for his scrawny build and sudden temper. Others simply called him Mad Murdo. He was disruptive and unreliable: prone to fury and drunkenness. When we left for Glasgow, he claimed it was because he had bested the farmer in a brawl and been dismissed, although the truth was less palatable.

On this stage, in my mind's eye, he was not present. He had secured employment at a mill, where he worked long hours, though he should have been home by now.

My mother stood at the sink, scrubbing clothes. She had little to her name but took pride in the appearance of her two girls.

Her belly was round, swelling with another child. She had borne two who did not survive infancy, both sons.

I was practising my letters upon a slate. My younger sister was playing at our mother's feet. I was eight years old, my sister six.

There was a pot upon the stove, cabbage and potatoes simmering within. It was beginning to smell, the odour provoking a feeling of unease, though it was not the taste that concerned me. I was hungry, we were all three of us hungry, but it was not yet time to eat. Or rather, it was past time to eat, but we had to wait for my father's return before the frugal meal could be served.

Mother was looking wan and tired. She wiped sweat from her brow with a hand reddened by scrubbing in the cold water. Then she spoke the words that I had been dreading.

'Go and look for your father, would you?'

There was no curiosity or concern in her tone, only a beaten resignation.

Upon the stage, there is now an outside scene, a street.

I walked along it, my dragging feet a measure of my reluctance to reach my destination. There was no mystery to this quest. He had finished at the mill more than two hours before.

On this occasion I did not find him in the tavern, but barrelling out through its door as I approached, propelled by a bigger man at his back. I recognised the fellow from being sent on this sorry errand before. A few others followed him through the door, sensing the sport to come.

My father was short and wiry, his gait unsteady. The man at his back was tall, brawny and calm.

'Go home, Murdo. You have already drunk more than your fill. See, here is your daughter come to fetch you home. Go while you still have a little money in your pocket so that you might be spared the wrath of your wife.'

The others laughed. There was a wildness in Murdo's eyes owing to more than drink. The bigger man saw it.

'And spare the girl the sight of me putting her father to the ground.'

His tone appeared to be one of reason, but even at that tender age I recognised the scorn within it. I knew what it was likely to precipitate. What it was intended to precipitate.

My father let out a cry and flew at the man, but no quantity of rage is a substitute for size and swiftness. It was this fellow's job to keep order in his tavern, and this was an angry bantam flying at a bear.

The bear did what he had offered to spare the bantam: put him to the ground in the sight of his daughter, rapid blows landing without reply.

My father was left prostrate, winded. He was staring down at the mud in his daze, spitting blood, his ears ringing with laughter from the men who had come out to watch. They did not tarry, though. They got what they came outside for. The show was done.

But this play is not.

I ran to my father's aid. He lashed out to ward me off, as though offended by my very intention. The back of his hand caught my mouth, my tooth piercing my lip.

I did not cry out, nor weep despite the pain. I knew this would anger him further: a show of weakness, womanly weakness, despised by a man not blessed with sons.

'What use are you?' he often demanded of me. 'What use are any girls to a father? Just a draw upon a man's pocket. Worse than worthless.'

My mother tried to convince him that the next child would be a boy, afraid of his disappointment should she be wrong, his wrath should another son fail to survive.

I remember my mother's keening grief as she held the little bodies of my brothers. I remember my mother seeking me out for comfort once they were cold, lying down on the bed with her arms wrapped around me as she wept. These were perhaps the only times I knew her tender embrace beyond infancy.

My father climbed to his feet. I told him Mother had dinner ready at home.

He eyed the tavern door with a glower that lacked intent, but this did not mean his anger had been doused.

He walked with me towards Cumberland Street, his head low. He said not a word. To any other spectators watching the stage from the circle, he might appear meek and chastened, but to his daughter, this lengthening silence only added to her growing fear.

The stage now shows a tenement stair, where I am climbing three steps behind my father.

Still he had not said anything. I scented it long before we had reached the top landing. The meal had cooked far too long. There was an acrid odour of burning, the water having boiled away. I feared Mother must have become distracted by her washing, or even worse, fallen asleep.

Sometimes Father would be too drunk to notice. That night, though, I sensed a quiet focus about him. It was not the drink that had put him in this mind. The rage was already there, and the ale gave it fuel. But nothing fed the flames of it like the beating he had suffered and the laughter of his fellow drinkers.

He wrinkled his nose as he reached the door to our room, an expression of distaste swiftly becoming something deeper. Then he walked across the threshold, and here the curtain closes upon the stage, for there are scenes that the Lord Chamberlain would not pass as fit to be performed.

I do not know if this is because I looked away in my fear, or if it is truly that my mind will not permit me to remember.

What I do know is that the next morning, though the blood on her face had dried, my mother woke to find she was bleeding from below. She dragged herself to the hospital, where the stillborn child had to be drawn from her. By nightfall she was dead.

ELEVEN

arvis had not killed the cook.

As Raven stood by the window in the professor's study, he thought about the events of the previous evening. Following the panicked entreaty from the butler, they had risen instantly from the table and hurried down to the kitchen, to discover that Mrs Lyndsay was not dead but merely anaesthetised. Encouraged (and quite possibly misled) by Jarvis, the normally abstemious and rigidly decorous woman had taken a large glass of the doctor's special champagne, shortly after which she had collapsed onto the floor. It took several hours for her to fully return to her senses, during which time Jarvis had required several glasses of the doctor's brandy.

Raven had never seen him shorn of his impermeable equanimity and wondered if his upset was primarily over Mrs Lyndsay's well-being or the ramifications of his own culpability. Raven noted that the latter would have been simple enough to conceal. Jarvis often gave off an air of detachment, but this indicated that there was something warmer beneath the surface.

More troubling to Raven was the question of how Dr Simpson reconciled his certainty that chloroform was safe if administered properly, with his practice of serving it as a recreational beverage. He was concerned too by how quickly Simpson had dismissed

John Snow's advocacy of precision in chloroform's dispensing. Simpson's passion and enthusiasm for anaesthesia was invaluable to a cause that required such an indomitable champion, but Raven questioned whether the professor might be cavalier to the point of reckless in his defence of it.

It didn't take Mrs Lyndsay laid out on the floor and Jarvis worried he had killed her for Raven to side with Snow in believing that powerful agents should not be treated lightly. Raven had seen what alcohol did to his father. It was the magic potion that effected an unfailing transformation from merely a selfish philanderer into an angry brute, and the man would surely have killed his mother but for Raven's intervention.

He had been only twelve years of age at the time. Raven had saved her life, but what that night had witnessed was a burden no child should have to carry.

The experience had in its own way transformed him. In a world where it seemed easy to serve injury and lay waste, he had made it his vocation to heal. In Dr Simpson he believed he had found the perfect teacher: a man driven by the stated desire to alleviate pain and suffering. But was his mentor falling to a different form of intoxication, deriving from the power of that which he had discovered? He had never struck Raven as a seeker of fame, but the goddess of reputation ruled over the field of medicine with a capricious hand, and there were few who did not relish the gilding of renown when it was bestowed upon them. If chloroform took Dr Simpson's name with it across the world, would that affect his judgment when it came to its safety?

He turned from the window and looked around the room. Dr Simpson's desk was piled high with papers and books, lecture notes were strewn about, and amid all of this sat an unfinished letter. The last sentence was abandoned halfway through, ink dripping onto the paper from the nib of a discarded pen. The appointing of Mr Quinton as secretary had made little impact here.

The letter was addressed to Robert Christison, Professor of

Materia Medica and Therapeutics at the university. Raven read the line '. . . the discovery of a large effusion of blood upon the bed of our lamented patient . . .', and fully intended to read further, but heard someone approaching and so he stood back, turning towards the window again.

The door to the study opened and the professor entered carrying more papers and a large leather-bound volume which he dumped heedlessly into the middle of his overcrowded desk.

'Come away now, we must get on,' he said. He looked at Raven, his brow furrowed. 'Are you ready?'

'Of course,' Raven replied with conviction. 'I am familiar with the procedure. I imagine it will have to be repeated several times.'

'That is highly likely,' nodded the professor. 'There was once a case, a Lady Paget if I recall correctly, who required sixty-seven tappings in five years, yielding two hundred and forty gallons of fluid! That of course was an exceptional case. Hopes of ultimate and complete cure for ovarian dropsy by paracentesis are faint and slight indeed. Usually all that can be achieved is temporary palliation.'

There was a small rap at the door and Sarah entered, followed by Mrs Glassford. Raven met Sarah's eye, and he felt a growing frustration about seeing her once more without having the chance to talk to her.

In the midst of the previous evening's chaos there had been no opportunity for him to ask more about her, but perhaps that had been for the best. What he most wanted to know – when and how she came to be married – would have necessitated inappropriate and intrusive questioning. And yet he was tormented by this lack of information. He had only been gone a year. How could such a thing have happened in such a short space of time? Who was this Dr Banks and why would a gentleman from a good family take a housemaid as his bride? It made no sense to him and he found, to his chagrin, that such questions had continued to torment him into the small hours of the night, keeping him from sleep.

Raven had to admit that Sarah had a glow about her, though he did not care to dwell upon why. This was in stark contrast to the woman beside her, who if anything looked worse than she had done the day before; sallow, drawn and feeble. Raven took the patient's hand and helped her up onto the examination couch, which had been placed against one wall, close to the window to capture the best of the available light.

Sarah moved about the room with purpose deriving from an evident familiarity with all that went on there. She removed a box from the cupboard beneath the bookcase and took from it a small glass bottle and a cloth. Approaching the patient, she removed the stopper from the bottle just as Raven turned to check the instruments he had laid out. He made clumsy contact with her forearm and knocked the bottle from her hand. It landed on the floor, the contents pouring out and rapidly seeping into the carpet. The sweet smell of chloroform began to pervade the room.

Sarah looked at the floor for a moment, then at Raven, then finally at Dr Simpson.

'I'm sorry, sir.'

'Accidents happen, Sarah,' he told her. 'Just fetch another bottle.'

Sarah blanched. 'That was the last one,' she said.

'Then perhaps you would be so kind as to go to Duncan and Flockhart's and replenish our supply.'

'At once, Dr Simpson,' she said, then hurried off.

Dr Simpson stood poised, knife in hand, and Raven feared for a moment that he was about to start the procedure without the anaesthetic. Instead he bent to the floor and cut out a square of the chloroform-impregnated carpet. He handed Raven the knife and then held the remnant above the patient's nose and mouth.

'Take a couple of deep breaths if you please, Mrs Glassford.'

Mrs Glassford, to her credit, did as she was told, unperturbed by this improvised method of administration. Raven stood motionless, trying to comprehend what the doctor had just done. He was unsure whether this was impressive or not. He could not readily imagine any other practitioner of his acquaintance doing such a thing and wondered distantly what Mrs Simpson would say when she saw the hole in her Brussels carpet.

After a few minutes, Dr Simpson was satisfied that the patient was suitably anaesthetised and indicated that Raven should start. Raven wiped the knife on the sleeve of his jacket to remove any adherent carpet fibres and then made a small incision in the taut skin of Mrs Glassford's abdomen, between the umbilicus and the pubic bone. Then he picked up a metal trocar and, unwilling to seem in any way hesitant, thrust the instrument into the patient's abdomen.

A large bowl had been placed across the patient's knees ready to collect whatever effusion was about to pour forth. Raven removed the spiked trocar from the metal cannula, bracing himself for the ensuing deluge, but nothing came. Not a drop. He felt a growing anxiety. It was the first task he had been allotted by the professor since his return and he was signally failing in it.

Determined that this should not prove to be the case, he rotated the cannula a little and lowered his head to examine its end. He chose to do this just as Dr Simpson sought to encourage the flow of fluid by applying gentle pressure to the sides of the swollen abdomen. The result was a voluminous gush which hit Raven full in the face, splashing over his clothes, his hair and the patterned wallpaper. It even reached up as far as the framed diploma which hung on the wall above the examination couch.

He stood, dripping, while Dr Simpson regained control of the situation by occluding the end of the spouting cannula with his thumb. Raven removed himself from the line of fire and with sopping hands positioned the bowl more suitably to catch the torrent.

Six pints of fluid were eventually obtained (minus the volume that had soaked into Raven's clothes), decompressing the patient's abdomen. This would, more than likely, alleviate her breathless-ness and markedly reduce her discomfort. Raven's discomfort was not so swiftly relieved. He had to fight a strong impulse to run from the room, but dutifully remained, fluid seeping into his trousers, while the professor monitored the flow. He stood his ground until Simpson had applied an adhesive plaster to the patient's wound, then excused himself with as much dignity as he could muster, determined to leave before the patient woke up.

As he climbed the stairs to his room, feet squelching in his shoes, he heard footsteps behind him. He sighed as he realised that his embarrassment was about to be compounded. Of course it had to be Sarah, returning from the druggists' with a basket containing several large stock bottles of chloroform.

'What happened?' she asked, concern morphing into amuse-ment. As he turned around, a glob of something left the ends of his hair and hit the wall.

'We managed to decompress Mrs Glassford's abdomen.'

'So I see,' Sarah said, unable to contain a snort of laughter. 'I am certainly no expert in complex medical procedures, but I suspect you may be in need of a change of clothes.'

Raven said nothing, turning away to resume his ascent. He realised with some confusion that she was following him. She continued to do so until he entered his room, where he was further disturbed to see her put down her basket and move towards him as though meaning to help him off with his saturated clothing. This intended resumption of a familiarity they had once enjoyed only served to remind Raven of what intimacies she now shared with someone else.

'I can manage,' he said, brushing her hand away from his shirt button.

Sarah stopped smiling.

'I'll bring some warm water and towels,' she said, and left him to remove the rest of his clothing alone.

TWELVE

hen Sarah returned, she found Raven already dressed, a pile of sopping garments at his feet. He accepted the ewer of warm water she had brought up from the kitchen wordlessly and unsmiling.

Raven bent over the basin on his washstand and, without ceremony, tipped the ewer's contents over his head before vigorously scrubbing at his face. He then dried his face and hair, and handed the wet towel to her, his expression inscrutable.

She had thought the levity deriving from his misfortune might help set a tone for them to speak again, but she reckoned without him feeling humiliated. She had forgotten how proud he could be, how sensitive about how he might be perceived. In his absence she had recalled only the things she liked about him. Small wonder she had suppressed the very thing that had driven them apart.

She stared at him for a moment, unsure of what to say. He looked well. His lean frame had filled out a little and he had lost his Edinburgh pallor. His face was burnished by the sun and the scar on his cheek had faded to a thin white line. She experienced an urge to reach out and touch him, but she suppressed it. She felt suddenly uncomfortable. He too looked as though he wanted to be elsewhere.

Sarah felt the need to say something, to acknowledge the awkwardness between them.

'You didn't write to me,' she said.

It was both a statement and a question.

'I did not think it appropriate to do so.'

'Correspondence is a private affair and seldom a scandal.'

He had no answer to this. He shifted his weight from one foot to the other and looked at his shoes.

'Well, you didn't write to me either,' he replied, his discomfort making him churlish.

'An address is usually necessary when engaging in correspondence, and I had none.'

'We moved frequently. We were seldom in one place for any length of time.'

'Did you not think that I might want to know what it was like? Visiting the great hospitals of Europe? An opportunity that I will never have,' she added, an edge creeping into her voice. Now she was the one becoming churlish.

He said nothing for a while, then looked up at her, his brow furrowed.

'I am sorry,' he said. 'More than you will ever know. But it is too late now, isn't it? You are married.'

'Marriage does not preclude friendship.'

'I think your husband might disagree,' he said and moved past her towards the stairs.

THIRTEEN

aven returned to the doctor's study. He could see no point in skulking about in his room and he needed to get away from Sarah. Talking to her had only compounded his misery, though if he sought a return to the familiar, he could look to the fact that badly handling a discussion with Sarah had been a leitmotif of his time here. Another was that work always offered a useful distraction, and he wished to discuss the likely pathology underlying Mrs Glassford's condition.

Mrs Glassford had been taken from the consulting room to one of the guest bedrooms to recover from her ordeal, although Raven was apt to think he had suffered more from the procedure than she had. At least she had been anaesthetised for the duration of her part in it.

'If the seat of the disease is the ovary, why then is no attempt made to remove it?' he asked as he entered the room, intent on putting his embarrassment behind him.

'Attempts have been made,' Simpson replied. Raven was grateful he made no mention of what had just occurred. 'A small number have even been successful. However, it is a procedure much frowned upon by our surgical colleagues. Any trespass into the abdominal cavity is deemed by them to be a death sentence, the risks too great to countenance. Here in Edinburgh some years ago, John Lizars attempted four ovariotomies; he was unanimously denounced by his colleagues for his endeavours. Liston called him a "belly ripper". Surgical opinion has changed little in the intervening time.'

'Anaesthesia has not quite been the boon that I thought it would be,' Raven confessed. 'I had expected great strides in surgery as a result.'

'I think you will find a vast number of grateful patients who would disagree with you most vigorously on that point,' Simpson replied. 'But with or without anaesthesia, few survive the opening of the abdomen. Hence Caesarean section being an obstetricians' operation of last resort. It is done only that we might save the infant when we know the mother is about to die.'

Raven sighed as he thought about the tumour in Mrs Glassford's belly, a malignant lump that was most likely already in the process of replacing the fluid they had just removed. Their therapeutic efforts would only produce a temporary relief. Suddenly everything felt hopeless. Perhaps, he thought, he should not have come back at all. Nothing was as he had imagined it would be and he now knew there was a wide world out there beyond Edinburgh.

Dr Simpson placed a hand upon his shoulder. 'All may yet be well, Dr Raven. We must not lose hope; without it how could we continue?'

How indeed.

FOURTEEN

llow me to open the curtains upon another play, not quite a year after the last. Three figures stand outside the Belmont Institute, a charitable establishment dedicated, according to its articles, to 'laying hold of and educating neglected and destitute children who, having no parents, or worse, whose parents are themselves living in vice and profligacy, leave their offspring to grow up in ignorance to become vagrants or criminals'.

Murdo MacDonald had nominated himself as a parent qualifying in the latter category. He stood upon feet rendered unsteady by beer and whisky, a sorry sight with matted hair, ragged clothes and his arm in a sling. He told his daughters it was broken in an accident involving one of the looms. He railed against the carelessness of his colleagues and the negligence of their employer, but his broken nose, swollen purple eye and a dozen older scars bore testament to a more likely explanation for his injuries.

One thing he said was undoubtedly true: with his arm broken, he could not work, and consequently he had declared that he could no longer afford to feed his family. He wished to entrust his daughters to the care of the Belmont Institute instead.

He told us we would be here for 'a time', my younger sister firmly of the belief that he would return at the end of the day.

I knew otherwise.

I was nine years old. Ellie and I had grown taller in the months since our mother died, but no broader. We mostly lived on bread when Murdo had the money and the inclination to bring some home, and upon thin porridge when there was fuel enough for the stove.

From up in the grand circle, the spectators might notice a redness upon the backs of my hands, but not the rough patchwork of raised lines and welts that had not yet healed.

A few weeks before, my father had come home from the mill directly, not having any money left for the tavern. His consequent sobriety was seldom an ameliorative. I was scratching upon my slate at the table when he became suddenly enraged and seized me by the wrist.

'Look at these hands, so pale and fair and soft. Is it any wonder I'm penniless? These are hands that have known no toil, hands that do naught but take from me, who works all the hours God sends.'

He went to the sink, from where he lifted the scrubbing brush.

'Who is it you think you are, to have hands so smooth and unblemished? Some rich lady of the quality? Fancy yourself the wife of a merchant or the mill owner? You were made to work, girl. I'll show you how your hands ought to look.'

He held each of my hands down upon the table in turn and scrubbed until my knuckles were bloody and ragged. He struck me about the head each time I cried out with the pain, telling me: 'I will not cease until you show the strength to endure this lesson in silence.'

The only mercy that night, with my fingers still bleeding and sticky and raw, was that he spared my hands the other task to which he often set them while Ellie slept.

Thus, despite my trepidation and my concern for my sister, I regarded our entry into the Belmont Institute as a form of deliverance. I could not imagine a life worse than with our father.

FIFTEEN

aven was about to cross Leith Street when he heard the clatter of hooves behind him and the rumble of wheels on the cobbles, loud and sudden. It caused him to halt at the edge of the road, an instinctive reaction to the sound of a carriage taking the corner at an injudicious speed.

The coach whipped past him, then was pulled to an impromptu halt, causing the horses to strain against their own momentum and that of the weight they pulled. Raven looked up to see what kind of fool was so recklessly driving the carriage with so little concern for his own safety and the welfare of the horses.

He was jarred by the sight of who held the reins, a wretched creature who looked more fit for a hearse than a carriage, and for riding horizontal in the back rather than driving the thing. More disturbing still, Raven recognised him, and with it the implications. The man's skeletal visage and grim pallor hauled Raven's mind back to a black night he would never forget, and two terrifying rides in a stolen brougham. He wondered whether the owner of this contraption was currently questioning its whereabouts.

'Mr Raven, it appears we are rightly informed that you are back in town.'

His voice was a rasp, but it carried a weight nonetheless, albeit borrowed from the man he worked for.

'If you were rightly informed you would know it is Dr Raven.'

'Either way, get in. Your presence is sought.'

'And politely declined. I have a prior engagement. I am expected imminently at the Maternity Hospital.'

Raven heard a heavy thump of feet hitting the ground, a figure having jumped from the other side of the coach. A shadow loomed across the cobbles, stretched not merely by the low angle of the sun, and a moment later Raven was reacquainted with another grotesquery. It was the fellow he had christened 'Gargantua'. He was by some distance the tallest and largest man in Edinburgh, but not proportionately so: it was as though he had been stricken by some abnormality that caused only certain parts of him to keep growing. His huge, stretched head accommodated features that were not in keeping with one another, a vast nose below two seemingly tiny eyes.

Raven to this day felt the reverberation of the man's hammer-like fist, driven into his head unseen in an ambush. Nor would he ever forget the crushing weight of him as he pinned Raven to the sodden ground in that alley where his nightmare premonitions of death were born. But mostly what he recalled was the inescapable grip of his massive hands, which had held him down while another of Flint's men, the one he called the Weasel, had taken a knife to Raven's face.

'It was not a request,' said the deathly coachman.

Raven clung on to his seat as the carriage resumed its breakneck progress, though the coachman's reckless driving was not the primary source of his discomfort. Sheer weight alone seemed enough to anchor the monster sitting opposite, who sat all the while eyeing Raven with undisguised malevolence.

Raven understood his resentment but still found it difficult to be quite as sympathetic as he ought, given Gargantua's role in that alley. His enmity towards the giant, however, was as nothing compared to his hatred for the man who had wielded the blade.

Raven's scar was like a physical manifestation of the anger he carried. It would never fade. He had been in many brawls, a good deal of which he had picked himself for no greater reason than a desire to unleash the turmoil within. He had felt pain after the fights he lost and shame after many of those he won – but no matter the outcome, he never bore a grudge against any opponent for the blows he dealt in combat. However, when a man was pinned and defenceless, defeated and posing no threat, to inflict pain and damage upon him was the act of a despicable coward. It was impossible to forgive, and the mere sight of Gargantua made him appreciate that his desire for vengeance upon the Weasel had not diminished – merely lain dormant.

After a singularly uncomfortable journey, seemingly hitting every pothole in Edinburgh, the Skeleton brought the vehicle to a halt outside a warehouse in a narrow alleyway off Lady Lawson's Wynd. The air carried the stench of decay emanating from the many tanneries situated along the length of the West Port. Somehow this seemed appropriate.

Gargantua approached a door with peeling green paint, the sign above it having long since lost its lettering to the elements. He made a series of knocks, evidently a code of some kind. The door creaked open on rusty hinges and Raven was confronted with the visage he had come to hate most in this world. The Weasel greeted him with a sneer that combined simmering aggression with an undisguised smugness that Raven was effectively under his heel.

The intervening year had not been kind. The few teeth the whelp once possessed were gone, causing his face to collapse in on itself, and there was fresh bruising on the loose flesh of his right cheek. The hat he wore was tattered and his clothes hung loosely about his skinny frame.

'Follow me,' he grunted.

The interior was dusty and dark, but the smell was mercifully less appalling inside than out. Raven was led into an office, where the man who had summoned him was reclining on a chair, feet up on a desk, puffing on a fat cigar. The Weasel remained in the doorway, blocking his exit.

Callum Flint was another person he had been happy to put from his mind while he was abroad. Raven cursed himself for his naivety in thinking that his return to Edinburgh might have escaped Flint's notice. In truth, he had sincerely hoped the man would be dead. He lived a dangerous life and was not short of enemies.

Flint was a money-lender, or at least that was how he would describe his means of income were anyone in authority to ask. He was a neat man, deceptively slight of build for one whose name carried such fear before it. Raven reasoned he did not need brawn himself while he retained Gargantua's services, but nor did he believe that Flint had got where he was without a level of martial prowess and ruthlessness in dispensing it.

Raven had once owed him a debt, which Flint had commuted instead to what he referred to as 'an understanding'. The oblique nature of this had troubled Raven from that moment forward, but he understood that when you do a deal with the devil, you generally don't get to dictate the terms.

He had thought that in the time he was away, Flint might have accrued greater concerns that relegated Raven to an insignificance. How foolish he was to think so. Such men had long memories and an eye for detail where it represented an opportunity to exploit their fellow man.

Flint did not get up.

'Do take a seat,' he said, indicating the chair opposite his desk. It seemed incongruous that he should have such a thing, Raven imagining the man to deal entirely in theft and violence. He realised he had forgotten the mundane practicalities attendant upon money-lending.

'I am not one of your employees, expected to jump when you snap your fingers,' Raven told him, sending a glance towards the Weasel. He was in no mood for conversational niceties.

'I wish to discuss your outstanding debt.'

'I was under the impression that I no longer owed you money.'

'It is my recollection that, in lieu of the money you owed, we had come to a mutually beneficial arrangement. Your debt is no longer a financial one, but an obligation to assist me – in any way I see fit – remains.'

'What do you want?' Raven asked, failing to keep impatience from his voice.

'Chloroform,' Flint replied.

'Then present yourself at Duncan and Flockhart's on Princes Street.'

The money-lender looked up at him with narrow eyes, a warning that his own patience was limited.

'They only sell it to doctors and dentists. You know that.'

'Yes. Because it is dangerous stuff, especially in the wrong hands. What would you want it for? Your more accustomed expedient of clubbing someone over the head produces much the same result.'

'Strikes me there are ample possibilities, if one has the imagination.'

The Weasel nodded sagely. 'I read in the newspaper about a man who woke up naked in a whore's bed, having had all of his money stolen,' he said. His voice was reedy and nasal, his diction not aided by the state of his mouth. 'He claimed to have been chloroformed in the street.'

'I find that extraordinarily improbable,' Raven replied.

'That a whore could be capable of such a thing?' Flint asked incredulously.

'No, that this specimen was reading a newspaper.'

Anger flashed in the Weasel's eyes, not ameliorated by Flint's obvious amusement at the remark.

'As for the content of the story,' Raven went on, 'I think we can both imagine a more likely explanation for how that came about. No less an authority than Dr John Snow has disputed these sensational accounts of the use of chloroform in criminal matters. It is nigh impossible to administer it against a person's will.'

'Then why would you have an objection to supplying me with it?'

'Because there are ample possibilities, if one has the imagination.'

Flint pulled his feet off the desk and stood up from his chair. He was shorter than Raven, but there was an energy about him that was intimidating.

'Are you refusing me, Doctor?'

'Yes. If you wish to restore my pecuniary debt, very well. I will see it paid to be rid of you. Minus the fees I would expect for having delivered your wife of her child,' he reminded him.

Flint stepped closer, their faces only inches apart.

'I don't think you understand. If I ask something of you, you do it, or there will be consequences.'

At that moment, Gargantua loomed in the doorway, demonstrating that he had been awaiting his cue, while before him the Weasel pulled out his knife.

SIXTEEN

arah put the last of the doctor's instruments back into the battered leather bag and put on her coat. Their patient – Mrs Sutherland – was now wrapped in blankets and seemed much relieved that her ordeal was over. She was a fragile and anxious old lady and Dr Simpson had asked Sarah to accompany him as he thought that chloroform might be required for the minor procedure that he wished to perform. In the end the lady had managed without the aid of an anaesthetic, Sarah's presence alone providing suitable reassurance and distraction.

'I shall return in a day or two, Mrs Sutherland,' Dr Simpson said, waving over his shoulder.

As they left the house, Sarah thought that this represented as good an opportunity as any to broach the subject that had been preying on her mind.

'Is there ever any bleeding when such a procedure is performed?' she asked.

'The procedure itself or when the lint is removed?'

'At any point. How likely would it be that there is significant bleeding?'

Dr Simpson stopped walking.

'Significant haemorrhage would be unusual in such a case. At any point in the proceedings. Why do you ask?' He looked at her with those piercing eyes which immediately told her he would not be fooled. He knew precisely why she was asking.

'I know about the letters in the *Monthly Journal*,' she admitted.

'Are you worried that what they say is true?' he asked.

'Of course not,' she said, hurt that he might believe that to be the case. 'But such slander should not go uncontested.'

Dr Simpson resumed walking. 'Do not concern yourself, Sarah. Their claims are groundless.'

'Even so, they ought to be challenged. Perhaps Dr Johnstone would be willing to intervene. He could write a letter of support, stating the facts of the case.'

'I have no wish to trouble the man. He has lost his wife and should not be dragged into this affair. The whole thing is unseemly. A scurrilous abomination.'

'But— '

'Sarah, I thank you for your concern, but I have no wish to discuss the matter further.'

As they proceeded down the High Street, past St Giles', there was a near-continuous volley of greeting. Dr Simpson was well known, and evidently, despite the efforts of his detractors, still well regarded. Truth be told, it would be hard to miss him. He was quite distinctive in appearance and unlikely to be confused for another man. He had a large head, somewhat out of proportion with the rest of his body, and wore a narrow-brimmed hat, always pushed back, leaving the whole of his face exposed. His large nose, wide mouth and exuberant whiskers would have made him intimidating without his ready smile. He had a discernible presence, like the gravitational pull of a planet, irresistibly attracting lesser bodies into orbit around him.

But how long could such esteem last in the face of a sustained assault on his character? Sarah remained concerned and she knew that Dr Simpson was too.

'We have one more visit to make,' the doctor said, leading her across the road, away from a rowdy gaggle. A group of young men, bounded by several constables, was being marched towards the police office. A small crowd seemed to be trailing in their wake, intent on seeing who it was that the constables had apprehended.

They turned into Jackson's Close, a narrow alleyway where daylight filtered through rows of laundry hanging limply from the windows on either side. Stepping over a puddle of stagnant, mucky water, they entered the crumbling edifice on the left side of the close and made their way to a door on the first floor. Their knock was answered by a worried-looking woman carrying a small, snot-nosed child.

'Dr Simpson, thank the Lord you have returned. I fear she is no better.'

Sarah thought that the child looked perfectly well – nothing that a bath and some clean clothes would not cure – but it soon became clear that the child the mother held was not the patient they had come to see.

They were led into a small, simply furnished room. Their patient was lying in a truckle bed in front of a modest fire. She was as pale as the sheets she lay upon and her breathing consisted of short, raspy little gasps. Sarah wondered about the diagnosis. Consumption? Some form of infectious fever? There was a myriad of possibilities but naming the disease was of little consolation if nothing could be done.

Dr Simpson knelt down beside the bed and laid a gentle hand on the child's head. There was no movement, not even a fluttering of the closed eyes in response. He removed the wooden stethoscope from his bag, placed it on the child's chest and bent his head to listen.

Sarah noticed that the younger child, still clasped in the mother's arms, was transfixed by this strange prostration. The mother, too, was watching intently, silent tears coursing down her cheeks. She lifted the corner of her apron with her free hand and wiped her face. As the doctor stood up, she put out her hand

and clutched his arm, pulling on the thick material of his coat as though afraid she was about to fall. She looked directly at him and said in a whisper: 'Doctor, what am I to do?'

Dr Simpson paused, then covered her hand with his and replied gently, 'You must give her back to the Lord.'

The woman began to cry in earnest, letting go of the doctor's sleeve and clutching the younger child closer to her.

'My little Maggie was the same age when He took her,' Dr Simpson said quietly. 'I know how it is: how hard.'

Sarah felt the tears coming to her own eyes and was powerless to stop them. As she stood in the corner, witness to this most tragic of scenes, she wondered who her tears were really for.

SEVENTEEN

aven settled in behind his desk in the consulting room, preparing himself for the tide that Sarah would unleash when she began calling the morning's patients. He tidied sheets of paper into neat piles, ensured his ink pot was full and noted the marked contrast between this desk and that of the professor. He imagined the inside of the professor's head would resemble his untidy desk: a jumble of thoughts, stacked one on top of the other, ready to be blown about by the next cerebral tempest.

He heard a cursory rap upon the door and looked up to see not Sarah but Jarvis, who wordlessly handed him the first post before turning on a heel. Raven was about to put it aside for reading later when his eye was drawn by the unexpected profile of Friedrich Wilhelm of Prussia upon the stamp, and, upon a closer look, Henry's handwriting.

He felt a strange sensation of longing and nostalgia for what already felt like simpler times, conscious of a distance that felt so much greater than the miles of the journey. He had such happy memories of his year abroad, learning and expanding his horizons with Henry. It had seemed a time of endless possibilities, when every day was new, and discovery lay around every corner. But what lay around one particular corner had soured everything, and its shadow fell upon him now as he realised that to have reached here so soon, Henry must have penned the letter perhaps only a day or so after Raven left. What could have occasioned such urgency? Nothing good, he would wager.

Raven opened the letter hurriedly, his eyes playing impatiently over the text as he skimmed past the polite enquiries after his health and the welfare of the Simpson household. His gaze alighted on the real reason for writing:

> We had a visit from the Berlin police. A man was found dead the morning after we were attacked, in the very alley where I was shot. The police said he had a kerchief wrapped around his face, covering all but the eyes, undoubtedly one of the same ne'er-do-wells.
>
> Perhaps our assailants turned upon one another in their anger, or perhaps having been unsuccessful in their attempt to rob us, they set upon someone else and fared even worse. Certainly it appears that one of them encountered someone with an appetite for mayhem.

So Henry knew. Without saying as much, he was telling Raven he knew.

> It seems one of our neighbours must have observed our unquiet ingress that night, noting my injury. After the uprising last year, sadly there are many locals who know a gunshot wound when they see one. They questioned myself and Liselotte, who informed them that you had bravely fought off our assailants.
>
> I am curious, and I would admit troubled, as to why the police should be concerning themselves with the death of some itinerant brigand. I wondered if there was any light that you might shed upon the matter?

Raven most certainly could not, beyond the aspect that Henry had already deduced. Then he thought about the masks, the kerchiefs wrapped around their faces. He had assumed this was to prevent their being subsequently identified. But rather, could it have been to avoid being recognised?

He had killed a man whose face he never saw, but until now Raven had not thought to consider that he had a name. Henry did not know it, or he would have surely said, but it seemed likely the police did.

He put the letter down as the door opened, then hurriedly set it aside as Sarah walked in.

'I need to speak to you,' she said in a low voice, as though mindful of being overheard.

Raven was immediately wary. He had no desire to discuss anything pertaining to the relationship between them. If she was seeking to explain herself, then it was surely only so that she could feel better about what had happened, and he didn't see how that would benefit him. He therefore saw no point in any further discourse upon the matter. She had decided to marry another man. He would have to accept it and move on, but that didn't mean he had to offer her some form of absolution.

'I cannot imagine there is anything that we need to talk about. Please bring me the next patient.'

'It's about Dr Simpson,' she said.

'What about him?'

'There has been a recent difficulty. A patient died under his care. He has been accused of negligence.'

'By whom? The family? Grieving relatives often wish to apportion blame when in fact the practitioner bears no responsibility for an adverse outcome. I doubt they have grounds for their complaint.'

'It's not the family.'

'Then who?'

'Dr Matthews Duncan and Professor Miller.'

Raven got up from his chair. 'I don't understand. A former assistant and the Professor of Surgery are accusing him of killing a patient. Why?'

'There is not the time to explain right now. Come to dinner this evening. We can discuss it then.'

Without waiting for a reply, she left the room.

Dinner. With Sarah. And presumably her husband. He would rather be back in Berlin facing the police.

EIGHTEEN

he dishes on the table looked and smelled inviting but Raven had little appetite. How could he eat? He was sitting opposite Sarah's husband.

Dr Archie Banks was not what he had expected. Or, if he was being honest, not what he had hoped for. He had thought – one of the many explanations he had entertained – that perhaps Dr Banks suffered from some form of physical deformity, a dowager's hump or a facial disfigurement, to account for his taking a wife from so far outside his own social class. However, this had proven not to be the case.

Archie Banks was, incontrovertibly, an attractive man. He was tall, with a full head of sandy-coloured hair, neatly trimmed moustache, clear complexion and strikingly blue eyes. He was perhaps a little thin, but this could hardly be construed as a defect. He did not gorge his food or consume too much wine – in fact he ate and drank with considerable moderation. He expressed himself well though he said little. He seemed content to let Sarah do most of the talking. For all that Raven had been prepared to detest him, he found Archie to be disappointingly deficient in objectionable traits.

Raven tried to engage in polite conversation while he pushed the food around on his plate, but all he could think about was the fact that Sarah had married this man – and all that this entailed. By the end of the meal he felt thoroughly dyspeptic and would have excused himself and gone home but for the fact that they had not discussed the issue which had necessitated his coming here in the first place.

'So,' Raven said as the housekeeper cleared away the last of the dishes, 'regarding Dr Simpson. Tell me what has happened.'

Sarah waited for the door to close.

'It all started with a rumour.'

'These things usually do.'

'Originating with Professor Henderson,' she went on.

'Henderson. The homeopathy enthusiast. Everyone knows he has an axe to grind. Simpson has always been vocally opposed to that nonsense.'

Sarah frowned at him and he realised that he should probably let her continue without further interruption.

'Dr Simpson performed a procedure on a woman who subsequently died. Henderson claims that her bloodstained mattress is proof that she died as a result of haemorrhage. According to him, she bled to death and the fault lies with Dr Simpson.'

Raven opened his mouth to speak but thought better of it.

'This rumour was then given credence when Dr Matthews Duncan and Professor Miller went to interview the upholsterer about the mattress.'

'The upholsterer?'

'The mattress had been sent to him to be cleaned.'

'That is very irregular,' Raven said, now finding it impossible to hold his tongue. 'It is most unprofessional to instigate an arbitrary investigation into another doctor's practice.'

'They denied that they did,' Archie said. 'They claim that they merely sought refuge in his shop during a downpour while waiting for the omnibus and happened onto the subject by chance.'

Raven snorted. There were multiple implausibilities to this explanation, chief of which was the notion of the two Edinburgh doctors in question clambering to the top of a crowded omnibus. In the rain.

'Tell me about the case itself.'

'I'll tell you what I know,' Sarah said. 'Mrs Johnstone, wife of Dr Johnstone at 34 Queen Street, was to undergo a straight-forward procedure. Something to do with the cervix, I think. Professor Syme had performed a similar procedure two years before. Dr Simpson maintains that there was little bleeding, that the patient did not die as a result of haemorrhage.'

'What was the cause of death?'

'Inflammation.'

Raven refrained from asking how she came to know these things. He knew she had a habit of listening behind doors.

'Syme must be enjoying this,' he ventured. 'Has he entered the fray?'

'Not that I'm aware of.'

'What did the post-mortem reveal?'

'There wasn't one. Dr Simpson wanted to spare the husband further distress. Although I think he regrets that now.'

'What does Dr Johnstone say about this? He must have formed an opinion.'

'I don't know, but I think we should ask him.'

'We?'

'Yes. We ought to find out what really happened, don't you think? Dr Simpson seems content to write a few letters and hope the whole thing dies down. But I am not prepared to stand by and let his good name be sullied.'

Raven was surprised that Sarah should seek to involve him and was about to ask why her husband couldn't perform this role when Archie stood and excused himself.

'I'm afraid I'm going to have to withdraw. Please do accept my apologies but I am suddenly terribly tired.'

He reached out his hand and Raven shook it.

'I'm really very pleased to have finally met you,' Archie said.

'From what I have been told, if anyone could get to the bottom of this queer business, it would be you.'

Sarah also got up from the table and went to the sideboard. She took a glass bottle from it and followed Archie out of the room.

Raven thought this rather strange. He would have taken the opportunity to leave himself, but his curiosity was piqued by Archie's sudden withdrawal. Despite Archie's politeness, Raven wondered if he had unwittingly caused offence in some way. He had a tendency to do that, though it usually ended in a threat of violence rather than the injured party taking to his bed.

Sarah returned after a short time and put the bottle back into the cupboard.

'What is that?' Raven asked.

'Chloroform. It helps him sleep.'

Raven's opinion of this must have shown on his face.

'Dr Simpson suggested it,' she said, as though the mention of the great man's name would dispel all doubt as to the propriety of using an anaesthetic as a cure for insomnia. 'Mrs Simpson uses it on occasion too,' she added, sensing further justification was required.

'The professor seems to prescribe it for everything, showing little concern for the dangers associated with such indiscriminate use.'

'That is not true.'

'What about the patients who have died as a result of inhaling it?'

'Sometimes the chloroform is not pure. It is not always correctly manufactured. And there are frequently errors in how it is administered.'

'You sound just like him.'

'If you are referring to Dr Simpson, I have no issue with that.'

Raven sighed. He couldn't help but think about the incident with the carpet.

'Don't you ever fear he can be a little rash? A little impetuous?' he asked, moderating his tone. He did not want to get into an argument. This was her household, after all.

'I would say fearless. Robust in his opinions.'

'I suspect his enthusiasm for chloroform may on occasion cloud his judgment.'

If he hadn't given offence before, the look on her face left him in no doubt that he had given it now.

'Will Raven, you're not the first to have toured the great hospitals and institutions of Europe and come back convinced you know everything. You might have been listening to great minds discussing hypotheticals, but I have been working with Dr Simpson on the practical realities every day. I think I'm in a better position to assess how "cloudy" his judgment is.'

Raven answered quietly, choosing his words with concision and care.

'No one is infallible, Sarah.'

He could see the outrage building in her eyes.

'Do you doubt him? Are you saying you believe he might be guilty of what he is accused?'

He answered swiftly to head off her ire.

'Of course not. I am simply warning you that even Dr Simpson has feet of clay. As for this business, I suspect it is merely an unseemly squabble among rivals that is less about the facts of the case and far more about personal agendas.'

'Then you'll help me?'

He looked at her for a moment. There was a time when she could have easily talked him into doing just that, but those days had passed.

He thought about the forces ranged against Simpson, and not merely the ones who had shown their hands here. Raven was trying to build a career, and needed to forge profitable allegiances, not make powerful enemies. He thought about his fragile reputation and how it could quickly be tarnished by association. If he were discovered taking sides in this dispute, he would be mere cannon fodder in a battle between generals.

'As I already mentioned, it is unprofessional to secretly investigate another doctor's conduct,' he said. 'It would be no more appropriate for me to go snooping about behind Dr Simpson's back than it is for Miller or Matthews Duncan. I am quite sure that if the professor required my assistance in this matter, he would ask me himself.'

NINETEEN

espite the trouble it was to bring me, I think the killing of Mrs Johnstone remains the one of which I am most proud. It continues to amuse me that her death should have become the centre of so much controversy, the great men of Edinburgh medicine playing out their games of blame and innuendo, speculation and accusation across the journals and the newspapers. What sport they had, what duels they fought, and yet none came close to the truth. Supposedly the greatest medical minds in the city failed to deduce why she should have suddenly deteriorated and would not respond even under the care of the esteemed Dr Simpson, a man whose name is known around the world.

If I had anticipated what this death would precipitate, perhaps I would have savoured it more. But is that not often the way of things: how the most significant moments pass us by, only revealing their value to us after the fact?

And in any case, I did relish Mrs Johnstone's death at the time, in and of itself. It could be said that we made each other famous, so it was appropriate that we should have had our intimacy, our exquisite coupling.

I recall the warmth of her body against me. How her breath hastened as our limbs entangled beneath the sheets. A perversity, you would no doubt say: a forbidden kind of love. But my God, the things I felt as she died in my arms, knowing it was by my hand.

TWENTY

aven took a deep breath of the cold, clear sea air through the open window of the carriage and imagined the soot and the smog of the city being swept from him. They were on their way to Portobello to visit a patient there: a child who had a recurrent problem with her ears, attributed to bathing in the sea too late in the season. Raven was enjoying the journey as a welcome respite from everything else that was going on, and a distraction from the pain of a sore tooth that had begun to trouble him.

He rarely accompanied the professor on home visits, his time being taken up with his other duties. Most days he saw patients at Queen Street in the morning and attended the Maternity Hospital in the afternoon. He mainly saw Dr Simpson at meal-times, though he had declined an invitation to participate in the doctor's ongoing post-prandial inhalational experiments. He decided that he had no stomach (or head) for such things and marvelled at the professor's enthusiasm for persisting with such a risky undertaking. Raven agreed with Jarvis that the professor was unlikely to find anything better than 'chlory'.

When on occasion he was invited along, Raven enjoyed the novelty of a change of scene, be it a Princes Street hotel or a jaunt further afield. He had ceased trying to impress the professor with the knowledge he had accumulated on his travels and was rediscovering the value of listening to his mentor hold forth on any number of topics.

He felt a little guilty that he had refused Sarah's request, and found himself seeking reassurance that he was right not to get involved.

'Pay no heed to idle chatter,' Simpson said. 'I have more important things to occupy my time. I remain busy in the defence of chloroform. Pockets of opposition still persist, and I am determined to root them out.'

Raven wondered if his own reservations about its indiscriminate administration were being referred to. And although Simpson's reply regarding the Johnstone case ought to have comforted him, paradoxically it had the opposite effect. It was often the things that Simpson did *not* want to talk about that were preying hardest upon his mind. Everything else was a pleasing diversion.

As they passed Piershill Barracks, Dr Simpson began extolling the virtues of sea air for all manner of complaints, indicating that their previous conversation was at an end. The cold wind which had initially seemed refreshing now felt distinctly icy, but there seemed little likelihood of the carriage windows being closed. Raven sat back as the brougham rumbled on, concerned that the end of his nose might succumb to frostbite by the time they reached their destination. The chill was proving no friend to his sore tooth either.

They drew up at a house situated on a wide avenue with an uninterrupted view of the sea. The sound of waves could be heard through the open windows of the carriage and Raven could taste salt on his tongue. Simpson sat for a moment before disembarking. Raven assumed he was enjoying the vista before them, but the professor sighed and said quietly to himself: 'How I yearn for an outing without the usual invalid at the end of it. I really must get a week or two free from the bell and sick folk.'

Raven wondered if the professor's workload was beginning to take a toll on the man, but any self-pity, if such it was, he quickly brushed aside. He turned to Raven and smiled.

'Come away now,' he said, stepping down from the carriage.

The front door opened as they ascended the steps and a worried-looking woman directed them to the room where their patient lay sleeping.

'She has been awake all night, poor lamb,' said the child's mother. 'She has only just fallen asleep.'

'Then we must endeavour not to wake her,' Simpson replied.

They entered a room, shutters closed against the brightness of the day, an oil lamp providing a dim glow in one corner. The child was lying propped up on several pillows, turned slightly towards them, her left ear uppermost. Her face was flushed, the ear a brilliant red, like glowing coals, and seemed to be giving out almost as much heat.

Dr Simpson removed his coat and quietly knelt down beside the bed. He placed his hand lightly on the child's head and then felt for the pulse at the wrist. Then he stood again, opened his bag and removed a glass jar containing several leeches.

Raven observed the mother's revulsion upon seeing the damp, black creatures. He masked his own surprise better, but hers was exacerbated by fear for her child. Raven had seen that look before when unpleasant treatments were prescribed: squeamishness at the prospect of what must be done, mixed with a greater dread that the diagnosis must be terrible to have necessitated such a course.

Simpson was about to unclip the lid when he paused and squinted at the ear.

'Will, bring the lamp over here if you please. Hold it up so that I may see.' Raven retrieved the lamp from a table in the corner of the room and held it above Simpson's head. The doctor pulled gently on the pinna of the child's ear and moved his own head from side to side as if trying to get a better view of something.

'Ha!' he said at last.

He rummaged in his bag for a small metal probe. (Raven always marvelled at the selection of instruments that could be mined from the doctor's bag.) He then prodded carefully within the ear canal, and after a few minutes extracted a round object which had been lodged within it.

Simpson placed the object upon Raven's outstretched hand to allow him to examine his find. Raven rolled it back and forth over his palm. It was a spherical concretion which could have been, in its original form, animal, mineral or vegetable.

'Is it a bead?' Raven asked, making what he thought to be an intelligent guess.

Simpson punctured the surface of the object with his probe and held it closer to the light.

'I think it is, or was, a pea,' the doctor said. 'Children have a great propensity for placing small items within the cavities of the nose and the ear. This curious behaviour defies any rational explanation, but the presence of such a foreign body does provide us with the reason for the child's recurrent ear problems. Mystery solved.'

Chuckling to himself, Dr Simpson then unclipped the lid of the leech jar and applied several of the creatures to the most inflamed parts of the ear.

Evidently, he had noted Raven's previous response.

'I am entirely sceptical about the efficacy of relentless purging, blistering and bloodletting,' he said. 'However, leeches do serve a useful function, if one altogether more limited and specific than our predecessors – and sadly still some of our peers – believe. They are most efficient at reducing engorgement, and they seem to purify the blood in some way, as if removing the poisons responsible for fever.'

When both his work and that of the leeches was done, he stood and indicated that they should all now leave the child in peace. Outside the bedroom door, he whispered something to the mother, handed her a prescription and then began making his way down the corridor.

Simpson halted suddenly and sniffed. Raven was momentarily confused by this until the aroma which had stopped the doctor in his tracks met his own nose, now happily defrosted.

'I smell toffee,' said Simpson.

The mother looked alarmed for a moment, as though the making of such confectionery would be frowned upon when there was a sick child in the house.

'It's for Christmas,' she said by way of explanation. 'I like to plan ahead.'

'Just so,' said Dr Simpson, smiling approvingly. 'I love toffee. Toffee's very wholesome.'

When Dr Simpson and Raven left the house, they carried with them several fat, satiated leeches and an abundance of toffee wrapped in paper. Almost as soon as they were ensconced in the carriage, Simpson unwrapped one of the paper parcels and offered Raven a piece.

'Thank you, no,' Raven said. 'I have a painful tooth.'

'You should have that attended to,' Simpson suggested.

Raven was about to say that his work commitments left precious little time for such things but thought the better of it. He did not wish to seem disagreeable or lacking in gratitude, especially when the professor's own workload appeared to be wearing him down.

'Does it pain you now?' Dr Simpson asked.

'Yes,' said Raven, putting his hand to his jaw. 'It kept me awake for much of the night.'

Simpson stuck his head out of the carriage window and called for Angus, his coachman, to stop. He then gave the man directions that Raven could not hear. A few minutes later the carriage turned from the main road onto a side street lined with a small row of shops.

Raven looked out and saw that they had drawn up outside a druggists'.

'Why have we stopped here?'

'A small amount of chloroform on a piece of lint applied directly to your troublesome tooth will provide relief until you see a dentist,' Simpson said, getting down from the carriage. 'Unfortunately, I have none in my bag.'

Raven was about to object that there was no need, but the throbbing in his jaw said otherwise. He was bemused, however, by Simpson continuing to suggest chloroform for every ailment. If he persisted, he would begin to look like a snake-oil salesman brandishing a cure-all. If he ever proposed its use as a treatment for baldness Raven would be compelled to intervene.

Somewhere gloomy in the back of his mind, he thought about the bottle he had been forced to supply to Flint, and worried what the money-lender and his crew of reprobates planned to do with it. It did not lessen Raven's guilt that he had been left with little choice but to acquiesce, though he did console himself with the truth of what he had told the man: chloroform would not do for them what they hoped it could – but that had not prevented misconceptions flooding the newspapers, and pharmacists regulating their supplies accordingly.

They entered the shop to find a small woman with grey hair vigorously scrubbing down the counter. Her shop was well-stocked and neatly kept, not so much as a jar out of alignment with its neighbour. The woman looked up at them and scowled, as though customers were a great inconvenience.

'What can I do for you gentlemen?' she asked, putting down her cloth and wiping her hands on her apron.

'I would like to purchase a bottle of chloroform,' Dr Simpson said, giving her his warmest smile.

It failed to have its usual effect. The woman sucked air in through her teeth and shook her head.

'I don't think I can help you,' she said. 'We don't sell it to them that kens nothing aboot it.'

TWENTY-ONE

he was not prone to such feelings, but Sarah was experiencing a profound discomfort about her surroundings. It was as though the chamber she found herself sitting in seemed to be closing in around her; or, even more disturbingly, that she was growing larger and all the more conspicuous within it. It was a small parlour dominated by a marble fireplace that was too big for the size of the room. There was also a surfeit of furniture: armchairs, tables, an elaborately decorated armoire, planters and plant pots. The curtains were closed and the mirror above the fireplace was draped in black crepe. The clock on the mantelpiece was stopped. Either the maid had failed to wind it, or it had been deliberately left that way to commemorate the hour of Mrs Johnstone's death. Were it the latter, then it was a strange custom for a medical man to observe.

Anxiety was beginning to contribute to her sense of slow suffocation. Perhaps she should not have come. The housemaid had looked at her askance when she had asked to see Dr Johnstone, thinking that she was a patient. She had assured the girl that she was not but had some difficulty explaining the reason for her visit. A private matter, she had said.

She was belatedly coming to appreciate that there was a form of safety in playing the restricted role of a maid or some other menial. Married or not, to present yourself as an independent woman on business of your own volition was to place yourself outside the protection of certain structures, and it was making her feel vulnerable.

Her mind turned to Will Raven and his refusal to assist her. She was surprised at his lack of concern for Dr Simpson, his reluctance to come to his mentor's defence. He seemed to have forgotten all that the doctor had done for him: taking him on as an apprentice, accommodating him under his roof, nurturing his talent; to say nothing of believing that he had talent in the first place.

Despite his outburst, she did not think Raven believed he had outgrown Dr Simpson, and that a year abroad had rendered further instruction superfluous. The professor was fond of saying that the medical practitioner should never cease to be the medical student, that professional distinction was dependent upon continuously extending knowledge by constant observation, reflection and reading. Raven would be quick to agree with Simpson that we are all works in progress, forever incomplete. He would not have taken on the role of assistant otherwise. Why, she wondered, was he therefore so reluctant to show loyalty to someone he apparently esteemed?

And thus, she happened upon the answer.

His indifference towards the professor was a mere proxy for the lack of loyalty he believed had been shown him. His disaffection was not with Dr Simpson: he was angry with her.

But why? For marrying someone else in his absence? He had no right to feel there had been any kind of disloyalty involved. He had left her in no doubt that he saw no future for them beyond simple friendship, and even indicated that that might not be appropriate once he was a practitioner in his own right. He had been, and still was, too concerned with the appearance of things and the possible repercussions for his standing.

Reputation. Character. These were currency in society. As a

woman she was just as constrained by them as he was; possibly more so. But to her mind that did not excuse his lack of concern for Simpson and his refusal to help clear the doctor's name.

The door opened, and Dr Johnstone came in. He had the look of a bloodhound about him: reddened eyes, droopy eyelids and the flesh of his jowls hanging loosely about his starched collar. He might have looked comical or at least benign had he been smiling. But he wasn't, for why would he?

'What can I do for you?' he asked, and then, without waiting for an answer, demanded: 'I'm sorry, who *are* you?'

Sarah was aware that it was only a few short weeks since his wife had died. A lack of civility was to be forgiven.

'My name is Mrs Banks.'

Her married name still sounded strange to her when she said it aloud, but, on this occasion, she thought that it might help lend her a degree of gravitas and respectability.

'Young lady, you have not answered my question.'

'I work for Dr Simpson.'

'In what capacity?'

Sarah wished, not for the first time, that she had some form of official title to explain what she did.

'I help with the patients.'

'I see.' It didn't sound like he did. 'Why are you here?'

'Accusations have been made about Dr Simpson.'

'Accusations?'

'Yes. That he was in some way responsible for your wife's death.'

Dr Johnstone drew in a deep breath. His brow furrowed and he began to look thunderous. The bloodhound was transforming into an attack dog.

She hurried on.

'I do not believe that, of course. That is why I'm here. I wish to try and establish the truth of the matter and put an end to hurtful speculation.'

'Is Dr Simpson aware that you have come here?'

'No, sir.'

'And what makes you think you have any right to ask questions on his behalf? Under other circumstances I would laugh. But I don't much feel like laughing.'

He was glowering at her. Sarah stood up and started backing towards the door.

'I am seeking to pursue this under the utmost discretion,' she told him, her voice faltering.

'Your presumption defies belief. As if I would discuss the death of my wife with you. Someone entirely unknown to me. A woman.'

'I am sorry. It was not my intention to upset you or cause offence,' she said.

'Well, it very much seems that you have. Good day to you, Mrs Banks. You can see yourself out.'

TWENTY-TWO

aven was finally ushering what he fervently hoped to be the last patient back into the hallway when the front doorbell rang. Dr Simpson was away, having agreed to make a visit to Hamilton Palace in Lanarkshire. Raven marvelled at Dr Simpson's ability to mix as comfortably with the aristocracy as he did with the fishwives of Newhaven. He had once described the Duke and Duchess of Sutherland and their daughter Lady Blantyre as 'good loveable plain folks', though given his subsequent description of Stafford House, with its marble pillars, enormous mirrors and walls and ceilings inlaid with gold, Raven found that he was disinclined to believe him.

Dr Simpson's absence had left them short-handed (and Raven short-tempered, still suffering as he was from intractable tooth-ache) on what proved to be a particularly busy morning, and the clinic had over-run into the brief time he had for lunch before he was due to head out to the Maternity Hospital. He and Sarah shared a look at the sound of the bell, acknowledging that it appeared this interminable trial was not yet at an end. It was the only time this morning that their feelings had been in concert.

Sarah had made a point of telling him how badly her

enquiries were faring, as though this was consequently his fault. She had gone to see Dr Johnstone and apparently been given short shrift.

'This is why I did not think it a wise course,' Raven had replied. 'The list of people likely to be antagonised by your enquiries only *begins* with Dr Johnstone.'

This had not gone over well.

'I might have made some progress had I been in the company of a doctor,' she insisted. 'Or at least a man.'

'Then in that case I am obliged to wonder why you did not engage the assistance of your husband.'

All exchanges between them thereafter had been chilly but professional, a cursory civility dictated by the needs of the clinic. Was this how it was going to be now?

Raven heard Jarvis open the door and explain to whoever had petitioned that Dr Simpson was not at home. 'Perhaps Dr Raven might be able to assist,' Jarvis suggested, his tone intending to discourage further enquiry. He might well have added, 'Or perhaps Glen, Dr Simpson's dog?'

Nevertheless, Raven heard a voice mutter: 'Very well, that will have to do.'

Raven stuck his head around the door in time to see a rather odd little man step into the hallway.

He was dressed in a suit that was no doubt once well made, but appeared to have served decades of wear. The buttons on his waistcoat strained to hold back a protuberant belly before what was otherwise a skinny frame, and Raven was uncomfortably reminded of Mrs Glassford for a moment.

'I am Dr Fowler,' he said. 'I was having difficulties with a patient and I hoped I might trouble Dr Simpson for his judgment. I gather he is from home.'

'As must I be very soon,' Raven tried to explain. 'I was just about to leave. Our morning clinic has over-run and I am bound for Milton House.'

'Then our purposes coincide. My patient is in Broughton Street. It will not be such a great detour for you.'

Raven suppressed a sigh, thinking of how Dr Simpson would respond were he here.

'Very well,' he said. 'I will be with you presently.'

Raven hoped Dr Fowler's command of matters medical proved better than his grasp of geography, Broughton Street being in utterly the opposite direction from Milton House. He calculated that this necessary detour would come at the cost of having any lunch at all if he was to be in time for his work with Dr Ziegler. He therefore made his own minor diversion to the kitchen to grab a bread roll for the road. Mrs Lyndsay's admonition was ringing in his ears as he left, prompting him to think that no good deed ever went unpunished.

It was a sentiment that returned to his mind a short time later as he stood at the end of the bed, contemplating Dr Fowler's patient. They were in a room denuded of all furniture save the bed and a solitary chair.

'The nurse who has been helping the family has a very strict policy about the management of the sick room,' the doctor explained.

Dr Fowler had said little on the walk along Queen Street, save for occasionally muttering about a 'terrible loss', which made Raven wonder how dire the situation was that awaited him. Raven had suggested hailing a hansom cab as his time was limited, but Dr Fowler objected to this extravagance. It was not a great distance, he said, and was therefore a journey best made on foot. The worn condition of Dr Fowler's footwear suggested to Raven that this was his primary mode of conveyance and reminded him that not all medical practitioners enjoyed the patronage of wealthy clients.

As it turned out, it was not an obstetric case that Dr Fowler was having trouble with, but this was not a surprise. Although Dr Simpson was a physician with a special interest in midwifery and the medical disorders of women and children, he was known to be a skilled diagnostician and his opinion was frequently sought by those dealing with cases outside this purview.

This patient was not even a woman. After spending a short time with him, it was one of the few clinical observations Raven would have trusted Dr Fowler to get right.

Raven stood with his arms folded and tried to think. Something was amiss, but he was struggling to identify what that something might be.

The patient's name was George Porteous. He was a young man with pale skin and a full head of red hair. He was lean but not thin, someone who had been well nourished. He looked to be in good health apart from the fact that he was soporous and could not be roused.

'He has been like this for two days,' Dr Fowler said. 'But at least the twitching has stopped.'

'The twitching?'

'Yes. Of the facial muscles. He was delirious for a while, muttering and clutching at the bed clothes.'

'You mean convulsions?'

'No, I would not say convulsions.'

'Any fever?'

'No fever. The pulse was elevated initially but not now.'

Raven approached the bed and laid a hand on the patient's forehead. It was warm, not hot, and free from perspiration. He gently lifted each eyelid in turn and found both pupils were normal in size. The patient's breathing was shallow, so shallow that Raven had to put his ear to the patient's chest to confirm that it had not ceased altogether.

'Is he a drinker?' Raven asked, although he thought it an unlikely explanation as there was no smell of alcohol.

'Not according to his sister.'

'Did he complain of any other symptoms? Headache, giddiness or palsy?'

'No. As far as I am aware, he experienced no unusual symptoms except for fatigue. He took to his bed and was then found by his sister to be at first delirious and then as you see him now.'

Raven had to admit to himself that he was mystified.

'I applied leeches,' Dr Fowler said, 'but rather curiously they all fell off and died. I did manage to bleed the patient, though,' he added, indicating a bleeding bowl on the floor next to the bed. 'Several ounces, but to no avail. My next suggestion was going to be a clyster to purge the bowels.'

Raven might have been at odds with Simpson on certain matters, but he was wholeheartedly in agreement about the limited usefulness of bleeding and purging.

'I think perhaps he has been drained of enough,' he said.

They opted to continue their discussion out of earshot of the patient, though he did not appear likely to hear much in his current state. Raven followed Dr Fowler into the hallway, a dark passage lit only by a small window into which little light was admitted due to the height of the buildings opposite.

'It is most perplexing,' Dr Fowler said. 'A young man, previously in good health. Clean living. Recently bereaved, poor soul.'

'Bereaved?'

'Yes, his mother died just last week. Heart failure.' Dr Fowler shook his head sympathetically. 'They say that a person may die of grief. Do you think that is so?'

Raven tried to keep a growing incredulity from his voice.

'Surely that would be a diagnosis of exclusion. There are many other possibilities to be ruled out before entertaining such a thing.'

'Perhaps they removed his mother's body head first,' Dr Fowler suggested.

'What do you mean?'

'A corpse should always be removed from the house feet first lest it beckon others to follow.'

Raven looked askance at the man.

'Did you, by any chance, obtain your medical degree from St Andrews?'

Dr Fowler looked momentarily confused. 'No, Edinburgh,' he replied, missing the veiled insult implied by this question. It had once been the case that, in their eagerness for funds, the University of St Andrews would issue a medical degree by post, without visit or examination, for the simple fee of ten pounds.

'What do you think is the diagnosis here?' Raven asked, hoping to redirect the man's thoughts and curtail this nonsense; although given what had just been said, he did not anticipate giving his opinion much credence.

'Some form of apoplexy?' Fowler suggested.

'Perhaps. His age would count against that and if there had been any kind of bleeding within the skull there would be other signs, would there not?'

The nurse appeared at the landing, a slight woman in a navy-blue dress.

'I'm just stepping out briefly, Dr Fowler,' she said. Her accent was not local. Raven thought she might be from Glasgow.

'I still think we ought to purge him,' Fowler said, repeating his earlier suggestion, perhaps for the nurse's benefit as she retreated downstairs.

'Absolutely not,' Raven insisted. 'You asked me here for my advice and that is it. Perhaps if you desist from relentless depletion, he might recover sufficiently for me to make a better determination of what ails him.'

The older man shrugged. 'Very well,' he conceded, though he didn't sound convinced.

Fowler went back into the patient's room and returned presently with his jar of dead leeches.

'A terrible loss,' he said, shaking his head.

Even in the dark of the hallway, Raven failed to conceal his disdain.

'Your leeches?'

'Why, yes. I've had them for some time, and they have served me well. I think of them as my little assistants.'

'Perhaps their working life was excessively extended,' Raven suggested, placing a hand on his colleague's shoulder. 'An earlier retirement from practice might well have saved them,' he added, hoping to plant a suggestion in the old relic's head.

TWENTY-THREE

arah poured tea into two china cups of expensive porcelain decorated with briar roses. The delicately painted pink petals made her think of the rosehip tea her grandmother had made them all drink during the winter months to ward off coughs and colds. She now spent considerably more time drinking tea than merely pouring it for others, but unlike the other married ladies of the New Town, could not imagine being satisfied by a future wherein tea drinking would occupy so much of her time. She preferred to work and to study, which was just as well as such solitary pursuits did not tend to garner many friends.

Mrs Glassford sat opposite her in a high-backed chair, a mound of cushions supporting her back, her swollen feet elevated on an embroidered stool. Sarah handed a cup to her companion and noticed as she did so that Mrs Glassford's tremulous grip caused a little spillage into the saucer. She was barely eating anything at all now, subsisting mainly on tea and thin soup. A pauper's diet.

'Have you thought any more about Dr Simpson's offer?' Sarah asked.

'Of moving into a room at Queen Street? It is kind of him to suggest it, but I manage well enough here. I have a housemaid to assist me.'

'Do you receive any visitors?'

'None in addition to your good self. I know so few people here that I am left entirely unmolested. I am at liberty to spend my time as I choose, which I consider to be a great luxury.'

'Your family are all in Glasgow?'

'My parents reside there, but I doubt that they know where I am. Family ties have been severed for some time.'

'I'm sorry to hear that.'

'It was the price I paid for choosing my own path.'

'Your own path?'

Sarah felt the usual tension provoked by such snippets of information – polite rectitude straining against a ravenous curiosity. When your own life had been so limited, the exploits of others became a source of fascination.

'I refused to marry the man my father had so carefully selected for me. A man of property who saw me in much the same way: an object to be owned, an acquisition. He was considerably older than I was, self-obsessed and controlling. I despised him.'

'Did your father know this? The reasons why you did not want to marry?'

'My opinion was irrelevant. Or so I was told. I was accused of being difficult, obstructive. But I had no wish to become an ornamental fixture with nothing to do but supervise servants and produce male heirs – "A toy of man who must jingle in his ear whenever he chooses to be amused." Wollstonecraft said that.'

Sarah was unfamiliar with the quote and the lack of recognition must have shown on her face.

'Wollstonecraft,' Mrs Glassford said again, as though repetition would invoke some kind of understanding. 'Don't tell me you have not read her *Vindication of the Rights of Woman*?'

Sarah shook her head.

'That is a deficiency we should rectify immediately. You must have my copy.'

'Thank you,' Sarah said. 'What happened after that?'

'I was sent to live with a maiden aunt as punishment. Father thought it would teach me about the lonely life of a spinster – a redundant woman, as he put it – but the experience had quite the opposite effect. My aunt opened my eyes to the world. She hardened my resolve. She was a committed bluestocking: enthusiastically devoted to academic pursuits and adamant that women were equal to men intellectually. She was an inspiration.'

'Was?'

'Yes. She died some years ago. I was inconsolable. My father suggested that she had overtaxed her brain, which left her vulnerable to bodily corruption or some such pernicious nonsense. I resolved at that point to have nothing further to do with him, to live my life on my own terms, free from male domination. But so few respectable occupations are available to a woman. It was a struggle; a lonely one at that.'

'How did you manage?'

'Private tutoring, piano lessons, that sort of thing. And my aunt left me some money, which was a help.'

'And then?'

'And then I met my husband. I had not thought to marry, but he surprised me. When we first encountered one another, I was terribly rude to him, and he later told me that was what drew him to me. He had not thought to marry either. He sought a life distant from convention, one full of excitement and challenge. "There is no room on this voyage for passengers, only crew." That was what he used to say.'

She smiled sadly at the memory.

'Our merry crew of two. We thought we were bound for a life of discovery and adventure, but alas, it was not to be. A few weeks in India was all that it amounted to in the end.'

Mrs Glassford sipped her tea, her eyes misting. Sarah felt a lump in her own throat. What was worse, she wondered: having the dreams of such adventures taken away or knowing already that your life together will be cut short?

She felt the need to change the subject, and to break the growing silence.

'What was it like, India?'

'Hot. So stiflingly hot. And dusty. But also exotic and invigorating. I was not there long, but it was enough to convey what a tiny corner of the world this is.'

'Did you see elephants?'

Mrs Glassford seemed surprised by the question.

'I did. Why do you ask?'

'I saw an elephant once, at the Edinburgh Zoological Gardens in Broughton Park. As close as I will ever get to India, I should think.'

'Nonsense. You are young yet. You do not know what your life will become.'

'They also had a lion. And monkeys. And an eighty-four-foot whale skeleton. It was found floating off Dunbar and was dissected on the beach by Robert Knox. Dr Simpson says that Broughton Park is far superior to the zoological gardens he visited in Surrey, where the lion had cataracts and the monkeys all had consumption.'

Mrs Glassford laughed. 'Well, it seems, Sarah, that you have seen more of the world than I without having had to leave Edinburgh. I shall have to go to this Broughton Park sometime.'

They sat in silence for a while, both knowing that such a trip was unlikely to occur.

'I do sometimes wonder if I am being punished,' Mrs Glassford said quietly.

'Punished?'

She indicated her swollen abdomen.

'That I have angered the gods in some way in failing to honour my father's wishes.'

Sarah thought of her own parents, and of the Simpsons' lost children.

'I have never found that death or disease discriminate in such a way,' she said. 'Good and bad, rich and poor, the sinner and the righteous man: all are vulnerable. No one is protected. And I don't believe that you are being punished. As far as I am concerned, you have done nothing to deserve such a thing. You simply lived your life as you wanted to, and I can see no fault in that. The sin is that more of us do not do likewise.'

TWENTY-FOUR

here were times when Raven wondered about the wisdom of his choice of profession: when a baby died; when a mother died; and on occasions such as this, when he found himself on his knees at a bedside, his hand deep inside a recently vacated uterus, trying to retrieve a reluctant placenta. By rights the thing should have detached itself with no assistance from him, but it had shown no inclination to do so.

'Just find the edge of it and peel it off the uterine wall,' Dr Ziegler suggested, having placed himself well out of range of any blood spatter at the patient's other end. 'Are you going to be much longer?' he added, lifting the chloroform bottle.

'No, I have it,' Raven said as he felt the placenta come away.

He got to his feet, a bloody, pulpy mass of tissue and membrane clutched in his hand. He felt like a distorted reflection of the nurse alongside him, who was clutching an altogether more welcome bundle.

'There must surely be an easier way of doing this,' Raven muttered.

'Some suggest injecting the umbilical vein with cold water, diluted vinegar or brandy but I have never found such interventions to be in any way effective,' Ziegler said. 'And never underestimate the skill required to do this procedure well. I read of a case recently where a surgeon removed part of the uterus and a small section of intestine in addition to the placenta.'

'And yet Professor Syme maintains that certain procedures should only ever be carried out by surgeons.'

Raven placed the now rather macerated organ into a bowl to examine it and ensure that it was complete. He noticed that Dr Ziegler was staring at him with a look of amusement, and realised that despite having rolled his sleeve up beyond the elbow, it was stained with blood all the way to the shoulder seam.

'I don't think you're going to get another day out of that shirt,' he said, laughing.

Raven usually enjoyed working with Dr Ziegler at the Maternity Hospital, but today Ziegler's good humour was wasted on him. He had received another letter from Henry, telling him that Gabriela had gone, and nobody knew where. Henry was subtly enquiring as to whether she might have followed Raven to Edinburgh as part of some secret assignation, though he could tell that his friend was clutching at straws. Raven replied to assure him that her disappearance so soon after his leaving was entirely coincidental, though he also expressed curiosity as to whether its coming so soon after the incident in the alley and the subsequent police inquiry could also be put down to mere happenstance.

It troubled him to think of what could have occasioned her sudden flight, as it troubled him to consider what Henry might believe or suspect of him. Raven had obliquely confirmed Henry's suspicions in a reply, stating how he concurred that 'the unfortunate brigand must indeed have encountered someone with a perverse appetite for mayhem'.

But even these were not the foremost among his troubling thoughts, being too far away and leaving no role for him by which to intercede. Primarily he was preoccupied with Sarah, an affliction he thought he had cured long ago. It had turned out to be merely in remission.

He was still trying to come to terms with the fact of her being married. He should have been happy for her, should he not? Grateful that he had been vindicated, and they had both got what they wanted.

That dinner at her home on Albany Street played out over and over in his mind, always climaxing with her expression of incredulous disgust. He had solid reasons for having refused Sarah's request, but he remained stricken with doubt over whether it had been the right thing to do. Nor could he be certain whether his judgment was actually flawed or whether he was questioning it simply because he could not endure Sarah's displeasure.

He knew that such a consideration should not mean so much to him, especially now. She was at most a colleague, an acquaintance. She was a married woman with her own life, and her disappointment or disapproval should not be an impediment to his abiding by his own decisions. And yet.

Perhaps it was Sarah's judgment that was giving him pause. For sure she was over-enamoured of the professor and blind to his weaknesses, but she also had an infuriatingly consistent habit of being right. He wondered if that was what prompted him to hold forth in ostentatious demonstrations of his own knowledge when in her presence: the fear that no matter how much he learned, she would still be wiser than him.

He returned to the task in hand, removing the soiled linen from beneath the unconscious patient before applying a bandage and compress.

'May I ask you about something rather delicate, Dr Ziegler?'

The older man's brow rose in curiosity. Raven took it as assent.

'What do you know about Dr Matthews Duncan and Professor Miller spreading rumours about Dr Simpson?'

Ziegler looked grave. 'A medical man relies on his reputation and there are those who seem intent upon destroying his.'

'Why, would you say?'

'Shifting allegiances. And I suspect jealousy plays a part.'

'How so?'

'Professional disagreements sometimes become acrimonious. Slights are deeply felt, grudges held.'

'Specific instances might aid my understanding.'

'I'm not privy to the nature of the dispute with Miller, but I know Matthews Duncan feels he has not been afforded the credit he is due for the discovery of chloroform.'

'He was there that night, I suppose,' Raven recalled, 'and he participated in many experiments to find a replacement for ether, albeit unsuccessfully. But Simpson doesn't deny he had a role, does he?'

'Regardless, it is always referred to as Simpson's chloroform, and I think Dr Matthews Duncan takes issue with that.'

'That's hardly Dr Simpson's fault, and surely not sufficient reason to propagate malicious gossip.'

Ziegler looked at him intently for a moment.

'In this case, I think it might be more than enough.'

Raven remembered previous encounters with James Matthews Duncan and thought perhaps Ziegler had a point. He was undoubtedly the possessor of a prodigious mind, but in order to accommodate his cleverness, the part of his intellect that negotiated relationships with other human beings seemed to have been diminished.

'And what of Miller? There must be some perceived iniquity or quarrel to explain his involvement.'

'As I said, I am unaware of recent unpleasantness between Miller and Dr Simpson. All I know is that Simpson did not support him when he applied for the chair of surgery.'

'Why not?'

'Syme was supporting Miller, which might have had something to do with it, but Dr Simpson said it was because Miller had been professionally dishonest.'

'That is quite the accusation. How so?'

'By publishing a report about the death of a patient he had

operated on without mentioning the pertinent and incriminating details of the post-mortem findings.'

'What was the case?'

'An orbital aneurysm. Miller ligatured the carotid artery, as was the recognised practice at that time, but when the patient died the post-mortem demonstrated that the vagus nerve had been included in the arterial ligature.'

'But that must have been such a long time ago. They are neighbours and always seemed to me to be on good terms. Surely that cannot be the cause.'

'Much can be hidden behind courtesy and politeness, especially by those waiting for their moment to strike. A case of "nursing his wrath, to keep it warm" perhaps. They do say you can take the measure of a man by the calibre of his enemies, and I predict that in time Dr Simpson will cross swords with greater men than these.'

Raven sighed.

'Can anyone be trusted in this profession? Can you count anyone as a true friend?'

'I would not have thought one so young could sound so weary,' Ziegler said. 'Instead of seeking an answer to that question, perhaps you ought to *be* the answer you would prefer.'

Raven tucked in the end of the bandage and checked that it was sufficiently tight. He placed a hand on the patient's abdomen, felt the now firmly contracted uterus and congratulated himself on a job well done. He thought about how many deliveries he had attended over the past few years, how much he enjoyed dealing with straightforward cases and how he was now able to manage the complex ones. He reflected upon how much he had been taught, most of it by Simpson.

He still marvelled at the swelling of the pregnant abdomen, a new life contained inside, at his ability to feel the position of the child through the abdominal wall, to hear the foetal heartbeat with a stethoscope, an innovation Dr Simpson was keen on. Not everyone was as convinced of the stethoscope's utility – some thought it had the appearance of quackery – but as usual Simpson was unconcerned with other people's displeasure. He would endure disapproval and censure if he thought that he was right.

When it came to the Johnstone case, though, it wasn't about being right, it was a question of honesty. Was Simpson being professionally dishonest, as he had once accused Miller? Was he attempting to cover up a mistake? Was he so concerned with his reputation that he would do such a thing? Raven found that difficult to believe. Perhaps he should have agreed to help Sarah after all.

She had been interrogating him about Mrs Glassford that morning, wanting to know details of the condition she was suffering from and the likely prognosis. He had skirted the truth as he had not wished to upset her. He knew Sarah had been spending time with Mrs Glassford, talking to her whenever she came to Queen Street, and visiting her at home.

He thought of Mrs Glassford's abdomen, the swelling of it portending death rather than new life. He pictured her drawn face, the growing tumour draining the vitality from the rest of her.

Raven was disturbed to find that this prompted thoughts of Sarah's husband: how thin he was, how little he spoke and ate at dinner, his use of chloroform to help him sleep.

Suddenly Raven understood what should have been obvious to him before. Archie Banks was dying.

TWENTY-FIVE

'arah, may I speak plainly?'

Sarah had been summoned to the drawing room, which was not an unusual occurrence, but the growing sense of suspicion and distrust amongst the household staff was causing her to feel unduly anxious about it. The look on Mrs Simpson's face when she entered the room had done nothing to assuage her concern.

'Things are not as they should be,' Mrs Simpson said, and then sighed. 'Oh, do sit down, Sarah. You're not on trial.'

Sarah sat on one of the upholstered armchairs, noticing as she did so that the embroidered antimacassar on the back of the chair was in dire need of washing. Such a thing would not have been tolerated when she was a housemaid here. She straightened her skirt, focused her attention on Mrs Simpson and reminded herself that she had done nothing wrong.

'I am beginning to feel that I am losing control of things. This house becomes more chaotic by the day. Problems seem to be mounting up and with Mina gone there is no one I can confide in.'

Under the circumstances Sarah was relieved that she was not being accused of anything, but was surprised by Mrs Simpson's admission. To her mind the house was no more or less chaotic than usual, grubby antimacassars notwithstanding.

'Dr Simpson is away from home so frequently he scarcely knows what goes on here, under his own roof. You know what he is like, Sarah; gathers up dinner guests on a whim as he makes his rounds, and anyone of importance who visits Edinburgh must come to see him, or so it seems. There are always visitors in the house, patients, the children to take care of. And now there is money missing.'

'Mrs Lyndsay has said as much to me,' Sarah replied. She decided it would be better to keep Mrs Lyndsay's suspicions about the culprit to herself for now. 'I gather Mr Quinton has uncovered certain discrepancies.'

'Yes. He was supposed to lighten the burden by bringing order to Dr Simpson's chaos, but he has merely added to my worries. I am supposed to oversee the running of this house, but I feel as if I am making a poor job of it. I worry that I am at fault.'

Sarah looked at Mrs Simpson and saw the dark circles under her eyes, the worry lines creasing her forehead. She realised that she had been concerned about the toll that the recent accusations against him might have been taking on Dr Simpson, but had failed to consider his wife. The loss of a doctor's reputation could have catastrophic consequences for his income. Was that why there was so much concern about the missing money? She had assumed that it was an insignificant amount that had gone missing, but now thought that perhaps it was a more substantial sum than she had initially supposed.

'I will do all I can to help,' Sarah said, though how such a thing might be achieved she wasn't sure. Her responsibilities seemed to be multiplying. 'However, my time is necessarily divided between here and Albany Street, and I suspect that I might have to be at home a little more now.'

Mrs Simpson looked sympathetically towards her.

'Is Archie getting worse?'

'He has good days and bad. More bad days of late.'

'I am sorry to hear that. It must be terribly hard for you. You are so young and so recently married. This should be a time of joy for you and I fear that it is not. But then we all have our crosses to bear, our losses to grieve, do we not?'

Sarah nodded, though she tried not to feel sorry for herself. Despite the likely difficulties to come, she had no regrets. She would rather have her time with Archie cut short than never have had him at all.

'If there is a further deterioration you should perhaps consider moving in here, where we can help you look after him.'

Sarah was touched by Mrs Simpson's thoughtfulness amid all the other problems she was wrestling with.

'You know that I am no stranger to illness,' Mrs Simpson continued, 'having nursed my children through the worst of diseases. Of course, you know this. You were here when Mary Catherine died.'

'Yes, I was,' Sarah replied. And unlikely to forget it. Carried off by scarlet fever before her second birthday.

'We lost a child before that too,' Mrs Simpson went on. 'Our first born, Maggie.'

Sarah knew the fact of this but not the details. She sat back in her chair, thinking that the best service she could offer Mrs Simpson today was to listen.

'It haunts me still. Before her fourth birthday, she was attacked with measles and then seized by a very bad form of sore throat. She could neither eat nor drink, took nothing for days. It was so heart-rending to witness her restlessness and distress, not being able to do anything to relieve her. Her demise was almost a relief to us all in the end.'

She looked at Sarah, tears in her eyes, the pain still raw despite the years that had passed since it happened.

'I remember her being laid out on a white bed in the parlour – this was when we lived on Albany Street, not far from where you are now. Her eyes were open, and she looked so beautiful. It seemed so strange that she did not breathe or move.'

Sarah had no difficulty imagining what had just been described. She had helped to lay out Mary Catherine's tiny body.

'She was the first to be buried in the family plot, at Warriston Cemetery. Now her sister lies with her and I wonder how many more of my children I will lay to rest before I die myself.' Mrs Simpson paused, looked down at her hands. 'And yet some mothers give them away. Hand them over to strangers.'

Sarah was confused for a moment until she realised that they were now talking about the foster children, illegitimate issue of patients in Dr Simpson's private practice who Mrs Simpson helped place with other families. It was seldom openly discussed but the household staff knew about it.

'I write to them, you know. The mothers who give their children up. Let them know about the child's progress. I don't know how they stand it.'

'I suppose they have no choice.'

Sarah felt the conversation was drifting into difficult territory. She had her own opinions about wealthy men who refused to publicly acknowledge their own offspring.

'I understand the Quintons have adopted one of your charges,' she said.

'Yes. They have no children of their own and so agreed to take the child. A little boy. They have moved into a large property on Castle Street. Took over the lease from a friend. I think that their intention had been to rent out rooms to students, but Mary Quinton tells me that so far no boarders of suitable quality have been found.'

'I can imagine Mr Quinton is exacting in the extreme with regard to the suitability of potential tenants,' Sarah said. 'He seems most fastidious in every regard. But is he quite sure about the missing money? Is it possible he could be mistaken?'

'He assures me he has checked the accounts several times over.' This was said emphatically, as though questioning Mr Quinton's book-keeping skills was in some way sacrilegious. 'He is in no doubt, and all of a sudden I don't feel quite at ease in my own home.'

Sarah felt uncertain of herself, wary of being given a role she was not prepared for, nor qualified to hold. Was she being spoken to as a friend? Was Mrs Simpson seeking counsel or merely a receptive ear? And when she felt in better spirits, would Sarah revert to being seen as housemaid and nurse? She felt the need to escape from this conversation and got to her feet.

'I will try to discover what I can,' she said. 'I'm sure that this whole matter will be resolved and that things will go back to the way they were.'

Even as she spoke these words, she didn't believe them. She knew better than most that some things can never be how they once were.

When Sarah left the room, a phrase from *Buchan's Domestic Medicine* came to her: 'There is no balm for a wounded mind.' More's the pity, she thought.

TWENTY-SIX

hough the stolen bread roll had done little to sustain him over the succeeding hours, and he could smell Mrs Lyndsay's cooking as he approached No. 52, Raven walked on past and continued to Broughton Street to check up on George Porteous, the stricken young man he had left there that afternoon. He was driven partly by the principle of what he thought Simpson would do in this situation, and as much by a wish to distinguish his conduct from the likes of Dr Fowler, a man more concerned with the welfare of his leeches than that of his patient. It was an attitude that was sadly not rare in the profession.

The door was answered by the patient's sister Greta, her face tear-streaked with grief.

'You are too late,' she said. 'George has died.'

'I am most sorry,' he told her.

She beckoned him inside and through to the parlour, where he found Dr Fowler still present, sitting in an armchair sipping tea. As soon as he saw Raven, the older man got to his feet.

'We should have purged him,' he insisted, jabbing a finger accusingly; as though an evacuation of the bowels would have saved the poor man. Raven thought that if he had prevented that last futile indignity, then his presence had perhaps served some purpose.

After further pointless conjecture about the potential power of an aperient to raise the near dead, Fowler turned his attention to the now doubly bereaved Greta.

'You have my condolences, Miss Porteous. I thought that were I to procure the intercession of Dr Simpson, we might save your brother. But alas, Dr Simpson's assistant merely obstructed the course that I recommended. It is my belief that George might live yet had I not followed his judgment.'

'I think I should go,' Raven said, pre-empting any further discussion. 'I will see myself out.'

He did not care for the insinuation that in dissuading Dr Fowler from administering an enema he had in some way contributed to the patient's demise. The man was clearly an imbecile, but he realised that, as an established practitioner, if Fowler chose to similarly denigrate his contribution to the case to the medical men of his acquaintance, Raven's nascent reputation would inevitably suffer, irrespective of the truth of the matter.

Greta followed him to the door.

'Dr Raven, my brother was sick for days and had the best care from the nurse throughout. I do not believe anything you did or did not do contributed to his death.'

'I am sorry I could not do more,' he replied softly.

'Is it contagious, do you think? Are there any precautions I ought to take?'

'Contagious? What makes you say that?'

'It is just that I fear whatever claimed George might spread to me next, like it went to him from our mother.'

'There is no need to be afraid. Your mother died of heart failure.'

'So says Dr Fowler,' she replied, sounding less than convinced.

As Raven walked back along Queen Street, his thoughts returned to his conversation with Ziegler regarding James Matthews Duncan's anger over his perceived lack of credit for the discovery of chloroform. It was said that success had many fathers, while failure was always an orphan. Both sides of this were never quite so true as in medicine.

Today was not the first time another doctor had tried to leave him with the blame for a patient's death. For that reason, he now saw that he ought to have been more sympathetic over the assault on Dr Simpson's character. He was reluctant to be a pawn on the chessboard, but now he was beginning to wonder what game was really being played. When someone was so keen to pin the blame elsewhere, that often suggested they had something to hide. In Dr Fowler's case it was merely the fact that his antiquated knowledge rendered him incompetent. But perhaps someone wanted to use Simpson as a scapegoat, and there was an agenda here beyond the one that Ziegler had suggested.

He thought of what Ziegler had told him, how he should *be* the answer he sought. He thought again about Sarah, how he had refused her his help, the hurt in her face when he did so, the fact that she was coming to him for assistance rather than relying on her husband.

It dawned on him that she knew how sick Archie was. Only too well, she knew. How could she not?

Sarah understood that some patients could not be saved, no matter the efforts of someone as brilliant as Dr Simpson. And Raven knew that sometimes, when you cannot fix something that is broken, you feel the need to fix something else in its stead.

TWENTY-SEVEN

he curtain rises upon the Institute's assembly hall, where the Reverend Gillies addressed the children each morning before classes and duties commenced. There were two hundred boys learning trades beneath the Belmont's roof, and half as many girls being taught sewing, knitting, cooking and other household skills.

It was a year later, and I was much changed: better fed and clothed, though I had not escaped the capricious rule of men. Nor had I found them to represent my only danger.

I had made friends, though. The Institute had provided an opportunity to reinvent myself in a place where my peers did not judge me as the daughter of Mad Murdo. I told them my father had been an adventurer and my mother an actress, both of them lost in a tragic sea crossing as they returned to me from America. I relished the way they looked at me in response. There was wonder in their expressions, but also sadness for me at what I had lost. It reminded them nonetheless that I was made of better stuff than they might assume.

Not everyone took to me for it, though. I had enemies there, not least Joyce Meechan, who was seated in the row behind as I sidled along the pew.

Joyce had arrived a few months previously, and I was dismayed to recognise her from playing in the back courts of Cumberland Street. Joyce was a year older, a pinch-faced girl who said I was a liar and a thief. She told people that my real father was a madman who killed my mother. If anything went astray, she accused me of taking it, and said I was getting fat because I stole from other people's plates.

On this morning, however, Joyce did not greet me with her usual sour sneer. Instead she wore a contrite expression and gave me a gentle, beckoning wave as I took my seat.

'I have urgent news,' she said, her voice low in recognition of the growing silence in the hall as the Reverend Gillies ascended his pulpit.

I turned and leaned across the back of the bench, impatient to learn what had led to this change in Joyce's demeanour. Joyce in turn leaned forward, presenting her ear.

'What news?' I asked in a whisper.

Joyce let out a shriek and recoiled, throwing her hands back dramatically in shock.

The Reverend Gillies' attention was immediately upon her and she was hauled to her feet by one of the masters, dragged to the front and was tearful by the time she was standing before the Reverend.

'What occasioned this indecorous outburst?' he demanded.

I did not hear her mumbled reply, but I did see Joyce raise her arm and point directly back towards where I sat.

The Reverend's face was crimson. He strode down into the body of the hall and grabbed me by the neck. I was dragged along the pew and forced into the aisle, where the Reverend whipped at my backside with his stick to drive me forward, sending me through the doors of the hall and all the way outside to the yard at the back.

I wanted to ask what I had done to merit such punishment, but experience had told me this would be folly. The impertinence of such a question would only anger him further.

He ordered me to lie face-down in the dirt. I obeyed.

'I will have you learn not to be so hasty with your tongue,' he said. 'And to that end, I would have you describe the shape of a cross with that tongue.'

'Where?' I asked meekly, raising my head.

'There. In the dirt. Let filth meet filth.'

The prospect moved me to protest.

'But I said nothing. I only asked what news.'

He struck me with the stick once more.

'Silence. You will use your tongue only for what I have commanded.'

I attempted to comply. I drew my tongue a few inches along the ground, wincing at the taste and the sensation, a horrible mixture of slime and grit. Then I repeated the ordeal, bisecting the first line to form a cross.

The Reverend struck me again.

'A cross such as the Lord died upon was greater than the length of Himself.'

I began to cry at the injustice of it. I had no notion what Joyce had accused me of, but it was clear that the Reverend Gillies believed it of me.

I did not know what dirt was made of. Though the Reverend stood over me as I washed out my mouth until every last speck was gone, that night I was ill with a terrible sickness, and in the following days I passed more soil than would cover the whole yard.

It was what happened when you ate filth. You were poisoned.

TWENTY-EIGHT

aven waited on the doorstep at Albany Street, trying to compose how he might best express his change of mind, while wondering how long it would be before he regretted it. He hoped the sunshine of being restored to Sarah's good graces was adequate compensation for the storm clouds likely to gather among his peers and superiors.

Mrs Sullivan, the housekeeper, answered the door.

'I am here to see Sarah,' he said, giving Mrs Sullivan what he hoped was a winning smile, a technique that Dr Simpson deployed with great success, and only possible now that his troublesome molar had been removed. A trip to the dentist the day before and a quick whiff of chloroform had seen to that. He had briefly contemplated braving the extraction without the aid of an anaesthetic, but his courage had faltered at the approach of the dentist armed with his tooth-pulling forceps.

'Mrs Banks is not here,' Mrs Sullivan replied, in a tone that suggested he had better be on his way. Raven wondered if perhaps she didn't recognise him from his recent visit. The alternative suggested that Sarah had not been generous in her accounts of him afterwards.

'Who is it, Mrs Sullivan?' called out a male voice behind her. Archie.

'It's Dr Raven from Queen Street.'

Evidently, she did know who he was.

'Do show him in.'

Raven was about to decline but the door was opened wide and he was ushered inside. He didn't particularly want to speak to Sarah's husband and certainly not without her present to moderate.

He was shown into the parlour, where Archie was already seated in an armchair by the fire.

'Do sit down, Will.'

He seemed open and friendly, as though they had known each other for some time. Raven was wary. He perched himself on the edge of a chair, hoping to give the impression that he was not at liberty to stay for any length of time.

He looked at the man sitting opposite: really looked, searching for confirmation of his suspicions. Archie was indeed thin, perhaps thinner than the last time Raven had seen him, but he couldn't be sure. He was pale but not uncommonly so. Raven had to admit that this was hardly conclusive evidence, but he felt intuitively that this man was far from well. Or did he merely wish that it was so?

'I am so glad that you called by,' Archie said. 'We haven't really had much of a chance to talk.'

Raven had been hoping that this was a state of affairs that might long endure. His instinct was to imagine that there was nothing they had in common to talk about, but if he were being honest, his reluctance derived from the opposite being true. They were both men of medicine, for one thing. But primarily the thing – or rather the person – they had in common was now Archie's wife.

'Sarah has told me so much about you,' he said cheerily. 'It seems you two had quite the adventure together, once upon a time. A secret alliance engaged in subterfuge and hazardous enterprises.'

Raven swallowed, wondering just how much Sarah had told Archie about their time together. Had it been anyone else, he could have been assured that common discretion protected his confidence, but this was Sarah. Little about her was common, and that included her relationship with her new husband.

'How did you two encounter each other?' Raven asked, eager to shift the focus of discussion. He was also impatiently curious.

'I was visiting the professor,' Archie said. 'I first crossed paths with James when we were both students here in Edinburgh. He was several years my senior, but we got on well and have kept up a regular correspondence since.'

Raven wondered if the visit being alluded to was as a colleague or as a patient but felt it would be impertinent to ask.

'When I arrived here from Perth in the summer, I left my card at Queen Street and then took a room at the Royal Hotel. I had only just begun to unpack my portmanteau when Dr Simpson appeared at my door in the company of Mr Gibb, the proprietor. He said that I must come and stay at Queen Street as his guest.

'Of course I protested, but he would not hear of my remaining at the hotel. I suggested Mr Gibb might have something to say in the matter, as I had planned to stay in his establishment for a week, but the hotelier simply smiled and shook his head. "We here in Edinburgh do rather much as the professor says," he told me. And so, within the hour I found myself comfortably ensconced at Queen Street. There I remained for some time – longer than I had originally intended – and there I met Sarah.'

'You live in Perth?'

'I had my practice there.'

Raven noted the past tense. He would not be returning, and nor had there been any talk of him setting up a practice elsewhere.

Archie paused for a moment and looked at Raven before continuing.

'I came to Edinburgh to consult with colleagues about a

medical problem. I have an ulcer on my tongue and came to seek advice and treatment.'

'I see,' Raven said. He knew now that his theory was about to be confirmed, but felt no satisfaction about being proven correct in his deduction.

'There have been a number of rather painful procedures performed in an attempt to rid me of it, but thus far they have only been partially successful. I met with Professor Syme again yesterday and he is recommending further surgery, a more extensive operation than before. Because such an operation comes with an attendant risk of considerable blood loss, the proposed procedure would have to be performed without the benefit of anaesthesia.'

Archie laughed, then added: 'I am of a mind to respectfully decline.'

Raven was unsure how to respond to this. One question was imperative, however.

'Does Sarah know?'

'Yes, of course. How could I have kept it from her? After all, it was her intellect and curiosity that attracted me to her in the first place. Was it the same for you?'

Raven was beginning to feel uncomfortable about just how much this man, this relative stranger, seemed to know about him. He was quite unprepared to be as open as Archie had been with him. Perhaps it was easier for Archie because he had greater worries. Or perhaps it was simply easier for him because he had been the one who married her.

He shifted in his seat. Archie seemed to sense his awkwardness and smiled at him benignly.

'If it's any consolation, I think one of the things that attracted her to me was that I reminded her of you.'

Raven got to his feet.

'I am not sure this conversation is entirely appropriate, or that Sarah would like us to be having it. I think that I had better leave.'

'Oh, don't be daft,' Archie replied. 'Sarah and I have no secrets from each other.'

'If you truly knew her, you would not be so sure of that.'

Raven had meant it to unsettle Archie, but it made him laugh instead.

'One of the great benefits of my condition is that I can be honest without fear of the consequences.'

Raven remained on his feet.

'Then you will indulge me if I am equally candid,' he said.

'Fire at will.'

'If you are as ill as you are implying, why did you marry her? Do you love her, or did you merely need someone who would be obliged to take care of you? She was a housemaid after all and is well used to hard labour.'

'Neither of us would be having this conversation had she been merely a housemaid,' Archie replied. 'But I suspect you think that I have taken advantage of her good nature. I don't suppose I can blame you for that.'

He got up from his chair and moved towards a cabinet in the corner of the room, from which he removed a decanter and two glasses. He poured a measure of what turned out to be rather good brandy into both and offered Raven a glass.

'I know that this is difficult for you, but I would like for us to be friends.'

Raven took the drink and sat down again, thinking to test Archie's new-found enthusiasm for honest conversation.

'Did she know how serious your illness was when she agreed to marry you?'

'That a cure is unlikely? Yes, she did.'

'And do you think that is perhaps *why* she agreed to marry you?'

'You think it was unfair of me to ask? I long pondered that question myself. There was a growing mutual affection between us. Plenty of people get married without that.'

'But in the circumstances, it would have been hard for her to refuse.'

'If you know her as well as you claim, then you will also know that she would not be forced into something against her will or better judgment. I have not deceived her in any way and there are a great many benefits for her in marrying me.'

'Guaranteed loss and pain do not seem like much of a benefit to me,' Raven muttered, downing the rest of his brandy in one gulp. The burn in his gullet felt good. Counter irritation.

'I have given her status,' Archie said, ignoring Raven's surly comment. 'Should the worst happen – *when* the worst happens – she will inherit my money, and with it certain freedoms and opportunities. Believe me, Will, I have her best interests at heart.'

Raven sat quietly for a moment as the truth of what Archie had said began to seep into his irritable mind. He knew his ire was being misdirected. He was angry with himself more than Archie. There was little point in resenting Archie or Sarah for seizing something he had lacked the fortitude to pursue himself.

'I have endured quite enough of the pompous prigs of my profession,' Archie said. 'And though I will surely not live to see it, my sense of mischief is tickled by the thought of their outrage on the day that a woman intrudes upon their so fiercely guarded domain. If any woman could, it would be Sarah.'

Raven was unsure exactly what was meant by this. Was Sarah planning some kind of battle with the medical profession in Edinburgh? If so, was her defence of Simpson imagined as a shot across the bows? He thought the notion fanciful but that didn't stop him worrying about his potential role in it.

'Don't you have any other relatives?' Raven asked. 'Surely they would contest such a bequest?'

'I have nobody else to leave the money to. No blood relatives. Or at least, none that I'll live to see.'

Archie's expression was curious. It seemed wistful and yet there was something proud, satisfied in it. Raven was about to disregard this last statement, thinking it a throwaway remark, when he realised what Archie meant.

If he did die, he would be leaving Sarah with more than his money. His legacy was going to be greater than that. Archie was under the impression that his wife was with child.

TWENTY-NINE

arah was replenishing the dressings drawer when Dr
Simpson entered the consulting room carrying a
sheaf of papers. He had just returned from his trip
to Lanarkshire and had barely crossed the threshold
before throwing himself into more work.

'Ah, Sarah. I am currently in the process of writing up some
notes for the *Monthly Journal* on the analogy between puerperal
fever and surgical fever, and I thought that Archie might like to
take a look at them?'

'Thank you, Dr Simpson. I think that he would like that very
much. Although I may have to read them to him. He is so easily
fatigued these days.'

'Then you must tell me what you think.'

'Me?'

'Yes. Why not? You have read half of the contents of my
library; you have tackled Gregory and Christison. Surely something I have written would not be beyond your comprehension.'

Sarah took the papers he held out to her.

'Thank you,' she said again, and wondered if he meant it.
Did he really consider her opinion to be worthy of note? She had
indeed read many of the books in Dr Simpson's library and, she
thought, understood them, but often doubted she would ever be

able to put the knowledge she was acquiring to any use. In such times she consoled herself with the adage that self-improvement was its own reward.

'You know the phrenologists say that examination of the skull reveals women to be the intellectual equals of men,' the professor said. He had a twinkle in his eye that Sarah had come to recognise: he was trying to provoke an argument, but Sarah had been over this course too many times before to be riled. She was also well versed in his opinions on this particular strain of quackery.

'I don't need a phrenologist to tell me that,' she said, smiling.

'You know I have never subscribed to the notion that women are in any way the weaker sex. I have been surrounded by remarkable women my whole life, and as Professor of Midwifery I know that women can withstand pain and distress as well as any man.'

'I fear that there are few men who would agree with you.'

'I think that Archie would.'

'Yes,' she smiled again. 'Archie would.'

'Did you know that when Her Majesty the Queen was born, she was delivered by a woman?'

'A midwife?'

'No. A physician.'

Sarah stopped what she was doing. He had her full attention now.

'When Queen Victoria's mother travelled from Bavaria to England in 1819, she brought her own doctor with her: Charlotte Siebold, who had received her doctorate in obstetrics from Giessen University two years before.'

Sarah was so excited by the notion Dr Simpson had just introduced that she had to seek clarification.

'The birth of our queen was managed by a female physician?'

'Yes. And then she promptly returned to Coburg where, if you can believe this, she delivered Prince Albert.'

There was only one aspect of this remarkable tale that held Sarah's attention.

'So, it is possible for a woman to study medicine in Germany?'

'I think Madame Siebold was an exceptional case. Both parents practiced midwifery and taught her all that they knew.'

'Is there anywhere in the world where a woman may study as she chooses?'

'On my last visit to London I met Dr Elizabeth Blackwell. Have you heard of her?'

Sarah shook her head.

'She recently qualified at Geneva Medical College in New York. She was on her way to Paris to further her studies there. I invited her to visit us here in Edinburgh.'

'Will she come?'

'She said that she hoped to, one day.'

'I should very much like to meet her. I did not know that a woman could go to medical school in America.'

'Well, yes, but it is not commonplace there either. Dr Blackwell is the first, something of a pioneer. She caused quite a stir among the medical brethren of the capital when she arrived there, but I think she is seen as something of a curiosity rather than as any kind of threat. Medical men can be very proprietorial. They do not like intrusions upon their professional territory. I suspect attitudes will harden should more women attempt to follow her example.'

'Do you think that it will ever be possible for a woman to study at the university here, in Edinburgh?'

Dr Simpson frowned.

'Despite being a leader in many fields, I doubt Edinburgh University will blaze a trail in this matter,' he said. 'Certainly not the Medical School. Knowing my brother professors as I do, I think it unlikely in my lifetime.'

Sarah felt her shoulders sag. Dr Simpson could usually be relied upon for his optimism no matter the subject being discussed. His doubts about this could not be readily dismissed.

'Things will change,' he said. 'There are few obstacles that will not disappear before determined industry.'

He smiled at her, but she noticed that, unusually, it did not reach his eyes.

THIRTY

thick fog had settled itself on the streets of the New Town as Raven and Sarah made their way along Queen Street. It was brutally cold, so they walked quickly, heads down. They had shared few words since leaving No. 52, Sarah rebuffing his conversational gambits with brief, terse answers.

Eventually, she spoke.

'What made you change your mind about helping me?'

There was an edge of accusation to it. He could tell she was still annoyed that he had refused her in the first place.

'It occurred to me that although Dr Simpson can be disorganised, he is not dishonest, and he is certainly not incompetent.'

'That is surely not news to you.'

'No, but it was brought home to me by a case I was asked to see recently. Unusual symptoms that I could not explain. Deep stupor preceded by delirium and twitching. I've never come across anything quite like it. The patient's usual practitioner, a Dr Fowler, was an old-fashioned type, determined to bleed and purge. He seemed more concerned about his leeches than the fate of the patient.'

'His leeches?'

'Yes, they all fell off and died shortly after they were applied. It seems he was quite attached to them, if you will.'

Raven paused, inviting her to share the joke. She did not look amused.

'I mean he had had them for a long time,' he explained. 'Given his adherence to the doctrine of depletion and blood-letting, the things probably succumbed due to exhaustion.' There was still no hint of a smile from Sarah and so he abandoned his attempts at humour and continued with the unadorned facts of the case.

'I had no idea what to suggest and the patient died shortly after I saw him. By the time I was involved it was probably too late to make a difference, but I still felt a terrible sense of defeat. Dr Fowler implied that I had been obstructive and was clearly trying to blame me for the outcome. It occurred to me that it is easy to make enemies in this town, and it troubles me that the death of a patient often becomes a battleground rather than an opportunity to learn.'

Sarah made no reply and they walked on in silence. Raven had thought that his change of heart would begin to melt the frostiness that had developed between them, but it appeared that a thaw might be slow in coming.

'How is Archie?' he enquired, and instantly regretted it. He didn't know how much her husband might have told Sarah about their conversation.

'Why do you ask?'

She sounded defensive. Perhaps she was merely wary of his suspicions, what he might have picked up on, being a medical man.

'Polite enquiry.'

Sarah seemed to realise she was being unnecessarily brusque.

'He is well,' she told him, her tone more even. 'And what about you? Aside from a few dead leeches, are you glad to be back in Edinburgh?'

'In some ways I am.'

He smiled at her, but her eyes were fixed ahead. She did not turn to look at him as he spoke.

'I feel I learned a great deal abroad,' he continued, 'but in practical terms, little seems to have changed with regard to my duties. I have yet to make headway in establishing myself as an independent practitioner. Working with someone as esteemed as Dr Simpson, it is tantalising to see the rewards that are still so far out of my reach. For instance, a lady from Brighton has been sending letters begging for a consultation. The professor always refuses, saying that she is not ill and that he has told her as much. Yesterday she sent a telegram offering a fee of a thousand pounds. A thousand pounds! And still he refuses to consider it.'

He waited for Sarah to respond but she said nothing, her face partially hidden by the thick woollen scarf she had wrapped round it.

'He said it would be better if she put her guineas into some struggling doctor's pocket,' he continued. 'I thought: there is a struggling doctor not three feet from you, sir. Honestly, I couldn't imagine ever being in a position to refuse such a sum. I've half a mind to go to Brighton myself.'

'What's stopping you?' she asked.

'I don't have the money.'

Raven hadn't intended it so, but he saw the joke when a hint of amusement finally appeared upon Sarah's face.

'Perhaps the doctor thinks he has wealth enough and his interests extend beyond lining his pockets,' she said. Her tone was sincere, but from the look on her face he could tell that she was teasing him. 'And the large fees he does collect allow him to treat those *with* nothing *for* nothing.'

'He could certainly treat a great deal of them if he acquiesced to the Brighton lady's wishes.'

Sarah rolled her eyes pityingly. Raven had to bite back a remark about her own new-found financial comfort.

As they neared the upholsterer's, Sarah softened her voice, as though concerned about eavesdroppers.

'Have you heard anything about money going missing? From Queen Street?'

This was the first he had learned of it.

'No,' he replied. 'Money is rarely discussed with me, for as you know I have none.'

Nor was he likely to for some time. What he earned now as Simpson's assistant would have to go towards repaying the debts he had incurred on his travels. Quinton had asked to borrow some from him the other day, a request he had greeted with wry amusement. It was clear the man was new to the place and didn't know him very well.

'What of it?' Raven asked.

'Just rumours. It's probably nothing.'

'Perhaps Jarvis has been forgetting to check the professor's pockets.'

Sarah's expression indicated she thought he was being facetious. He wasn't, entirely.

'You are right that the professor cares little about his wealth,' Raven said, 'and it is my contention that it makes him somewhat careless about money. He can be careless with other things too; forgetting appointments and visits.'

'He never forgets anything that is interesting or important. Imaginary megrims are another matter.'

'He's not infallible, Sarah,' Raven said, thinking that this was worth repeating.

'None of us are.'

They had finally reached Mr Hardie's shop.

'Thank goodness,' Sarah said as she pushed open the door. 'I'm freezing.'

They entered the premises, Sarah breathing into her cupped hands to warm them. The shop was clean, tidy and smelled of wood shavings. A small man stood behind the counter, a large leather apron covering his clothes.

'Good morning,' he greeted them. 'How may I be of assistance?'

'I am Dr Raven, assistant to Dr James Young Simpson.'

Mr Hardie's smile disappeared as soon as Simpson's name was mentioned.

'I have already provided Dr Simpson with the letter that he requested,' he said. 'I had nothing to do with the rumours regarding the late Mrs Johnstone. I never stated, and could not state, that she died of bleeding. I am a simple tradesman, why would I say such a thing?'

Raven opened his mouth to reassure the man that they had not come to accuse him of anything, but Mr Hardie was not done.

'I heard that she had died of inflammation after some operation, and I casually remarked to a medical gentleman who came into my shop that she must have been very ill, as there was some staining of blood on the surface of the mattress. I thought it to have been the result of bleeding from the arm. This medical gentleman and another afterwards came and asked me about the size of the stain on the mattress, and I answered them. I do not consider myself responsible for what occurred after that.'

Raven wondered how many visits the man had been subject to regarding this mattress. It did seem odd that the medical gentlemen should take such a keen interest.

He smiled at Mr Hardie, hoping to calm him a little. The man seemed to be unduly harassed given that Raven had yet to ask a question.

'Where is the mattress now? Might we take a look at it?'

'It's been sent to Mr Harrower.'

'Mr Harrower?' Sarah asked.

'Yes.' He looked at them as though it should be obvious what he was talking about. 'He has charge of an establishment where beds go to be steamed and cleaned after people die. Whatever might be the cause of death,' he added quickly, seemingly afraid of further incriminating himself.

'When was this?' Raven asked.

'Sometime last week.'

'So, it is likely to have been cleaned by now?'

'Oh, it has been. Won't do to leave these things lying about for any length of time. Mr Harrower said that when he opened it up, little or nothing of it was spoiled, only the surface was stained with a small amount of blood. Just as I said. No clotting or anything like that. Most beds he sees are in a thousand times' worse state.'

'Thank you, Mr Hardie,' Raven said. 'You've been a great help.'

Mr Hardie visibly relaxed at this, loosening his grip on the counter.

'I sincerely hope that's the end of the matter,' he said. 'I haven't seen so many doctors since my youngest got run over by a cart and broke his leg. Bit of bone came right out through the skin. Was in the Infirmary for months.'

Raven thought it best not to enquire about the outcome of that but thanked the man again as he and Sarah left the shop. They walked away from the door and then stopped.

'What now?' Sarah asked. 'Obviously that vindicates Dr Simpson, but with the mattress having been cleaned, we have no proof.'

'I doubt it would make much difference if we had,' Raven admitted. 'Matthews Duncan and Professor Miller heard the same from Mr Hardie as we did. So I am now curious as to why two medical men would so misinterpret the upholsterer's account.'

THIRTY-ONE

n pursuing his investigation on Dr Simpson's behalf, Raven stood by the wisdom that – Edinburgh medicine being something of a snake pit – he ought to avoid making new enemies. To that end he reasoned it would be best to continue his enquiries with someone who never thought much of him to begin with.

He intercepted his quarry coming out of the grand building where he now lived on Wemyss Place. James Duncan was unquestionably a bright and gifted doctor, but one who had an arrestingly high opinion of himself and who was impatient for the renown he felt was inevitably his due. He had famously been something of a prodigy, having procured special dispensation to allow him to gain his MD at the age of only twenty. He had then continued his studies in Paris, making use of his fluent French, into which he had translated one of Dr Simpson's papers on the use of ether. Raven knew these details because he had been repeatedly availed of them when they worked together at 52 Queen Street.

Despite his obvious pride in having advanced so far so young, he had always struck Raven as a man in a hurry to seem older. To that end, since last Raven saw him, he had attempted to grow a beard. This undertaking had met with a success sufficiently partial as to merely draw attention to his difficulty in completing the project. He wore a three-piece tweed suit that looked expensive and seemed not so much the style of an older man as of a bygone era. Raven suspected this was merely affectation rather than lack of attention to current fashions. Much like the 'Matthews' he had, in Raven's opinion, unnecessarily appended to his name, it was an attempt to seem more august and distinguished.

'Dr Matthews Duncan, I would trouble you for a brief word.'

Raven hailed him using his augmented moniker, having decided upon a strategy of flattery and friendliness. Given the man's dismal social graces, it would not serve to be confrontational.

Duncan sighed, indicating he was a busy man and that such an interruption had better be of valuable import.

'Very well. And you are?'

When they last saw one another, Raven had himself worn a beard to hide the swelling and stitches upon his recently ravaged face. Nonetheless, he had no doubt that Duncan recognised him without it. He masked his annoyance behind a warm and enthusiastic smile.

'I have not been away so long, surely, James. I'm Will Raven. We worked together at Queen Street.'

'Of course, yes. Will Raven. You must forgive me my confusion. I have had so many apprentices working under me that it can be hard to keep track.'

Raven noted the implication that he'd been Duncan's apprentice rather than Simpson's. Duncan then proceeded to tell Raven how his own practice was now well established and expanding at such a rate that he thought he might have to recruit an assistant.

Belatedly he appeared to remember that Raven must have had some purpose for apprehending him.

'I believe you had an enquiry. Are you looking for a position?'

He said this in a weary tone, as though it was a bore to be fending off would-be assistants.

'No. I am recently returned from studies abroad and have

accepted the position of assistant to Dr Simpson. However, there is a matter that is troubling me, as I am concerned that I might be tainted by association. News comes to me of a patient of Dr Simpson's who died, and I believe there is some controversy over his treatment of her.'

'Indeed. A most disreputable affair. One does not like to impugn the judgment of a fellow practitioner, but it appears Dr Simpson might have been gravely at fault.'

'Can you tell me how?'

'He conducted a procedure that went badly wrong, and there was haemorrhage. The mattress was soaked in blood.'

'How awful. Where did you see this mattress? Did you visit the house?'

'No. But I spoke to the upholsterer who took it away.'

'Is it possible he exaggerated, or misremembered? Lay people can be easily shocked by a little blood and imagine it to be a great deal more.'

'He told us the mattress was soaked, and yet Simpson claimed there was very little blood. I find the inconsistency highly suspicious.'

'But presumably you had reason to enquire about the mattress because of some other aspect of the case?'

'Indeed. Professor Syme carried out a similar procedure on the patient with no such dire complications as were precipitant from Simpson's work. Mrs Johnstone died three days after Simpson left her. It appears obvious he botched the operation and has sought to conceal the truth of it.'

Raven was bemused by Duncan's mention of truth. He and Professor Miller were effectively in conspiracy, as they were both lying about what the upholsterer had told them.

'It is a pity there was no post-mortem examination,' Raven suggested.

'I find that highly suspicious also,' Duncan replied with great vehemence.

Raven had dangled this before him for a purpose, and he had seized upon it, confirming what he suspected. They had nothing else.

'I gather you and Dr Simpson have had an unfortunate parting of the ways during my time abroad.'

'His conduct has been unconscionable, and I would thus warn you to be wary if you are working for him. He has been striving to make his name synonymous with chloroform and chloroform synonymous with his name. He is bent on erasing my part in its discovery.'

Raven would have to concede that there was some truth to this. Despite Sarah's unshakable faith in Dr Simpson's righteousness, Raven knew that all medical men sought recognition, and were disinclined to share the glory when it shone upon them.

'The world ought to know that it was I who suggested and produced the sample we used in its discovery. I had been experimenting for months, trying all manner of compounds and mixtures.'

Duncan perhaps did not remember that Raven had been there that night, possibly because he had been unconscious at the time Raven made his entrance. Consequently, Raven doubted this part of his claim, but it would do no good to tell him as much. It would serve only to antagonise him. People often misremembered and reassembled the facts in a way that suited what they already wished to believe. Though Duncan had indeed worked with Simpson for months to find an alternative to ether, Raven did not believe that he had suggested or provided the successful sample on that famous evening. In fact, they had narrowly missed inhaling something rather toxic that might well have killed everyone in the room. It was a happy accident that this draught was misplaced and a bottle containing chloroform was tested instead.

What was clear was that he knew precious little about the treatment of Mrs Johnstone and had merely seized upon the outcome as a stick with which to beat the man he perceived as his foe. In this enterprise he had happily joined with two other, more senior medical men who, as Dr Ziegler suggested, held their own grudges. Raven suspected neither would be any more inclined to respond to contradictory evidence than the man before him now.

If he truly wanted to clear Dr Simpson's name, he would have to go to a first-hand witness.

THIRTY-TWO

arah entered the darkened bedroom with a tray bearing Archie's breakfast. She told herself it was an affectionate indulgence to be bringing it to him in his bed, but in truth she was trying to spare his energy by delaying when he had to get up. As always the meal itself was an exercise in optimism. He rarely ate much of it, whatever it was. This morning: a soft-boiled egg and tea. She put the tray down and helped him to sit forward, plumping up his pillows. He looked tired but then so was she. He was having disturbed nights, only managing to sleep for short periods. Sarah, more often than not, slept in a chair beside the bed.

'Good morning,' she said and kissed his forehead.

'You look exhausted,' he responded. 'I fear you're getting less sleep than I am.'

'Not exactly what every young wife wants to hear,' she replied as she pulled open the curtains. A thin grey light entered the room, doing little to cheer it. She sat on the bed beside him and he took her hand.

'Perhaps I should consider moving to Queen Street as Dr Simpson has been suggesting,' he said. 'It would let you sleep at night, let one of us get their strength back at least.'

Sarah shook her head, but he continued.

'It won't do for you to become ill too.'

Sarah had been resisting this, seeing it as her duty to look after him, but she knew that she couldn't keep going on in this vein indefinitely. She thought of Mrs Glassford's refusal of the same offer. She had said it was to preserve her autonomy and the comforts of home, but Sarah suspected that her reluctance was down to the knowledge that it would mark the beginning of the end.

'I prefer having you all to myself,' she said.

Archie smiled and then sipped his tea, grimacing slightly as it went down.

She knew they would be revisiting this topic soon enough, but for now felt some relief at heading it off.

'Nonetheless, there will come a time when you won't have me at all. We should talk a bit about the future. Your future.'

Sarah shook her head again.

'You need to start thinking about life without me.'

'It may not come to that.'

'Sarah,' he said simply, an appeal for her to acknowledge what they both knew.

'We still have time,' she said, 'but as we do not know how much, I would sooner not spend it talking about what will happen when it is at an end and I am left on my own.'

'But you won't be left on your own, will you?' he said softly. 'And that is why we must talk about it.'

Sarah swallowed. She felt guilty to be so lacking courage in facing a future Archie would not get to share. A child he would not live to see.

'That is the aspect I least wish to think about,' she admitted. 'I am scared, Archie.'

'You will be provided for. Have no fear.'

'That is not the greatest source of my fear. I do not think myself ready to be a mother.'

He squeezed her hand. Was his grip weak, she wondered, or was he merely being tender?

'I'm sure you had a good example set you, or you would not be the woman you are. Tell me about your mother,' he said, resting back against his pillows.

Sarah looked at his handsome face and wondered how she would feel if she saw it reflected in a son once Archie was gone. And if it was a girl, would she see her mother again? The thought was simultaneously cheering and melancholy.

'She was kind,' she told him. 'She worked hard. She suffered a great deal.'

'In what way?'

'Multiple pregnancies that ended badly: miscarriage or still-birth. I was born early and thought too weak to survive.'

'How wrong they were.'

'It weakened her. She was frequently ill, and I missed a lot of time at school to stay home and look after her. It made me impatient when I was there. I was a constant source of irritation to the schoolmaster.'

Archie grinned eagerly. It reminded her of the times when they first met, discovering each other through intimate conversation.

'Why?'

'I finished my work too quickly. It made the boys look bad.'

Archie laughed, sipped his tea again and then placed his cup and saucer on the small bedside table where it would probably remain.

'Tell me about the women who inspire you,' he asked.

It was Sarah's turn to laugh.

'They are mainly women who refuse to do as they are told,' she said. 'Who ask questions and demand answers. I have been exposed to all manner of unconventional types at Queen Street.'

'Such as?'

'Elizabeth Rigby, Catherine Crowe. Women who supported themselves through writing. Forthright in their opinions. I remember Mrs Crowe scandalised Hans Christian Andersen by inhaling ether after dinner one night.'

'Were they not mothers too? I know that your Mrs Wollstonecraft was.'

'Mrs Crowe had a son, I think. And no husband because she left him. He was a brute, apparently.'

'Unconventional indeed,' he said, though his mind was clearly racing. He paused for a moment, then said: 'If you have help with the child, you could continue to study. I am not alone in thinking that a broad education is necessary for women if they are to be properly equipped for raising their offspring.'

'But surely a broad education should be put to greater use, beyond the home? If the intellectual faculties of women are equal to that of men, should they not be encouraged to do more than merely oversee the education of their children?'

'Of course. I only meant that not everyone objects to female self-improvement.'

He spoke softer now, begging her candour.

'If you could do anything, what would you do?'

'I don't know.'

'I think that you do.'

'If I were entirely free to choose? If my gender was no impediment?'

She paused as though contemplating the question, but he was right. She already knew the answer.

'I would like to be in Will Raven's position: a doctor working alongside Professor Simpson.' Then she sighed. 'But such a thing is impossible.'

'And yet you work alongside the professor now.'

'It's not the same.'

'No. But it is a start.'

She got up and started straightening the blanket on the bed.

'Dr Simpson says that a woman has obtained a medical degree in America. Perhaps I should go there.'

She thought he would dismiss the notion as fanciful. Instead

Archie said: 'Perhaps you should. If you have the means and there is nothing to keep you here.'

She found his sincerity arresting. It was something that hadn't occurred to her before, not a circumstance that she had entertained, yet he truly believed it a possible course of action. Her head spun. To travel beyond the narrow confines of Edinburgh!

She thought of Mrs Glassford's words: *You are young yet. You do not know what your life will become.* It cheered her to imagine other possible lives beyond what was about to happen. Her immediate future seemed to portend little but difficulty, loss and pain. But perhaps there would be better days to come.

She looked at Archie and felt guilty for contemplating life without him. But this kind of introspection brought with it other unanswerable questions. Would Archie be suggesting these things if he were well? It would be highly irregular for a medical man with any social pretensions, however modest, to allow his wife to work. Would he have married her if not facing a life-threatening illness? Such thoughts threatened her very sanity.

As she stood up, she glanced out of the window, and the sight of the grey November streets jolted her back into the coldest reality. She saw all these musings for what they truly were: the consoling fantasies of a dying man. This was a city where his fellow doctors were conspiring to do down no less a man than James Young Simpson. What chance had a woman of ever taking them on?

'Eat your breakfast, Dr Banks,' she commanded, indicating that the conversation was at an end.

THIRTY-THREE

r Johnstone entered the room with the look of a man unmoored. He seemed uncomfortable in the heart of his own house, a disoriented look in his eye as though his surroundings were strange to him. Raven recognised it. This was someone to whom familiar spaces no longer made sense. A vital part of the equation by which he understood the world was missing, and now nothing added up.

Raven could not help but think of Sarah and what lay in her near future.

But perhaps these were not so easily compared. Dr Johnstone and his wife had been married for more than twenty years. Sarah and Archie had been married but a matter of weeks. When he learned that, he had wondered whether he ought to have returned from his travels sooner, but he couldn't fool himself into thinking that would have made a difference. The time to change something was before he left, and back then he had been too concerned with what people thought.

Too meek. Too cowardly.

Perhaps weeks or decades made no odds in matters of the heart. Perhaps he merely wanted to tell himself Sarah and Archie's love was a lesser thing. He ought to admit to himself that it was surely otherwise. They were happy together, despite knowing they would not be together long.

Was it different if you knew in advance that your spouse's life was limited? Did that make it easier to prepare yourself for his loss? Or did that make it more painful, seeing him every morning, perhaps looking upon him for a joyful moment before remembering?

Dr Johnstone carried with him a glass of whisky but did not offer one to his visitor. Raven didn't interpret it as impolite; more that it had slipped his mind that he ought to. Perhaps his wife had been the one who played host in such times.

'The housekeeper told me your name, but I have quite forgotten it.'

'I am Dr Will Raven. I am Dr Simpson's new assistant.'

Dr Johnstone nodded, briefly closing his eyes. 'Of course you are.'

His tone was irritable, on the cusp of annoyance. Raven inferred that he had little margin for error before he might be shown the door.

Dr Johnstone strode purposefully across the room, proceeding past him to the sideboard. He produced from it several news-papers and journals, which he slapped down deliberately hard to emphasise their collective heft.

He was telling Raven there was no need for him to state his business. He was also telling him precisely how welcome he was.

'My wife's death has become a mere football kicked around in a game between men who ought to know better.'

Raven spoke softly. 'Believe me, Dr Johnstone, sir, there is nobody who regrets that more than Dr Simpson.'

Johnstone opened one of the journals and stabbed a finger at the page.

'I'm sure that . . . Professor Miller and Professor Henderson were they here would profess their regret too.'

'Not with any sincerity. While I have no doubt that they

would *profess* regret, I believe there is an unseemly alacrity with which they have seized upon your wife's demise. They are men who have various grudges against Dr Simpson. You are right that it has become a game, but one which Dr Simpson has been too courteous to play. Which is why I am taking it upon myself, unbeknownst to him, to ascertain the truth of the matter and hopefully put an end to it.'

Dr Johnstone fixed him with a sour look.

'You are not the first. There was a woman here recently, asking the same thing.'

'Mrs Banks,' Raven stated, to confirm they were working together. It felt like a retrospective attempt to confer some credentials upon her, as he could now well imagine how she must have been received.

'Yes, though I didn't see the point. These are complex medical matters, so how could she have understood them? In truth I was relieved to learn that Dr Simpson didn't send her, as it would have shown a level of disrespect I would consider beneath him.'

Raven was surprised by the strength of his urge to correct Dr Johnstone on Sarah's knowledge and capabilities, and felt disloyal that he chose to suppress it. However, he was trying to get the man to open up, and ruled it an occasion when discretion was the better part of valour.

'Mrs Banks and I have elsewhere discovered that some of the claims made in these letters are baseless. What we don't have is a first-hand account, which is what may be necessary for this issue to be . . . laid to rest.'

Raven had searched momentarily for a different phrase, before judging these words the most effective.

Dr Johnstone sipped from his whisky, eyes glazed, almost as though he had forgotten Raven was present. Then he seemed to come back into the moment.

'I have worked in this city a long time. I know the game they are playing,' he said. His voice was low, tinged with weariness and not a little anger. 'Every time they write about this, they make it sound worse, and I know they will wring it out for every last drop it might shed. The reason I have not written to the papers already is out of concern that my own testimony would not be credited by these individuals. I have nothing but gratitude for Dr Simpson's kind attention, and like him it was my intention to maintain a dignified silence, but nonetheless putting my account on record might be the only way to draw a line under it.'

When he eyed Raven again, his expression was softer.

'I confess, the other reason I have been reluctant is that my involvement was limited. I entrusted my wife's care to Dr Simpson and to the nurse I employed.'

Raven thought of the disdain with which Dr Johnstone had just referred to Sarah and to women's grasp of medical matters. He couldn't see how this sat with him handing the care of his wife to a nurse when he was a doctor himself.

These reflections must have been more legible upon his face than he intended, for Dr Johnstone looked at him with an expression that was challenging yet sincere, and said: 'You are asking yourself why I delegated such duties to a nurse when I am a medical man.'

Raven thought it unwise to deny it, and best to say nothing.

'You are not long qualified, are you, Dr Raven?'

'No, sir.'

'And nor, I would wager, have you children or a wife.'

'No, I have neither.'

'When you do, pray that you are never required to treat them. It is not done. One's judgment is utterly askew, confused at every turn by emotion. Every doctor encounters a sense of helplessness on occasion, an absolute impotence as circumstances overtake one's knowledge and ability. Now imagine the magnitude of that helplessness when it is with regard to the health, to the *life*, of the one you love the most.'

Raven nodded solemnly, acknowledging his understanding.

'I have no regrets over employing a nurse, and certainly not this nurse. She was a caring and diligent woman, and she was with my wife to the last. She, in fact, is the one you ought to speak to. She will remember more clearly because I did not see a patient. I only saw Dorothy.'

'What was the nurse's name?'

'Mary Dempster.'

'Do you have her address?'

Dr Johnstone turned briefly to the sideboard as though it might be written down.

'Actually, no. I advertised for help in the newspaper. There were two respondents and I chose her because she came with excellent references and had worked on the surgical wards of the Royal Infirmary.'

Dr Johnstone finished off his whisky and seemed far away once again. His subsequent words told Raven where his thoughts had taken him, and it couldn't have been a pleasant journey.

'What I can say is that the amount of blood Dorothy lost never made me uneasy. Considerably more was lost when Syme performed a similar procedure two years ago. Nor was there significant bleeding when Simpson removed the lint plug he had put in place at the time of surgery. The nurse will be able to corroborate that.

'Dorothy seemed to be recovering after the operation, but then deteriorated over the coming days. I am not convinced this ailment was entirely related to the surgery, though perhaps that hindered her strength to fight it off. She was tormented: delirious, grasping at phantoms, her breathing shallow. It was as though she had fever, but her temperature was not elevated. She was at times unrousable, as though narcotised, and yet her pupils were normal in size. An odd combination. I do not think that I have seen it before.'

Raven felt something course through him as he realised that he had, only a few days ago. Dr Johnstone was describing the same symptoms George Porteous exhibited before he died.

He recalled Greta Porteous's fear that she might develop the same disease, because their mother had died shortly before George fell ill. He had missed it at the time, but he now understood that her mother's symptoms must have been similar for Greta to be so concerned.

Raven had previously thought that had Dr Simpson been present at the Porteous house, he would have known what to do. Now it appeared Simpson had been confronted with the same symptoms here and been equally confounded.

As Raven was shown to the door and bade his farewell, he had to suppress his excitement. He had deduced that in their eagerness to go after their enemy, these supposedly great medical men had missed the true significance here. There appeared to be a new, previously undiagnosed disease at large: one that spread rapidly and killed within days. It potentially represented a danger as large as cholera or typhoid. And no one had laid claim to its discovery.

Rather than the blackening of Simpson's name, this could be the making of his own.

Raven's Malady.

He liked the sound of that.

THIRTY-FOUR

eputation and renown: these are precious things, are they not? More so than anything else you own, for nothing is harder to replace. They are a currency, as surely as the money in your pocket. But just like money, they are not the value they represent: they are mere tokens, promissory notes. Reputation is a guarantor of your character, but not the truth of it. Like any other currency, it can be forged.

I learned a painful but valuable lesson at the hands of Joyce Meechan, when she lied about me. It is important to be in control of what people believe of you, especially those who have power over you. That is why I endeavoured thereafter always to please the Reverend Gillies. Witness how my obedience was demonstrated in his private office.

He was playing host to Mrs Josephine Kirkwood, a benefactor of the institution, and her friend, a woman I only heard referred to as 'Olivia'. Formal introductions were not a courtesy extended to the likes of me. The purpose of the visit was to allow Olivia to see the good work undertaken at the Institute in the hope of her becoming a donor like Mrs Kirkwood.

Mrs Kirkwood enjoyed a reputation as a woman of great charity. You may judge for yourself whether that was her true nature.

I stood silent and still, with my hands clasped in front of me and my head bowed. I noted that Mrs Kirkwood was in her stockings, her boots sitting upon the floor next to the desk that dominated the room.

'You will see demonstrated the civilising effects of our methods,' the Reverend said. 'Mary, come forth and write for us from Hebrews, chapter thirteen, verse seventeen.'

Obey them that have the rule over you, I wrote in my best hand, *and submit yourselves: for they watch for your souls, as they that must give account, that they may do it with joy, and not with grief: for that is unprofitable for you.*

Olivia watched with interest, while Mrs Kirkwood beamed with satisfaction.

'Mary here was brought to us by her destitute father,' Mrs Kirkwood said, 'making one of the few wise and selfless decisions of his life. He was the worst of drunkards, with an erratic and volatile nature. What you see here is proof that, in our care, even the worst of that which is inherited can be overcome.'

I put down the pen and stepped back from the desk.

'Now, lace my boot for me,' Mrs Kirkwood said.

I knelt down, took Mrs Kirkwood's right foot and eased it into the corresponding boot, patiently and delicately threading the laces through the eyelets and tying a neat bow. While I was about this business, Mrs Kirkwood placed her left heel upon my back, as though it were a footstool.

Olivia laughed, incredulous. 'Josephine, a compliant nature is desirable, but allow the girl her dignity.'

'You misunderstand, Olivia. A certain indignity is good for her. Humility is a vital part of what is imparted here, and thus soothes the more savage instincts that only cause conflict within the self. Knowing one's role and accepting one's place is the only path to peace for all of us.'

It was to prove an appropriate introduction, for Olivia overcame her reservations, and was to have her foot upon my back for several years thereafter.

THIRTY-FIVE

aven found himself standing in another alley, but on this occasion felt no threat bar that posed by the rubbish heap emitting an unmerciful variety of noxious odours. His companion was being discreetly sick, if such a thing were possible, but it was daylight and no strong drink had been taken.

He handed Sarah his handkerchief and she wiped her mouth. Raven wondered how she planned to explain this sudden illness: would she attempt a lie, or would she come clean, confirming what he already suspected?

'Are you all right?' he asked.

'I am fine.' Her reply was emphatic, defensive.

'Emesis is not usually a sign of good health,' he said gently, offering her the chance to explain.

She ignored this, refusing to be drawn. He decided not to push her; it would be better that she tell him in her own time. But why was she keeping it from him? He was a doctor after all, a man-midwife no less, and so unlikely to miss the signs. Was it the pregnancy itself or the fact that she was refusing to confide in him that bothered him more? In truth he could not say. He missed how they used to be, how open they were with each other. He could not expect otherwise now that she was married and carrying another man's child. A child she would probably have to raise alone. Another thing she would not talk about.

They emerged from the alleyway onto Broughton Street. At the end of the morning clinic, Sarah had seemed unusually quiet and Raven suggested that she accompany him. He had a visit to make and thought some air might do her good. He realised it would also provide a chance for them to talk, there being little opportunity for uninterrupted conversation during working hours at Queen Street. She readily agreed, which had surprised him.

As they walked, they resumed the discussion which had been abruptly curtailed by Sarah's sudden need to void the contents of her stomach.

'Have you heard anything more about the missing money?' he asked.

'No. Have you?'

She sounded eager, clearly hoping his question had been a mere overture to revealing a significant discovery.

Raven shook his head.

'Mr Quinton has Jarvis in his sights because he empties the doctor's pockets every night,' she said. 'Meanwhile Mrs Lyndsay continues to believe one of the new housemaids is to blame. She came from the Lock Hospital, and as far as Mrs Lyndsay is concerned, she is a fallen woman and therefore morally irredeemable.'

Raven thought that any such accusation levelled at Jarvis was absurd, but the notion forced him to confront just how limited was his knowledge of the man. For all he knew, the butler could have been getting away with helping himself for years, particularly as Dr Simpson paid no mind as to how much money was in those pockets.

'I suppose we know little of what Jarvis does when he's not working at Queen Street, do we?' he said. 'Though it hardly seems likely he'd be spending Simpson's money in some den of vice. But Edinburgh is a place where all men have secrets.'

'Indeed. So what might be your covert agenda?'

'Me? Surely I am not under suspicion?'

'If I were a detective, you'd be the first I would question. Someone who is always complaining about his financial situation. Bemoaning your lack of opportunities to earn more while Dr Simpson is ambivalent even when a thousand pounds is dangled before him. You would surely fit the bill for someone inclined to steal from his employer.'

Raven was relieved to see that she was smiling as she said this.

'I suppose if anyone might get to the bottom of it, it would be this Quinton fellow,' he observed. 'I doubt I have ever encountered anyone wound so tight or so humourless, but I suspect those traits are the perfect antidote to Simpson's tendency towards the chaotic. What do you know of him?'

'Only what I have heard from Mrs Simpson. He keeps himself apart from the other servants. I know that he is married and lives with his wife in a house on Castle Street. He and Mrs Quinton have fostered a baby, a little boy called Rochester. Mrs Simpson arranged it.'

'Rochester?' Raven scoffed.

'Yes. And I really don't think you are in a position to criticise given names.'

She was laughing now, a sound Raven found immeasurably pleasing.

'Perhaps you could try to find out more about him?' she suggested. 'You are better placed than I since he shuns the company of those below stairs.'

Raven thought it unlikely that the bloodless creature he had been introduced to would deign to converse with him either, but did not wish to appear unhelpful.

'I will try,' he said, hoping he did not sound as noncommittal as he felt. 'In the meantime, I have some progress to report on our investigation.'

'That is welcome news,' Sarah said, turning to him and putting a hand on his arm. 'Number 52 is not as it should be. Dr Simpson is barely himself. He is pretending that this mattress business is not upsetting to him, but the opposite is true. It's plain for anyone to see. And Mrs Simpson is struggling to cope despite the new staff. She seems overwhelmed and I worry for her.'

Sarah belatedly noticed where her hand had strayed and removed it. Their eyes met briefly as she did so, which served only to add greater significance to the touch.

'I think that we might be able to clear this matter up once and for all,' Raven said, giving stridence to his tone to dispel the awkwardness. 'I have spoken to Dr Johnstone and discovered more about his wife's illness.'

'He received you?' Sarah asked. 'Cordially?'

'He was as affable as could be expected in the circumstances, but yes. He was most helpful.'

'He all but threw me out for my impertinence in daring to be there asking questions. He took great exception, I think, to being interrogated by a woman.'

'The man is grief-stricken and his sorrow has been compounded by the indignity of his wife's death having become the subject of debate. In going there alone, did you really expect it would be otherwise?'

Sarah glared at him, so he hurried on.

'I prevailed upon him to help us clarify the matter. He said that he will write a letter stating that his wife did not die of haemorrhage and that he had nothing but gratitude for Dr Simpson's kind attention. He suggested that his account of events could be corroborated by the nurse who attended Mrs Johnstone after the operation until her death.'

'Then we must find her,' Sarah said. 'We should amass as much evidence as possible to prove beyond doubt the baselessness of these damaging accusations and show those foul peddlers of fiction to be the craven gossip-mongers that they are.'

Raven was a little taken aback by her vehemence and thought that the whole matter would have been resolved long ago if someone had thought to put Duncan and Miller in a room alone with Sarah.

'Perhaps more significantly,' Raven said, 'I might be able to prove that her death was entirely unrelated to Dr Simpson's procedure.'

Sarah stopped walking.

'What do you mean?'

'The symptoms she experienced were similar to a fatal case I was involved with recently. I think I might have mentioned it to you. It was perhaps the second such case within the same house-hold. It is my theory that this might be a dangerous and perplexing new disease. I am on my way now to speak to the doctor who had treated both patients first. I thought him old-fashioned and outdated in his practice, though I might have judged him harshly, as Dr Simpson was also powerless to identify or intervene in what appears to be the same condition.'

'Then I am glad that I have come with you,' Sarah said. 'Perhaps I can learn what it is about your manner that makes you welcome in the home of a gentleman while I am sent away with a flea in my ear.'

'I think we both know which quality of mine makes the difference.'

'Yes, and you flatter yourself if you think it is your being a doctor.'

THIRTY-SIX

s they turned into Broughton Place, Sarah wondered if Raven was right. Had he discovered a new disease? He certainly seemed to have convinced himself, as he was unusually animated, describing the common symptoms the patients had experienced. He was still in full flow when they arrived outside Dr Fowler's residence. It was a neat little dwelling in the middle of a terrace, similar in appearance to No. 52 but on a much smaller scale.

'How will you explain my being here?' she asked as they approached the door.

'It hadn't occurred to me that I would have to do so,' Raven admitted, frowning slightly. 'I'll say that you are my assistant, a nurse who works with me.' He seemed satisfied with that and knocked on the door. 'It might be best if you refrained from speaking,' he added as the door was opened.

They were shown into a small parlour by a young girl who bade them wait while she sought out her master. The space was rather spartan, in stark contrast to the overstuffed room Dr Johnstone had thrown her out of. The few bits of furniture had an air of neglect about them, stained and shabby. An unmarried man lived here, Sarah thought. Or a widower. She immediately felt sorry for him, perhaps because she too would soon be alone, left behind to fend for herself. Then she remembered that Archie was not going to leave her entirely.

She noticed a pile of papers on a low table next to a seat by the fireplace, which upon closer inspection appeared to be hand-written. Sarah edged close enough to take a look, expecting to find medical notes. To her surprise she discovered that Dr Fowler appeared to be writing a story, perhaps even the early stages of a novel. She skimmed a paragraph, further surprised to discover it written from the point of view of a woman. It appeared to be a tale of anguish and deprivation. She wondered if he had been reading Charles Dickens. She wondered also if Dr Fowler was not merely unmarried, but lonely.

The parlour door opened, interrupting her reflections. She took a guilty step away from the table as Dr Fowler entered, looking to all intents and purposes like the human embodiment of his care-worn fixtures and fittings. His clothes appeared to be as old as he was, all frayed edges and loose threads. He seemed surprised and not entirely happy to find Raven standing at his fireside. Sarah was ignored so completely that she might as well have been invisible, her worry about how she might be introduced rendered superfluous. He prefers his women fictional, she thought.

'Dr Raven. I had not expected to see you again.'

'I apologise for this impromptu visit, Dr Fowler, but there is an important matter that I must discuss with you.'

Their host indicated that they should sit. Sarah lowered herself into a chair, fully expecting a plume of dust to rise up from the upholstery as she did so.

'I have some questions about the Porteous case,' Raven began.

Fowler shifted in his seat, clearly uncomfortable.

'I regret ever having involved you in it,' he said.

Raven pointedly ignored this and continued: 'Greta Porteous said her mother died shortly before George, and she seemed concerned that she also might become ill. She seemed to believe her brother and her mother succumbed to the same disease. And yet she told me you had informed her that it was a failing heart that led to her mother's death.'

'Mrs Porteous was ill for a longer period than George, a number of weeks. The family engaged the services of a nurse to help look after her and it seemed as though she would recover. But her illness was of a relapsing and remitting kind. At times she seemed to rally – under my instruction, of course – and then she would worsen.'

'Did you notice any similarities in the symptoms?'

'There was a degree of delirium, I suppose. Some days she would seem quite lucid and other days she was tormented as though haunted by spectres. They do say that those who are closest to death are most able to see the world that lies beyond it.'

Sarah snorted and then attempted to cover it up with a sneeze. The proliferation of dust at least made this seem plausible enough.

'Excuse me,' she said.

'Were there other symptoms? What of her temperature, her heart rate?' Raven asked.

'There was no fever. The pulse was irregular at times. All quite consistent with my diagnosis.' Fowler shook his head and smiled at Raven, suddenly more at ease. 'I see no evidence of contagion here. If there was, the nurse would surely be affected, as she spent more time with either of them than I did, or Miss Porteous.'

Raven straightened in his chair.

'Of course. The nurse. We should establish whether she is suffering any of the same symptoms. Do you know who she was?'

'Yes,' Dr Fowler replied. 'I have recommended her to several patients before. Her name is Mary Dempster.'

Raven looked astonished.

'Did you say Mary Dempster?'

'Yes. What of it?'

'That is the name of the nurse who treated Mrs Johnstone.'

Dr Fowler's expression quickly progressed from smugness to confusion as the significance of the exchange was lost on him.

'Three of her patients have died exhibiting similar symptoms,' Raven went on.

'Then she is in danger,' said Sarah. 'She might already be ill.'

Dr Fowler looked at her as though she had just materialised in front of him, like one of the spectres he claimed had tormented Mrs Porteous.

'Or perhaps she is merely serving as a conduit,' Raven suggested. 'The unhappy medium carrying the contagion of disease from one patient to another.'

'Like puerperal fever?' Sarah asked.

'Exactly!' Raven said, delighted she was following his logic.

'This is nothing like puerperal fever,' Dr Fowler protested.

'It is not the disease but the contagious communicability that might be the same,' Raven insisted.

Fowler slumped in his chair, completely at a loss.

'Where does she live?' Raven asked. 'Do you have her address?'

'Not to hand,' he said, getting to his feet. He wandered towards the door, leaving Sarah unconvinced he would remember what he had gone in search of by the time he reached the hall.

'The nurse is the key to this,' Raven said.

'What makes you so sure?'

Sarah was concerned that his enthusiasm was getting the better of him, clouding his judgment in much the same way that he himself suggested the professor's had been compromised with respect to chloroform.

'Simpson has written about this very thing, in his paper comparing puerperal and surgical fever. In 1840 in Manchester, four hundred women in different parts of the town were delivered by twelve midwives. Sixteen died of puerperal fever, all sixteen having been delivered by the same midwife. There must have been something connected to that one midwife which meant that all of her patients took the disease while the patients delivered by the other midwives escaped it. Some form of morbific principle attached to her hands.'

Sarah opened her mouth to tell him she had read this very paper but Raven was in full flow.

'Several years ago, Dr Simpson attended the post-mortem examination of a patient who had died from puerperal fever. He and another practitioner handled the diseased parts. The next four midwifery cases that Dr Simpson attended were all affected with puerperal fever. The next three cases the other doctor attended were attacked with the disease. There is something that adheres to the hands. Common ablutions will not remove it; chloride of lime must be used.'

'Doesn't everyone use chloride of lime then?'

'Dr Simpson favours cyanide of potass, but that is of no matter. Not all are convinced. There are those who still favour the miasma theory: epidemics of disease occurring as a result of noxious air.'

'But Dr Fowler is right. This is not puerperal fever,' Sarah said.

'No. But it might be Raven's Malady.'

And there it was, the reason his fervour alarmed her: his hunger for professional acclaim was driving this now more than his desire to rescue Dr Simpson's reputation.

Regardless of his motivation, they did need to speak to Nurse Dempster. Sarah felt sure that finding her would conclude their investigation with regard to Mrs Johnstone's death. Whatever other avenues of enquiry Raven wished to embark upon, he could do so himself.

Dr Fowler reappeared, looking perplexed.

'I must apologise. If I ever had the address, I have misplaced it. However, I believe it is to be found by consulting the Post Office directory. How many Mary Dempsters can there be in Edinburgh?'

THIRTY-SEVEN

here was an easterly wind whipping off the water of Lochend as Sarah strived to match Raven's long stride down Easter Road. She could feel moisture in the air and hoped it had been picked up from the loch rather than being an indicator that the dark-grey skies were about to unburden themselves.

It was a Sunday afternoon, one of the few occasions when neither she nor Raven had duties elsewhere, and they were spending it in an attempt to locate the nurse who had worked for both Mrs Johnstone and the Porteous family. Raven had suggested Sarah might prefer to spend the day with her husband, which had made her uneasy. It might have been an idle remark, or even motivated by his own preference to go alone, but she could not help worrying that it indicated he was aware of Archie's condition. Was he implying she ought to make the best of what little time they might have left together? Or was that her own guilt speaking?

She felt compelled to play a part in clearing Dr Simpson's name, for reasons she could not rightly articulate. She had told herself that it was imperative she accompany Raven so that Dr Simpson's plight was not forgotten in Raven's eagerness to pursue his own agenda. However, she could not deny that a part of her sought an excuse to leave the house. Time with Archie was increasingly bittersweet. He was weakening before her eyes, and every moment spent with him carried the promise of pain to come. God forgive her for thinking so, but there were times when she could not bear it.

She heard Raven let out a frustrated sigh as they rounded a bend in the road and a neat little cottage came into view, sitting in isolation amidst a well-tended garden with a view of the Forth.

'Something irks you?' she asked.

'This does not look like the kind of home a nurse could afford to rent.'

'Perhaps she has a husband who earns a good deal more,' Sarah suggested. 'There are some men who are happy for their wives to work, after all.'

She enjoyed landing this blow upon him, but her pleasure was tempered by it returning her thoughts to Albany Street, where perhaps she ought to be right then.

'A woman married to such a man would not choose to work as a nurse, believe me,' Raven replied. 'Any more than you would choose to keep working as a housemaid.'

They had found three listings for 'M. Dempster' in the Post Office directory, and had come straight from the first one, who had turned out to be a retired book-keeper in Abbey Hill. From Raven's misgivings about this cottage, it appeared he believed their quest would take them all the way to the third address, in Leith.

'We have come this far, so we might as well enquire,' Sarah reasoned.

'Very well,' he responded, with little enthusiasm.

The cottage was set back from the road. Sarah thought she saw a flash of movement at one of the windows as they approached, but a cloud of blackbirds had flown past at the same time and she dismissed it as merely a reflection.

Raven rapped on the door, his knuckles firm but not peremptory, as though aware he had little right to be disturbing anyone.

He still had not developed the self-importance of the typical professional gentleman, a trait she found endearing in him.

They waited in vain for a response, throughout which time Sarah became more convinced that the black flash in the window had indeed been birds.

'Do you remember what she looked like?' Sarah asked, it occurring to her that if she was disinclined to receive them, this Mary Dempster could very easily deny who she was, and they might be none the wiser. Sarah had once learned a harsh lesson concerning an individual presenting himself as someone he was not.

'I saw her briefly when I first visited George Porteous,' Raven replied. 'A slight woman with dark hair. She sounded as if she was from Glasgow.'

He tried knocking a second time.

'I don't think anyone is home,' he said.

'I thought I saw someone at the window, but I might have been mistaken. Perhaps we should leave a message asking her to come to Queen Street, if indeed this is the right address.'

As she said this, Sarah heard movement from within. She and Raven shared a look, a moment of renewed optimism.

A moment later the door was opened by a bespectacled woman in a wool dress and knitted shawl, fair hair spilling from beneath a lace-trimmed cap. She was a little portly, an ample bosom filling out her dress.

'I am sorry to keep you,' she said. 'I was not expecting visitors.'

'Not at all,' said Raven. 'We are the ones who should apologise for calling on you unannounced. We might even have the wrong address. We are in search of a nurse by the name of Mary Dempster.'

The woman wore a regretful expression, shaking her head in a way that had Sarah preparing her weary feet for the walk to Charlotte Street in Leith and then all the way back to the New Town.

'My sister is not at home,' the woman said.

'But this *is* her house?' Raven inferred, optimism in his voice.

The woman's brow furrowed in brief annoyance.

'It is *my* house. I am Martha Dempster. Mary is my sister.'

'I see,' said Raven. 'We were told a recent employer had procured Mary's services by means of the Post Office directory, but the M. Dempster listed there is you.'

'Indeed, though my sister does live here. Well . . .'

She seemed about to elaborate then changed tack.

'Do you seek her for nursing work?'

'No, though we do wish to speak with her concerning some of her previous patients. I am Dr Will Raven and this is my associate, Mrs Sarah Banks. May we come in?'

Miss Dempster seemed reluctant, fetching a glance behind her as though perhaps the house was in a state of disorder.

'It is a matter of some importance,' Sarah added.

'Very well,' she said. 'But allow me a moment.'

She closed the door, leaving them on the threshold to ponder the delay.

'Why would she keep us here?' Raven asked, his impatience evident.

Sarah wanted to tell herself it was because he was desperate to save future patients from this new ailment, but she knew his motivations were less altruistic. Raven did not share all of the less admirable traits of his fellow professionals, but he was a medical man nonetheless, and he had the scent of glory in his nostrils.

She was more sanguine about the reason for the wait.

'She is house-proud, I imagine, and we have caught her unawares. Tantamount to being intruded upon half-dressed.'

A short time later, they were shown inside, through a neat hallway into a bright parlour at the back of the house. Sarah surveyed it with a maid's eye for what might have been urgently tidied away, but nothing leapt out at her. Her gaze was more pressingly drawn to the herb garden she could see through the window, as the relationship between plants and medicine had become a passionate area of study. The beds looked carefully tended. She spotted mint, sage and rosemary as well as yarrow and comfrey, suggesting that whoever tended this garden shared her interest in medicinal plants. There was one plant which looked familiar that she could not identify.

'Is Mary expected home soon?' Sarah asked as she took a seat.

There was uncertainty in Martha's expression, as though she was not sure quite how to answer.

'She tends to reside with the patients she works for,' Martha said. 'She left a few days ago to take up a new appointment. I do not know how long she will stay.'

'Do you know where this appointment is and who it is with?'

Again the uncertain expression.

'She does not always discuss these matters with me. Suffice to say she comes and goes, but I seldom have notice of either. What is this matter you wish to discuss with her?'

Raven sat forward in his chair, that eagerness animating him once again.

'We have reason to believe that three of the patients she recently attended might have died from the same illness. We are concerned that she is at risk from it too, or that she may somehow be unwittingly instrumental in transferring it.'

Martha visibly bristled at this last, and rightly so. Raven really ought to have phrased this more delicately, but his enthusiasm for his theory over-rode such considerations.

'My sister is an excellent nurse, and much sought-after,' she said. 'I am sure nothing that she did would have played a part in this.'

Sarah knew she had to ameliorate the situation, and quickly.

'Mary's reputation indeed precedes her. She was spoken of most highly by the doctors who worked with her in these cases.'

Raven picked up on her tone and attempted to make amends of his own.

'Quite. It appears that these patients died of a new disease, not encountered before in this city. Mary is therefore the person best placed to provide accurate accounts of how the disease progressed in each case. She is in a unique position. She may be able to provide evidence vital to our understanding.'

Martha's demeanour softened a little.

'Yes,' she said. 'Mary did mention a young man who had died soon after his mother. She was most upset about it, as they had both appeared to grow stronger under her care, only to decline and then succumb. It was distressing for her. She is very particular in her care and takes pride in her work. We both do.'

'You are a nurse too?' Raven asked. Once again, he could have moderated his tone to perhaps sound less incredulous.

'Yes. It was not the life I envisaged for myself, but I had to find a purpose after everything that happened.'

She looked away briefly, as though her thoughts had gone elsewhere.

'You have a fine house,' Sarah said. If Raven was going to express his surprise at the incongruity between her job and her surroundings, she reasoned she ought to balance things by complimenting the latter.

'Thank you. Mary and I moved here after my parents died. I was fortunate enough to inherit some money. We could not hope to rent such a place on a nurse's earnings, though certainly private nursing is far better paid than in the hospitals.'

Sarah wondered at her reference to 'my parents', rather than 'our'.

'I encountered your sister briefly at the Porteous house,' Raven said. 'I might be mistaken, but by her accent I took her to be from Glasgow. And yet you sound— '

'Edinburgh born and bred,' Martha interrupted with a proud smile. 'I ought to clarify: Mary came to us when I was thirteen and she was twelve. She was in an orphanage in Glasgow.'

'She is your adopted sister,' Raven stated.

'Yes. Though it amused us down the years how often people would say we had a resemblance while they thought we were true sisters. Introduce an idea into someone's head and they will soon start to paint a picture around it.'

How true, Sarah reflected, her mind inevitably turning to poor Miss Grindlay, Mrs Simpson's sister, who had paid a high price for painting just such a picture.

Quiet settled upon the room, and with it the awkwardness among people with nothing left to say to each other. It prompted Raven to get to his feet. He produced a card and handed it to Martha.

'I would be obliged if you would ask your sister to contact me at her earliest convenience when you do see her. It is particularly imperative that she speak to me should she or any of her patients exhibit similar symptoms to those of George Porteous.'

'Of course, Dr Raven.'

As Sarah stood, her eye was caught once again by the plants in the garden, particularly the one she was unable to name.

'I see that you have some medicinal plants in the garden, but there is one I cannot identify, to the right of the rosemary.'

Martha had a look through the window, her expression strained.

'Mary is the one who has a passion for horticulture. Having grown up in a Glasgow slum, the very notion of a garden has always held great appeal. I think the plant you are referring to is potatoes.'

'Of course,' Sarah said, feeling rather foolish. She ought to recognise potatoes. Perhaps it was her own instance of painting a picture around an idea. She had been searching her mind for something medicinal and missed the obvious as a result.

Martha showed them to the door, assuring them she would pass Raven's card on to her sister as soon as she returned. He seemed relieved to have made a form of contact, but Sarah could sense his frustration at not being able to speak to Mary directly.

Sarah had a portion of that too. She wanted to amass all possible evidence in Dr Simpson's favour.

There was definitely rain in the wind as they retreated down the garden path.

'When did you get those cards printed?' Sarah asked, unable to keep a note of amusement from her voice. 'May I have one?'

Raven looked self-conscious, as though she had caught him in an affectation. He handed over a card.

'Why doesn't it say "Wilberforce"?' she chided him.

'Only my mother gets to call me that.'

'It looks a little sparse. Did you not think to print a little raven silhouette on there?'

'As a doctor, it behoves me to eschew symbols synonymous with death.'

'Perhaps you should have considered that when you changed your surname.'

'I dropped my late father's name and took my mother's. That was as wide as the choice extended. Though I do take your point. It is a pity her name was not Goodfellow.'

'No. That would be fraudulent. You are no more a good fellow than you are a raven.'

He smiled, something she had seldom seen him do since his return from the Continent. She had missed it.

'I knew a fellow at medical school by the name of Slaughter,' he said. 'I cannot think that will enhance his practice.'

Sarah glanced back at the cottage for a moment.

'What did you think of Martha?' she asked.

'Pleasant enough. But under the circumstances, a poor substitute for her sister. I may have to return to Dr Fowler in case he knows which family she might have gone to work for now.'

'I got the impression she was holding something back. That she and her sister do not have an easy relationship.'

'Adopted or not, which pair of siblings does?' he replied.

Sarah thought of that look of uncertainty in Martha's expression before she answered questions. Thinking back, it seemed not so much that Martha was unsure of what to say than that she was worried about what she *ought* to say.

As though concerned her sister might be listening.

She wondered again about that flash she saw at the window. Could it have been a dark-haired woman? Or was Sarah painting another picture?

THIRTY-EIGHT

arah entered the downstairs waiting room to find the new housemaid filling the coal scuttle.

'Morning, Lizzie,' she said, her greeting startling the poor girl and causing her to spill a few lumps of coal onto the hearth rug.

Lizzie bent to pick them up and then rubbed at the area with a rag, causing the coal dust to become more deeply embedded.

'You'll need to lift that and beat it,' Sarah said. Lizzie looked up at her and scowled. 'I'm trying to help you,' Sarah explained, surprised by her surliness.

Lizzie said nothing. She tucked the rag into the pocket of her apron, then lifted her brush and the bucket containing the rakings from the fireplace.

'Remember to sift the cinders out of that,' Sarah said, indicating the bucket. 'Mrs Lyndsay hates to waste anything.' She smiled at the girl, hoping that her advice would be accepted with good grace rather than discarded out of hand. Sarah felt that the girl was in need of an ally and would be happy to fill the role if Lizzie was willing to let her.

'There's no end to the things that Mrs Lyndsay hates,' Lizzie replied, spitting the words out. 'There's not much that pleases her as far as I can tell.'

'Mrs Lyndsay is a good woman, but you have to work to earn her favour.'

'I work from morning till night as it is. What more am I supposed to do?'

'Just give it a little time.'

Lizzie snorted. 'Sure, what else can I do? Go back to what I was doing before? Sometimes I think it would be better than this.'

'You don't mean that.'

'What would you know about it?'

Sarah did not think that her lack of first-hand experience of Edinburgh brothels made her ineligible to hold an opinion on the matter.

'I know that this is a safe place to be,' she said, 'where people will take care of you if you let them.'

Lizzie gave her a penetrating look, as if assessing the truth of what she said.

'That include the old witch in the kitchen?'

'Mrs Lyndsay is just a bit set in her ways. She'll come round. Just show her that you're a good person.'

'Perhaps I'm not,' Lizzie said, walking towards the door, swinging her bucket. As she pulled the door closed behind her, Sarah began to wonder if Mrs Lyndsay was right to be suspicious.

Sarah heard the doorbell ring out and wondered if Lizzie would deign to answer it. She tried to imagine the girl dropping her bucket and rushing to the door, bristling with undisguised hostility. Perhaps it would be better if she didn't. She might get herself dismissed.

Sarah looked out into the hallway and watched with some relief as Jarvis opened the door, his frame blocking her view. She thought she heard the voice of a young woman, timid and quiet. Jarvis's greeting was, as always, polite and implacable but with a hint of weary stoicism.

'Dr Simpson is from home, attending a patient. Would his assistant, Dr Raven, be suitable?'

Sarah heard a mumbled response in the affirmative.

'Do come with me. I will take you to him presently.'

As Jarvis stepped aside, Sarah recognised the woman who was following him in. She was Mrs Glassford's housemaid. She had a grave look about her, the significance of which Sarah immediately understood.

Sarah found herself following them along the corridor, drifting like a wraith as though propelled by an unseen force. She loitered in the doorway while the maid stood before Raven in his consulting room. The conversation was brief, the young woman stumbling over the few words that were required to deliver the news.

'Can I offer you some tea?' Sarah asked her as the maid turned towards the door, though she was barely conscious of the words issuing from her mouth. She felt numb, present but not truly here.

The girl declined politely and went to leave, her errand at an end, her message delivered. She seemed anxious to extricate herself, though Sarah doubted she had any reason to hurry back to her place of work. What future for her, now that her employer was dead?

It was this thought that somehow rendered an abstract notion into something tangible.

Mrs Glassford was dead.

The numbness lifted and she felt a wellspring of grief rise up and engulf her. Raven was by her side now and she leaned towards him. His arms folded around her as tears began to stream down her cheeks. It felt safe there, a place she could let go and give in to what she was feeling. She sobbed loudly, her shoulders heaving. Then she heard footsteps and was aware of a presence nearby.

She lifted her head from Raven's chest and saw Quinton standing a few yards away. They broke apart, but the speed and suddenness with which they did so served only to emphasise that they were doing something they wished to hide.

Quinton, for his part, looked mortified, both by having

intruded and by what he had intruded upon. He had never struck her as a man well equipped to comprehend other people's emotions, as he barely ever registered any of his own.

'My apologies,' he muttered, then turned on his heel and retreated.

Raven beckoned her into his consulting room and closed the door to give them some belated privacy.

'Sarah,' he said softly, 'what grieves you?'

And that indeed was the question. Who were these tears really for?

Mrs Glassford had been an inspiration. She had shown by example that a woman did not have to accept her lot, rejecting the husband picked out by her father and choosing instead a life on her own terms.

Sarah had devoured the book she had given to her, *A Vindication of the Rights of Woman*. Mrs Glassford had referred to it simply as the *Vindication*, which seemed apposite, as it served that purpose regarding so many of the beliefs Sarah had come to hold. How well had it described the diminished lives accepted by even the most privileged of women: 'Confined then in cages like the feathered race, they have nothing to do but to plume themselves, and stalk with mock majesty from perch to perch. It is true they are provided with food and raiment, for which they neither toil nor spin; but health, liberty and virtue are given in exchange.'

It had made Sarah think mournfully of the wasted potential of Mrs Simpson's sister, Mina, her talents and intelligence unnurtured as she sought only to marry well. And this was to say nothing of the wasted potential of all those women who inhabited the realm below stairs, where she, until recently, had been confined. How many Shakespeares, how many Newtons – how many Simpsons for that matter – had we lost because they were born of a gender that was denied the chance to shine?

Sarah had been fond of Mrs Glassford. She had only known her a short time, and throughout all of it she had been aware she was likely to die, but the reality of her death was shocking, a portent of a greater loss yet to come.

She looked up at Raven.

'It is Archie,' she said. 'He is dying, Will.'

Raven nodded solemnly.

'I know.'

Then it struck her: how could he not? Raven had seen him, had spent time with him and was a doctor. He did not need to be told. She had deceived herself about this, and Raven had played along out of politeness.

'Have you and Archie talked about it?' she asked, suddenly appalled by the notion.

'Yes, but he only confirmed what I had suspected. I did not think it my place to raise the matter with you.'

She nodded in acknowledgement.

'But I am always here to listen,' he added.

Sarah swallowed, his solicitude threatening to prompt more tears.

'It's easy to think you can cope with the prospect of impending loss until you are actually confronted with it,' she said. 'I knew Mrs Glassford could not be saved. And nor can Archie. It is possible to hide from that reality when you don't know how much time you have. But now Mrs Glassford is dead . . .'

She closed her eyes a moment.

'I am so afraid, Will, but I cannot tell Archie how scared I am. He needs me to be strong. He should not have to comfort me. It must be the other way around.'

'Archie would not wish you to bear your fears alone.'

'You do not understand, Will. I cannot tell him my fears, for they are shameful. There is a cowardly part of me that wishes he was already gone, because I cannot face what lies ahead.'

Tears came once more, and again she sought solace in Raven's embrace. She felt the warmth of him, an easy familiarity about his touch, his smell, and something stirred in her: something that had not been forgotten. She had a glimpse of comfort, of a companion who would help her carry the burden of her coming pain, and of a future that might lie beyond it. Then it vanished when she remembered the reason such a future could not happen: a burden she would have to carry alone. Quite literally.

The last time they spoke, Mrs Glassford had expressed her fear that she was being punished for wanting more. For her defiance. Sarah had assured her otherwise, but now she feared that she was being punished too. She would be left on her own, not merely a widow, but a widow with a child on the way.

It had been easy to fall for Archie, because it felt like there would be no risk in doing so, and that was the danger. She had told herself that it was a noble friendship, offering him comfort while she enjoyed his company. Looking back, it was impossible to trace the point when friendship no longer felt enough. No single increment had seemed like a step too far, and with each little step she had fallen a little further in, still believing it was something transient, something temporary. By the time she saw how far she had come, it was too late to turn back.

With Raven, it had not been tiny increments. It had been giant leaps into the void. He had made her reckless in a way she could not bring herself to regret. He had made so many things seem possible, but then he had withdrawn it all, retreating behind his studies as an excuse. A man who had seemed so dangerous, so unlike other medical men, had suddenly become fearful, acquiescent of all their rules and strictures; reeled in by convention, by concern for what others might think of him.

With Archie, there was no fear of it all being withdrawn because, paradoxically, that was a certainty. She had thought that knowing it was temporary would make it easier. In practice, the opposite was true. Every day she saw the life they might have had together; how good they were for one another (though all the while there hung the question of whether they would have been together had Archie not known what was approaching).

When he asked her to marry him, she had no doubts, no second thoughts. How could she deny him? How could she deny herself? It was true that she had glimpsed the pain to come, but it seemed a speck of cloud on the distant horizon when all around was sunshine and warmth.

Now the sky was black, and when the rains, the thunder and the lightning commenced, she would be alone.

THIRTY-NINE

he rule of man is consolidated by structure, by the erection of institutions. And though a woman might sometimes rule an institution, it is the laws of men that she upholds, and primarily she does so to protect her own position. She prosecutes the laws of men more strictly than men themselves because she knows her power is merely borrowed. She is in permanent fear of the power that has been entrusted to her, and she is merely its vessel and their instrument. As long as she is wielding power in the interests of those who handed it to her, then she knows she will not find herself on the wrong end of it. This is true whether she be in charge of a schoolroom, a hospital or indeed a household, and I can testify to the truth of this in all cases.

Upon the stage in my memory is a parlour in Canonmills, Edinburgh. It was bright and airy, with a view to the Water of Leith from the windows. On this day the chairs were turned from the fireplace towards a low table upon which tea would be served. As though counting down the time to this decorous moment, a recently polished clock was ticking on the recently polished sideboard. All was neat and ordered, a world away from Cumberland Street or the Belmont Institute.

The audience might believe it to be the set for one of those lighter plays about social mores, replete with competing suitors and comic misunderstanding. They would not realise that what they were looking at was in fact an arena for blood sport.

This was the living room of Mrs Olivia Dempster, wherein a number of ladies would soon gather: old friends, good friends. They would sip tea. They would nibble delicately at cake. They would smile warmly at one another. And all the while, they would be vigilant of their own defences and gimlet-eyed in the lookout for a weakness in someone else's armour that might let them slip a blade between her ribs.

Mrs Emily Robertson would not be attending today, though in her absence she would be the focus of more attention than her presence ever commanded. She had had to withdraw from polite company because her youngest daughter had been caught reading something inappropriate.

Everyone would be sympathetic, everyone would be sorry for her trouble, and everyone would be secretly delighted. Thrilled, in fact: not merely relieved that it did not happen to them, for the retention of mere equilibrium was no cause for excitement. Every time someone else fell, they embraced it as proof that they were better than she, and a vindication of the way they each ran their own homes and raised their families.

It was like a dance: it made its own self-contained sense, and required a grace and skill to execute it. But equally, if you could not hear the music, the movement and posturing would seem absurd, the orchestration slavish.

It took me a long time to hear the music, though I quickly understood that I would never be permitted to partake of the dance itself.

Martha was already in the parlour, waiting for me to join her in making final preparations for the guests.

She called out as I descended the stairs: 'Mary, time waits for no man!'

It was a knowing remark, urging me to make haste by using a favoured expression of her mother's.

I was fastening the last button on my dress as I came in. It was cornflower blue and a little baggy because it belonged to Martha first, but I nonetheless enjoyed having the occasion to dress in something fine. I had just changed out of my working clothes. My morning had been busier than normal, preparation for Mrs Dempster's at-home supplementing my usual duties. As well as helping the cook, I had been beating carpets, dusting furniture, polishing tables and cleaning up after the household's three dogs and two cats. Having been raised in the country, Mrs Dempster liked to have animals around her. She also rode, though she did not own a horse. She did, however, own a horsewhip.

Martha's preparation for this gathering had been to spend the morning practising the pianoforte for the recital she was to give. She was nervous about the prospect, concerned about disappointing the guests and terrified of letting her mother down. She did not understand that the guests would be disappointed only if she played flawlessly. Martha had been too cosseted to see the real world that rotted beneath the painted façades.

I remember the first time I laid eyes upon Martha, though more vividly I remember how she smelled. She emerged red-cheeked from the warmth of the kitchen, the happy odours of fresh baking enveloping her. She looked at me with an anxious curiosity, excited in her anticipation but a little apprehensive too.

'This is Mary,' Mrs Dempster had said. 'She's going to be living here now.'

I often thought back to this choice of words, how I hadn't been described as Martha's stepsister, nor as being adopted. The blurring of status had begun immediately.

It took me a long time to realise that when Mrs Dempster had queried the propriety of her friend Mrs Kirkwood's foot upon my back, it wasn't because she was appalled. Rather, she was excited by this demonstration of submissiveness.

The adoption rendered me no better than an indentured servant. It was through the diligent efforts of Mrs Kirkwood that many a household was able to procure a maid they might otherwise struggle to afford.

Mrs Dempster got to bask in her peers' admiration for her charity in taking me in, but her friends also understood that she should not be expected to treat this foundling as an equal to her real daughter. In their eyes, Mrs Dempster had raised me far above my origins, and I ought to be grateful for that much.

Olivia adopted her from an orphanage in Glasgow.

I've heard the father was a derelict.

What of the mother?

I can but imagine the worst.

I wanted to tell them that my father had been a captain in the army, a hero of Waterloo, and that my mother was an actress said to be the equal of Madame Vestris. I wanted them to question the stories they were telling themselves by providing an alternative narrative of my own. There was no opportunity to do so. No one ever asked. No one was ever interested enough.

I always had the impression that Martha was fond of me, though it was in the same way as she was fond of the dogs. She was by turns affectionate towards them and amused by them, but there was no question that they were creatures for her to take or leave as she pleased.

Martha laughed at me when I entered the room.

'What is amiss?' I asked.

'You have soot upon your forehead,' she replied, amused.

I automatically reached towards my head with my sleeve, but Martha's hand restrained me. She produced a handkerchief and wiped the mark away.

'Whether on your face or on your sleeve, a sooty mark is not to be tolerated when presenting one's girls in company.'

Martha wore a knowing smirk as she spoke. If we enjoyed a degree of sorority, it was in having a common foe.

'You mean as though I've just arrived here fae a manky back court,' I replied, reverting to my original accent.

The way I spoke now was a token of Mrs Dempster's 'civilising' of me.

I remembered some of the teachers at the Institute correcting mistakes in the children's grammar, and insisting upon what they called the proper words for things in place of the terms we had grown up using. Some of the children were merely confused by this. Others, such as myself, understood the status of the new terms, but continued to use the old ones in everyday conversation.

To Mrs Dempster, however, my very pronunciation gave offence. It sounded 'coarse and uncouth', as she put it. 'Your accent is redolent of the gutter. It is a stench we must scrub away.'

I found it easy enough to adapt. At the Institute, I had sometimes amused my friends by speaking in the manner of the Reverend Gillies or one of the teachers. I soon learned to speak to Mrs Dempster's satisfaction, but a part of me felt I was being tamed and resented it. I resolved that one day I would go out in the world and speak as I pleased.

In the meantime, my old way of speaking was always guaranteed to make Martha laugh; though seldom as much as when I exaggerated my new elocution and pretended to be Mrs Dempster.

I put the back of my hand to my newly clean forehead, feigning shock and outrage.

'I will not suffer you to speak in such a manner beneath my roof.'

I bathed in the glow of Martha's amusement. At such times I understood what it must feel like to be on the stage, for one's performance to delight an audience.

'Any young woman evincing such shoddy enunciation might just as well present herself in rags, for she will be making plain the squalor of her provenance, no matter if she be wearing the finest silks from Kennington and Jenner.'

Then I saw the change, the brief flash of alarm in Martha's face, the reddening of cheeks as her eyes turned to the floor.

Mrs Dempster was behind me. She had heard every word.

I turned around slowly. Mrs Dempster did not even speak my name.

'To your room. At once,' was all she said.

I retreated up the stairs, one of the dogs scurrying after me.

My room was little more than a cupboard, space only for a bed and a washstand. Nonetheless, I recall how pleased I once was that this little space was mine alone, never having had such privacy. There were times when it served to make me feel isolated, however – no more so than when I had been banished there, awaiting punishment.

I had assumed that my insolence would guarantee exclusion from the afternoon's events, but I soon realised my error. I could not be excluded, for I was an important part of the tableau. I was to be the polite, smartly presented and grateful stepdaughter who had been elevated by the supreme charity of Mrs Dempster in taking me in and providing me with the opportunity to better myself.

I heard one of the dogs on the boards outside, then the heavier tread of Mrs Dempster, who shooed the creature away. It obeyed, as all the house's lower creatures did.

She came in, closed the door behind her and turned to face me, only feet away in the cramped little room.

I felt a familiar tightening in my chest. I knew it was pointless to protest or even to express my penitence. Nothing would stop what now must be done.

Mrs Dempster gestured with the horsewhip.

I assumed the position, bending over the bed as I had done so many times before.

'Pull up your dress,' Mrs Dempster commanded. 'I have guests coming and I do not wish to leave a mark.'

On the fabric, she meant.

It was a fiercer thrashing than I had endured in some years. The earliest ones had been the worst. 'Like breaking in a horse,' Mrs Dempster had said.

On this occasion, there seemed to be real fury in the strokes and in the duration. She only desisted when blood was drawn, and even then, I suspect, only because it might seep through and become visible. Appearances had to be preserved, after all, because within a half hour I was to be downstairs, pretending all was well.

I played the part that was expected of me: smiling, content and grateful before the guests. Having learned to mask my suffering, I was dry-eyed, giving no indication of pain or injury.

As it happened, there were tears shed at the end of that day, though they were not mine.

One of the dogs became ill sometime in the evening, writhing and squealing on the floor of the kitchen. The creature's agony would not pass, and it was in a state of such conspicuous distress that in the end Mr Dempster had to despatch it. I heard the awful keening and yelping suddenly silenced, though it was soon to be replaced by Martha's own howling lamentation.

'She must have eaten something she shouldn't,' Mr Dempster opined, commencing an enquiry as to precisely what and how, in case any of the others might soon fall victim to the same affliction.

He discovered that the pantry door had been left unlatched, and in its hungry curiosity, the animal had dislodged some items from the only shelf it could reach. One of those was a basket of stale crusts, which it had upended. Unfortunately, another of the things it had toppled was a paper bag of arsenic, purchased the previous year when Mrs Dempster spied a rat in the pantry. The contents of the bag had partly spilled among the crusts, and it appeared the poor dog had poisoned itself.

Mrs Dempster had not seemed particularly moved by the loss of the dog, but she did appear stricken at the sight of her daughter's distress, and her inability to assuage it.

For my part, I observed the reactions of both with a detached fascination, the appeal of which I could not at first apprehend. But as I watched Martha's tears and the helplessness of a mother unable to comfort her daughter, I came to understand the effect it was having upon me.

I found their anguish nourishing.

FORTY

rs Glassford's remains arrived at 52 Queen Street towards the end of the morning. She was brought there upon a cart, which had to sit in place until the clinic was over so that the patients would not witness the body being carried inside by Raven and Jarvis. The butler's face was unreadable throughout the short journey, with no hint of discomfort or clue as to what introspection might be going on regarding the unusual duties his appointment required of him.

The man was indeed a mystery to Raven, but, despite an air of cold detachment often bordering on disdain, he found it difficult to believe anything truly wicked or deceitful of the fellow. Of course, he reminded himself, the ability to present such a façade would provide the perfect disguise for such wickedness and dishonesty.

The small waiting room at the back of the house had been closed off to allow a post-mortem to take place. Dr Simpson had requested Raven carry out the examination himself, having received an urgent summons to attend to a lady at Tait's hotel. An examination table had been placed in the middle of the room and several lamps lit due to the dullness of the day. The bleak weather seemed appropriate to the task that Raven had been given, congruent with his mood, but as he rolled up his sleeves a shaft of winter sun broke through the cloud, illuminating innumerable motes of dust as they spun in effortless spirals above the shrouded corpse on the table.

Raven paused for a moment, considering how fleeting our existence could be, how suddenly death could arrive. He thought of Archie Banks, who had seized life with unrestrained vigour once presented with its cruel shortening. He could not help but reflect upon the comparative wisdom of certain choices he himself had made; though ultimately his doubts all came down to one choice in particular.

Holding her in his arms had brought back so many feelings he had thought lay buried. Though it hurt to see her upset, and the thought of her torment to come caused an ache in him, the warmth of her embrace made him aware of how cold he had been. It took a burst of her sunlight to remind him he had been living in darkness.

While Raven was abroad, he had told himself that what he felt was merely an infatuation: two people who had been thrown together in straitened circumstances, an unlikely dalliance from which they both would be wise to move on. But upon his return, when he was confronted with how Sarah *had* moved on, he realised how deep his feelings truly ran.

He had been a fool.

Raven had reasoned that if he wished to have a successful medical practice, it would be expected that he marry and have children, and that he take a respectable wife from a good family. If he were to marry a housemaid, it would be assumed that this was because he had got the poor girl pregnant and was doing the honourable thing by her. Even if no child was forthcoming, it would simply be assumed that she had lost the baby, and subsequently it would be expected of him to fade from prominence as a matter of decency. Marrying a housemaid would be the thing that defined him in the eyes of medical society, and he would not be permitted to rise far beyond it.

If he were being honest, had Sarah not been a housemaid, he still could not imagine her as the kind of obsequious and compliant wife of which society approved. That, after all, was what had drawn him to her in the first place. In fact, since meeting Sarah, he had found such obsequious and compliant women to be insipid and dull. The very reason he had struck up a rapport with Gabriela in Berlin was that she was a woman who would not meekly accept her place.

Raven had just begun to lay out the instruments he would require when Sarah walked in unannounced, as though his thoughts had summoned her.

'What are you doing here?' he asked, surprised. Surely she knew what he was about to do.

'I've come to assist,' she answered, as though it was the most natural thing in the world.

'I am about to perform a post-mortem. You cannot be here.'

'How am I to learn otherwise?'

Raven indicated the shape on the table, shrouded beneath a sheet.

'But this is Mrs Glassford,' he told her.

'This *was* Mrs Glassford,' she replied. She was calm and dry-eyed, in contrast to the day before.

Raven found this change in her demeanour disconcerting. He didn't want her here. Her presence would be a distraction, and if he was honest, he feared a sudden dissolution of this new-found composure as soon as the sheet was removed.

'Does Dr Simpson know you are here?' he asked, thinking it unlikely that the professor would have sanctioned this.

'Dr Simpson says I should grasp every opportunity to increase my knowledge.'

Raven noted that she had not answered his question and was thinking he was going to have to manhandle her out of the room, when she walked over to the desk in the corner and picked up a piece of paper.

'I will sit over here and make notes,' she said. 'Simply tell me what you find.'

Raven stood with his hands on his hips in front of the examination table, trying to think of a way to dissuade her.

'You knew this woman,' he implored. 'Only yesterday you wept for her.'

'But this is not her, merely her remains. The body is no more than a vessel. We are both of us fascinated by its workings, but our bodies are not who we are or who we were. As a woman, I know better than you what a mistake it is to define a person by their physical form.'

Raven hesitated for a moment, wondering how best to proceed without making a scene. Perhaps she will change her mind, he thought.

He pulled the sheet from the body. Sarah remained where she was, her face betraying no response.

The corpse lay completely exposed, leaving Raven to concede the wisdom of Sarah's observation. As with all dead bodies, it bore only a passing resemblance to the person who had so recently given up residence within. There was something strangely unhuman about it, reminding him of an anatomical model rendered in wax. That thought quickly dissipated as he became aware of the smell. There was a distinct whiff of putrefaction and he decided that for the duration of the examination he would breathe through his mouth.

The body was extremely bizarre in appearance: shrunken extremities and a swollen, globular abdomen rising up as if in triumph over its emaciated host. It looked as though the wrong pieces had been put together to make up the whole. It brought to mind a book Sarah had been telling him about, persisting as she did with her habit of reading in spare moments at the morning clinic. The tale concerned a scientist who created a man from constituent parts of different people. He did not recall the details, but it had not ended well.

Raven lost little time in contemplating the task before him – prevarication would not serve. He looked at Sarah once more, hoping to see doubt written on her features, but she appeared resolute, sitting by the desk, pen in hand. It seemed he had no choice but to proceed.

He made a visual inspection of the body, recounting the relevant details for Sarah to note down, and then proceeded to open the abdomen.

As his blade sliced into the late Mrs Glassford's skin, he thought back to his discussion with Simpson regarding how little they could do for her condition, and how John Lizars had successfully performed precisely the procedure that might have saved her – the removal of an ovary – but had been vilified for his actions, despite the recovery of his patient.

If you performed a procedure against conventional wisdom, and the outcome was bad, then your reputation would never recover because calamity had resulted from your being reckless and arrogant. And if you performed a procedure against conventional wisdom and the outcome was good, you would be condemned equally for the same recklessness and arrogance. You could expect censure, investigation and condemnation. They would say that it was more by luck than judgment that you succeeded: that it was an anomaly, and therefore did not change anything. Perhaps they needed to reassure themselves that they would have been right to do nothing in the same circumstances, and tell themselves that their inaction was something other than cowardice.

When a patient would surely die without intervention, how could it be wrong to try?

Raven knew the answer: it was the same one that forbade hastening a patient's end. It would be argued that the patient's condition was 'almost universally fatal', and a great weight rested upon the first of those words.

It was *almost* certain that the patient would die, but what if she didn't? Intervene to save her or to end her suffering, and you were taking it upon yourself to decide her fate. It was not yours to make such a decision, they would say, because how could you be sure?

The possibility that such a patient might rally and recover if you did nothing was the bedrock of the moral case against attempting anything outside of established practice. But how did something ever become established practice? Someone had to take the risk, not merely in terms of outcome but of reputation, and very few doctors were prepared to place that stake.

Raven peered into the cavity he had opened up, curiosity suppressing all other emotion, and stated precisely what his examination revealed.

'The abdomen contains a quantity of semi-purulent fluid, and on the right side a large cyst is attached to the ovary.'

He cut into the cyst. A thick fluid began to ooze out.

'The cyst contains a considerable amount of gelatinous matter.'

He could hear the scratch of Sarah's pen noting down what he said.

As he continued to poke about at the bottom of the cyst, he momentarily became aware of her standing at his shoulder, craning her neck to see. He could feel her breath on his neck. Raven closed his eyes for a moment, his concentration interrupted. He took a deep breath – through his mouth – and forced himself to focus on what he was doing.

'Look,' he said, pointing out what was encased in the heart of the tumour.

Sarah's composure finally broke and she gasped, but it was in fascination rather than shock.

'Hair, bone and teeth,' she stated.

'Indeed. One incisor, one bicuspid and one molar.'

'How bizarre . . . and revolting.' Her face puckered in distaste. 'Are you all right?'

'I'm fine,' she insisted, sounding annoyed by his solicitude. 'Stop asking me things and start telling me things. What *is* that?'

'Certain types of morbid growth may contain within them highly organised structures,' Raven responded, enjoying a solicited opportunity to demonstrate his knowledge. He must not become verbose, he warned himself, though in the event, Sarah's subsequent question would have prevented it anyway.

'Why are teeth and bone present in some types of tumour?'

'Pathological investigation has yet to provide an answer,' he replied meekly.

'You mean you don't know,' she said, staring closer.

'No one does,' he admitted. Raven felt a certain disappointment, as he always did whenever he was forced to confront how much of medicine remained shrouded in mystery. Each feat of progress or discovery was another candle in the dark, but sometimes all they let one see was the vastness of the void.

FORTY-ONE

he unmistakable odour of putrefaction still hung in the air, even though the corpse had been removed. Sarah observed Raven raising a hand to his nose, indicating that he suspected the smell might be coming from him. His subsequent expression confirmed that this was indeed the case. He moved to the sink and began running his hands together beneath the tap.

'I've washed my hands three times already,' he said. 'It's impossible to get rid of the smell.'

'"Common ablutions are not enough", remember?' Sarah said, adding chloride of lime to the water in the bowl.

The resultant chemical scent was a relief. Sarah had begun to feel queasy again. Curiosity and her keenness to be involved had made her determined to suppress any squeamishness she might feel, and for the most part the knowledge that it was Mrs Glassford's remains had not been a problem. She was able to look at the body in abstract, particularly once Raven opened it up and revealed the organs within. However, the lingering smell was prompting an instinctive revulsion, and she did not wish to appear weak by being sick.

It was not her only reason, either. Raven had seen her vomiting a few days ago. He had been sharp enough to deduce Archie's condition, so perhaps it was folly to think that, as an obstetrician, he was not already suspecting hers too.

She did not like to think about it, and yet it was always there, waiting, inexorable, like Archie's illness. She knew this was one of the reasons she was so motivated to pursue her investigations. She needed some kind of distraction, a purpose to consume her in the here and now, because in the future there lay only the daunting certainty of Archie's death and the daunting uncertainty of the new life growing inside her.

Archie had said her future would be assured, and she did not doubt his sincerity, but it was the nature of that future that worried her. Assured also meant inescapable. Was a widow and a mother now all she would ever amount to? A life defined and dominated by raising a child was better than one defined and dominated by domestic service, but she had allowed herself to hope for so much more. For all Archie's talk of wishing her to educate herself and to put that education to practical use, she did not envisage how that could be compatible with the demands of raising a child on her own.

She thought of Mrs Glassford, of the strange and disturbing entity that had consumed her, and could not help but see it as a twisted, grotesque parody of her own condition. She carried inside her a creature that would swell her belly and then devour her, leaching from her the many lives she had dreamed for herself.

The image shook something loose from her head that jolted her back into the present, a terrible possibility forming in her mind.

'The leeches!' she said.

'What leeches?' Raven asked, understandably confused by her random exclamation.

'The ones Dr Fowler was bemoaning the loss of. You told me they had fallen off George Porteous and died.'

'What about them?'

'Isn't it strange that they all died at the same time? Have you ever heard of such a thing?'

Raven's face took on a sudden glow of excitement.

'Sarah, I believe you have made a crucial observation. It could be that this new malady is a disease of the blood. Perhaps that is in fact how it is carried. As you just said: common ablutions are not enough. If Mary Dempster has been less than scrupulous in washing her hands, tainted blood adhering to them might be the conduit by which the illness is being transferred from one patient to another.'

The excitement in his expression wilted as he failed to see it mirrored in her own. He had leapt, with great energy and enthusiasm, to a predictable but entirely wrong conclusion.

'Don't you follow?' he asked, sounding frustrated. 'As Simpson found regarding puerperal fever— '

'Will, permit me to ask you something,' Sarah said, cutting him off. 'How many diseases have you observed in gravely ill patients to whom leeches were applied?'

His nose wrinkled in irritation. 'Dozens. What of it?'

'And what happened to those leeches?'

'Nothing. They became engorged and fell off.'

'After feasting on the blood of patients suffering every variety of disease, the leeches were unaffected. And yet the leeches attached to George Porteous all died. What does that tell you?'

His enthusiasm was rekindling, as though she had merely needed to grasp a principle in order to properly understand.

'That this is what makes it such a dangerous new manner of disease. If it can spread so quickly to the leeches, then perhaps by investigating that, I might ascertain how it spreads to other people.'

Sarah could not believe she was having to spell it out. Raven was an otherwise rational and intelligent man. However, she understood what was impeding his thinking.

'Do you recall what Martha Dempster said about what happens

once an idea gets lodged in one's head? You are so intent upon finding this new disease that you are missing what is obvious. There is a far simpler means by which Mary Dempster could be directly responsible for her patients becoming ever sicker and then dying. The leeches died because George Porteous had something in his blood that proved poisonous.'

'Are you suggesting that the nurse administered something in error?'

The possibility of such a simple but deadly mistake had crossed Sarah's mind, and she would have welcomed this less disturbing explanation. However, the numbers were against it.

'One fatal misadministration would be unfortunate. Three suggests something less accidental.'

Raven took a moment to consider this, but that proved long enough to reject it.

'I could say that your judgment is equally affected by a tenacious notion. Because of that horrible business last year, you are too easily inclined to see the possibility of poison.'

Sarah had to concede that if it was true of Raven, it could equally be true of her. Nonetheless, her theory chimed with the unease that had been in her mind since they visited that cottage at Lochend.

'It struck me there was something awkward and oddly wary about Martha Dempster's manner when we spoke to her, and it has taken me until now to deduce what that was. The woman was afraid of her sister.'

'I got no such sense, and even if I had, it would be quite the leap to extrapolate that she must be a poisoner.'

'Isn't it suspicious that she cannot be found?'

'We have barely looked. But even were we to entertain your notion for a moment, what poison would have produced such symptoms, leaving no sign of its administration?'

'There must be a few possibilities.'

Raven fixed her with an unblinking look, like an impatient

schoolmaster waiting for a pupil to admit she doesn't have the answer.

'Prussic acid?' she suggested.

'When it kills, it kills quickly and is not something easily procured,' Raven responded dismissively.

Sarah ignored his tone. She was not yet ready to abandon her thesis and attempted to work through the problem logically.

'Well, if procurement is an issue, the most commonly available household poison is arsenic.'

'But arsenic produces symptoms of abdominal pain and vomiting, which were not observed in these cases.'

Sarah cursed inwardly. She ought to have remembered this. Nonetheless, there were still other possibilities.

'Laudanum?'

'The pupils would have been small. Pinpoint. They were normal in size.'

'What about chloroform?' she suggested, though she knew she was getting desperate. 'Could it produce stupor or delirium that lasts for days?'

'No. Its danger is that it kills quickly. There have been fatal accidents due to its abuse: a druggist's assistant in Aberdeen developed a habit of sniffing it from a towel at his place of work and was found dead face-down on the counter; and at Duke Street Hospital in Glasgow a doctor was found dead after inhaling it. But in both cases, it was obvious what had occurred.'

'What if the victims were given it to drink? I know that Mrs Lyndsay recovered from drinking Dr Simpson's chloroform champagne, but what if she had taken more? It's relatively easy to get hold of,' she added, anticipating Raven's previous objection.

'Unless you're Dr Simpson,' he muttered cryptically.

'What?'

'Never mind. Anyway, you would be able to smell it. Furthermore, it would be highly irritant to the mouth and throat unless very diluted. I observed no such marks on George Porteous, and if there were any on Mrs Johnstone, you can be damned sure Professor Miller and James Matthews Duncan would have seized upon it.'

Sarah frowned by way of admitting she was exhausted of suggestions, but Raven was not exhausted of arguments as to why she was wrong.

'Even if the symptoms matched a known poison, what reason would a nurse have to murder her own patients? A private nurse, no less. She would be killing her employers and putting herself out of work. This is not like some scheming wife poisoning her rich husband so that she might live off the inheritance.'

Sarah could offer no response. The image rather uncomfortably made her think of Archie and his assurances that she would be provided for once he was gone. A hundred times a day she would enjoy the relief of forgetting, her mind focused upon something else, and then it would be dragged back. Remembering hurt every time.

'I must be on my way,' Raven announced, rolling down his sleeves and putting on his coat. He seemed content that the conversation was at an end, his case made irrefutably.

She would have to concede that she had no further arguments with which to present him. She remained suspicious of Mary Dempster and convinced that her sister Martha had not been entirely truthful with them. However, a sense or a feeling did not carry the weight of evidence, and nor could it make up for a lack of answers to the questions Raven had posed. Nonetheless, her instinct was to find the evidence rather than dismiss her theory.

Men often talked about a woman's intuition. Ostensibly it sounded complimentary and yet its intention was usually patronising and dismissive: a term for irrational flights of fancy that these silly creatures would occasionally dream up from nowhere. Sarah understood the true nature of what they were describing. It was not irrational, and nor was it a mystical sixth sense resultant of a uniquely feminine sensitivity. It was a simple, practical consequence of observation. When you put them in a room, women paid attention to the subtle signs people were sending, while the men concerned themselves only with the impression they were making.

Raven thought he was looking for a new disease. Sarah thought that something more sinister was afoot.

If Mary Dempster had made her own sister afraid, she had made other people afraid before her. Her deeds would have left a trail, and Sarah knew where she might pick it up.

FORTY-TWO

here was frost beneath Raven's feet as he walked along Princes Street, a glistening unwelcome harbinger of the harsh months ahead. Raven was prompted to think back to the unprecedented heat he had endured during his summer in Berlin, but was grateful not to be there now. He had heard stories about the winter in that city and had no desire to witness it first-hand.

A few yards ahead he saw a smartly dressed gentleman emerge from one of the hotels, and recognised him as Dr Alison, Professor of Medicine at the university, and, more pertinently for Raven's purposes, the author of an influential pamphlet on the spread of infectious disease.

Fortune was smiling upon Raven, and not before time. It was a chance encounter, but one which Raven decided to put to good use. He approached the man and tipped his hat.

'Professor Alison, I am Dr Raven, assistant to Dr Simpson.'

It came as a relief to see Professor Alison's eyes widen in positive affirmation of the name. Given the bad blood emanating from everything that Simpson had become caught up in, it was easy to forget how many of his peers in the city held him in the highest regard. And to Raven's further delight, it seemed Simpson's was not the only name familiar to him.

'Yes, of course. Will, isn't it? I recall we dined together at Queen Street when you were studying under James as his apprentice.'

'How kind of you to remember. And what a stroke of luck that I have run into you today. If you have the time, perhaps you would be good enough to bestow upon me the benefit of your wisdom? I have recently had to contend with several cases of what I believe might be a new form of transmissible infection.'

Professor Alison looked intrigued.

'I have an idle moment right now. Perhaps we might retire somewhere out of the cold and avail ourselves of tea, or something stronger, while we discuss it?'

Raven's heart surged. Then Professor Alison's nose suddenly wrinkled, an unpleasant odour in his nostrils. Raven caught it too and turned to see that a cart had pulled to a halt on the road alongside them. It was covered in muck, having been used to transport God knew what, but the most appalling aspect was that the Skeleton sat at the reins, and, inevitably, Gargantua was with him.

Raven felt a rage kindle within him as the giant leapt from the vehicle. On this occasion, it was not the mere annoyance of being summoned once again, but of being thus confronted and his most unsavoury associations laid bare before no less a figure than the Professor of Medicine.

Alison looked Gargantua up and down as he crossed the pavement towards them with his lolloping gait, the professor's disdain at being imminently importuned not quite disguising his concurrent professional fascination. At that moment, Raven felt his own outrage ameliorated by an unaccustomed feeling of sympathy for Gargantua. The man had probably been subject to cruel and invasive regard most of his days, but Raven knew that he particularly resented the scrutiny and assessment of medical men. He feared what Gargantua might say as a result. The giant was, however, remarkably polite.

'Pardon the intrusion, sirs, but my employer, Mr Flint, urgently requests the attendance of Dr Raven here.'

Professor Alison's eyes narrowed at the mention of Flint's name.

'Flint?' he asked with incredulous distaste. 'He is the money-lender, is he not? Dr Raven, surely you are not in debt to such a man?'

Raven did not know quite how to respond. The words 'after a fashion' floated in his mind unspoken, but there seemed no way to describe any arrangement he might have with Flint that would reflect anything other than badly upon him. This would surely tarnish his nascent reputation with not only Professor Alison, but anyone who might learn of this through him, a constituency comprising everyone who was anyone in Edinburgh medicine.

'Dr Raven is sought on a medical matter,' Gargantua said. 'He was good enough to deliver Mrs Flint of her first child and has no qualms about who he is prepared to treat.'

Raven felt an unexpected gratitude towards Gargantua. Though it was his and the Skeleton's presence that had precipitated this disaster, his careful words were nonetheless a mercy he had not been obliged to extend. He could have played it other. He wondered what lay behind this thawing of the animosity the giant held towards him. Prior to this he would have believed all the salt in the world incapable of melting that ice.

'Most admirable of you, doctor,' Alison said, politely but uncomfortably. 'I will let you away.'

With that the professor swept onwards, visibly relieved to extract himself from their encounter, while Raven was left to get on with whatever Flint wanted of him.

Raven climbed delicately onto the back of the cart and sat himself on the least filthy part he could find. He pulled his collar up and his hat down and counted his blessings such as they were, a voice inside quelling his haughtier instincts. Was he so far above these people? He was, after all, literally a cut-throat, and by now quite possibly a wanted man.

He wondered again at the identity of the man he slew, the

unexpected efforts of the police, and the subsequent disappearance of Gabriela, but these were futile musings upon matters far away.

The cart trundled along, Raven oblivious to the route taken until it pulled up at the rear of a building in Fountainbridge. He knew he had been here before but did not recognise it, as he had been ushered in under rain-lashed darkness. Daylight did not flatter the place. It was a five-storey tenement as teeming and overcrowded as any in the city. Raven had no notion who actually owned it, but he knew who it belonged to in every practical sense.

He was all but marched inside and up the stairs to a small third-floor apartment, two storeys above the larger accommodations he had visited before. The man who occupied those was waiting for him in the hallway.

'I have an injured man in urgent want of treatment,' Flint said.

'I am not the only doctor in this city,' Raven replied. 'There are many better, and I would wager many nearer, whose attendance would not have occasioned retrieval from Princes Street.'

'I don't doubt it. But let's just say that I trust you in a way that I would not trust others, Mr Raven.'

'Dr Raven,' he corrected, not with much conviction. He wasn't sure Flint heard, or whether he would care.

He was shown into a cramped, gloomy and foul-smelling room, his nose immediately recognising the odours of blood and faecal matter. Upon the bed was something else he recognised with equal distaste.

The Weasel.

'Alec here is in a bad way,' Flint said. 'He is in dire need of a surgeon.'

It was odd to hear his real name. Raven had never been curious as to what it was, and now that he knew, he struggled to associate it with the man lying before him. He was squirming, sweat-lashed and panting in his pain.

'He's been shot,' Gargantua added.

'Where?'

Flint and Gargantua looked back and forth between each other. Clearly there was something they did not wish to disclose.

'What does the location matter?' Flint asked. 'Just do something.'

'I meant, where upon his person?'

Gargantua pulled back the covers, causing the smell to instantly worsen. An improvised dressing, none too clean, had been applied across the Weasel's abdomen and the material was heavily bloodstained, but this was not Raven's primary concern. The smell alone told Raven the intestines had been breached.

Flint read his expression and did not like what he saw.

'I have faith in you. Do not prove it ill-judged.'

He winced. These were not words of encouragement so much as an implied threat of retribution should he fail.

Raven knew immediately this would be a far different prospect to digging a bullet from a shallow wound in Henry's leg, but one didn't say that to a man like Flint. He thought about protesting his relative lack of experience in the management of gunshot wounds but quickly changed his mind. It would be better to display a supreme confidence in his own abilities in order to forestall any suggestion of incompetence should the worst happen. To that end, he decided it best to inspect the wound, even if only to confirm his suspicions.

Raven took in the room, with its one tiny window giving onto the back court.

'Can we move him to where there is better light?'

Flint muttered something to Gargantua and withdrew. He returned momentarily with another of his men, the squat individual Raven thought of as Toad. Between them he and Gargantua lifted the bed with the Weasel on it, while Flint led them across the close to an apartment on the other side. A mother was escorting her children out of the way, clearly told to vacate so that Flint could commandeer her home. Her table was moved, and the bed placed down in its stead before a wide, south-facing window.

The Weasel whimpered as Raven approached, recognising him now that there was enough light.

Words of reassurance came to Raven's mind, but they would not pass his throat.

'Help me move him,' Raven said, addressing the giant. When the man seemed reluctant to assist, he explained: 'I need to look for a second wound, to ascertain whether the bullet has passed through.'

Raven knew it was academic whether the bullet remained inside the Weasel's abdomen or not, but he felt obliged to provide a convincing performance. It was important to give the impression that he knew what he was about. His own life might very well depend on it.

Gargantua, with an unexpected gentleness, turned the whimpering man onto his side. The image transported Raven back to that alley off the Canongate. There, it had been he who was helpless, gripped in those massive hands while the Weasel looked on, ready to wield a blade. It ought to have felt like a fitting reversal, but as the movement caused the man to cry out Raven felt guilty about inflicting this unnecessary pain.

Suddenly there was no history between them: he was only a doctor dealing with an injured patient.

'The ball has not passed through,' he said, indicating that Gargantua should release his hold on the patient.

'Can you get it out?' Flint asked.

Raven sighed. He knew it would make no difference if he did. 'Let me have a look.'

Raven lifted the sodden dressing from the front of the abdomen. There was a small oval wound, the edges torn and blackened, a dark and malodorous fluid oozing out of it over his fingers. To his dismay he was jolted back to a different alley: the one in Berlin. That had been another moment in which he had instantly shed the person he was and become something else, but that night in Prussia the transformation had been driven by something less noble and more primal.

The image passed and he pulled himself back to the here and now.

He replaced the dressing and turned to face Flint and Gargantua.

'This man was shot last night. One bullet. From a pistol. At close range.'

'How can you know that from looking at a hole in his belly?' Flint asked.

'There are lacerations and bruising around the entrance wound. The edges are blackened as if they had been burnt. This arises from the heat and flame of the gunpowder at the moment of explosion.'

Flint and Gargantua seemed intent upon what he was saying, so he continued.

'A bullet fired from a moderate distance produces a well-defined round or oval wound without blackening or burning. The feculent matters escaping from the wound indicate that the bowel has been perforated. There are signs of inflammation suggesting some time has elapsed since the injury occurred.'

Raven was relieved that he could recall these details from the Medical Jurisprudence lectures he had attended as a student. Flint looked impressed but that was unlikely to last.

'What can be done?'

'Given the fluid leaking from the wound, and the smell . . . there is no doubt that the intestine has been damaged.' Raven lowered his voice. 'Whenever the contents of the stomach or any of the bowels are effused over the surface of the peritoneum, death is the inevitable result.'

Flint and Gargantua looked at him in an uncomprehending silence. Raven sighed. He thought he had been perfectly clear.

'There is no point in guddling about in this man's guts. Surgeons only open the abdomen as a last resort, for the patient seldom survives it. In midwifery it is sometimes done to save the baby when there is no hope for the mother. Because once we have opened the belly, the mother will surely die.'

'Why?' Flint asked. There was no anger in his voice, only a bleak curiosity.

'It would seem nature does not tolerate the exposure of organs it has seen fit to keep covered. Infection is the inevitable result. Much like gangrene in a leg, except in this case amputation of the infected part is not an option. However, the situation is immeasurably worse if the bowel itself has been injured. Hence there is no point in attempting to retrieve the bullet. The damage cannot be repaired. There is nothing that I or any surgeon, including Syme himself, can do in a case such as this.'

Flint thought about this for a moment. He looked towards Alec and nodded, accepting what he was being told.

'I must leave now,' Raven said. 'There is nothing more I can do here, and I am needed at the Maternity Hospital.'

Flint put a hand on his arm.

'There *is* something you can do,' he said.

Raven was about to protest when Flint leaned in closer. He could smell stale alcohol and onions on the man's breath.

'Give him something for the pain. Ease his passing.'

Having issued his command, the money-lender left the room, leaving Raven with the dying man and the giant, whose presence seemed intended as Flint's guarantor that Raven would do as he was bid.

He dosed the Weasel liberally with laudanum and then packed up his things, hoping to leave and never darken the door of this place again.

Gargantua blocked his path.

'You will return,' he said.

Raven nodded, but it was not good enough. Two huge hands gripped his lapels.

'Give me your word that you will return.'

'You have it,' Raven replied.

FORTY-THREE

arah stopped outside a house on Castle Street and checked the address on the letter she carried. It was the correct number but seemed rather too grand an establishment to house Dr Simpson's secretary and his wife. It was considerably larger than the few rooms she shared with Archie on Albany Street.

The door was answered by Mrs Quinton herself, a neat woman, well dressed if not expensively so. Sarah was shown into a bright room at the front of the house, illuminated by large windows that faced onto the street. There was a large black marble fireplace with enamel panels, and several sofas and armchairs upholstered in expensive-looking fabrics. When invited to sit, Sarah was unsure where to put herself. Framed portraits adorned the walls and suspended over it all was a huge crystal gasolier.

'What a beautiful room,' Sarah said as she handed over the letter along with a parcel of baby clothes Mrs Simpson had asked her to deliver.

'Yes. It's a wonderful house. So well located,' Mrs Quinton replied. 'Sir Walter Scott lived at number 39.'

'An auspicious address, in that case,' Sarah said.

'Quite so,' Mrs Quinton replied, smiling broadly. 'The house is rather too large for just the three of us,' she continued. 'Well, four, if you count the nursemaid.' Her tone implied that she did not. 'We took over the lease from a good friend of ours. The furniture belongs to her too. It was left for our use,' she added, indicating the contents of the room with a wide sweep of her hand. 'A woman of great taste.'

'You are very fortunate to have such a friend.'

'Yes. It is so important in this world to make the right kind of connections, to move in the right circles.'

Sarah wondered how they could afford it. An inheritance or some form of annuity perhaps. She noticed that Mrs Quinton had placed the parcel on a side table but wasted no time in opening the accompanying letter. 'I was beginning to doubt whether this would ever arrive,' she said petulantly, scanning the contents. She folded the letter again and placed it on top of the discarded parcel before sitting down beside Sarah and straightening her skirts.

'Between you and me, there is a deplorable lack of organisation in that place.'

'What place?'

'Well, Queen Street, of course. Mr Quinton says that the household accounts are in a dreadful state. They are very fortunate to have found him as he will surely arrange things as they should be. Although I feel he is being sorely ill-used.'

'In what way?'

'He is at Queen Street from early morning until late. Sometimes it is after midnight by the time he returns to us. I do not believe that his salary is sufficient recompense for such excessive demands being made upon his time.'

Sarah felt words of defence rising to her lips, but before she could speak the door opened and a young woman entered carrying a red-cheeked infant.

'Is it that time already, Nancy?' Mrs Quinton said as the child was handed to her. 'I insist on spending at least an hour with young Rochester before lunch.'

Young Rochester did not seem particularly enamoured with

this arrangement and began to wail when relinquished by his nurse.

'Now now, young man. That is no way to behave,' Mrs Quinton said. She turned to Sarah. 'Would you care to hold him?'

Sarah stood, took the proffered child and began to rock him gently, his crying quickly subsiding. Mrs Quinton waved her arm to dismiss the nursemaid, who retreated rapidly, leaving the two women alone again.

'You might be wondering at his name,' Mrs Quinton said. 'Young Rochester here is of noble lineage. I know who his parents are, but of course that information must remain in our keeping. It would be quite the scandal if it were ever to be divulged. Fortunately, I am the soul of discretion,' she said, placing a hand over her heart in emphasis. 'I felt it was my Christian duty to offer the poor child a home, my husband and I having no children of our own.'

Sarah wondered if such charity would be forthcoming had the child been a street urchin rather than the progeny of the upper orders, but then chastised herself. Agreeing to take responsibility for someone else's child was no small matter. She looked at the baby in her arms and wondered what her own child would be like; wondered, not for the first time, if she was equipped to be a mother.

As though sensing her ambivalence, Rochester screwed up his face, turned a rather disturbing shade of puce, and began to cry again. His crying this time was loud and insistent, not easily soothed. Mrs Quinton reached for a bell on the side table and summoned the nursemaid to take him away. The poor girl looked harassed and Sarah wondered if her pay was sufficient recompense for the demands placed upon her.

Mrs Quinton indicated that Sarah should sit again and then began to enquire about her own situation. Sarah was becoming used to this. She was a conundrum, representing a deviation from the norm that seemed to cause a degree of disquiet in the bosoms of those wedded to the notion of a rigorously imposed social hierarchy. In some this disquiet was expressed as curiosity, exposing her to probing questions that she was sure her interlocutors would find inappropriate should they be similarly interrogated. In others, her effrontery at presenting herself as above stairs when her origins were unequivocally below provoked outright hostility, so she put up with gentle questioning as best she could.

'So, you were a housemaid?'

'Yes.'

'But no longer?'

'No. I work as an assistant to Dr Simpson.'

'I don't understand. I would have assumed that the doctor's assistant would also be a medical man.'

'He has one of those as well.'

'So, what do you do?'

Her tone was becoming imperious, as though she was beginning to doubt the veracity of Sarah's claims.

'I help to organise the patients in the waiting room— '

'If his waiting room is anything like his account books, I imagine it is in grave need of organisation. But you are married, are you not?'

'Yes.' And here it was, the thorniest part of the issue.

'And what does your husband say about you continuing to work? Mr Quinton would never permit such a thing. It would reflect very badly on him. Very badly indeed. What would people think? I will tell you what they would think, and more importantly what they would say. They would say that he had utterly failed in his duty to provide for his family.'

She stopped suddenly, her diatribe interrupted. She put a hand to her mouth, a look of concern upon her face. 'Is he terribly poor, your husband?'

Sarah was sorely tempted to make something up, something salacious about gambling debts or misappropriated funds that she felt would gratify this woman more than the truth. But she thought better of it.

'My husband is a doctor and understands the value of what I do,' she stated, her even tone belying the irritation she was feeling.

'A doctor? Really? Well, that is most irregular.'

'Yes, I suppose that it is.'

Mrs Quinton changed topic at this point, preferring to discuss the difficulties of child-rearing, how demanding it all was. As the conversation continued – Mrs Quinton seeming in no hurry to be elsewhere – Sarah wondered if the woman lacked acquaintances in Edinburgh. Perhaps she had yet to make many friends. Sarah could empathise if this was the case. She herself belonged precisely nowhere, which made establishing and maintaining friendships difficult, if not impossible. Who could she confide in? Who could she share her innermost thoughts with? Only Archie. And, of course, Will Raven. In fact, she was confiding in Will more now as Archie was becoming increasingly unwell. There was a connection growing between them again. Given the circumstances, she was unsure whether this was a good thing.

Sarah became aware that she was being less than attentive, having lost the thread of the conversation. Mrs Quinton was expounding upon the subject of wet nurses, nursery nurses and the expense associated with finding the right help. Sarah's distraction had gone unnoticed as she was not expected to respond, merely to listen. She thought that she should perhaps feel sorry for this woman but could not bring herself to do so. There were so many women who managed so much more, with so much less. She decided she could not sit and listen to this any longer and wondered at her lack of patience. A lack of sleep, perhaps.

'I'm afraid that I must be going,' she said, standing up. 'Duty calls.'

Mrs Quinton looked a little put out that their conversation

had been so suddenly terminated, but Sarah was adamant that she could not stay.

Mrs Quinton walked her to the front door. She paused before opening it, a thin smile on her face.

'Please thank Mrs Simpson for the letter and for the package,' she said. Her smile faded. 'Also tell her I expect the next payment to arrive on time.'

FORTY-FOUR

t was dark when Raven was once again shown into the room where Alec lay. He remained by the window, but no light shone through it. The room was lit now only by candles and a single lamp.

A vast shape moved in the gloom, and once he got over his shock he saw that the giant was keeping vigil, seated by the wall. It seemed an odd sight, and it was only in that moment that Raven saw that Gargantua and the Weasel were friends. He had not imagined that there was anything to connect them beyond their common circumstances, comrades in criminality.

Alec was writhing, and doubtless would be writhing all the more had he the strength to do so. He was making a pitiable and unsettling keening sound, a combination of moaning and weeping. The man was in agony.

Now that he knew his given name, what others called him – what his mother must have called him – it changed how Raven perceived him. He thought of the revenges he had fantasised for this man, the strength of his desire to see him suffer. Now he was suffering beyond Raven's imaginings and the sight shamed him for ever wishing it.

There was no sign of the family who lived here, still banished at the money-lender's command. No sign either of the man himself.

'Where is Flint?'

Even in the little light there was, Raven could see that Gargantua was uncomfortable at the question. He guessed it was for the same reason they did not wish to disclose where the shooting took place.

'He's away on some business that's none of yours.'

Raven approached the bed. Alec was fevered, covered in a clammy sweat, his face contorted in the throes of his suffering. His hands were cold, his pulse small and frequent.

'Take away . . . the pain,' he implored.

'Didn't keep his medicine down for long,' Gargantua grumbled from the corner, evidently unimpressed by Raven's ministrations thus far. 'You must give him something else, something stronger.'

Their eyes met. They both understood what Gargantua was asking.

Raven opened his bag and looked through the contents. The strongest thing he had was chloroform: destroyer of pain, gateway to oblivion. Should he use it? It would relieve the man's suffering, no doubt about that, but wouldn't it also hasten his demise? It was forbidden to deliberately kill a patient. The sacred Hippocratic injunction was *primum non nocere*. First, do no harm.

He thought once more of that alley in Berlin. He did not want the burden of knowing another man had died by his hand, but in this case not to act would be to hide behind the pretext of morality. A sin of omission was still a sin.

He had long desired to avenge himself upon this creature, to end the man's life in retribution for the violence he himself had suffered. But this would not be vengeance. Vengeance would only be served by allowing his suffering to continue, and Raven did not wish that. He only had to think of the reason he bore his grudge, reflected upon earlier that very day. When a man was pinned and defenceless, defeated and posing no threat, to inflict pain and damage upon him was the act of a despicable coward. In similar circumstances, failure to relieve a man's suffering felt equally craven.

Gargantua stepped closer, his heavy tread creaking the boards, bending the very floor.

'What are you waiting for,' he demanded, 'a miracle?'

Raven removed the amber-coloured bottle from his bag and examined the contents. There would be enough.

'What is that?' the giant asked.

'Chloroform. Considered by some to be miraculous.'

He poured a few drops onto a handkerchief and held it above the dying man's face.

'Sleep now, Alec,' he said.

FORTY-FIVE

can speak now of a time beyond childhood, in which
my memories do not feel at one remove. My mind
puts up no barriers between the woman I am now
and its recollections of the mere girl I was before,
and for the most part I enjoy remembering. I did not enjoy all
that was happening to me, but there is pleasure in revisiting the
stations on a journey towards my becoming someone greater,
someone stronger.

At each station I became less afraid.

I started work at the Royal Infirmary in Edinburgh when I
was sixteen years of age. That was not merely when I became a
nurse, but when I became defined by something other than those
who had control of me, the people I belonged to.

Mrs Dempster was reluctant to spare me, but Mr Dempster
proved my advocate and over-ruled her wishes. I have not spoken
much of him, but I will say now that he was always fair towards
me. He never for a moment regarded me as a daughter, but he
did regard my upkeep as his responsibility. Consequently, he saw
that were I to find employment of my own, in time I would be
able to leave, and his obligation would be discharged.

Mrs Dempster deferred to his wishes, of course. His might
have been the word of God, so obsequious was she in executing

his authority over his household. I recognised it from how many of the women at the Institute had deferred to the Reverend Gillies: if he was God's instrument on Earth, then they would be *his* instruments, and by extension a functioning part of His divine order.

Yet Mrs Dempster never demonstrated affection towards him, or even gave the impression she was fond of him as a person. I believe she merely liked the idea of him, all he represented and how that reflected upon her. He was a living totem of what she regarded as her achievements, the sum of which was being his wife.

I heard her talk to her friends about his position at the bank, exaggerating his importance, embellishing his achievements. I was sure everything they said of their own husbands carried the same weight of gilding upon the truth. It was all part of the dance, this institution of the family: revered and hallowed by all, yet clearly constructed upon lies and artifice and pretence.

The first days at the hospital were a punishing purgatory of drudge work, but many of the tasks were not so different to my duties at home: serving meals, emptying chamber pots, laundering bedsheets, washing floors, dusting furniture, stoking the fires and ensuring the lamps were filled. The head nurse, Miss Peat, was an austere and mirthless presence, constantly critical and enforcing her will with the threat of dismissal. I had been well prepared for the regimen of institutions through my years at the Belmont, and for working under harsh authority wherever I went. It was under her stern eye that I was then taught how to dress wounds, bathe patients and treat bedsores.

I was paid a pittance, and there was even less in my pocket after Mrs Dempster deducted a portion too.

'You will contribute to the household while you remain under my roof,' she insisted. 'If you no longer have the time to carry out your previous household duties, then you must pay your way.'

It perhaps goes without saying that Martha was not required

to contribute, unless one allows the endeavour of preparing herself for life as a wife and mother. Mrs Dempster was tirelessly on the lookout for a suitable match, talking about it as though the fate of the nation depended upon her success.

Her view of the world seemed so small, while mine was becoming ever wider. I shared responsibility for dozens of patients and my knowledge was rapidly expanding. I learned how to make and apply poultices, how to administer enemas and prescribed medications.

The medicines themselves fascinated me, the effects these liquids, pills and potions produced. Through careful listening I absorbed as much information as I could and purloined several medical textbooks from inattentive students, which I studied in their entirety until I fancied myself as wise as those who taught me.

'The difference between a medicine and a poison is the dosage,' we were warned, by way of impressing upon us the responsibility we had in dispensing powerful compounds such as mercury, quinine and opium.

I took pride in the care of my patients, and seeing a sick person restored to health partly through my ministrations gave me a sense of purpose and achievement like nothing I had known before.

The patients' appreciation meant a lot to me too. They valued my cheerful manner, as did the other nurses, and as a result I earned the nickname 'Merry Mary'. I got on well with most of my colleagues, though there were those who took a dislike to me for no clear reason, such as Gertie Cupar. Gertie was a haughty and self-possessed young woman who had started work at the hospital around the same time as I had, but who seemed to regard herself as my superior. I could not help but reciprocate her antipathy.

Nor did I like all my patients. Some of them just seemed so hopeless, so pathetic, particularly those advanced in years.

Nothing seemed to make any difference to them, because the main thing ailing them was simply the decrepitude of old age, for which there was no treatment. It bothered me that they were taking up my time.

When I reminisce about those days I prefer to dwell upon the pleasant patients, the ones who demonstrated an appropriate degree of gratitude. I remember Arthur, a railway labourer admitted with painful legs and bleeding gums on account of the poor provisions supplied to the railway construction camps. I looked after him for some weeks, and from early in his stay I noticed how his face seemed to light up whenever I appeared on the ward. He always said his pleases and thank-yous, but more importantly, he spoke to me deferentially, as though I was a person of substance, someone who was entitled to his regard.

I was particularly diligent in my care of him and took pride in watching him recover. I recall my sadness at the prospect of losing him when the doctor pronounced him cured. I did not want Arthur to leave.

I altered the ward journal, ascribing symptoms to him that he did not have, and consequently delayed his dismissal. I was pleased with the outcome itself, but more so that I had been able to effect it so simply.

I subsequently did the same with other patients whom I found it pleasant to look after, especially when there remained the danger that the bed would otherwise be filled by some faltering ingrate who was a better fit for the cemetery.

Some of the physicians were more diligent than others, relying upon the evidence of their own observations rather than merely acting upon what was written in the journals. One such was Dr Hewitt, an ambitious and busy-minded young man who queried the accuracy of what had been recorded, noting that it bore little resemblance to what he could plainly observe. He demanded to know who had been responsible for these erroneous reports.

I lied and told him the patient had been under the charge of another nurse. It first occurred to me to blame the self-regarding Gertie, but I had learned well from Joyce back at the Institute. I had to choose my scapegoat with care. The doctor would never have believed it of Gertie, for she was fastidious in her habits and more importantly I knew she would have been vociferous in denying her involvement. Instead I blamed Nelly Campbell. I liked Nelly well enough and she me, but she was known to be clumsy, and furthermore was sufficiently timid. She meekly disputed that the patient in question was ever under her care, but was not listened to, and was summarily dismissed before the day was out.

Even so, this incident served as a warning. When next I wished to keep a patient longer, I knew I could not rely solely on presenting falsified documentation of troubling symptoms. I would have to induce them.

I administered doses of medicines that made my preferred patients demonstrably sick when they were due for examination. It was easy enough to do. It proved evidence enough to satisfy even the like of Dr Hewitt.

More so than when I merely altered the ward journal, I marvelled at the effects of my actions. It appeared I had the ability to bend matters to my will simply by the administration of medicine. It created in me an ever-deeper curiosity, an insatiable thirst for greater knowledge.

I watched the doctors carefully. It seemed to please them that I was showing such a keen interest by asking them about dosages and the effects of the various pills and potions that they prescribed.

There was a limit to how much first-hand experience I was permitted, however, which was why I liked being on the ward at night. With the doctors largely absent and nurses sparsely spread about the hospital, I was free to experiment. I dosed patients with morphine in ever-increasing amounts and paid close attention to the results. I watched as their breathing slowed and their pupils shrunk in size.

The next station upon my journey was marked by a dock-labourer from Leith by the name of John Robertson. He sustained a burn to his upper chest on account of sleeping too close to the fire while under the influence of ardent spirits. The burn extended to the front of his neck and caused him to experience a restriction in his breathing, for which he was prescribed warm-water dressings and morphine three times a day. I gave it more frequently than that, watching as this brute of a man became drowsy and incapable.

In the midst of my experiment I was called away to assist another patient who had had a seizure, and when I returned, I found that Mr Robertson's breathing had stopped altogether, and he was quite dead.

I did not mean to kill him. But nor did I have any regrets about having done so. Rather, I felt powerful that I had wrought this. A man so mighty, felled by my small hand.

That sense of power only increased the next day when his newly widowed wife came to claim his remains. I watched her weep and wail, this gushing, uncontainable outpouring of grief. A drastic change had been wrought upon not one but two people: one life ended, the other altered for ever, and all of it precipitated by actions that were unknown and unsuspected.

I felt like I wanted to hold Mrs Robertson, as I had been held when I was taken into the bed alongside my mother in her sorrow at losing each of her sons. On those nights, though I was sad to see my mother in such torment, part of me was grateful for what had happened, because it had given rise to this tenderness. Such affection was otherwise not permitted by my father. He did not like it when she coddled us.

As I had experienced before, something in Mrs Robertson's grief gratified me.

FORTY-SIX

aven was woken by a knock on the door, coming to with a start as he heard his name spoken by a female voice. It was one of the new maids. He bid her come in, by way of letting her know he was awake.

She stuck her head around the door tentatively. He noted the contrast between her shyness and the liberties Sarah used to take when she held the same position.

'I was sent to enquire as to why you are still in bed. You have missed breakfast.'

Raven reached for his pocket watch to confirm this, though the girl would have no reason to misinform. He had indeed overslept. He had been very late in returning from Flint's place in Fountainbridge the night before, and it had taken him a long time to fall asleep as he considered the implications of his course of action.

He quickly pulled on some clothes, concerned at the prospect of facing the rigours of a morning clinic without so much as a bite of toast to fuel him. He just hoped Mrs Lyndsay was not in an obstreperous mood.

He was descending the stairs hurriedly when he heard a familiar voice rising from the hall below. It was the northern Irish accent that made it unmistakable, though the gruff confidence was distinctive also. The mere sound of it pricked the hairs on his head and urged him to spin on a heel, but it was too late. His approach had been seen, and such a volte-face would be conspicuous in precisely the way he wished to avoid.

It was not wise to invite the suspicion of James McLevy, the city's foremost policeman. The detective prided himself on solving all of his cases, by which he meant seeing someone convicted for every crime he investigated. He was also concerned with the recovery of stolen property, an activity for which he had a less complete success rate. There were those who believed a failure to locate that which was stolen ought to cast some doubt on the guilt of whoever was apprehended for stealing it, but McLevy was more sanguine about such discrepancies.

Raven knew there were very few people in prison who would claim other than that they were wrongly accused, but he had heard enough tales in the Old Town to make him extremely wary of McLevy's methods and the power he wielded. And whether the property he did recover ever ended up back in the possession of those from whom it had been stolen was a matter of further conjecture.

The detective was standing in the reception hall, wrapped in his familiar black frock-coat and top hat, flanked by one of his men and speaking with Dr Simpson. Raven caught a whiff of alcohol coming from both the policemen before he had reached the foot of the stairs. The staleness of it suggested they had only stopped drinking a few hours ago, most likely having been in a tavern after concluding a late night's work.

'Ah, here he comes now, though not looking his most sprightly,' Simpson said. 'You remember Will, don't you?' he asked McLevy.

Raven was rather hoping McLevy didn't.

'Indeed. I recall you took a keen interest in that unfortunate business down in Leith. I am hoping you might be able to assist me.'

This came as something of a relief, as a less rational impulse

had Raven fearing the man might be here on behalf of his counterparts in Berlin.

'I have been telling Mr McLevy about your position at the
Maternity Hospital,' Simpson said. 'He has a question for you.'

Raven observed that the professor was full of outward
bonhomie, but he had been around the man long enough to know
when it was merely a show. Simpson had always been friendly and
cooperative with McLevy, advising Raven that it was useful to
have such a man owing one favours. Raven saw the wisdom of it,
but that was easier for someone like Simpson to say, as he could
expect the ledger to be accurately kept, and a debt of favours
honoured.

'I gather you were working there yesterday,' McLevy said.
'Did you have to deal with any unusual patients?'

'Well, there was one woman with obstructed labour, which
gave me no end of difficulties, but I can't see how that might be
a matter for the police.'

'I was thinking more unusual in terms of being the wrong
sex. We are enquiring at all hospitals and among doctors in the
city as to whether they were asked to treat a patient yesterday
who was shot.'

Raven hoped his involuntary look of discomfort was interpreted as mere shock at hearing about such an incident.

'Shot? That certainly would have been unusual. To my knowledge no one has ever presented at the Maternity Hospital with
a gunshot wound. What happened?'

'An unfortunate consequence of Dr Simpson's famous
discovery,' McLevy said. 'A gang of masked men robbed a carriage
on its way north from Berwick. They surprised the guards and
attempted to subdue them by the highly unusual – and as it turns
out highly ineffective – method of holding cloths to their faces.
The cloths were discarded at the scene and when recovered still
retained the characteristic smell of chloroform.'

Now there could be no question McLevy was talking about

Flint's men. This had been what he wanted the chloroform for. The arrogant fool must have assumed Raven's warnings were mere bluster. Now he knew otherwise, and to what cost.

'The cloths failing to have the effect this crew presumably imagined, there ensued a struggle, during which one of the coach guards discharged his weapon.'

'And what of the guards themselves?' Raven asked, concerned as to how grave this crime might be to which he was now connected. 'Were they injured too?'

'They were beaten and bound, but they will recover. My concern is with what was taken. If I discover who was shot, it ought to be enough to lead me to the goods.'

This was why Flint had brought Raven in. They could not take the Weasel to another doctor, for fear word of the injury might spread and thus betray them.

'What did they take?' Raven asked.

'A strongbox being transported to the Exchange. It contained certificates of stock holdings.'

'What use are such documents?' asked Simpson. 'They bear the owner's name, do they not?'

'They bore no name as yet: that is why they were targeted. They were being transported from a printing works in Newcastle ahead of a stock offering. With the aid of a talented enough – and corrupt enough – calligrapher, they could be rendered indistinguishable from legitimate documents.'

'I do hope my Mr Quinton isn't eavesdropping,' Simpson said, 'or I will have to offer him a raise in order to keep him from temptation.'

Raven laughed, though he was barely listening. He had only asked the question in order to appear natural and to conceal the turmoil going on inside his head.

If he told McLevy what he knew, it would surely rid him of Flint for ever. But no sooner had this possibility opened before him than he saw that it was not so simple. Flint was too clever to keep the stolen goods anywhere that could be tied to him. That was probably where he had gone last night when Gargantua responded so anxiously to Raven's question as to Flint's whereabouts.

Furthermore, they would surely have disposed of the Weasel's remains by now. There would be no evidence, but were the police to come enquiring, Flint would know who had pointed them there. And there would be repercussions. Reprisals. Much worse than anything he had experienced before.

He was also conflicted by the humanity he had witnessed from Gargantua, and from Flint for that matter. The moment he was shot, Alec had become a liability: a millstone that would drag Flint down. Raven had thought of Flint as entirely ruthless, but if that were true, he would have finished Alec off and disposed of his body, never to be found. Instead they had endeavoured to save him, not knowing it was hopeless.

McLevy fixed Raven with his penetrating stare.

'You are quite sure you did not treat such an injury yesterday?'

'I think it would have stood out in my memory,' Raven replied, hoping the casual nature of his answer served to cover its falsity. Also, he had technically not yet lied outright.

'In truth it is as well,' said Dr Simpson.

'How so?' McLevy asked, picking up on the gravity of his tone.

'There is a bond of trust between doctor and patient. If an injured man, even a criminal, knew his physician might tell the police about injuries that would put him under suspicion, it could discourage him from seeking medical help. He might die, though death is not the sentence for his crime.'

McLevy's face twisted into a parody of compassion.

'Criminals dropping dead as a result of their misadventures,' he said. 'Aye, what a tragic loss to all of us that would be.'

FORTY-SEVEN

arah stood outside the main entrance to the Infirmary, the imposing scale of the building prompting second thoughts about the wisdom of pursuing this solo investigation. She recalled how it had gone when she attempted to question Dr Johnstone and did not welcome the prospect of being vehemently rebuffed again. She was growing weary of being dismissed and had at least, on this occasion, obtained an appointment rather than arriving unannounced. Miss Peat, the matron, had agreed to see her, though Sarah had been vague about the reason for the interview.

She had considered asking Dr Simpson to vouch for her, as he had recently been appointed as physician to the hospital, but that would have required divulging the reason for her visit. She and Raven had thus far managed to keep their investigations from him, though their relationship had not entirely escaped notice.

Quinton had intruded upon them when Raven was comforting her, which might have meant little to him in isolation. However, it transpired that he had witnessed them together again in the immediate aftermath of Mrs Glassford's post-mortem examination, both being too caught up in discussion of what they had seen to notice when he stuck his head around the door. Quinton had made a remark this morning about the time she was spending in Raven's company, as though there was something improper in what they were about. Sarah had dissembled rather than rebuke the man for his impertinence, having no wish to make an enemy of him.

She felt slighted, but it had served as a timely warning. She regarded her behaviour as beyond reproach, and yet it was enough to make Quinton feel he had the right to pass comment. What might the consequences be if she dared do something that was actually reckless or radical?

Looking at the size of the place, it was easy to envisage herself wandering the corridors of the Infirmary, getting lost. She decided to head first to the porter's lodge to ask for directions.

The porter was a squat man with heavy whiskers, loquacious in his response to her enquiry, supplying more information than she required.

'Miss Peat. Lovely woman,' he said. 'Very good at her job as far as I can make out. Not that it's made easy for her.'

Sarah made no reply, which he took as reason enough to continue. She quickly got the impression he liked to talk and was starved of much opportunity to do so.

'Between you and me,' he said, lowering his voice conspiratorially, although there was no one in the vicinity to overhear, 'the resident doctors try her patience. Complain about the food, destroy hospital property in a wanton manner, use improper language. It has got to the point that she refuses to sit at the dinner table with them.'

Sarah opened her mouth to ask, again, where she might find this poor woman, but the porter had more to say.

'The chaplain and the treasurer won't sup with them either. Supposed to be gentlemen but doesn't sound like the behaviour of gentlemen to me.'

Sarah was beginning to think she would have found Miss Peat's office herself by this point, but she saw an ally to be had, for the cost of merely listening awhile.

'Such behaviour sounds truly brutish,' she said. 'Perhaps we should be training young ladies to be doctors instead.'

The porter gaped, momentarily confused, then let out a great belly laugh at what he assumed to be her joke.

'Young ladies,' he repeated, wiping his eyes. 'Most amusing. Anyway, my apologies, but I've quite forgotten what you asked me.'

'Miss Peat?' she reminded him, smiling. 'I do not wish to keep her waiting.'

'Of course, of course.'

The directions, when they came, were straightforward enough: through the main door, turn left, end of the corridor.

Sarah marched up the curved driveway, the towering edifice now surrounding her on three sides. It accommodated some two hundred souls in various states of disrepair, while the surgical hospital contained a hundred more. She was grateful that she had never had to enter either part as a patient. 'Once you go in, you never come out,' was the prevailing wisdom. She had at one time considered seeking employment as a nurse here, but Dr Simpson had dissuaded her. She would be left to empty bedpans and scrub floors, he said. She would be better employed at Queen Street. As she was a housemaid at that point, she had been dubious about this, but time had since proven him right.

She walked through the main door into the entrance hall, its grand staircase built wide enough to accommodate street chairs bearing the ill and the injured. It was beginning to show signs of its age in places but was clean and reasonably well maintained. 'The want of cleanliness is a fault that admits of no excuse,' her mother had been fond of saying, and it appeared Miss Peat shared this view.

Sarah had once asked Raven about the position of matron, wondering if it might be a suitable occupation for her to aspire to, but he had been dismissive. He had told her that a prerequisite of the job was being an unmarried woman or a widow with no dependents. This stipulation had been made after a previous incumbent and her daughter made off with several items of hospital furniture and four dish-covers purchased from Sibbald's.

Sarah wondered how long would pass between the events that would make her eligible and then subsequently disqualify her.

She found the matron's room at the end of the ground-floor corridor and paused before knocking. She straightened her coat and hat, hoping to present herself in the best possible light.

'Come in.'

The voice sounded calm and even-tempered. She had braced herself for something more aggressive and hoped that her subsequent questions would not provoke the woman she was about to meet.

Sarah opened the door and entered the room. Miss Peat looked surprised to see her.

'Oh. I was expecting Mrs Chilvers from the laundry.'

Miss Peat was sitting at a desk, a leather-bound ledger open in front of her. She was a woman of indeterminate age, wearing a grey cotton dress, a white apron and a cap. She had a long, thin nose, at the end of which sat a pair of spectacles.

'I am Mrs Banks. We have an appointment.'

'Yes, of course. Mrs Banks. Do sit.' She indicated an armchair by the fire. 'You are seeking employment, I presume?'

'No. I am an assistant to Dr Simpson. I have come at his behest. An urgent matter.' Sarah felt her cheeks flush at this glaring falsehood. She hoped the matron would not notice.

'Assistant? To Dr Simpson? How unusual.'

Sarah wondered if she was going to be questioned further – about her claim to be the professor's employee or why the doctor had seen fit to send her – but Miss Peat merely waited for her to be seated and then offered her a cup of tea.

Sarah declined the refreshment but took it to be a favourable sign. Miss Peat manoeuvred herself out from behind her desk, poured herself a cup from a large brown enamel teapot and sat down in a chair opposite. She took a sip of her tea and waited for Sarah to speak.

Sarah wondered where to start and decided it might be prudent to keep the details of her quest to a minimum.

'I am seeking some information regarding a nurse whom I believe used to work here. Her name is Mary Dempster.'

Miss Peat's teacup stopped halfway to her mouth. She placed it down upon the saucer calmly, but it was obvious that the very mention of the name had unsettled her.

'What kind of information do you require?' she asked, trying just a little too hard to appear unperturbed.

'It is of a sensitive nature. I am curious as to whether there were any disciplinary issues, or whether any matters regarding this nurse's conduct ever gave you concern.'

'I run a tight ship here, Mrs Banks. It would be inappropriate to discuss disciplinary issues with a member of the public.'

'There *were* disciplinary issues, then?'

Miss Peat took another sip of tea, allowing herself a moment before she responded.

'As I said, it would be improper to answer that question in discussion with someone who has just walked in off the street.'

Sarah feared this was as far as it would go. She could tell Miss Peat had a fierce sense of propriety, as necessarily fastidious about her position as she was about the cleanliness of her hospital. Nonetheless, there was a hint of regret in her demeanour, a distinct sense of conflict within.

Sarah was inspired to persevere, realising that there was a way to make that very propriety work in her favour.

'I appreciate your discretion, Miss Peat,' she said. 'However, were I to inform you that I was perhaps enquiring as a prospective employer of Mary Dempster, as someone possibly intending to take her into my household . . .'

Miss Peat nodded eagerly. 'Then I would be duty bound to

tell you of the grave reservations I would have about you employing someone I had cause to dismiss.'

'Let us imagine, then, that I am indeed making such an enquiry.'

Miss Peat's gaze flicked left and right, as though she suspected there were other eyes upon them.

'I had recently taken up the position of head nurse when she began working here, and initially I believed she would make an excellent addition to the staff. It is exceedingly difficult to attract the right type of woman to the job. Despite what is generally held to be the case, nursing does not come to all women by intuition.'

'What altered your opinion? Why was she dismissed?'

'She was dismissed for dishonesty and theft. A locket belonging to a recently deceased patient was found in her possession. But in truth, what troubled me about Mary was not what she was dismissed for but the multiplicity of incidents for which she was not.'

'I'm not sure that I follow.'

Miss Peat cleared her throat, sipped her tea again and continued.

'Things could never be proven against her. There was always someone else positioned to take the blame. My suspicions would point towards her, but evidence and accusations always fell upon others; often people to whom she bore ill will. A thief is not to be tolerated, but I believed Mary to be something far more sinister. She was a practised deceiver, a manipulator who sought to conceal her true actions.'

'We are not merely talking about theft here, are we?' Sarah asked.

Miss Peat shook her head.

'Initially she made herself indispensable; she was cheerful, hardworking and was popular with the medical staff, who spoke highly of her abilities. She joined the hospital apothecary on his rounds, expressing a desire to learn as much as he was willing to teach her. She was uncommonly knowledgeable as a result. But as time went on it became clear that she was often less than truthful, and she frequently displayed a reckless disregard for doses of prescribed medicines. It was my suspicion that she also tampered with fever charts and the ward journals.'

'Why would she do such a thing?'

'I think she fancied herself a doctor.'

Miss Peat's words hung in the air a moment.

'There are few things as hazardous in a hospital as one who believes herself clever and does not comprehend the depths of her own ignorance. I believe she was instigating treatments that had not been sanctioned by the medical staff and that she preferred to work at night so that her actions could be hidden. There was a concern that more deaths occurred when she was on duty, but such a thing is difficult to prove when death is such a frequent visitor to the wards already.

'She covered her tracks well, I'll say that for her. But I will tell you this, for this much I do know – she is a dangerous woman. For surely there is nothing more dangerous than a woman who has ambitions above her station.'

FORTY-EIGHT

aven was finishing off a hurried lunch when Jarvis appeared and handed him a letter. He reached for it eagerly, anxious for news of Gabriela. He looked at the stamp in the hope of seeing King Friedrich Wilhelm, but was disappointed.

'From Albany Street,' the butler said pointedly.

He opened it hurriedly and immediately recognised that the hand was not Sarah's. The signature confirmed that it had indeed come from Archie, asking Raven to bring him a stock bottle of chloroform at his earliest convenience. Raven wondered why the man had not asked his wife to pick up a bottle from Duncan and Flockhart's. It was equidistant and she was well enough known at the pharmacists' premises as not to be denied. Then it struck him that perhaps Archie did not wish her to know how much of it he was getting through.

Raven suppressed a sigh and started upstairs to retrieve a bottle from the sideboard in Dr Simpson's office. It being the afternoon, the professor was at the university giving a lecture. If Raven recalled correctly, at this point in the syllabus it would be about fibroid tumours of the uterus. The professor continued to be one of the more popular lecturers at the university. He was an engaging speaker whose skilful use of anecdote and personal experience illumined what in another's hands would be deathly dull. Raven recalled how inspired he had been by Simpson's words and his manner when he sat before him as a student, and then how proud he had been in assisting at those same lectures as his apprentice. He had dutifully collated and carried the copious notes for each talk, never to see the man refer to them.

These thoughts served to emphasise how the professor was lacking his usual sparkle. Raven felt again a degree of shame that he had been slow to come to his defence, and grateful that Sarah had been so insistent. He was impatient to tell Dr Simpson about how they intended to exonerate him, but was wary of being premature in his announcements. He did not have the hard proof he required yet, but once he did, the denials and objections of the likes of Miller and Duncan would surely be swept aside as their peers digested the significance of Raven's discovery.

He strode into Simpson's study and was startled to find it occupied, Mr Quinton seated at the professor's desk. Quinton looked up from the document before him, peering over his spectacles like some feather-bare raptor.

Raven recovered from his fright and made for the sideboard, bending to retrieve the bottle he required.

'What are you doing?' Quinton asked, with a tone that implied he had the right to know.

'I might ask you the same question,' Raven replied.

'I am attempting to bring order to this chaos,' Quinton said, gesturing to the storm of papers that was Simpson's desk. 'And you?'

'I require a bottle of chloroform.'

'Then you must fill in the ledger to say you have removed it.'

'What?' Raven asked, though he had by now noticed the book that was sitting atop the sideboard.

'It is important that we keep track of the consumption of supplies, particularly those which might be expensive. Have you any idea how much money is spent on medicines in this household?'

Raven had to rein in his incredulity.

'That's because we treat patients, Mr Quinton. We are doctors. I appreciate that such extravagances might be inconvenient when totting up the numbers, but treating disease is not something that ought to be subordinate to the exactitudes of petty accountants.'

Quinton ignored this outburst.

'Without a record being kept there is no way of knowing whether those purchases are being dispensed appropriately, or whether they might have been misused or even resold.'

Raven stood up, the bottle of chloroform gripped in his hand.

'Are you accusing me of selling on medicines at a profit? Would that I had the time.'

'It is for the protection of your own reputation then that every purchase henceforth should be logged, and each item that is removed for consumption be logged too, with the reason noted, that I might ensure the figures correspond. Who is this chloroform for?'

'A patient. One who is in great need of it.'

'I wish to have a name.'

Raven felt exasperated that this self-important cypher should be proving an impediment to taking care of a sick man.

'I am taking it to Dr Banks, Sarah's husband. Are you content that I should dispense it to treat him, or would his suffering make for neater figures on the page?'

Quinton narrowed his eyes. 'Ah, yes. I have observed that you and Mrs Banks have quite the rapport. Is Dr Banks aware of how much time you have been spending with his wife?'

'We work together. And what damn business is it of yours?'

'You might have heard that I have discovered serious financial discrepancies. I am making it my business to be vigilant. I am on the lookout for impropriety and immoral conduct. Compromising behaviour is often at the root of financial dishonesty.'

'I would recommend you visit the kitchen,' Raven told him.

'Does Mrs Lyndsay have specific information, or are you making an accusation?'

'She usually has a large stock-pot on the stove around this time of the day. The ideal size and temperature for you to go and boil your head.'

FORTY-NINE

s Sarah made her way back out of the Infirmary, she passed the entrance to one of the wards, beds lined up either side. She saw a doctor making his rounds surrounded by a gaggle of young students, all jostling for position, trying to hear what the great man said. A nurse stood to the side, awaiting his command. She imagined the place much later in the day, all but deserted, lamplit and quiet, and thought about Mary Dempster recklessly experimenting with medicines, the effects of which she did not fully understand.

Sarah had mixed feelings about putting all of this before Raven. Was it enough to convince him that the nurse was somehow implicated? And if she was continuing to instigate her own treatments, what was she administering that was proving to be so detrimental to the health of her patients? On the other hand, it did provide an answer of sorts as to why she was doing it and why the symptoms experienced by the patients did not correspond with any of the commonly known poisons. And yet, even if all that were true, it did not explain why her sister seemed afraid of her.

Her thesis about deliberate poisoning seemed to be floundering, but the elusive nurse still seemed to be key to the whole thing.

As Sarah strode across the courtyard, she noticed movement from the porter's box. He had seen her approach the gate and was coming out to talk to her again.

'Are we going to be seeing more of you, then?' he asked.

Her blank look invited him to elaborate, though she suspected that little invitation was ever necessary.

'I assumed you were speaking to Miss Peat about taking up a job here,' he continued, pointing back towards the Infirmary as though she had forgotten where she had just come from.

'I was merely making some enquiries.'

'Well, if you're interested in working in this place, Miss Peat is not really the one to give you the full picture. A good woman, for sure, and a formidable one, but she doesn't know everything that goes on under her nose, much as she'd like to think so. If you want to know how things really are, you ought to eavesdrop on the nurses' common room. It's on the second floor. I say common room, for that's what they call it, but it's merely a disused storeroom – one they make sure nothing ever gets stored in. A little cubby hole where they sit and drink tea. Or more likely gin if they're there overnight.'

Sarah thanked the porter and turned back to the hospital again, this time climbing the stairs to the second floor. A pair of orderlies were transporting a patient along the corridor, the patient uttering oaths about what he considered to be rough handling. Beyond them she saw two women in aprons and caps hurrying towards a door at the end of the corridor. They disappeared through it before Sarah could reach them.

It was roughly where the porter had described, but with nothing to identify it, there was no way of knowing what lay beyond. She was about to knock when the door opened again and a young nurse emerged dressed in a plain cotton gown and the same apron and cap as the previous two women.

Behind her, Sarah could see half a dozen nurses sitting and standing inside the cramped space. It did indeed look like a store cupboard. There was no window, though in its favour it did seem warm and snug.

'I think you might be in the wrong place, ma'am,' the nurse who had opened the door told her. 'The wards are back there.'

Sarah drew some confidence from being addressed as ma'am.

'I think that I am in exactly the right place,' she said. 'I'm not here about a patient. I am attempting to locate a nurse who used to work here by the name of Mary Dempster.'

'Never heard the name,' the nurse said, then turned and asked the room: 'Somebody here asking after a Mary Dempster. Anybody remember her?'

A heavy-set, stony-faced woman stepped forward.

'What do you want with her?'

Sarah fought off an urge to turn and retreat, instead stepping fully inside the room.

'I need to ask her some questions regarding her care of a patient.'

'A fool's errand,' the woman told her. 'Even if you find her, you're unlikely to prise any truth from her.'

'That's unfair,' said a red-haired woman standing against the wall. 'You never took to her because the patients liked her more than they liked you.'

'The patients like an enema more than they like you, Gertie,' chimed another, prompting much laughter.

'Merry Mary, they called her,' the red-head went on. 'She was always cheerful on the ward. Small wonder they were going to like her more than Grumpy Gertie.'

'She was a snake,' Gertie said, fixing her eyes on Sarah and ignoring the rest. 'She got my friend dismissed for a thief. And all the time it was her that was stealing things. Or have you forgotten that, Mhairi?' she demanded of the red-head.

'I am told she works privately these days,' Sarah said. 'Might there be any way of discovering who she is working for now?'

'Why don't you ask Nora, there?' said Mhairi. 'She was Mary's little sweetheart after all.' She laughed, a scoffing, almost snarling quality to it.

Sarah looked at the older woman Mhairi had indicated, sitting in the corner, sipping from a mug. From the smell of it, she was drinking something other than tea.

Gertie announced that she had to be getting back on the ward.

'I hope you're not after her for work,' she said, brushing past. 'You'd be wiser inviting the devil himself into your house.'

'Or your bed,' said another voice, to further giggling.

Sarah drew closer to the woman in the corner.

'You're Nora? You were Mary's friend?'

Nora's face became pinched. 'No, I damn well wasn't. None of them believe me, and yet still they have their sport.' She looked past Sarah to address the others. 'Can't have it both ways. Can't say it didn't happen and then call me names like it did.'

'Believed you about what?' Sarah asked softly.

Nora waved a dismissive arm. 'I'll not throw myself open to anyone else's ridicule.'

Sarah cast an eye around the gathering, clearly a harsh jury of Nora's peers. She remembered from the schoolyard how people sought any kind of weapon they could use against you: something you said, something you did, something you wore. Making up a story and pretending they all believed it. Pretending not to believe your own story just so that they could call you a liar for telling it. Most people quickly learned not to draw attention to themselves, for fear of supplying ammunition.

Sarah spoke loud enough for all to hear.

'It strikes me that if you were willing to tell me this story, then that would be proof enough that it must be true. For why would you subject yourself to further scorn if it were a lie?'

Nora appeared to draw some promise of vindication from this logic. She paused for a moment, staring into her cup. Then she spoke slowly, quietly, as though telling her story required effort.

'It happened when I was here as a patient. I had to have

treatment for a problem,' she said. She nodded at her lap. 'Down below.'

She paused again and looked at Sarah to ascertain whether she understood. It was an ongoing source of bemusement to Sarah that most people lacked the rudimentary vocabulary necessary to accurately describe their own anatomy, or if they did know the correct terms, were disinclined to use them.

'There is no need to be delicate about it,' Sarah told her. 'I work for Dr Simpson, the obstetrician.'

'I had a cancerous ulcer,' Nora clarified. 'It was treated with silver nitrate. The night after it was done, I was suffering dreadfully. The pain was terrible. Mary Dempster was the night nurse. She gave me some medicine to drink. I took it, but she kept coming back and bade me drink more. Said it would put an end to my suffering.'

'Can you tell me what the medicine was?'

'I don't recall. I was beside myself with pain.'

'What happened then?'

'Here we go,' Mhairi muttered. Sarah shot her a look, fiercer than she intended. Her curiosity was making her bold.

'My eyes became heavy and I had a drouth like you wouldn't believe. My mouth was parched, all the moisture in it dried. I could barely speak; my tongue couldn't form the words. My arms and legs felt heavy; I couldn't move them however much I wanted to. And then I was aware of the covers being pulled back and I felt the mattress sag.'

Nora swallowed repeatedly as though the reminiscence was causing her throat to dry again. She took a sip from her cup.

'She got into the bed beside me.'

'You must have been delirious,' argued Mhairi. 'No one in their right mind would get into bed beside you.'

'It happened,' Nora insisted. 'I felt her hands caress my face and she spoke to me.'

'You were probably full of laudanum, right enough. But it revealed your darkest desires, didn't it?'

With that, Mhairi turned away, having had her fun.

'What did she say?' Sarah asked, ignoring the others.

'That I should sleep, that it would soon be over. Something like that but repeated over and over.'

'And then?'

'I remember footsteps in the corridor. I think someone else was coming along. She jumped out of the bed good and quick after that. Then I fell asleep.'

'That is most peculiar,' Sarah said.

Nora looked urgently at her.

'You don't believe me, do you? Same as the rest.' She was becoming agitated. 'She gave me something to drink, something to make me sleep, and then climbed into bed alongside me and I'm the one said to have lost my reason.'

'I do believe you,' Sarah assured her. 'But what I fail to understand is why? Why would anyone do such a thing?'

Nora spoke in barely a whisper.

'I think she meant to kill me.'

FIFTY

aven was still feeling aggrieved by the time he reached Albany Street; being tasked with such a menial errand had done nothing to improve his black mood. However, when Archie himself answered the door, he realised his error. The chloroform was merely a pretext. It was Raven that he wanted to see.

'I'm so grateful you have come,' he said. 'There is something I would like to discuss with you.'

Archie ushered Raven into a small study opposite the parlour. He accepted the bottle of chloroform and placed it on top of his desk, then indicated that his guest should sit. Archie remained standing, albeit restively, in front of the fire. Raven noticed that he was unshaven, coarse bristles speckling his chin. He looked wan, and possibly thinner than the last time he had seen him.

He didn't speak for a few moments, long enough for Raven to become concerned that the subject of their discussion was going to be his comforting Sarah when she had learned of Mrs Glassford's death. His exchange with Quinton had unsettled him. Was it possible that Quinton had spoken to Archie about his disquiet at finding them together in an embrace? Or had his words merely been intended as a warning?

Obviously, Archie did not represent any kind of physical threat

– pistols at dawn were unlikely – but Raven was appalled to think of Archie being wounded by a twisted account of his wife taking solace in another man's arms.

'I don't know how to begin,' Archie said finally.

Raven swallowed. 'Take your time,' he said, though his discomfort was becoming acute.

'There's the rub. Time is not something I can afford. I think that the end is approaching rather faster than I had anticipated.'

'What makes you say that?'

'My disease is advancing. I am getting weaker.' He spoke firmly and with conviction, dispassionately stating the facts of the matter. He did not seem to be inviting contradiction, was not seeking the false reassurance that a contrary opinion would bring.

'I know that everyone feigns optimism for my sake. I know that no one wants to admit that all hope is exhausted, but it is quite evident that all that can be done for me has been done.'

He paused for a moment, allowing Raven to absorb what had been said.

'I have endured three painful operations which have brought me some relief, but the symptoms always return. There is a firmness at the back of my tongue that extends into my throat, and the nodes in my neck are hard and immobile. There can be little doubt about what that means. I know I am not long for this world, and I have accepted it, but I have one lingering concern. I have no wish to become a burden to Sarah.'

Archie looked directly at Raven in a way that made him feel distinctly ill at ease. There was another pause.

'We are both medical men,' Archie continued. 'We know how it is likely to go for me now. Speaking and eating will become increasingly difficult. The pain will worsen. Death will come slowly. I will succumb as a result of starvation, suffocation, or the tumour will erode into an artery and I will bleed to death.

Unquenchable haemorrhage. You know how that will be. What that will look like.'

Raven could well imagine. As an obstetrician he was no stranger to sudden and dramatic blood loss but the prospect of exsanguination from the mouth, blood filling the throat, perhaps drowning in the stuff, added a uniquely horrific dimension.

'I would not have Sarah witness such a thing.'

'No. Of course not,' Raven said.

'I want to be able to talk, to eat, to kiss my wife, to laugh and to enjoy the time I have left as much as I can. But when that is no longer possible . . . I see no point in prolonging the inevitable.'

An image of Archie kissing Sarah was suddenly all that Raven could see, and he cursed himself for his shallow selfishness. A dying man was taking him into his confidence, and yet he could not fully banish his own desires.

'That is why I hope I can count on your assistance.'

'Assistance? With what?'

Their eyes locked, the intensity of Archie's gaze conveying the gravity of his request.

'I do not wish to wait helplessly for the end.'

Raven's mouth dried. He tried to grasp what Archie meant, his mind struggling to acknowledge what was being said. Was he asking Raven to ease his passing, smooth his pathway to the grave, or was he suggesting something more deliberate, something anticipatory? Was this man, his rival for Sarah's affections, asking Raven to kill him? Coming so soon after his intervention with the dying Alec, it was as though the gods were toying with him. His facetious thought about a duel at dawn returned to mock him, then to make matters worse, propelled him back to Berlin.

He saw the pistol aimed at his head, loaded quicker than he could have anticipated. He saw the spray of blood hit the wall as he opened the gunman's throat. He had cheated death then by taking a life, using a surgeon's blade designed for acts of mercy.

Was there some perverse price to be paid for evading his destiny in that alleyway? Was he now fated to end lives rather than to save them?

I do not wish to wait helplessly for the end.

Sleep now, Alec.

'I understand you might wish to think about it,' Archie said, interrupting Raven's tormenting thoughts. 'How best it might be achieved.'

Archie glanced towards the bottle of chloroform. Or at least Raven thought that he did. He was beginning to feel dizzy, an unpleasant vertigo settling upon him, as though he had been inhaling the stuff himself.

Archie swallowed.

'That is not all. I have a further request.'

Raven reasoned that nothing he might ask for now could possibly trump what had been asked for already, but was wary of making assumptions.

'After I am gone, I will need someone to look after Sarah. I have seen to it that she will be provided for financially, but there are things she will need other than money. She is a strong woman, a remarkable woman, but I am under no illusions about how difficult life will be for her. She will need a man's protection.'

Raven thought that Sarah may well disagree with this statement.

'What about the child?' he asked, thinking it best that everything be brought out into the open.

'She told you?'

'No. My deduction.'

Archie smiled. 'Of course. It is after all your area of expertise and you have been spending a considerable amount of time with my wife.'

Raven wondered if there was a barb within this remark but decided against seeking clarification.

'If you know that, then you will understand why I am so

concerned. To leave her to bring up a child alone: it pains me to think about it, almost as much as it pains me to think about all that I will miss. Will you help her?'

'To raise your child?' Raven asked. The words came out before he could censor himself.

'To assist her, advise her. To ensure she is not left alone.'

He looked at Raven unflinchingly, as though he had an unassailable right to make these demands of a man he barely knew.

'I got to have her just a little while. I am grateful, so very grateful for that much. But I am sure I will miss the best of Sarah. She will achieve remarkable things if she has the help of her friends.

'I would not ask any of this if I did not know how much you cared for her already. And though I have not known you long, I have the confidence that you are a good man because of how much she cares for you.'

Raven bowed his head. He did not feel worthy of Sarah's care or Archie's confidence.

'You are wrong about me, Archie. I am not a good man. If I was, we would not be having this conversation.'

'What do you mean?'

'I mean that if I was a good man and not the coward that I am, Sarah would be my wife, not yours.'

'What were you afraid of? What stood in your way?'

'I feared for my position, my status were I to marry a housemaid. It seemed important at the time.'

The folly of it all seemed so stark now that he had admitted it.

'You deserved her more, Archie, and you deserve far longer with her. You were the better man. The stronger man.'

Archie's expression softened and he put a hand on Raven's shoulder.

'Perhaps there are truths that you can only tell a dying man.'

'I apologise if I was indiscreet,' Raven said, his sense of foolishness deepening.

'You miss my meaning. The consolation of my plight is the clarity it affords, to see what is truly important and to help others see it. We make different decisions when we know life is short. And yet life is always short, for all of us.'

Raven felt dazed as Archie accompanied him to the door. He could not fathom how things had become so complicated so quickly. He had only been back in Edinburgh a matter of weeks.

'Think about what I have said,' were Archie's parting words.

Raven considered them unnecessary. It was unlikely he would be able to think about anything else.

FIFTY-ONE

t was beginning to get dark as Sarah walked towards Princes Street, the failing light hastening her stride. She had spent longer than she intended at the Infirmary. It was her policy never to be out alone after nightfall, and though she would likely be home before the lamplighter appeared on Albany Street, she did not want Archie to worry.

Fear was prominent in her mind, though. She was wary of what might lurk in each close and alley that she passed, imagined horrors that grew all the more frightening as the sun set. She thought of Nora's fear too, that look of terror revisited as she recounted her story.

Mhairi had attributed it all to delirium, possibly an effect of the medicine Nora had been given. However, delirium by its very nature was transient, and the phantoms it summoned were as quickly dismissed. Sarah knew from her own experience that though demons could sometimes assail her in the dead of night, the fear she felt was dispelled by morning, its source instantly forgotten. The traumatic nature of the event Nora had described was evident in her retelling of it. That she still felt such fear all this time later suggested that it was born of something tangible.

But equally, Sarah could understand Mhairi's scorn. She knew that the night nurses could be a law unto themselves. Raven had said as much on numerous occasions – poorly paid drudges who helped themselves to the laudanum on occasion and rested their weary bones in empty beds. But what would make anyone get in beside one of the patients? Thinking about some of the poor souls she had encountered in Dr Simpson's waiting room, Sarah couldn't imagine ever being tempted to do such a thing.

With frustration she realised that, despite this new information, she was still stuck with Raven's seemingly intractable questions. The symptoms Nora had experienced did not match the ones described in any of Raven's cases, but that was a mere detail in comparison with the equally obstinate issue of motive. Was Mary Dempster deliberately killing people? And if so, why?

As she approached the High Street, she saw that her route across to the North Bridge was obstructed by an overturned dray. The wagon had shed its load of beer barrels and was attracting a sizeable crowd. As she skirted round the back of the Tron Kirk, she sifted once again through the reasons people usually had for killing one another – greed, lust, envy, anger, vengeance, power – but none of them seemed to apply. Unless they applied in some obscure way that she could not see. How did killing her patients, and latterly those who employed her, profit or satisfy Mary Dempster?

This is not like some scheming wife poisoning her rich husband so that she might live off the inheritance, Raven had said.

As Sarah marched up the High Street, she passed the *Scotsman* newspaper office and the sight triggered another memory, something that Archie had said on the very day Raven had returned to Queen Street. He was reading an article about four members of the same family who had died within two weeks of each other.

I wonder who's to inherit . . . I'd be checking their pockets for arsenic.

Archie had said it in jest but might have spoken more truth than he realised.

FIFTY-TWO

t is sometimes a source of anger and sometimes of amusement that for much of my adult life I have been surrounded by doctors who considered themselves above me. They had no notion of how far I was always above them.

Doctors flatter themselves when they talk of holding the power of life and death over a patient. By their rationale, any child at the table holds the power of life and death if she so much as lifts the knife from her plate. The knife, the scalpel, and indeed the medicine, is merely an instrument. Power lies not in the object itself, nor even in the hand that holds it. Power resides in the will to use it: not in the knowledge that one has the means of taking a life, but the knowledge that one has the fortitude to do so.

Nobody truly holds the power of life and death if they have only exercised it in the service of the former.

I must stress that I bore Mr Robertson, the dock-labourer, no ill-will. Indeed, I bore no ill-will to many of the patients who died at my hand: in certain instances, I wished only to provide for them an easeful death, sparing them an agonising end or what I could see would be a squalid future. Others were casualties of my experimentation, a means to an end. In many instances I had no feelings towards them one way or the other, much as I felt towards the dog I poisoned with arsenic. It was merely the means by which I sought to hurt Mrs Dempster.

I most certainly felt ill-will towards her, an enmity that did not diminish in accordance with my seeing less of her.

I recall how, in a moment of forgetting myself, I spoke to a patient from Glasgow in my own voice, rather than the one she had beaten into me. I was initially alarmed to realise that I had done so in front of a doctor, and expected some form of rebuke, but none was forthcoming. It became clear that nobody was judging me for it. It had simply been another exercise in Mrs Dempster bending me to her will.

As I had once vowed, I began to speak as I pleased when I was at work. This in turn led to me sometimes forgetting myself before Mrs Dempster, but her ire only increased my determination not to let her eradicate the person I perceived myself to be. And nor did I let her actions go unanswered.

I saw to it thereafter that when she beat me, one of her animals died. I was patient in my retribution, lest she too quickly understand the correlation between the two events.

Why did I not simply kill Mrs Dempster, you may well ask, and the answer lies partly in what I have just told you. Back then I had the means but not the fortitude. Drugging some pathetic specimen in the hospital was a different prospect to poisoning a robustly healthy woman in her own home, particularly one who loomed so large in my perception. However, I was growing stronger all the time.

I was paid a little more by this time but chose to continue living at the house in Canonmills. I had seen the kinds of low places my fellow nurses inhabited, as well as the little they could afford to eat, and decided that living with the Dempsters was preferable. It must also be acknowledged that I had unfinished business in that house.

Martha was still living there too, though finally, to Mrs

Dempster's delight, there was a healthy and indeed handsome prospect of that changing. Mrs Dempster would always talk about her real daughter as though she was quite the beauty, but betrayed her true perception in the surprise she showed in having secured for her a match. It goes without saying that she had made no such efforts on my behalf.

I knew what fair looked like in a girl, having seen it in my real sister, Ellie. It had always been clear that she would be a beauty, and at the Institute it was already becoming apparent that she would use this to find favour. I had not seen Ellie in years. She was 'adopted' too, though Mrs Dempster took delight in dropping hints that she had caused trouble for her new family and was likely to be put out as a result.

Martha was as plain as me, if not plainer, and certainly a good deal plumper. Nor was she as clever as me, but nonetheless, all of Mrs Dempster's efforts and aspirations were coming to fruition. Her daughter was engaged to be married to a gentleman by the name of Colin Flett, who worked for the General Steam Navigation Company in Leith.

He had been invited to the house for dinner some months before because he was a client of Mr Dempster at the bank. That was when he started to take an interest in Martha, an interest she heartily reciprocated (though not as heartily as her mother).

I thought him handsome. I liked the sound of his voice, the stories he told. His accent was unusual. I suspected it had been altered by living in all manner of different places. He was from Orkney originally, and told us his family had always had an association with the sea. Through his job with the shipping company he had travelled many times to London, to Dublin, to Amsterdam and even to New York. He was a man shaped by travel and by many and varied experiences. Calm and knowledgeable, gentle and wise: the opposite of my father in so many ways. He was ten years older than Martha, a man who had seen his fill of the world and was now ready to take a wife and start a family. Marriage was proposed, and Mrs Dempster was beside herself with joy. One could say all her ships were coming in.

He came to the house on a cold Sunday afternoon in January, after church. He had recently returned from the port of Hamburg and he talked fondly of the beer he drank there, so I served him some local ale with his meal. Mrs Dempster objected, saying he might prefer wine as that was what she and Mr Dempster were drinking. However, he assured her that the ale was most welcome and delighted everyone by thanking me in German.

He began to feel ill that afternoon, and by early evening it was clear he was in no condition to return home. Mrs Dempster insisted he lie down in the guest-room, a large chamber she had never seen fit to offer me, despite me 'paying my way'.

There was some concern that Colin's illness was the result of his recent travels, as nobody else was showing any ill effects after eating the same meal. It was suggested that a doctor be summoned, but being a nurse, I convinced them that such a measure was premature, and that Colin would most likely improve after a good night's sleep.

Unfortunately, sleep proved impossible for him. As he lay there, as restless and disoriented as any storm-tossed sailor, he complained of being stricken by a fierce thirst. I prepared a drink for him, and bade Martha serve it to him.

'You will look after him in sickness when you are his wife,' I told her. 'Best that you begin now.'

This notion seemed to please her, and she swept off with urgent purpose, the glass clutched between her hands. Thus, though she would never know it, Martha administered a large dose of poison to her betrothed.

I recall sending Mrs Dempster to fetch me some towels soaked in cold water for Colin's growing fever, and it pleased me to reverse our places, to be the one commanding her. She did as she was told because she was afraid for Colin, though mostly for her daughter and for her own grand vision. More than her obedience, though, I enjoyed her distress.

I will confess I was envious of Martha, and the life she was looking forward to with her husband-to-be, but that was not the motivation for what I did. She was not my target, any more than Colin was.

Once upon a time I had the means but not the fortitude to kill Mrs Dempster. However, by the time I had the fortitude, I had come to realise that I did not so urgently wish to end her life. I had seen people slip away, oblivious of their fate, and she did not deserve such mercy. I wished Mrs Dempster to suffer. It remained my intention to kill her, but first I wanted her to see everything she cared about destroyed.

FIFTY-THREE

here was a cold mist enveloping Edinburgh, the kind that caught in one's throat with every breath and made one wish for high winds to disperse it. When he was a schoolboy, on such days Raven would often climb Arthur's Seat or Salisbury Crags, as sometimes it was possible to get above the fog. Not only was the clear air a relief, but it was quite the spectacle to look down upon the clouds. It was even possible to imagine that Edinburgh had vanished, and that there was no city hidden beneath the shroud of grey. No Callum Flint to entangle him in criminality, no Archie Banks to request of him that he end his life.

Nor were his worries confined to Scotland any more. He had received another letter from Henry late yesterday, and though correspondence from his dear friend was always welcome, there had been little in it to comfort him.

I understand now why Gabriela has fled. The police returned yesterday, and I finally learned the identity of the man slain in the alley. His name was Javier Salazaro, and, as suspected, the man was no vagabond. The name was not familiar to me, but Liselotte informed me that Gabriela's estranged husband is called Ignacio Salazoro.

It seems that Ignacio regarded Gabriela as an ongoing source of shame and disgrace, living what the police described as an immoral life. It appears Javier came here seeking to abduct her and return her to his brother's household.

Given his status and influence, there can be little question but that Ignacio now knows the name of the man who thwarted those plans, and who killed his brother.

Raven recalled Dr Ziegler saying that you could judge a man by the calibre of his enemies. He reflected grimly that this at least indicated he was finally going up in the world.

He hoped that Gabriela's disappearance was an effort to avoid a subsequent attempt rather than evidence of a successful abduction, though it angered him that she should be forced to uproot herself just to maintain her autonomy. No husband should consider a wife his property.

On this particular Sunday, much as he needed it, he could not afford the luxury of a recreational expedition. He and Sarah had to venture north through the murk to learn more about certain tragic events that might shed further light upon their investigations. Four deaths in one household in a matter of weeks – spanning three generations – was highly unusual and might well be another instance of the disease he was hoping to identify. If the symptoms were consistent with what had been described before, then this household could go down in history as the place where Raven's Malady was verified. Three cases would be insufficient to convince anybody, but seven? That would be hard to refute.

Sarah had still not been dissuaded of her notion that the nurse had been taking an active role in the demise of her patients, though they were at least united in agreement that Mary Dempster might be a crucial common factor in this series of deaths. In her stubbornness, she had taken a trip to the Royal Infirmary and was still refusing to relinquish her wayward theory despite learning nothing more substantial than that Mary Dempster had been dismissed for being light-fingered; and that she might once have climbed into bed with a patient whose self-confessed delirium at the time made her the epitome of an unreliable witness.

Raven had begun preliminary work on a paper but would have to admit that a lack of primary evidence was undermining him. He cursed the fact that he had only begun to identify the illness after George Porteous died, meaning he had missed the opportunity to more closely examine a live sufferer. For now, all he had were sketchy second-hand accounts. Two of these were occluded by the fog of emotion, and neither Dr Johnstone nor Greta Porteous had been closely involved in their relatives' care. The third witness was Dr Fowler, whose judgment was clouded by altogether different factors.

As a medical man Raven had been appalled by Dr Fowler's obtuseness and superstition, though he suspected his disdain paled in comparison to Sarah's. Her anger at the absence of opportunities for women to educate themselves was only matched by her resentment at the privilege and preferment extended to men she considered her intellectual inferiors. Raven had little doubt that a bumbling anachronism such as Dr Fowler would have fallen into this category; he suspected it to be a wide field, one in which he was probably included too. For that reason, he would have to admit to deriving some satisfaction from setting her straight on her flawed poisoning hypothesis. She was clever, but like her revered Dr Simpson, her judgment was not infallible.

It might have been due to the pallor of the day, but as they trudged along Inverleith Row he thought that Sarah was lacking colour about her face. Raven was loath to enquire as to how she was feeling, because she clearly did not wish to confide in him regarding her condition, and thus any enquiry, no matter how sincere in its intentions, was likely to be met with hostility.

Their destination was Trinity Grove, according to the relevant page of the newspaper which Sarah had rescued from the basket of kindling by the fire. The house they sought was a handsome one that would have enjoyed an uninterrupted view all the way across the Forth had the day been clear. From a distance, it offered no suggestion of the suffering that must have been endured within, but as they drew nearer, an unkempt garden was the first sign that all was not as it should be.

'It looks disappointingly empty,' Raven remarked.

'It does,' Sarah agreed. 'I fear there will not be anyone with whom to leave a card.'

Raven was unsure whether this was intended as a slight, which usually meant that it was.

'We should knock anyway, for what it is worth,' she added. 'Perhaps we could enquire at the neighbouring houses. Surely they will have visited the family during a time of so many bereavements?'

Raven lifted the heavy brass door knocker and beat it against the plate. He could hear the reverberation inside, and imagined it echoing through the empty house, unheard. However, moments later he heard footsteps approaching from around the side of the building.

The man who appeared did not seem dressed for the weather, accoutred only in frayed trousers and a filthy shirt. Raven observed beads of sweat upon his forehead and recognised that he had been toiling, hence the lack of a coat.

'You are too early,' he said. 'The sale of furniture and other goods is not until next Saturday.'

'Are you the gardener?' Raven asked.

'I am today,' he replied. 'I am attempting to tidy things up a bit before winter falls. And before the sale, which as I say, is next week.'

'We are not here for the sale,' Raven stated. 'I am Dr Will Raven, and this is Mrs Sarah Banks. We are investigating the spread of what we believe to be a dangerous new disease. Having learned of the unfortunate events that occurred here recently, we wish to ascertain whether there may be a connection. Are you a relative of the Eddlestone family?'

The man grimaced and let out a weary sigh.

'My name is Iain McKinnon, and I'm afraid you will find nothing new here. Not unless this disease you seek is what we already call heartbreak and grief.'

'You knew the family well?' Sarah asked.

'My sister Julia died here. Her husband Stuart was my closest friend.'

Iain pointed across the street to the house diagonally opposite.

'I live there. Always have. We grew up together. Known the Eddlestone family all my days.'

'If it is not too painful, can you tell us a little about what happened?' Sarah asked, her voice softly appellant. She had a gift for putting people at ease: the same talent that calmed the most obstreperous patients at Queen Street no matter how busy the waiting room. 'The newspaper said three generations had died but they often get these things wrong.'

'No, that part is true enough. Old Mrs Eddlestone was the last to go. She spent much of the past few years bedridden, and yet I often said to myself that she would nonetheless see the rest of us buried. It was closer to truth than I intended.'

'A hardy specimen, was she?' Raven suggested with an encouraging smile, though he had detected little affection in Iain's tone.

'She was not an easy woman. I had not envisioned mourning her death, but in the event I was already grief-stricken. I was wary of her as a child and that never diminished. Her husband was lost at sea when her children were small, which I will own made things difficult for her, though, God forgive me, I sometimes wondered whether he was merely hiding.'

Raven wondered at the unguarded nature of the conversation, but traumatic events often rendered people more open than they would be otherwise.

'Her son Stuart and my sister Julia were sweethearts from childhood. It seemed inevitable that they would marry, but I had my concerns about Julia moving into this house, fine as it is. In truth, I think she did not expect the old woman to live so long. Mrs Eddlestone was often ill, though I suspected it sometimes suited her to be so. Each time we thought she was nearing her end, she would wax strong again, bitter and spiteful as ever.'

'Julia and Stuart had a child?' Sarah asked.

He wore a sad smile.

'Yes. Eleanor. A beautiful girl, although she was strong-willed and used to getting her own way, the only one of us who was any match for old Ma Eddlestone.'

The smile faded, and only the sadness remained.

'A few weeks ago, she fell suddenly and profoundly ill. We all feared the worst, and then she appeared to recover. Unfortunately, her recovery was not sustained. The illness returned to claim her.'

Raven was aware of Sarah glancing at him but he kept his attention focused on Iain. Remittance and relapse: these were stages he had expected to hear about. However, he was cautious. Many a child had fought a brave battle with illness, raising their parents' hopes only to succumb.

'As I say, she was always strong and determined. They kept having to put her back to bed because she was impatient to be well. Perhaps in the end that was what did for her: she was vulnerable because she would not rest as she was supposed to. Nor did it help that she kept refusing her medicine. She said she didn't like it. She was too young to understand. If only she had taken more of it . . .'

He swallowed back tears, his voice trailing off.

'It stole the life from my sister. I saw her fade away before my eyes. Within a week of Eleanor's death, she was bed-ridden herself. Tearful and wandering, as though the world no longer made sense to her. You could say she died of a broken heart.'

Raven turned to look at Sarah, as he knew that this would be hard for her to hear. He knew her father had passed away shortly after her mother died in childbirth, and Sarah maintained that it was his grief that had killed him.

'And what of your friend, Stuart?' Raven asked. 'Did he die of a broken heart too?'

Iain glanced in the direction of the Forth, though there was only fog to see.

He cleared his throat. 'Stuart . . .' he began, then winced and looked away again.

The thought appeared to be too painful. They had been friends since childhood after all. But Raven detected another element to his reticence, and suspected he knew what it was. He thought of Archie's request for perhaps the twentieth time that day.

'You are a doctor, you say?'

'Aye.'

'Then I can speak to you in confidence?'

'We can promise you the utmost discretion,' Sarah assured him. Raven wondered if she suspected too.

'Surely nobody could blame him for what he did,' Iain said, almost as though talking to himself. 'He had already been through so much. But people can be harsh judges when they sit at a distance. He had lost all; all but his mother, I suppose. But she was provided for, so he was not abandoning her . . .'

Raven was certain now of what Iain was reluctant to divulge and reasoned it would be easier if he said it for him.

'He took his own life.'

Iain nodded solemnly.

'We found him in his bed with Julia's locket clutched in his hand.'

Raven was beginning to feel like an intruder upon a stranger's sorrow. With every word spoken it looked less like this was a piece in the puzzle he hoped to solve, and thus they had little business troubling the man further.

'How terrible for Mrs Eddlestone to find her own son that way,' Raven said. Iain had not painted her well, but nobody would have wished her to witness such a thing. Family – even interfering in family – was often the thing that kept older people going. Now that she had lost everything, it was unsurprising that this proved the beginning of the end for her.

'No, the mercy was that she did not,' Iain said. 'She was confined to bed at the time, and in fact was never to leave it.'

'It's just that you said "we",' Raven reminded him.

'I meant myself and Mrs Eddlestone's nurse. She lived with us for several weeks. She was recommended by Dr Fowler. Personally, I had little faith in the man, but he had been Mrs Eddlestone's doctor a long time and she was not to be argued with.'

'This nurse,' Sarah said. 'She didn't happen to be called Mary Dempster, did she?'

Raven thrilled with anticipation at what was about to be revealed, sensing triumph in the air around him as he calculated the implications.

'Yes. How do you know that?' Iain asked, clearly surprised by her perspicacity.

'Call it a woman's intuition,' Sarah replied.

'We know Dr Fowler,' Raven added, eager to assuage any curiosity. There was no time for detailed explanations about what it was they were trying to uncover.

'Well, I'll concede that his judgment was sound in this case,' Iain went on. 'She is a good woman, not just a good nurse. Bless her. Truth is, she found Stuart first, though only by a few moments. He had killed himself with morphine. When I came in, she was disposing of it in the hope that we would never know and might thus be spared the ignominy on top of the loss.'

Raven felt the ground shift beneath him as Iain spoke, vividly seeing what the man could not. Seeing what he himself had been wilfully blind to, despite Sarah's efforts to reveal it. His triumph turned to ashes in a twinkling.

Mary Dempster had killed Stuart, and Iain had walked in on her getting rid of the evidence.

'The pity is, had I been but a minute later, I would have believed he went the same way as Julia,' Iain said. 'I was grateful for Mary's solicitude nonetheless.'

'Indeed,' agreed Sarah, flashing Raven a look. 'We may never know how many such acts of mercy she has committed without acknowledgement or reward.'

'As I say, Mary is a good woman. If she hadn't been in the house to look after Mrs Eddlestone, I doubt Eleanor would have held on as long as she did.'

'We are so sorry for your dreadful loss,' Sarah said. 'But can I ask one more question? You said earlier that Eleanor was too young to understand. Understand what?'

His countenance took on a look of profound regret.

'She wouldn't take her medicine because she said it was making her sick. She didn't understand that she was already sick and even if it tasted nasty, the medicine would make her better.'

'I see.'

As did Raven. Finally. Belatedly.

Iain glanced back to the garden.

'If that is all, I ought to return to my labours. I am sorry I could not assist you.'

'Not at all,' Raven told him, the words catching in his throat, but not for the reasons that might be assumed. 'Thank you for your candour at such a difficult time.'

They watched him walk away with a heavy tread. He looked weighed down, and small wonder, but he had no notion of the burden he had just passed to them. The man had been more helpful than he could possibly know, and certainly more helpful than he could be *permitted* to know. Raven suspected that it was only for that reason that Sarah was able to wait until he was out of earshot to announce her vindication.

'The trail left by Mary Dempster grows ever longer. Do you still think she is transferring some morbid principle to these patients on her hands?'

Under the circumstances, she at least had the decency not to sound proud.

'Her hands are almost certainly responsible, but not in the way I had envisaged.'

'I trust you are no longer optimistic about diagnosing a new disease?'

'No,' he conceded. 'I think we can add Raven's Malady to the list of fatalities attributable to this Mary Dempster.'

'I shudder to think just how long that list might be. She must have been working as a nurse for at least a decade. How many patients might have died leaving nobody the wiser to her being the reason why? We must tell someone: Dr Simpson, or James McLevy.'

'Not yet,' Raven cautioned. 'If word gets out that a nurse has been murdering patients – whole families, even children – then there will be mobs on the streets. We don't want every nurse who ever lost a patient to be held accused by angry relatives.'

'She must be stopped, though.'

'As soon as possible, but to do that, we need more than simply to find her. We will require the strongest proof, for who will believe something so monstrous? I certainly did not before now. More than ever, we need the how and the why.'

FIFTY-FOUR

he air remained unsettlingly still and consequently there was no hint of the fog lifting as Raven proceeded alone through the city, bound once more for the cottage in Lochend. Sarah had again offered to accompany him, but on this occasion he had insisted she go back and spend the rest of her day with Archie. He left it unspoken that her time was limited and she should not waste it.

She had acceded, but he detected a degree of reluctance and recalled what she had confided in him. Every moment she spent with Archie was precious and yet simultaneously painful. The idea of her suffering made him want to hold her, but he had to put such thoughts from his mind. That way lay only confusion and anguish. He had missed his opportunity and he would have to learn to live with that.

Also unspoken was Raven's concern that he now knew they were dealing with someone highly dangerous, and therefore he did not wish to put Sarah in harm's way. He had woken up many a night tormented by thoughts of how close she had come to death once before – how close they both had – due to Raven failing to see what was right in front of him.

He had missed so much that ought to have been obvious in this recent enterprise too. Raven wondered how many enduring misapprehensions in medicine (and other fields, for that matter) were down to ambition and the desire to be vindicated. How many proud men had only sought out the evidence in support of their own hypotheses and eschewed that which might inconveniently put their ideas to the test?

The world needed fewer such proud men, or perhaps it merely required more women like Sarah. An increase in the latter would guarantee a reduction in the former.

Raven had been foolish, he could see that now, and he was grateful to Sarah for revealing it. His visions of being lauded for finding a new disease were unworthy, for in truth he had hoped such a discovery would hasten his elevation. There were no quick paths to success or renown, and nor should he seek them.

Simpson had discovered chloroform not by mere happenstance and serendipity, but as a cumulative consequence of a lifetime's endeavours and its accumulated wisdom of judgment. That was what James Matthews Duncan ought to grasp too. 'No man can ever reach great reputation or great excellence without great exertion,' as Simpson often said in his lectures.

As he strode along Easter Road, Raven reflected that the pursuit of medical knowledge could also take quite a toll on one's shoe leather. What made it even harder on the feet right then was the possibility that this was likely to be a wasted trip. In that respect he was grateful for the fog, for it might be what kept Mary Dempster indoors on a Sunday after church; if, that is, she was not still resident with her new employer.

He had no other reason to be grateful for the murk, as it was a considerable impediment to his navigation, obscuring the landmarks by which he would normally get his bearings. He wasted a good ten minutes walking up the wrong road, taking a turn too soon. Then, once he had doubled back and corrected his course, he realised he had walked past the cottage he was looking for, as it was set back from the road.

His approach being obscured, he wondered whether he might

benefit from catching his quarry unawares. Sarah had spoken of her suspicion that Mary had been in the house when last they visited. She thought she had seen someone at the window, and there had been a delay in Martha answering the door: long enough for Mary to instruct her sister to conceal that she was home.

The question this posed, however, was how Mary would have known to be evasive of two strangers. Then Raven remembered that she had seen him, albeit briefly, at the Porteous house. It was therefore possible that she had spied him from the window, and though she could not extrapolate from that the reason he was there, she had not evaded discovery for this long by being careless and taking chances.

The front door was opened without delay on this occasion. Martha Dempster looked at him a moment, as if trying to place from where she knew him.

'Dr Raven?'

Perhaps it was merely in contrast to Iain McKinnon's understandably dour demeanour, but he thought she seemed pleased to see him.

'Miss Dempster. Sorry to trouble you again, but I wondered whether on this occasion your sister might be home?'

'No,' she answered, Raven reading her countenance in vain for any hint that this might not be true. 'But do come in out of the cold,' she added.

She ushered him into a small drawing room at the front of the house, the door of which had been closed last time. Raven wondered what had been behind it on that occasion. The room looked expensively furnished, though many of the fixtures seemed overly grand and out of scale for the room. He had previously assumed that this had been the Dempster family's home but now thought that he had been mistaken. The furniture must have belonged to her parents and been brought here from another house after they died.

'Can I offer you some tea?' she asked.

As long as your sister isn't preparing it, Raven thought. How vulnerable we all were when we placed our trust in others, how exposed when others harboured evil intent. How much more so in the case of a nurse, when they were entrusted to administer medicines.

'That would be most welcome,' he answered.

He was thirsty, and, after his long walk through the fog, in need of something warming. But another reason he readily accepted was that it would keep Martha busy in the kitchen while he took a look around. This time he was determined to be mindful of evidence that Mary was in fact present: two used teacups, for instance, or two place settings at the table.

As soon as Martha left the room, Raven put his hands upon the two chairs by the fire to test whether they might both be warm from having been recently occupied. Only one was but that did not surprise him. He suspected he would find no such clues today, as Martha seemed altogether less anxious. If Sarah's notion was correct, then on this occasion her sister truly was not at home.

Nonetheless, he crept out into the hall on light feet and gently pushed open the door opposite leading into the room where Sarah thought she had spied movement at the window. It was a spacious and brightly decorated bedchamber, its sturdy double bed seeming likely to have belonged to the late Mr and Mrs Dempster. The bed was neatly made, and thus there was no way to determine whether it had or had not been slept in the previous night. He lifted the counterpane. The sheets were tucked under the mattress with military precision and he recognised the handiwork of someone trained at the Royal Infirmary.

There was a plain gown laid out on the bed, a clean apron placed on top of it. The gown was dark blue with white braiding on the cuffs. He thought it similar to the one he had seen Mary wearing at the Porteous house, though he could not be certain as he had seen her only briefly on that occasion.

There was a row of books upon the window ledge. Raven's

eye was caught by the spine of one that he thought might be a copy of Christison's *Treatise on Poisons*, though he could not read the lettering clearly from where he stood. He was about to step closer when he heard a voice at his back.

'What are you doing in Mary's bedroom?'

Raven jumped.

'My sincere apologies, Miss Dempster. I was in search of the water closet.'

He noted that she seemed almost as alarmed at her discovery as Raven had felt at being discovered. He thought of Sarah's contention that she was afraid of her sister and could barely believe he had failed to see it before.

She directed him to the privy, a small, dimly lit closet at the back of the house. As he relieved himself, he thought again about the bright and spacious bedroom he had just seen: at the front of the house, south-facing and enjoying a view had it not been fog-bound. Although it was Martha who had inherited money from her parents, it appeared Mary had the master bedroom. He considered what that implied with regard to who held the whip-hand in the house.

When he returned to the drawing room, Martha had already brought in a handsome tea service on a tray and was beginning to pour.

'Have you spoken to Mary since last I visited?' he asked.

'Yes. She did come back, albeit briefly. She came to retrieve clean clothes and left again within the day. I gave her your card, though I assume from your visit that she has not made a point of speaking with you.'

As she said this, Raven realised that leaving the card had been a mistake. Once again, his judgment had been skewed by chasing the wrong cause. Martha would have told Mary that her visitors were investigating the deaths of three of her most recent patients. As a result, she most certainly wasn't going to get in touch. More likely she had run to ground.

'I have not had contact with her, no.'

'And how goes your quest to identify this new affliction? Are there further sufferers?'

'Four more, I believe.'

'I was worried for Mary after we spoke, though I was not sure what to be looking for. She seemed well enough, physically, though she was irritable. She was far from forthcoming when I asked about the symptoms exhibited by her recently deceased patients.'

Raven got the impression this had been a fraught exchange. It also confirmed that Mary knew what he and Sarah were looking into.

'I stressed that there was no implication that her competence or methods were being questioned, but she seemed angry none-theless.'

'Did she happen to mention the name of the family she is working for now?'

Martha's expression became meek, the look of one not enjoying being made to revisit a memory.

'I did enquire, but she scolded me for asking too many ques-tions. "What business is it of anyone but mine who I work for?" she said. She was . . .' Martha shook her head. 'Mary can be rather short-tempered and aloof, but this was different. You said that this new illness made the sufferers delirious. Would that include being so defensive and suspicious towards the honest enquiries of her own stepsister?'

'No, no, I am sure she is quite well,' Raven assured her, though everything Martha said confirmed that there was something far wrong with Mary Dempster: just not the affliction that had claimed her victims.

'How is your relationship with Mary generally, if you don't mind my asking?'

Martha composed her face into a smile, but in the moment before, he witnessed a glimmer of concern. It was as Sarah had observed: a fear of what she was permitted to say. However, as

Martha warmed to the subject, it was clear that she remembered she did not need to fear being overheard.

'We have our ups and downs, like all family I'm sure; blood relations or not. Sometimes we are like the oldest of friends, and other times I am grateful she has gone to live with her patients. Doubtless she is grateful to get away from me too. She once struck out on her own for a time after we had a falling out. She stayed in some squalid place, all she could afford. I convinced her to come back, but only by apologising. I can't even remember what for, but it only mattered that it was me who admitted I was wrong. Mary never apologises. Mary is never wrong. I think it is because she had such a harsh childhood that she finds it hard to concede ground.'

'Am I right in saying that this was not the house where you grew up?'

'No. We lived at Canonmills: a much finer house than this. My father worked for the bank.'

'Do you have other brothers and sisters?'

'No. I was alone until my mother adopted Mary.'

Raven wondered at this way of putting it: that it was her mother who adopted Mary, not the family.

'That must have been a disruption and a difficult adjustment, for all of you.'

Martha paused, considering her answer.

'Like Mary, my mother was a strong-willed woman, and not to be defied. She saw it as her role to civilise Mary. To break her in, like one might do a horse. And it should be said, the instrument was the same.'

Raven had to conceal his reaction. The whip-hand indeed.

'My mother succeeded, to some extent. She even changed the way Mary expressed herself, forbade her to speak as though she was from Glasgow. As you remarked the last time we spoke, she reverted and does so with all the greater pride now.

'At the time I accepted much of this. I was oblivious and, I will admit, somewhat spoiled. I realise how hard it must have been for Mary, as I was the focus of so much more attention. It was my mother's primary purpose in life to ensure that I married well, while Mary was shown no such consideration. She had already embarked upon a career as a nurse by the time I became engaged.'

Raven failed to mask his surprise.

'You were married?' he asked.

'No. My husband-to-be died before we could be wed. His name was Colin, Colin Flett.'

She seemed to savour the sound of his name, a wistful look upon her face.

'He was in shipping, a client of my father's at the bank. Though you'd have thought it was my mother who was marrying him, so overjoyed was she at all her ambitions, schemes and stratagems coming to fruition. But her hopes were dashed. Colin became ill on a visit to the house, on a Sunday afternoon just like this one. He was dead by the morning.'

She looked away with an expression of equanimity that must have taken many years to attain. Raven could not disrupt that by explicitly voicing his suspicions, but nonetheless, he needed to know.

'Did Mary nurse him?'

She smiled. 'Of course. That is my great consolation: that he was cared for by someone who knew all that he meant.'

Raven finished his tea in the growing silence, Martha lost in her recollection.

He put the cup down, the sound enough to bring her back to the present.

'Martha, how did your parents die, if it is not intrusive to ask?'

'Not at all. After all, you are far from the first doctor I have encountered. My father passed away first. He became ill very suddenly. He had seemed in the peak of health, but as I had witnessed with Colin, disease can strike down anyone at any time.

Poor Mary allowed herself no rest, tending to him every hour she was not working at the hospital, but it did no good. Our doctor did not know what ailed him. Nobody was able to help him.

'My mother was devastated. He was her sun and her moon. More than that: being his wife was what gave her purpose and status. She was such a proud woman, fiercely outspoken, so haughty in how she carried herself, and yet she was so diminished after that. She became poorly and took to her bed, never to leave it again. After that, though we were stepsisters, Mary and I were the closest people each other had. The *only* people each other had.'

Raven had to suppress his reaction, for there it was, a mirror of events he had already heard about this very day: a cruel and spiteful matriarch who died last, only after seeing the people she loved pass away beneath her own roof and her family's future annihilated. Long before working for the cantankerous Mrs Eddlestone, there had been Mary's stepmother. Mary had killed her daughter's betrothed, and with him her dreams, then killed the husband she adored, before killing her last.

But as he looked at Martha, calmly contemplating her painful past, he asked himself why Mary had spared her. Would she not have wished to inflict that bereavement upon Mrs Dempster too: the death of her only child?

Clearly there had to be some kind of bond between them: something that still endured, despite the fallings out and the fear Martha evidently felt towards her stepsister. Or perhaps Mary needed her somehow: if she had spared Martha for a purpose, it might prove crucial if he could work out what that purpose was.

Raven got to his feet.

'Miss Dempster, thank you for your time and your hospitality, but I must get back to Queen Street. Before I go, I would like to stress that it is imperative I speak to your sister, and soon.'

From her face he could tell she had inferred much from the seriousness of his tone.

'Do you fear for her, Doctor? Are you quite sure my sister is not in danger from this ailment?'

Raven had to think carefully about how much he could say without putting her in danger. Mary had spared Martha thus far, but that did not guarantee the latter's safety if Mary felt her sister had betrayed her or become a threat. Equally, he did not wish Mary to know just how much he and Sarah had uncovered. He had already alerted her to their investigation by leaving his card.

'Do you truly have no notion where she is, or is it perhaps that you do not wish to say?'

She looked worried, as Sarah had observed: uncertain of what she was permitted to reveal.

'She left in a hurry. She told me little.'

Little wasn't nothing.

'If you hear from her, or you learn where I might find her, please do not delay in contacting me.'

Martha put a hand on his arm.

'What are you not telling me, Dr Raven?'

He looked her in the eye, trying to gauge what might be hidden behind her fearful face. He could see how she was torn between loyalty to Mary and troubling doubts about what her sister might be keeping from her.

'I could ask you the same question.'

She withdrew the hand, folding her arms about herself.

'I do not know what you mean,' she replied.

'When first we visited, my associate Mrs Banks thought you seemed afraid of your sister.'

Martha looked meekly at floor.

'I am not,' she said, her voice quieter.

Raven stepped through the front door then turned to face her one last time.

'You should be.'

FIFTY-FIVE

aven walked through the open door into Dr Simpson's study, where he had been summoned. The professor had just returned from a trip to London and Jarvis was remonstrating with him about various items missing from his luggage.

'Several woollen vests have disappeared: lost or misplaced, presumably,' the butler was saying as Raven entered the room.

'They're not lost,' Simpson countered, as if this should be obvious. 'I've got them all on.' He turned to Raven. 'Train carriages are ferociously cold this time of year.'

Jarvis left the room muttering and shaking his head.

'He's in a mood because I leave again tomorrow,' Simpson said as the door closed. 'He's concerned that I am travelling too often, tiring myself out.'

Raven thought that Jarvis was probably right. The professor did not seem to rest. His burgeoning practice seemed to keep him busy at all hours of the day and night despite Raven's employment as his assistant. There were so many things that he insisted on doing himself.

As soon as they were alone, Simpson brandished a letter, waving it in front of Raven.

'Do you know what this is, Dr Raven?'

The use of his formal title made Raven wary. He had evidently done something to provoke Simpson's ire: not unheard of, but far from a common occurrence. Raven was not afraid of him, not like he had been of his father, but he disliked disappointing the man. His disapproval could be crushing.

'Perhaps it is a trick question, but it looks very much like a letter to me,' Raven answered.

Dr Simpson did not smile in response. Another bad sign.

'It is a letter from Dr Johnstone, whose wife died under my care some time ago.'

'What does it say?'

'I think that you know.'

'I would hope that he has written in support of you, to vindicate your professional character, to defend you against the egregious comments that have been made by your colleagues.'

'That is a remarkably accurate assessment of what this letter contains. Dr Johnstone delivered it himself, apologising for the delay in supplying it, hoping that it would prove to be enough to put a definitive end to the matter. He told me he had been encouraged to write it after a visit from my assistant.'

From his tone Raven reasoned that gratitude was not about to be forthcoming.

'Did you visit Dr Johnstone?' the professor asked.

'Yes, I did.'

Raven was relieved that Sarah's name had not been mentioned.

'I thought I had asked you to leave this matter alone. That I would deal with it in my own way.'

'With all due respect, Dr Simpson, your own way was proving to be ineffectual.'

'How I chose to address the issue was up to me. It is my professional reputation that is at stake.'

'And unjustly so. I couldn't bear to see their slanderous accusations go unchallenged.'

'So you disregarded my wishes. I did not want a grieving man dragged into this regrettable affair.'

'Even if that was precisely what was required to clear your name?'

Dr Simpson sighed. 'Much as I appreciate the sentiment that spurred you into action, I cannot condone what you have done. You have interfered when I asked you not to. You have added to a grieving man's burden.'

Raven could find nothing more to say in his own defence. If this was his offence, he was guilty of it.

'Do not always assume that you know best,' Dr Simpson said, more gently now. 'An over-inflated sense of your own capabilities will lead you to trouble. Guard against complacency, Dr Raven. Or there will be hell to pay.'

FIFTY-SIX

aven could feel the sweat cooling on his skin as he reluctantly shed his coat. The room was surprisingly cold for somewhere so small, particularly a chamber in which an expectant young mother had laboured so long. She was in her first confinement, its extended duration causing a neighbour sufficient worry that she had sent out for help.

As Assistant Medical Officer to the Maternity Hospital, the majority of deliveries Raven attended were 'outdoor' patients: assistance provided by the hospital, but the patients delivered in their own homes. Often these outdoor cases could prove challenging, even when obstetrically straightforward, given the lack of heat and poor lighting in the crowded dwellings to be found here in the Old Town. Raven often wondered whether he should start carrying coal and paraffin in his bag in addition to his forceps.

The effort of his ascent to the fifth floor of the West Port tenement had warmed him, but it would not last against the coldness of the room. As he climbed, he thought of how often he had heard Dr Simpson stating cheerily, 'It's always the top.' Raven wondered about the truth of this, reasoning that it seemed that way because only the occasions that affirmed it brought the notion to mind. Those cases on the lower floors did not, so their plenitude was forgotten. He wondered again at his folly in pursuing his imagined new disease.

Louis XIV of France said that only the small man desires always to be right. It struck Raven that the route to discovery and knowledge lay not in the desire to be right, but in one's preparedness to be wrong. Perhaps seeking proof that tested one's contention was as important as garnering proof to support it. Only if the latter outweighed the former could one be certain of its soundness.

Raven cast an eye over the suffering woman before him. Alone, with no one to support her in her time of trial but her neighbour.

'Her husband died six months ago, poor thing,' the neighbour told him. 'He caught a fever. A decent man.'

His thoughts turned to Sarah. She would not be left to labour alone, not with him and Dr Simpson keeping an eye on her, but she too was faced with raising her child without its father.

Archie had asked for his help in that matter, an easier request than the other intercession he sought. Of course, Raven would gladly assist, but what he offered would not be – could never be – the help of a husband, the help of the child's true father. He wondered, in fact, how much assistance he would be permitted to give: how close Sarah would allow him to be, to her or her child.

Raven looked in his bag for the chloroform bottle and couldn't find it. The prospect of attempting a delivery like this without it was not in any way appealing. He recalled giving a bottle to Archie and panicked briefly, but his fingers grasped what they sought just as he remembered where he had got that one. He thought then of Quinton, that supercilious cadaver of a man, but perhaps he was wrong about him too.

There was something to be said for bringing order to Dr Simpson's chaos. Perhaps simple book-keeping might yet cast an unexpected light upon his practice. He wondered what knowledge might be found were he to look back at a definitive tally of how much of each medicine they went through over the course of a week, a month or a year; what patterns and tendencies might reveal themselves.

Raven administered the chloroform to the woman with practised ease and made a preliminary examination. He had become so accustomed to this work that he felt a sudden alarm when he couldn't fathom what he was feeling. It was something boggy and swollen, and after poking about for a bit he realised that the presenting part was not the head but the breech. It was not usually so difficult to make a distinction between the two, but the mother's pelvis was too narrow to allow the breech to descend into it and as a result it had become impacted and grossly swollen.

He glanced up at the exhausted and sweat-soaked young woman, rendered oblivious for now by the chloroform. For all she had gone through, he felt it unlikely that she would be presented with a living child when she came around.

With a considerable amount of manoeuvring, he managed to pull down the legs and then the arms but significant force was required to deliver the after-coming head. Under other circumstances Raven would have been concerned about the resultant compression of the skull, but he was in no doubt that the death of the infant had preceded all of his efforts.

As anticipated, the infant was well beyond any attempt at resuscitation when finally delivered, but with a bit of luck (and the fact that he had washed his hands) the mother may yet survive her ordeal. He would have to be content with that.

As he lay the infant upon the bed, the neighbour knelt down beside it, said a short prayer then got to her feet and made for the fireplace.

'Flora put some coins aside in case she needed the doctor,' she said.

Raven told her to leave the money where it was.

'She'll want to hold the bairn,' the neighbour said.

'Of course.'

There was still some warmth in the infant's tiny body. He wrapped it in a blanket and held it to his chest, hoping it would not be entirely cold by the time the mother woke.

As he cradled the dead child, something in him changed.

There were so many children he had delivered into poverty, a new burden to those who already had nothing, and yet it was a burden that they ached to bear.

A burden *he* ached to bear.

What might a child who was raised by someone as special as Sarah be like, imbued with the values and perspective she would give?

He felt a pang of angst and regret, initially thinking it was on behalf of Archie, who would not get to witness these things, but then realising it came from his own heart. The role Archie had offered him would not be enough. He wanted it to be his child that was raised by Sarah. Raised *with* Sarah.

Then, to his surprise, he realised he did not care that the child was the fruit of another man's loins. After all, there had been times when he took solace in the possibility that his mother had secretly lain with someone other than his father: that he had not inherited the man's brutish and destructive nature. (Unfortunately, all subsequent evidence pointed to her fidelity.)

He had made one terrible mistake with Sarah, and it had cost him dear, but perhaps there was redemption to be had yet. Archie had shown him the error of his judgment, of his cowardice. Archie's offspring would therefore be a permanent reminder of what truly mattered in this life. Raven would be proud to raise that child as his own.

FIFTY-SEVEN

t was raining when he came back out onto the street, and there was a bite in the wind. Raven pulled his coat tighter about him, grateful for its heft and warmth. He had many vivid memories of being on these same Old Town streets when he could not afford such a garment. He had felt particularly cold and vulnerable during his days at George Heriot's school, scurrying between buildings to minimise his exposure. As a student at the university, though he had been no better clothed, there had been many nights when a skinful of ale at least made him heedless of the weather. He had never been heedless of *all* the elements, however, for on these streets there lurked more brutal things to assail you than wind and rain.

When he was a child, he used to look forward to being a man, because he believed that when such a time came, he would no longer feel so much fear. Now he understood that to be a man was to feel fear and to proceed nonetheless. As Sarah had told him and Archie had shown him, he would rob himself of the life he ought to live if he let fear restrain him. That obtained whether it be fear of violence from men such as Flint and Gargantua, or fear of disdain from men such as James Matthews Duncan and Professor Miller.

Such fortitude was easier preached than practised, for he felt the hand of caution upon him as he observed that he was approaching Lady Lawson Wynd and recognised the alley where Flint had his business premises. A tingle in his scar was telling him to take a different route, in wariness of figures who continued to loom large in his mind. He realised that it was purely a reflexive response, for he was on good terms with the money-lender for now. He had even less to fear from the man he now forced himself to think of as Alec, yet his pulse still quickened at the thought of his sneering face and his grotty knife. This was the true nature of what people called ghosts: being haunted by a presence when there was nothing physical left to fear.

In defiance of this, Raven made himself walk down that lane, but his courage faltered as he heard a creak ahead indicating that Flint's door was opening. He pressed himself tight to the wall, heart thumping as he waited to see who would appear. He half expected to see Alec emerge, with his wrecked mouth and rodent-like features. But it was not he who came through the door, nor Gargantua or Flint himself.

Flattened against the brickwork, it took Raven a moment to recognise who he was looking at, confused by the sheer incongruity. It was like finding a face he knew in Bosch's *Garden of Earthly Delights*: familiar but jarringly out of place and unexpected in this underworld realm. He watched Quinton walk out into the street and swiftly on his way. There was something furtive in his stride, as though trying to give the impression he was merely passing and had never been inside that building.

Many things slotted into place, but Raven had learned not to draw conclusions from limited evidence.

He waited for Quinton to disappear from sight then rattled at the door. It was answered by another of Flint's henchmen, the squat one who looked like a toad.

'I want to speak to your boss.'

'He's not to be disturbed just now,' Toad replied curtly. 'Come back another time.'

'I'm here now. So why don't you go and ask if he'll indulge an interruption to discuss the correct use of chloroform?'

Toad shut the door in his face, but Raven knew he would relay his remark, and that Flint would infer its significance. He returned forthwith and showed him in.

Flint was standing next to his desk, a strongbox sitting on the floor beneath it. Raven made a point of staring at it. Flint glanced down too, perhaps checking that the lid was closed. He didn't want Raven seeing what was inside.

There was a pistol on the desk, a far more modern piece than the one he had faced in Berlin. That Flint definitely wanted him to see.

'Dr Raven. Always a pleasure. To what do I owe this unannounced visit?'

He spoke flatly but Raven detected a wariness.

'Yes, apologies for the unheralded nature of my call. Normally I prefer to be conveyed to you against my will, but I happened to be passing and I saw Mr James Quinton leaving here with the look of a man not keen that anyone should know his business. I am curious as to the nature of your relationship with him.'

'That's what we respectable men of business refer to as confidential,' Flint stated with barely contained aggression, a warning to back off. 'A matter between me and him.'

Raven did not flinch from his gaze.

'I might suggest it was a matter between you, him and some stolen stock certificates.'

Flint reached for the pistol, but before he had it cocked, Raven had his knife resting on the money-lender's throat.

Their eyes were locked upon each other, Raven pressing gently with the blade, Flint's weapon an inch from Raven's belly.

'This pistol has a Forsyth percussion lock,' Flint stated. 'It uses fulminate of mercury instead of priming powder. So there is no delay between my pulling this trigger and the charge firing. You saw what a lesser weapon did to poor Alec.'

'And this is a Liston knife. The man could take a leg off through the thighbone with such a blade in twenty-eight seconds. Imagine what it would do to the soft flesh of your throat should my wrist twitch in response to you pulling that trigger.'

Flint pointed the gun away. He backed off a step, putting the pistol back down on the desk.

Raven lowered the knife, though he kept it in his hand.

He knew there could be no winning such a stand-off. The same applied to the discussion he wished to have. With a man such as Flint, you had to make him believe he had the upper hand, or you would remain in stalemate.

'We had an agreement. I honoured my side of the bargain in supplying you with chloroform. I am asking you to reciprocate by supplying information. What is Quinton doing for you?'

Flint laughed. 'Primarily he is doing precisely what he does for your Dr Simpson. He is keeping my books.'

'And what else?'

Flint glanced at the strongbox. They both understood that Raven wouldn't be asking this question if he didn't already know the answer. This wasn't the part he was most interested in.

'His skills as a calligrapher and his knowledge of the stock market are also proving useful.'

'Why did he need to borrow money from the likes of you?'

Flint gave an amused shrug. 'I never ask,' he said. 'But I always collect. And sometimes I take payment in kind, as you well know. Services rendered.'

'How much is his debt?'

'I can't see how that is any business of yours. Now, be on your way. If I need you, I know where to find you.'

Raven took a step closer to him.

'I am no longer some student or apprentice. I have a certain status and I have connections of my own in this city. I might be inclined to inform James McLevy that I recently treated a man for a gunshot wound. That would rid me of you for good, wouldn't it, Mr Flint?'

This gave him pause, but like a practised brawler Flint did not reel from the blow for long. He nodded, calculating.

'Dr Raven, just so you understand, if you were to tell McLevy who you treated, I would have to tell him where I got the chloroform. And that's not the worst thing I could talk about, is it?'

Flint's mouth curled into a cold smile.

'It is true you delivered my wife, and for that I remain grateful. Admiring, even. You delivered Alec too, one could say. You were unable to save him, though it was a mercy what you did for him in the end. What they call a mercy killing: but a killing nonetheless.

'I have witnesses to what you did. Witnesses who will say what I tell them to. You might claim it was an attempt to ease his pain, but they will argue that you went further than that and it was not your place to hasten his end. They might contest that his end was so assured. Some might even call it murder.'

Flint ran a finger along Raven's scar.

'After all, this was a man you bore a grudge, the proof of which any judge can see etched upon your face. If you stop prying into matters that don't concern you I am sure neither of us will have reason to make good on our threats.'

FIFTY-EIGHT

arah watched as Raven and Jarvis hefted Archie's brass-studded leather trunk into the house.

'What does he have in this thing, ship's ballast?' Raven complained as they manoeuvred the trunk down the hallway. Sarah followed them inside and closed the door, thinking as she did so about the first time she had ever crossed this threshold. No. 52 Queen Street had been an intimidating prospect then and she remembered feeling scared and alone.

Little wonder. She had been sixteen years old and had just lost both of her parents. She had no experience of domestic service and was unsure what her new life would be like. She knew how to cook, to clean, to sew, this last skill being forced upon her at school when she would have preferred to continue with mathematics and Latin. She was sure that a lifetime of performing domestic chores would serve her well, but there were other aspects of her new situation which concerned her. She had heard the rumours of course; about hard labour and cruel treatment at the hands of unscrupulous employers.

She was unafraid of physical work – having grown up on a farm she was well used to it – but harsh punishments were unfamiliar to her. She had never been beaten as a child and had no desire to experience such a thing now. Having lost her family, she felt that she had surely suffered enough already.

She need not have been afraid. What she found here was kindness and inspiration. A household, as it turned out, full of remarkable possibilities, and through which remarkable people passed. Doctors, of course, but also writers, artists, politicians. She had been exposed to worlds that, until then, she had not known existed.

She watched as Raven negotiated a bend in the stairs, taking care not to make contact with the walls, as though he was carrying Archie himself and not just the sick man's luggage.

She remembered when she had first seen Will Raven, when he had first moved in. What a terrible first impression he had made. She had expected a gentleman, similar in style and manner to the apprentice he was to replace. He had turned up on the doorstep inexcusably late, in stained clothes, reeking of alcohol and with evidence of a recent altercation etched indelibly upon his face. It was obvious that he was a man apart, unlike the others who had gone before. This made her wary of him. Understandably so. And yet they had become friends. More than friends.

Circumstances had thrown them together. She had thought that their attachment would continue, saw no reason why it should not, but Raven had seen things differently. She had been abandoned. She could think about it in no other way and it had been a source of pain to her for some time. She would be shy of any such connection in the future. Or so she had thought until Archie arrived.

In contrast to Raven, Archie was the epitome of respectability. A good man from a good family. Yet this façade disguised a radical heart. His egalitarian views put the liberal sensibilities of Dr Simpson in the shade. Sarah found his company intoxicating and even from an early stage he seemed to encourage her interest. Dr Simpson had prescribed fresh air and exercise as part of the treatment for Archie's ailment and he often invited Sarah to join him in his perambulations around Edinburgh.

She remembered the day they had climbed to the top of Calton Hill, the view along Princes Street, and of course of the Bridewell and Calton Jail. He took her to the tearoom at Nelson's Monument and paid the fee so that they could climb to the top of the tower. Afterwards they sat outside on a stone bench and talked about their plans for the future. She had been cold, and he had put his arms around her. He had suggested to her that perhaps they could face the future together. He had kissed her then, which had sealed their collective fate.

She was aware even then that a barrier had been crossed. She was mindful that many would have viewed this as a seduction and that she had been foolish to go along with it. She knew of the dangers facing housemaids who had relations with those above stairs, clandestine trysts behind closed doors. But their relationship was no secret; it had been conducted in the open, and thus was potentially more damaging to Archie than to herself. As a result, she had been convinced that his intentions were good. There was no subterfuge or coercion. There was no deception. Theirs was a union of equals. There was no shame in what they had done.

Things moved rapidly from that point on. It was never acknowledged but seemed mutually understood: they did not have time to waste.

She vividly remembered her joy at leaving this house not so long ago, to be married and live with her husband in the home that they had made together on Albany Street. How happy she had been to find herself not yet twenty and mistress of her own house. Her happiness was only tempered by the knowledge that it would not last.

Archie soon followed his luggage and was helped up the stairs to his new quarters, Raven providing a shoulder for him to lean on. Sarah could not help but smile at the sight of it. She had not thought to see these two men become so close.

Archie stumbled at the top, but Raven grabbed him before he could fall, strong arms encircling Archie's emaciated frame.

'I thought I told you to lay off the brandy at breakfast,' Raven said.

Archie laughed, but then began coughing, and their progress was halted for a few minutes until it subsided. He had become so frail, a hollowed-out husk bearing little resemblance to the man that she had first seen here not so many months ago. The rapidity of his decline was terrifying to behold, the disease consuming him voraciously and without pity, merciless in its ferocity.

'I am sorry to be putting you through this,' Archie said to her once they had managed to get him into bed. Raven had left them, sensing that they needed to be alone.

'I would not have had it any other way,' she replied. 'These have been the best days of my life, times I never thought I would have – marriage to a doctor, in charge of my own household. Mistress of my own domain.'

Archie looked at her with a sad smile.

'I know there is a question that troubles you,' he said. 'But you are too kind to ask it.'

'I don't know what you mean,' she said. But she did.

'You wonder whether love would have been allowed to blossom between us had we met under different circumstances. Would I have asked you to marry me had I not been ill? I know this, because I am equally troubled by the question of whether you would have accepted my proposal had I been well.'

'How could I have refused?' she replied, laughing, but Archie remained serious. She sighed, sitting down on the bed beside him. 'I suppose neither of us can answer that question, for the truth is we can never know.'

'I was very nearly married to another,' Archie said.

Sarah had never considered this before and realised that she should have done. Archie was handsome and successful: it was unusual that he had not married before now.

'What happened?' she asked, curious but also afraid of what he might say.

'For various reasons we had a long engagement. Too long, as it turned out. Her affections were transferred to another. She claimed that she had never really loved me. I felt that I had been subject to an unforgivable deception. I was deeply hurt by it. It felt like a physical wound that would never heal and I did not think that I would ever let myself love another as I had no desire to experience that kind of hurt again. But then I met you.'

Sarah wondered at the events upon which fate could turn. How different might things have been if Will Raven had returned from his travels a few months earlier than he did. Or was she deceiving herself to think he would ever have rushed back from abroad into her waiting arms?

'I did not allow myself to become close to anyone after I lost her,' Archie said. 'It was only when I feared life might be short that I let myself be open to love once again. That is why there cannot be a definitive answer, for if I had met you before I became ill, I would doubtless have suppressed any feelings that might have developed.'

They sat in silence for a while, Sarah thinking that there was nothing more to be said.

'Perhaps what you really want to know is whether I would have done things differently from Raven.'

Sarah was shocked by his insight, as though he knew what she had been thinking.

'He spoke to me of this,' Archie continued. 'It made me ask myself, as you too are presumably wondering, would I have acted in defiance of the judgment of my peers in order to be with you? At such a fledgling stage of my career? All I know of the difference between Raven and me is that I was not tested in that way. In my case the disapproval of my peers was no threat.

'If you find him wanting because of this . . . I would say,

do not judge a man by his mistakes, but whether he learns from them.'

Sarah left him to sleep, troubled by their conversation. She decided she would go home for a while as she needed time alone, time to think.

She had offered to move to Queen Street with Archie, but he would not hear of it. He wanted her to have some respite from his illness. He wanted her to remember him in a better condition, how he was in happier days. He was trying to make it easier to adjust; it would be a separation in stages.

'I do not know how long I have left,' he said. 'But I know that you have to prepare for the future. That future will be at Albany Street, should you choose to stay on there. You ought to get used to being there without me.'

As she was preparing to leave, he had made a rather unexpected request.

'I would like you to consider reverting to your own name, when I am gone,' he said.

'Why would I do that?'

'There was never any requirement for you to change it in the first place. I have no jurisdiction over you, nor did I ever wish to have. You do not belong to me. I want you to be your own person.'

FIFTY-NINE

aven watched Sarah as she descended the stairs to the hallway and reached for her coat. He could tell she was trying not to cry. He wanted to give her privacy and was about to walk away, but she called to him.

'What news of our elusive nurse?' she asked. 'Have you located her?'

'She returned briefly to the cottage at Lochend,' he said, 'but her current whereabouts remain unknown.'

'Do you still entertain any doubt that she killed those people?'

'None,' he replied. 'In fact, I believe that she might also have killed her stepmother, her stepfather and her sister's fiancé.'

Sarah's face, already pale, blanched further.

'What makes you think that?'

'They all died quickly, unexpectedly, while under the same roof as Mary. The stepmother, who Mary detested, died last. A perfect precursor of what happened at Trinity.'

'You suspect her motive to be what? Vengeance?'

'She was treated cruelly by her stepmother. She killed those the stepmother loved, and then the woman herself.'

'But why would she then go on to kill her patients? What motive would she have for that? And why did she spare Martha?'

Raven admitted he'd been asking himself the same question.

'I think that you were right when you suggested Martha was afraid of her sister, but there is undoubtedly a bond between them. I suspect Martha is useful to Mary in some way, but I cannot fathom precisely how.'

'I do not think that bond would survive were Martha to learn that Mary had murdered three of the people she loved. Perhaps if we apprised her of our suspicions, she would be more forthcoming.'

'That occurred to me, but I did not feel it was the time to tell her. Nor did it seem likely she would be convinced.'

'Certainly not without better evidence,' Sarah said. 'The truth of it seems plain to us, but we remain without solid proof that Mary has poisoned anyone.' She began to button up her coat. 'And if we are to take our suspicions to the authorities, we need to build a case that would merit investigation. We need more than supposition and coincidence. People die all the time. How can we prove that she is killing them?'

Raven had been grappling with the same question. His proposed motive of vengeance would not explain all the deaths that had come to their notice, and he had no idea what method she was using to achieve her nefarious ends. She had presumably killed Stuart Eddlestone with morphine, but that did not match the symptoms of her other victims.

'We might never know how many have died at her hands,' Raven said, giving voice to nothing more constructive than his vexation. He paused for a moment, his brow creased in thought. 'What *do* we know for sure?'

'We know that people die in numbers when Mary is around, and the death of Dr Fowler's leeches is suggestive of mischief,' Sarah replied. 'According to Christison, there have been reports of leeches dying when they were applied in cases of poisoning with oxalic acid and opium.'

'But our cases do not fit with either.'

'We need to find out what she is giving them.'

'And how do we do that?' Raven's voice had grown louder in his frustration. Sarah put a finger to her lips. This was not a conversation that either of them wished to be overheard.

'It is unfortunate that there have been no post-mortem examinations carried out,' Sarah observed. Raven wondered if this was a veiled criticism of himself: he had not pushed for one in the Porteous case, though convincing Dr Fowler of its necessity would have been difficult.

'Even if there had been post-mortems, they might not have shown anything,' he replied. 'In order to detect poison in a corpse, we need to know what poison to look for.' Back to that again. They seemed to be going around in circles.

'We should speak to Dr Fowler again,' Sarah suggested. 'Find out who Mary has worked for in the past and what happened to them. If he was Mrs Eddlestone's physician, perhaps he can shed some light on what happened at Trinity: what the cause of death was in each case and whether he prescribed the morphine Mary was seen disposing of.'

'I would be wary of giving too much credence to his answers,' Raven warned. 'But even though she was caught disposing of it at the Trinity house, I doubt that morphine was her modus operandi. It does not match the other patients' symptoms, and its effects would be too obvious, even to an old fool like Fowler. I think that our Nurse Dempster is far more cunning than that.'

Sarah's face suddenly contorted. She bent over and grasped at her side.

'Sarah, what is it? Are you unwell?'

She took a couple of deep breaths and straightened up again.

'It's nothing. Just a twinge.'

'Has this happened before?'

She looked at him. Paused for just a little too long.

'Once before,' she admitted.

'I should examine you,' Raven said.

'There is no need.'

'How far along are you?'

She gaped at him in surprise, which he hoped did not betray a lack of confidence in his abilities as an obstetrician. She looked as if she were about to deny it but seemed to change her mind.

'I haven't bled for two months now. There is no need to worry about me, though. I am quite well.'

Raven hoped that this was the case but resolved to look again at the obstetric textbooks he had been studying in the wake of the Glassford case.

'At least come and sit for a moment,' he said, leading her to his consulting room.

He sat her in a chair and closed the door.

'I am wary of Quinton seeing us together again. He seems to miss nothing that goes on under this roof. He has even taken to monitoring our use of medical supplies. Counts out drops of chloroform as if they were gold coins.'

'He is not so all-knowing,' Sarah stated emphatically. 'He has yet to find his thief.'

'I think that he has been busy with other things,' Raven replied.

He sat down in a chair beside her.

'Are you planning on moving in here with Archie?'

'No. He wants me to stay at Albany Street. He says I need to rest, and I know that he is right, but I feel guilty.'

'Why?'

'Because it is a relief to get away. It's so hard to watch him suffer.'

Raven felt a twinge in his own guts as she said this. Now that Archie was here, he would be able to press Raven about his request.

He noticed that Sarah had begun to weep and offered her his handkerchief.

'I have been trying not to cry when I am with Archie,' she

said, 'but I feel that I can cry in front of you.' She leaned towards him, but Raven drew back. She looked surprised and then hurt.

'It doesn't feel right with Archie here, under the same roof,' he said by way of explanation.

'Is it more unseemly to be seen comforting another man's wife or to be seen in a dalliance with a housemaid?'

Raven sighed. She was never going to forgive him for leaving her, was she? For not doing what Archie had done.

'The world of medicine is not forgiving,' he said. 'It is a snake pit. You have seen that. There are people who would use any weapon they can to do down their rivals.'

'Why don't you just admit it?' she said. 'You did not love me enough to suffer the disapproval of men such as James Matthews Duncan, men you do not even respect.'

'There is more to it than that,' Raven replied, looking down at his clasped hands. 'There is a part of my nature that I fear, and I have battled to tame it. Simpson always tells his students: "Let your own professional character be the one great patron to whom you look for professional advancement." I have been trying to cultivate a professional character that invites trust and respect.'

'And you needed to leave me in order to do that?'

'I thought that I did.'

'You fear you have the devil in you,' she said. 'You told me that once. The truth is, Will Raven, I admired you *because* of your devilment. But now I can see you are afraid to be yourself.' She sighed as if weary. 'All men have the devil in them to some extent. The ones I distrust are the ones who would deny it.'

SIXTY

arah felt a twinge in her side again as she waited at Dr Fowler's door. It passed as it had on previous occasions, but she wondered if she should have let Raven take a look at her after all.

There was no reply to her repeated knocking. He must be out on visits, she thought, and wondered if it was worth waiting to see if he returned. Perhaps she should have delayed her visit until Raven could accompany her – he had been detained by a patient – but she had felt in need of air and was gravely concerned about the unsuspecting soul that might currently be under Mary Dempster's care. She felt a spit of rain and decided she would return later rather than risk standing outside in a downpour. The walk home would be exhausting if her skirts and petticoats became too wet.

She had turned to walk away when she saw Dr Fowler approach, striding hurriedly along Barony Street.

'Dr Fowler, I wonder if I might speak with you, if you have a moment?'

'Mrs Banks, isn't it? You were here with Dr Raven, Simpson's assistant.'

'That's right.'

'Do come in.'

He opened the door and led her inside. She was struck once again by the peculiar nature of his home. The rooms she glimpsed as she passed them were a strange mix of the spartan and the cluttered. Piles of books, ill-sorted collections of objects. It was a self-curated museum of a strange and solitary man's life. She wondered where he kept his leeches, the new ones he had presumably recruited to his service. She had to suppress a smile as her mind conjured up an image of their much-mourned predecessors beneath a row of tiny headstones in the garden.

He showed her into the small parlour at the back of the house where they had spoken before.

'You work for Dr Simpson too, if I recall?'

'Yes. I do.'

'You are a nurse?'

Sarah answered in the affirmative. It seemed easier that way.

'You were here asking about a nurse, weren't you? Mary Dempster.'

'Yes,' Sarah said.

He seemed alert, sharper than she remembered. Not quite as doddering as the first impression she had garnered of the man.

'Did you find her?'

'We have been trying to do so but have yet to track her down. The address we found in the Post Office directory was that of her sister. Mary lives there too, but she has not been at home.'

'She is working, I presume.'

'Yes, but her sister couldn't tell us where. I was wondering if you could tell me who she has worked for recently, who you have recommended her to? Perhaps she is back working with one of them now.'

'That is certainly possible. When it comes to care of the sick, reputation is everything. People want someone they know and trust.'

He went over to a table in the corner and spent a few moments locating a blank piece of paper. He noted down some names and addresses, the scratching of his pen the only sound in the room. On the edge of the table Sarah noticed the manuscript she had seen on her previous visit.

'There have been others, no doubt,' Dr Fowler said as he handed the scrap of paper to her, 'but these are the ones that come most readily to mind.'

'Thank you,' she said. She pointed to the manuscript. 'I see you have been turning your hand to prose. Are you writing a novel?'

Dr Fowler grabbed the pile of paper and held it to his chest, clutching it to himself as though afraid she might try to take it from him.

'Have you been looking at this? How much have you read?' he said, suddenly hostile.

Sarah hurriedly apologised. 'I didn't mean to pry. I merely caught a glimpse of it the last time I was here.'

Dr Fowler looked sheepish, as though aware that he had over-reacted.

'What a poor host I am,' he said, conspicuously changing the subject. 'Do forgive me. I must get you some refreshment.'

Without waiting for a reply, he bustled out of the room, taking his manuscript with him, and returned with a glass of cordial which he insisted that she drink. Sarah took a tentative sip.

'I would drink it all if I was you,' he said. 'You will be grateful for it later if you intend to visit all the houses on that list. Uninvited guests are seldom offered tea. This is Edinburgh, after all.'

She did not understand this last remark: she was never done serving tea at No. 52, whether guests had been specifically invited or not.

Dr Fowler seemed to sense her confusion and smiled.

'That was a little joke,' he said. 'Though one born of a weary doctor's experience making house calls in this city. I am from Glasgow originally. Hospitality is a little more forthcoming there.'

He seemed to be more amenable now that his manuscript had been safely stowed somewhere. Perhaps he is starved of company, she thought. She saw this as an opportunity to ask more about Mary Dempster, but she knew she would have to tread carefully. She dared not share her suspicions with this man who had recommended the nurse to so many patients.

'I believe Mary Dempster is from Glasgow,' she said.

'I deduced as much from her accent. She told me a little about her upbringing, the tremendous obstacles that she has had to overcome. She and her sister were orphans. Her sister ended up in the asylum after becoming a prostitute, which is a testament to how it might have gone for poor Mary had she not been adopted. It is most impressive, I think, her choice of occupation, her compassion for others.'

'And yet being a nurse exposes her to further suffering, and to death. So many of our patients die, and so many of Mary's patients have died recently. How does she cope, I wonder, when she has had to endure so much herself?'

Sarah had hoped to provoke some acknowledgement or comment about all the recent deaths, some of which Dr Fowler had been involved with himself. But he did not respond in the way she had hoped.

Rather, he seemed energised.

'It is something one learns to come to terms with. Sometimes the best you can do for your patient is to give them a good death. It can be a great blessing. It is often said that it is a privilege to be present at a birth, but I believe that the same could be said about a death. In both cases we bear witness to the moment when an individual passes from one realm to the next. At that precise instant we are closer to God than we will ever be until we die ourselves.'

Sarah felt a little disturbed by this pronouncement and decided it was time to leave. There was something distinctly odd about this man, and she could not bring herself to ask any further questions. He was unlikely to discuss the details of the patients he had attended with her anyway. She would leave that to Raven. She downed what remained of the cordial by way of indicating that her visit was at an end.

'Thank you for your time,' she said as she made for the door.

'Until we meet again,' Dr Fowler replied, following in her wake.

Sarah rather hoped that they wouldn't.

SIXTY-ONE

arah was finally on her way home to Albany Street when she began to feel weak. She was now, as he had predicted, grateful for the drink Dr Fowler had given her. She had walked further and for longer than she intended, trying to visit as many of the addresses on Dr Fowler's list as possible.

She had spoken to people in two households who had employed Mary Dempster and had visited three others where nobody had been home. By the last of these, she had resolved to follow Raven's example and have calling cards printed.

She wondered what she would put on them. Should she be Mrs Sarah Banks or Sarah Fisher? A part of her thought it would be disloyal or ungrateful to reject Archie's surname after he had done so much for her. And yet, it is what he wanted, and therefore the truly disrespectful thing would be to refuse his wishes. She knew that it hadn't always been this way: a wife taking her husband's name. Not in Scotland anyway. Perhaps it was time to revisit the old ways of doing things.

She was making her way back up from Stockbridge, where she had spoken to a Mrs Haldane, who told her how Mary Dempster had nursed her sister back to health after a bout of enteric fever. Sarah had concocted a story about trying to find the nurse to give her a gift bequeathed by a recently departed relative, in gratitude for services rendered. Mrs Haldane was effusive in her praise of Mary, hardly supporting their theory that she was in fact a ruthless killer.

Before that, however, she had spoken to a Mrs Guthrie, who was the cook in a house where Mary had also been employed. The lady of the house, Mrs Bennet, was from home and in her absence, Mrs Guthrie told Sarah how Mrs Bennet's 'illness' was in fact a result of her late husband being quick with his fists. She had recovered under Mary's care, but her husband had fallen ill and died shortly afterwards.

Mrs Guthrie's description of his deterioration was familiar. A sudden illness to which he quickly succumbed. Delirium, coma and death in rapid succession. This brought her back to the unresolved issue of how this might have been achieved without arousing suspicion. Why kill some patients and not others, and why risk killing so many in one family, as in the Trinity case? The questions continued to mount up and they seemed to be no closer to answering any of them.

As she ascended the slope of Dublin Street, around the corner from her house, she passed a grocer's shop which had a variety of vegetables displayed in the window. She stopped to look, giving herself a moment to catch her breath.

She thought about Mrs Lyndsay's cooking and hoped that Archie would be tempted to eat a little of it. A forlorn hope perhaps. It was unlikely that he would have the strength to sit through meals with the rest of the family.

She thought too of Mrs Lyndsay's resistance to change, her adherence to the established order of things. Like her recipes, she understood what worked and feared altering any of the components. She seemed to think that the whole of society worked that way too.

There was a pile of potatoes in the middle of the window display. Sarah was reminded of the garden at Lochend and the plant that she could not identify. The plant that was still flowering so late in the season. The plant that Martha had said was potatoes. She had accepted Martha's suggestion but now she realised that Martha had been wrong. The plant was not potatoes, though it did look similar, because it was from the same family.

It was deadly nightshade. *Atropa belladonna*. Atropine.

She saw now why they could not identify the poison Mary was using from the symptoms being exhibited. It was because she was using more than one.

Raven had said she was too cunning to use morphine or opium as the signs would be obvious: pinpoint pupils a clear indicator. Atropine dilated the pupils. Each drug counteracted the signs of the other.

Other things began to slot into place, other symptoms and signs that could now be explained: the thirst that Nora complained of at the Infirmary; the delirium, the muscle twitching, the grasping at phantoms that had afflicted other patients. All effects of excessive amounts of atropine.

As she hurried home, she thought about what she had learned about Mary Dempster: her following the apothecary around the wards of the Infirmary, her willingness to learn and her disregard for the prescribed doses of the medicines she administered. She was not using a poison as such, but killing her patients with excessive amounts of prescribed medicines.

Rounding the corner onto Albany Street, Sarah felt suddenly light-headed but put it down to the excitement of her revelation. As she opened her front door, however, she began to feel her legs give way. Staggering into the hallway, spots began to form at the periphery of her vision, fading to blackness as she collapsed onto the floor.

SIXTY-TWO

t was starting to rain as Raven contemplated the impressive front door of Quinton's home on Castle Street, and he could not help but wonder what part a talent for forgery might have played in the book-keeper's affording such a handsome address. It was not envy that had motivated him to come here, though; rather, his concern for a man who had no idea how deep and treacherous were the waters he was wading into.

It was Mrs Quinton who opened the door, a baby in her arms. The child looked sleepy, blinking at the light from the street, though Raven could not discern whether it was in the throes of waking up or nodding off.

From what he could see of the hallway behind her, the interior promised to be as grand as Sarah had described it. Raven wondered whether Quinton was not so new to the worlds of fraud and criminal enterprise, in which case his warnings were like to fall on deaf ears. Nonetheless, he was bound to try, and he had a duty to all at Queen Street.

'This must be Rochester,' he said, offering Mrs Quinton a broad smile.

She did not reciprocate and seemed wary of his familiarity.

'Indeed. And you are?'

'Dr Raven, assistant to Dr Simpson. I need to speak to your husband.'

She glanced behind briefly, then back at Raven, anxiety in her expression. He could tell she was thinking about telling him Quinton was not present, but she knew she had given herself away. One does not look to check when one knows someone is from home.

'Now is not convenient,' she said instead.

'Believe me, the urgency of this matter trumps all convenience.'

Mrs Quinton did not formally invite him in, but rather stood meekly to the side so that he might step past her.

As he strode through the various downstairs rooms in search of Quinton, he was presented with part of the reason she was reluctant to admit him. The place was bare. It looked like it had been looted in a siege. Sarah had made mention of expensive fixtures and furniture, yet it appeared they hardly had a stick.

As Raven swept into the drawing room, James Quinton rose from where he had been squatting on the floor in front of the fireplace. He wore a look of indignation at the effrontery of Raven inviting himself inside, but Raven recognised it for a mask, as he had glimpsed Quinton's face before he donned it. It was the visage of a man caught naked: exposed, vulnerable and ashamed.

Mrs Quinton followed Raven into the room, Rochester beginning to cry in her arms.

'What are you doing here?' Quinton demanded of Raven, a share of his anger directed at his wife for admitting him.

'It is imperative that we speak regarding your employer.'

'And I will be at Queen Street in the morning. You have no business importuning me at my home.'

'Your other employer,' Raven clarified. 'Mr Flint.'

Quinton's haughty indignation was extinguished. He looked instantly wan.

The child's crying grew noisier.

'Leave us be,' he told his wife, his voice quiet but urgent.

'What is the matter?' she asked, her concerned tones barely audible over the growing volume of Rochester testing his little lungs.

'I said leave us in peace,' Quinton commanded, louder now.

Mrs Quinton looked back and forth between her husband and Raven, then departed, closing the door. Raven guessed she would have waited behind it to eavesdrop were it not made impossible by the child.

Raven looked around the empty room, conspicuously bereft of furniture.

'Are you preparing to host a dance?' he asked.

'What do you want?' Quinton replied tersely.

'There is no thief at Queen Street, is there? But there is one at Castle Street.'

Quinton swallowed, unable to mount a response.

'I gather you are having some financial difficulties. It would also be my deduction that you have borrowed some money from a mutual acquaintance.'

'I have no idea what you are talking about,' Quinton said, but his response lacked conviction. He looked cornered, as though afraid of where the next threat might be coming from. His secrets were known. The roof was falling in on him.

'I was lied to,' he said, veering from denial to explanation. 'I was offered the lease on this property by a friend. Or someone I believed to be a friend. Soon after arriving here we learned that everything had been purchased on credit, and the rent was in arrears. Unbeknown to us, in taking over the lease we had also assumed the debt, and all of it was gathering interest. We had creditors at the door almost immediately.'

'Why didn't you explain your situation to Dr Simpson? He could have helped.'

Even as he asked this, Raven cringed a little. He had been in the self-same position once, and had proceeded just as unwisely, but this was why he wanted to help.

'His new book-keeper, telling his new employer that he is in debt and has been duped after failing to do his due diligence?' Quinton asked. 'How would that have looked?'

'Better than the view from here now, I would wager. How on earth did a man like you end up crossing paths with Flint?'

'Am I to assume you are familiar with the fellow?'

'More than I would care to be.'

'I did not seek him. It happened the other way about.'

Raven's expression betrayed his confusion.

'Flint purchased my debt. It is one of the ways he operates. He approaches creditors and offers them a figure that is less than the sum owed, but more than they think they may ever get.'

'And he has a greater success than such creditors when it comes to motivating his debtors to pay,' Raven said. 'I know this from experience.'

'His men took our furniture. I feared what they might take next, but happily an opportunity arose.'

'For you to render services in lieu of payment.'

'My debt to him will be redeemed once I have helped him sell on some stock certificates. In fact, I am due to receive a share of the takings. I will make good on everything after that, I give my word.'

'That is not how it works with a man like Flint. That is why I came here. Once he has his hooks in you, there can be no escape. He tells me you are keeping his books too.'

'Only while I remain in his debt. Once the stocks are sold, I will have no need to deal with him.'

'You will always be in his debt: that is my point. He now has leverage over you. You are involved in fraud, forgery and theft.'

'I haven't stolen anything.'

Raven raised an eyebrow.

'To Flint's knowledge,' he clarified.

'You are complicit, though: forging the signature of the registrar of the exchange, on documents stolen in a robbery which saw guards assaulted and a man shot dead.'

This last detail seemed to drive home the depths he was sinking into. Quinton was a man used to dealing with gentlemen in fine tailoring trading numbers on paper.

'What would you have me do?'

'Not make the mistake I did when I first came to Queen Street, similarly in debt to Flint. I concealed my situation out of pride, and fear of making a poor impression. You must come clean and ask for help.'

'I have little faith we would get it. My wife pressed Mrs Simpson for more money for looking after Rochester, but she refused.'

'She did not know your circumstances. Dr Simpson and his wife are reasonable and compassionate people. If you are honest and contrite, I am sure this can be resolved. I would not see you trapped in Flint's clutches. But I will not permit you to persist in your deception, or in sowing suspicion about Dr Simpson's household, leading people to believe their colleagues might be dishonest.'

'I just need more time,' he pleaded.

'What you need is to tell the truth and confess to Dr Simpson that you are the one who has been taking money. It would be better coming from you, but if it does not, I will have no choice but to inform him myself. He is with a patient in Dunblane and will be back in two days. I will give you until then.'

The door was closed behind Raven with more force than he considered seemly. Perhaps once he had time to calm down, Quinton would appreciate that Raven had his best interests at heart, but for now he did not blame the man for feeling raw.

The rain had become heavier and the wind blustery. He bowed his head and pulled his coat about him as he strode down Castle Street. A carriage clattered past on his right, giving him a moment's concern. Every time one drew near, he was apt to recoil in case the Skeleton should turn out to be at the reins. This one continued on its way, leaving him unmolested, but once the noise of hooves began to fade, he became aware of being hailed with some urgency.

'Dr Raven? Dr Raven!'

He glanced up to see the plump figure of Martha Dempster hastening along Queen Street to intercept him at the junction. A gust of wind whipped up from the east, causing her instinctively to grab at her hat, strands of her fair hair escaping from beneath.

She produced his calling card as she approached, gripping it in her fingers and holding it up as though to establish her credentials.

'I was coming to the address on here in the hope of speaking to you. It is regarding my sister.'

'You have found her?' he asked eagerly.

'No. Quite the opposite. I am growing concerned that I have heard nothing from her.'

Raven eyed the calling card. These were not matters he wished anyone at No. 52 to overhear. He led her instead down the slope in the direction of Albany Street.

'We must get in out of the rain. Mrs Banks's home is nearer.'

It was his intended destination anyway as he had decided to keep a close eye on Sarah after witnessing her episode of pain. Something about it troubled him despite Sarah's insistence that all was well.

'I thought long after your last visit,' Martha said. 'About you saying I ought to be afraid of Mary. Though right now I am increasingly afraid *for* her.'

Raven knew she would not be bringing up his warning if it had not struck home. She had come to talk, but she would still need to be delicately coaxed.

'I cannot help Mary unless I am in possession of all knowledge that might be relevant, and that particularly includes matters you might consider unsavoury. In all truth, Martha, is there anything about your sister that has ever given you pause?'

Martha frowned, her head bowed against the rain.

'She could be coarse. That always set her at odds with my parents. Mother said she was wanton. I don't know about that, but she was certainly defiant. She seemed to court my mother's ire, which troubled me because I always endeavoured to avoid precisely that.'

As she said this, it struck Raven that Martha was the opposite of all he admired in Sarah. Though it was an uncharitable thought, he wondered if her late fiancé would have run a mile had he been presented instead with a woman who challenged everything.

'And over your whole lives together, is that the sum of it?' he asked, trying to keep the frustration from his voice.

Martha hugged herself and briefly bit her lip.

'Well, there is something. I've never said this to anyone, though. It seems disloyal. Shameful, in fact, even to have thought it.'

She shook her head and Raven feared she was about to clam up again.

'There is nothing disloyal about it if it helps us find her. Tell me, Martha.'

'All our animals kept dying. The dogs and the cats. Our pets. And God forgive me for thinking it, but I sometimes wondered if Mary had something to do with it.'

'Why?'

'Whenever Mary was punished by my mother – and by punished, I mean beaten – sometime later, one of the animals would die. Not immediately, but it would happen. I might be wrong, though, or misremembering. Pets die all the time, don't they?'

There was a look of uncertainty on her face. She had been wary of him but now she needed someone to trust, and perhaps the knowledge that someone trusted her. This would be the time to tell her what they had discovered, and what they suspected about Martha's own family. He had to get her in out of the rain, though: put her at ease in Sarah's parlour with a warm fire and a cup of tea. He could see her front door up ahead.

As they closed in on it, something wasn't right. He felt some instinct seize him as he noticed that the door was not closed. Hurrying towards it, he could see a pair of feet within the hall, the toes pointing upwards.

Sarah was laid out on the floor, unconscious.

SIXTY-THREE

arah was pale, drifting in and out of consciousness. Raven lifted her up and carried her through to the bedroom, where he placed her on the bed. Martha followed, looking blank-eyed at what had confronted them.

Raven loosened Sarah's clothing. Her face was blanched, her pulse rapid, her abdomen swollen. His worst fears had been realised. He had not a second to waste.

'Can you wait with her?' he asked Martha.

She nodded. 'Where are you going?'

Raven did not answer, already tearing off into the rain, bound for Queen Street as fast as he had ever run.

His recent reading about ovariotomy had reacquainted him with the current thinking regarding all ovarian and fallopian-tube pathologies. In response to Sarah's episode of pain he had scoured the books and journals searching for a possible explanation, hoping to exclude the one he had immediately thought of, seeking reassurance but finding only cause for concern. Since then his bag had been packed with everything that he might need should the worst happen.

Raven bolted inside No. 52 and fetched the bag from his consulting room. He was almost to the front door again when he recalled his recent moment of apprehension visiting one of the outdoor patients. He checked to ensure he had chloroform. There was indeed a bottle, but it was close to empty.

Raven ran to Dr Simpson's office and seized a replacement from the store cupboard. As he emerged with it gripped in his hand, he encountered Quinton coming up the stairs. Raven's look was enough to warn him not to even open his mouth.

'What is wrong with her?' Martha asked when he returned to Albany Street, her features expressing a combination of horror and fascination.

'I think she has an extra-uterine pregnancy,' he said. 'The foetus is growing in the fallopian tube instead of the uterus. Now the tube has ruptured, and she is bleeding.'

'What can be done?'

Raven wondered how to explain the complexities of the situation that they had found themselves in: that Sarah was bleeding into her abdomen, that what was happening was almost uniformly fatal, that although the pathology was relatively well understood, suggestions as to how such a catastrophe might be managed were few. One such was in a passage he had read just a few days before: 'Here is an accident which can happen to any wife in the most useful period of her life which good authorities have said can never be cured, but the bleeding vessel through which the stream of life is rushing away can be ligatured.'

The only problem was, to his knowledge, no one had ever done it.

From his discussions with Dr Simpson he knew that the concept of ovariotomy was contentious enough – some even suggesting that the opening of the abdomen to remove an ovarian cyst was tantamount to homicide – but this was more contentious still.

He had thought about summoning help. Another practitioner more experienced than he was. A surgeon. Another obstetrician. But he hesitated. They might not agree with his plan of action, might attempt to prevent him doing what he wanted to do, what he felt he must do in the circumstances.

He wondered what Dr Simpson would do in his place, but couldn't convince himself that he would agree with Raven's somewhat reckless plan of action. The opinions of other obstetricians were not encouraging either. Some of his reading on the subject was, in retrospect, more hindrance than help. Charles Meigs, the eminent American obstetrician, had discussed the management of tubal pregnancy as a hopeless endeavour: 'We could make an incision in the abdomen and clear away the coagula and serum. But who is bold enough to do so? Who is astute enough to discriminate betwixt all possible causes of such phenomena to warrant him in the performance of gastrotomy for fallopian pregnancy? There is no such wise and bold surgeon. Nothing remains but for us to extend all relief and calmly await and submit to the inevitable end.'

No such wise and bold surgeon? Not wise perhaps. But bold certainly. Especially if the alternative was to stand by and watch Sarah die. Calmly submit to the inevitable end? Such a thing was not possible.

'Martha, she is bleeding,' Raven said as calmly as he could, despite a sense of rising panic. 'The only way to save her is to open the abdomen and arrest the haemorrhage.'

Martha looked appalled by this suggestion. 'Are you sure?'

The question caused him to ask himself how certain he was about the diagnosis. He went through the symptoms and signs again. No menstruation for eight weeks, recurrent pain and then collapse. She was pale and cold, with a weak pulse. There was a considerable amount of effusion in the abdomen. However, there was no way of knowing for sure, no way to confirm it without actually going in. The only alternative would be to wait until she was dead and confirm his diagnosis at post-mortem, as had been the case in Paris, and that he was not prepared to do. Not again. It was always better to do something than nothing.

He had to act, and he must do so immediately if she was to have any chance of survival. The fallopian tube and its vessels would be secured and divided in much the same way as during an ovariotomy, as he had done when he removed the ovarian cyst from Mrs Glassford's abdomen post mortem. The operation itself should be relatively straightforward. The result, however, would be quite another matter.

'Yes. I'm sure,' he said, trying to speak with confidence and authority.

'Is there no other way to help her?'

'No. But I can't do this alone. I'm going to need your help.'

Martha hesitated for a few moments then nodded.

'Tell me what to do.'

'Go to the kitchen and fetch me hot water, a basin and some towels. I think I have everything else now.'

Martha left the room and Raven began to lay out the instruments that he would need: scalpel, clamp, ligatures, piles of lint, sponges and the chloroform. In Sarah's depleted state she would not require much of the latter. Her pulse, still rapid, felt a little stronger now that she was in bed, her feet elevated on pillows. She was groaning a little, not fully awake.

Martha returned with a large bowl of water and an empty basin. Raven added chloride of lime to the water, dropped his scalpel in and then washed his hands, almost scalding himself.

'Christ, Martha, I said hot, not boiling.'

Martha bit her lip but said nothing. She stood silently by the bed awaiting further instructions. Raven proceeded to give the chloroform. As he had expected, only a small amount was required. He rolled up Sarah's chemise and paused, quickly running through in his mind what he had to do. Most basically, get in there and stop the bleeding. But how different the theory was to the practice.

He took a few deep breaths, forcing himself to think of everything in an abstract way. It was a procedure, a process, a series of steps to be followed: incision from umbilicus to pubis, enter peritoneal cavity, pass ligature around broad ligament and divide it.

Even if he succeeded, he knew he would be criticised for this. It was unjustifiable in the eyes of the profession to perform hazardous experiments, for surely this is what he was about to do. Those who challenged established rules were always harshly dealt with. Only those whose professional stature had been recognised and rewarded could expect a fair hearing. Someone at his stage would be condemned out of hand. He thought of Dr Simpson, the scandal of the bloodstained mattress, the criticism he had endured over nothing but unsubstantiated gossip. This mattress was going to be a thousand times worse. But there was no time to think about such things. His reputation be damned. If he had to choose, then he chose Sarah.

Without further thought, he began. His mind cleared, his focus became preternaturally acute. He opened the abdomen, scooped out a huge amount of clot, filling the basin that Martha had brought him. The source of mischief was easily identified: an ovoid swelling in the left tube, ruptured and full of clot. He clamped and tied the broad ligament, arresting the haemorrhage just as the textbooks suggested it would, and removed the ruptured tube. He worked quickly, knowing that Sarah would be weakened by blood loss.

He washed out the remaining clots, bloody serum and debris and closed the abdomen using interrupted sutures. Martha helped him apply a bandage. It was done.

As soon as he was finished his hands began to shake uncontrollably. He sank to his knees, grasped Sarah's arm and felt for the pulse at her wrist. It was there: just palpable to his tremulous fingers. He kissed the back of her hand and then let his forehead rest upon it.

'Don't die, Sarah,' he whispered. 'Please don't die.'

SIXTY-FOUR

artha helped him change the sheets on the bed, Sarah groaning a little as they moved her. She had been busy around him as he worked, dealing with the worst of the mess. He thanked his good fortune that there had been a nurse in his company when this happened, though in one respect it would have been better if he had been alone.

'I would ask you not to discuss this with anyone,' he said. He wondered how he would explain himself if she asked why, but she did not.

'I may be less experienced than Mary,' she said, 'but I have worked as a nurse long enough to understand the need for discretion.'

Having thus reassured him, Martha asked if she could be spared. She was anxious to continue her search for her sister, though she vowed to come back later in the day.

Mrs Sullivan arrived shortly after Martha's departure. She had been out on errands when Sarah collapsed, an absence which Raven had initially been grateful for, given the necessarily clandestine nature of his intervention. Her return required Raven to provide some explanation for the alarming quantity of blood on the soiled sheets. Martha had performed a near miracle cleaning up, but there was only so much that she could do. He informed the housekeeper that Sarah had suffered a miscarriage.

'Some things are just not meant to be, are they?' Mrs Sullivan said, revealing a philosophical bent that Raven had not suspected she possessed. Then she added, less than charitably, 'It seems that I have traded one invalid for another.'

Raven stayed by Sarah's bed – ignoring Mrs Sullivan's suggestion that he go home – giving her small amounts of brandy and water when she could manage it. The fact that she roused sufficiently to take anything at all was reassuring but he knew there was likely worse to come. After what he had done, inflammation was inevitable and he knew that her survival was still very much in the balance.

Some hours later Raven felt a chill, and was suddenly aware of how cold the bedroom had become now that his sweat-soaked shirt was sticking to his skin. The fire had gone out at some point, he knew not when. It could have been hours ago.

He felt a gentle hand on his shoulder. Martha. He had not been aware of her return. Perhaps he had fallen asleep.

'There's someone here to see you, Dr Raven,' she said.

'Thank you, Martha.'

He got to his feet, aware that his hands were still shaking a little. They had remained steady when he needed them to, but it was as though a dam had broken and all the anxiety being held back was now slowly seeping through his system. Or perhaps it was merely the cold.

He stepped into the hallway, where he was surprised to find Jarvis standing before him. It seemed incongruous to see him anywhere but Queen Street, and looming in the gaslight he could almost have been a vision conjured by Raven's over-wrought mind. There was no question but that he was real, though, and he was looking even more austere than usual.

'I need to speak with Mrs Banks,' he said firmly, taking off his hat.

'She is indisposed.'

'It is a matter of some importance, Dr Raven.'

The fact that Jarvis addressed him this way made Raven wary.

'In truth, she has been taken ill. She is not fully conscious.'

Jarvis turned the hat in his hands, looking uncertain of himself. It was a sight Raven had never witnessed before.

'Perhaps it is best that it comes from you,' Jarvis said.

He cleared his throat.

'Dr Banks is dead.'

SIXTY-FIVE

rchie's was one of the more peaceful-looking bodies Raven had been confronted with. He was propped against his pillow, eyes closed, no evidence of writhing torment or the choking agonies Raven had feared might attend his passing. It would be important to convey this to Sarah. He could tell her Archie looked as though he had simply fallen asleep and never woken up. This was ostensibly true, but the actual nature of his death was more problematic, as indicated by the strong smell of chloroform pervading the room.

It was early morning. The sun had only just started to penetrate the mist as Raven and Jarvis strode briskly from Sarah's home to 52 Queen Street, and the warm scents of Mrs Lyndsay cooking breakfast had greeted them as they entered the house. It had struck Raven that in an hour or so he would be expected to see patients as usual at the morning clinic. The house and the city beyond it were preparing to get on with a normal day, indifferent and oblivious.

'I found him when I came in to ask if he felt strong enough to get up for breakfast,' said Jarvis.

Archie's right arm was extended, palm-up, a stock bottle of chloroform lying on its side a few inches from his fingertips. It had fallen from his grip, the stopper sitting in Archie's lap. Half of the volume had soaked into the sheets and the mattress.

'You had best let some air in here otherwise the pair of us will soon be on the floor,' Raven said.

Jarvis assented with a nod, drew back the curtains and slid open the window.

In the brighter light, Raven could see from Archie's pallor that he had been dead for hours. A wave of sadness passed through him as he reflected that he never really got to know the man, and now he would not have the opportunity.

Raven picked up the bottle and replaced the glass stopper.

'What was he doing with the chloroform?' asked Jarvis.

'He had been using it to help him sleep. I suspect that last night it had its effect quicker than he anticipated, before he could put the bottle back on the bedside table. It spilled and he was overwhelmed by it.'

He wanted to place this explanation firmly in Jarvis's mind. Raven did not want him, or anyone else, to guess what he truly suspected. One of the hardest things about what Archie had asked of him was the possibility that someone – but particularly Sarah – might deduce that he had deliberately ended his own life. She didn't want to see him suffer, and she was preparing herself for life without him, but no one is ever prepared when the loss becomes real and final. To think that Archie had denied them more time together might only add to the pain.

It occurred to him that she never got to say goodbye, but his greater concern was whether she would live long enough even to find out. He would have to break it to her that she had lost the unborn child too. The one consolation was that Archie had gone to his death without knowing that. But for the chloroform, it might have been Raven's painful task to inform Archie that Sarah had died, rather than the other way around.

Exhaustion was starting to hit Raven now, and with it the sense that everything was falling apart. Sarah had lost her baby,

THE ART OF DYING   *345*

lost her husband, and might yet lose her life. There was no new disease to make Raven's name, and the only fruit of his investigation might be that Simpson would dismiss him from his employ for going against his instructions. But he knew that he had to keep his wits about him, for there was still work to be done.

'We should attempt to conceal what happened,' he said, indicating the bottle. 'Change the sheets, air the mattress. It would be easier on Sarah . . . on Mrs Banks,' he corrected himself. 'Easier on everyone if they simply believed that Archie's time had come. He was, after all, very ill.'

Jarvis nodded solemnly, but as he did so, Raven noticed Quinton lurking outside the door. Looking, listening, taking note, as always.

Raven walked out of the bedroom and thrust the chloroform bottle into Quinton's hands. 'Here. Put this back in your stock cupboard,' he said bitterly. 'But before you do, perhaps you'd like to measure precisely how much is left in it, to keep your precious records straight.'

SIXTY-SIX

aven hurried back to Sarah's bedside as soon as the morning clinic was over, just as he had done the day before. Mrs Sullivan had been good enough to sit with her. He knew there was little she would be able to do other than rush to Queen Street to summon him if Sarah suddenly deteriorated, but he would not have been able to pull himself away to attend the clinic otherwise.

'There is little change,' Mrs Sullivan said when he arrived.

Raven wondered whether this was good news or not. He could hardly expect her to be up and about her usual business given what had happened to her. Little change was better than sudden sinking. He would settle for that.

Sarah was still deathly pale, but her pulse was lower than the day before and there was no sign of fever. The abdominal dressing was dry, which concerned him. He had expected some drainage from the wound and the absence of any effusion could mean that pus was collecting inside.

Raven had sent word to Dr Ziegler that he could not come to the Maternity Hospital that day. Ziegler was an understanding fellow, but Raven knew he would have to find someone to look after Sarah soon. Perhaps he could send her to Queen Street when she was well enough to be moved. That would not be for some time, though. If ever.

He was finding it difficult to be optimistic, concerned that any complacency on his part could lead to disaster. But he also knew that all he could do now was await events, hope that he had done the right thing and that Sarah would recover.

'I have made a pot of soup,' Mrs Sullivan told him. 'You should get something warm down you. You look nearly as bad as she does.'

As she said this, Raven tried to think when he had last eaten. After returning from Milton House yesterday, he had stayed at Sarah's bedside and woken in the night having once again fallen asleep in the chair. Mrs Sullivan had made a meal for him at some point in the evening, but it had lain there and gone cold while he slept.

He ladled himself a bowl of soup and carried it from the kitchen into the bedroom, eating it from his lap as he sat in that same chair. He did not wish to admit it to himself, but he preferred to stay here and watch Sarah breathing, in case these proved the last times he might do so.

He had wolfed down half of it when he heard the jingle of the doorbell. He put the bowl down and was on his way to answer when Martha Dempster appeared in the hall, having let herself in.

'How is she?' she asked, an anxious look upon her face as though she expected bad news.

'No worse. Some signs of improvement,' he said, although this sounded more hopeful than he felt.

Martha stood before him quietly for a moment, nodding. Then she spoke.

'Dr Raven, enquiring about Mrs Banks is not the whole of my business here. I have received word about my sister.'

Raven was jarred by how Mary Dempster had vanished from

his mind. It was as though he hadn't thought of her name in weeks rather than days. All he had thought about was Sarah, and it felt as though nothing else mattered. And yet if he didn't find Mary, he would never be able to prove to Simpson or anyone else what he and Sarah had discovered.

'She is staying in the place she ran off to once before, when we previously had a falling out. I received a letter from her. It was waiting for me yesterday when I returned home. She asks for me to visit her, which seems odd to me. Why would she not simply come home?'

'Where is this place?'

'Off the West Port. A building in Warnock's Close. In truth I am afraid to go there. It is a notorious part of the Old Town.'

Is there any other kind?, Raven thought.

SIXTY-SEVEN

he Lawnmarket was teeming as Raven crested the Mound, the throng spilling down onto Bank Street. It was a market day, stalls lining the street from the Esplanade to the Tron.

As he crossed towards George IV Bridge, Raven passed spatters of vomit and blood, interspersed with the mounds of horse dung that choked the gutter. Some people had evidently cracked open the ale casks early, or perhaps they had simply been drinking all night. He saw a fight break out or possibly resume, heard the crack of fist upon cartilage, saw blood spurting from a burst nose. Another staggering combatant was cradling a broken arm, his inebriation a greater impediment to his perambulation than his agonies. Drink was muffling the pain for now, but when it wore off he would likely be presenting himself at the Infirmary. Would that the vintners and tavern-owners spared a thought for the doctors whose task it was to fix the damage wrought by their customers, he mused.

Then he chided himself for this thought. How many times had he himself drunk deeply of their wares before ending up in a brawl? As many times as he had gone into a tavern in the express hope of starting one. Was this new perspective a sign of maturity or merely hypocrisy?

The brawl attracted the notice of a policeman on the other side of the throng. Raven watched him hurry to a colleague, one he recognised from being in McLevy's company when he came to Queen Street. The first was speaking animatedly and pointing Raven's way, then they both set off towards him, negotiating the bodies, stalls and barrows.

Their haste warned Raven that it might not have been the fight they were interested in. He didn't think Flint would have said anything, as it would only rain down greater trouble upon his own head, but it was possible someone else had told McLevy about Raven's visits to Fountainbridge after the robbery. There had been plenty of witnesses: the family decanted from their home to accommodate his patient, for instance.

He did not wish to wait and find out. He ducked out of sight behind a stall, keeping his head below the crowd as he ran towards a close off the Lawnmarket. He glanced back and confirmed that it was indeed him they were pursuing. Perhaps McLevy planned to prevail upon him to give up what he knew.

He stood tall so that they would see him enter the close, then ran down it at full pelt before skirting left when he emerged. He turned into a parallel alley and doubled back, describing a full loop before proceeding down the new West Approach Road.

Martha was correct that the West Port was an insalubrious part of the town, and no respectable lady would wish to venture into it alone. It wasn't particularly safe for a respectable gentleman either, but Raven wasn't sure he yet qualified. There were times when he was haunted by the vision, the fate that might await him down some gloomy alley, but also times when there was a dark want in him, a desire to *be* the thing good people feared when they ventured into such places.

He was familiar with Warnock's Close from his schooldays not so far from here. It was one of the places he knew to hurry past should his route take him this way. The passage was barely wide enough for two people to pass each other, the clogged channel in its centre wholly inadequate to draw the contents of soil buckets out to the street. The walls were buckled, the building on his right looking in danger of collapsing into the equally creaking tenement on the other side.

As he hastened towards the door Martha had specified, a figure emerged to block his path: a scrawny, malnourished and filth-caked specimen gripping a blade. It looked like a common table knife that had been sharpened to a point, its handle no more than a wad of rags. He held it up before Raven's face, a blast of alcohol accompanying his words.

'Give me what money you have, or you will feel my knife.'

Raven held out his hands in a gesture of surrender. The would-be thief eyed his right hand eagerly as Raven reached into his coat.

He produced the Liston blade.

'That wee skelf isn't a knife,' he said. '*This* is a knife.'

The cutpurse did not tarry to argue the point.

'Run along,' Raven muttered. He would likely encounter him again soon enough, or one of his colleagues would. It only remained to be seen whether it was in a hospital bed or in the mortuary.

He put the knife away but reckoned it might not be the last time he would have to defend himself before he left this neighbourhood.

Raven stepped into a stairwell on the right where the smell of urine was at least a change from faeces in the gutter. As he ascended, he heard retching behind one door, the sounds of congress behind another: male grunts and exaggerated yelps of female pleasure. He identified a professional performance, intended to hasten the conclusion.

The address he had been given was on the sixth floor. Simpson's words were a mockery in his head as the climb tested his thighs, but the sixth floor wasn't even the top of this ramshackle construction. It might have been once, as might the fifth or fourth, but more storeys had been added over the years, hence the buckling of the walls below.

He knocked on the appointed door, immediately hearing some movement in response to the thumps, but the source sounded lighter than a human on the move. It was not the tread of footsteps, but a sudden scuttling: birds perhaps, or cats. He thought again of the oddness of Mary's request, which had rightly unsettled Martha.

The door was locked but it was a rotten, ancient-looking thing. It took very little effort to force it, the wood crumbling away from the lock, which clattered to the floor.

The smell hit him as soon as he opened the door, but it was not the only thing to come rushing his way. The scuttling sound had been at least two dozen rats, initially disturbed by his thumping and now startled by the sight of his presence. They were scurrying to get away, but he was standing before the only exit. He had to kick and stamp as they flowed towards him, though not all of them were skittish in the face of human interruption.

A hardy few were proving themselves reluctant to give up their feast.

She was lying with her back to him before an overturned chair, from which she must have tumbled. She was wearing the same style of dress he had seen draped over her bed: dark blue with white braiding on the cuffs. Raven stepped around to the other side of the body, causing the last of the vermin to scatter. He did not recall much about her face from their brief encounter at Broughton Street, but that would have made no difference. The rats had nibbled away at the exposed areas first.

He looked around the sorry little room. There was a makeshift bed upon the floor, only a pile of straw and some filthy sheets. There was a gin bottle and two glasses next to it on the bare boards, alongside a plate and a knife. Barely a crumb remained of whatever she had been eating. The rats had seen to that too.

The room's only other piece of furniture was the table Mary had been sitting at when she fell. It had on it a pen, a bottle of ink and a pile of papers. Raven picked the first sheet up and read the heading:

MY TESTIMONY AND CONFESSION
MARY MACDONALD

He rifled through the leaves, too impatient to focus in depth, individual phrases and details catching his eye. A brutal childhood in Glasgow, abandoned to an orphanage, adoption by Mrs Dempster, further cruelties inflicted upon her there. But it was not merely a catalogue of how she was sinned against. It was a stated admission of her crimes. A confession indeed.

Raven turned hurriedly to the final page.

I am about to take my own life because I am afraid of what I have become, and afraid of who I will hurt next. When Martha told me people had been asking questions about the deaths of my patients, I was forced to confront how I would feel were she to discover what I am and all that I have done. I write this not in the hope that Martha will forgive me, or even understand, but because I have come to accept that she deserves to know the truth.

He flipped back through the sheaf and started reading more closely. The stench in his nose was telling him he should take the pages and resume reading somewhere else, but he was impatient to find out all he could. However, he had barely begun before he became aware of the echo of voices from in the stairwell, the hurried thump of feet upon wood. He looked up to see McLevy's man bound through the door. His colleague almost ran into the back of him as he stopped to take in the gruesome sight he had encountered.

'Dr Raven, I am John Soutar, police officer and assistant to Mr James McLevy.'

'I know who you are. It is as well you are here, as you can see, though you don't know the half of it.'

'Bind him, Tommy,' Soutar commanded the other man. 'And take care to bind him well. He is wanted for murder.'

Raven reeled, looking from Soutar to the corpse. He wondered for a moment whether Martha Dempster had somehow laid a trap for him but didn't see how that could be or how it might profit her.

'What are you talking about? This one's been dead for days. I just got here. She took her own life. She has even left a testimony explaining why.'

Soutar picked up a page and briefly glanced at it.

'We will investigate this in due course, but it is not why we're here. You are being apprehended on suspicion of the murder of Dr Archibald Banks.'

SIXTY-EIGHT

hey marched him down the High Street through the crowds, a man either side. Amidst the chaos of the crowd, there seemed ample opportunity to run and disappear, but aside from his hands being bound, where would he go? Best that he remained cooperative and acquiescent, then he could calmly and rationally explain why the accusation was false.

He just wished he had heeded Dr Simpson's advice in seeking to have McLevy owe him favours.

They passed Parliament Square, the police office coming up on the right-hand side. Raven noticed a policeman at the door gesture to Soutar with a shake of the head and a pointed finger.

They kept walking.

'Where are we going?' Raven asked. The police office had been a troubling enough prospect, but somewhere unknown was far worse. His fear was that he was being taken directly to Calton Jail, schoolboy tales of which had haunted his nightmares ever since.

'No room at the inn,' Soutar told him. 'All of the holding cells are full. It's been a busy old day. Often happens after a full moon. We are using the Night Asylum for the Houseless as an overspill.'

Raven was led past Gun Tavern and through a heavy door,

where he was greeted with a sight akin to that which greeted Heracles on his errand to retrieve Cerberus. Behind a gate barred from floor to ceiling there had to be at least forty men confined inside a single chamber. From the fact that the smell of alcohol was strong enough to be detected over those of sweat and urine, it was evident that most of them were drunk.

A few sat on benches lining the walls, but most were milling around, conversing, laughing, arguing. They could have been in the tavern next door except there was no more drink to be had, and they could not leave. He saw several lying on the floor, unconscious, but not all from the drink. Some were out cold in puddles of vomit, others in puddles of blood. Somewhere in the gloom he could hear a sonorous, stentorian snoring, like some terrible beast was asleep in the dark. He could not see where.

Tommy undid Raven's bonds while Soutar patted down his pockets, removing his Liston knife.

'Better we take this from you than one of them. It would not serve the ends of justice were you to be gutted before we have the chance to hang you.'

Raven was surprised he didn't take his money too. It seemed certain he would be relieved of it soon enough.

He was thrust through the gate by Soutar while Tommy pulled it shut again with a reverberating clang.

Raven turned to face his jailer.

'On whose authority am I being held?'

Soutar turned his back and walked away.

'On what evidence?' he shouted as the policemen headed for the exit. 'I demand to talk to McLevy.'

The door was opening as they approached it and he recognised the booming northern Irish accent before he saw the speaker.

'You don't get to make demands in here, Dr Raven.'

Raven gripped the bars as McLevy wandered over. 'There has to have been some kind of misunderstanding, Mr McLevy. I was not even present in the house when Dr Banks passed away.'

'You can prove you were somewhere else?'

'It is well known where I was. Jarvis the butler knew to come and find me at number 7 Albany Street. I was tending to Mrs Banks, who had become ill.'

'Tending to her?' McLevy said with a knowing leer. 'Yes, I am informed that you and Mrs Banks have become very close. I am also led to believe that Mrs Banks stands to inherit handsomely from her late husband. Furthermore, I am told that Dr Banks died from the over-inhalation of chloroform, an agent with which I believe you are particularly familiar.'

Raven saw it now.

'You've been talking to Quinton. The man is a thief and his testimony cannot be trusted.'

'My informant is a most respected and reliable individual. He tells me that not only were you indeed present at 52 Queen Street on the night that Dr Banks died, but that he saw you in an agitated and hurried state, impatient to lay hold of chloroform.'

'I required the chloroform for a procedure I was carrying out at Albany Street.'

'So you admit you just lied to me about being present.'

'I was there but a few minutes.'

'But a few minutes. And just how long would it have taken to render Dr Banks unconscious and then to pour the bottle over the sheets so that it appeared an accident? For Mr Quinton witnessed you the next morning discussing with Mr Jarvis how you wished to conceal the fact that chloroform had been responsible for Dr Banks's death.

'You have the reason, you had the wherewithal, and you had the opportunity, but even more than that, you sought to disguise what was wrought. There is no question that you will answer for this crime, Dr Raven. To me, the only doubt that remains is the extent to which Mrs Banks was party to this, and whether she is likely to hang too.'

SIXTY-NINE

aven slumped disconsolately to the floor, McLevy's words winding him as surely as a punch to the gut. He squatted against the bars, fortunate to have dropped in one of the few spots not spattered by something that used to be inside someone else. He was reeling not merely from the words themselves but from the malevolent glee with which McLevy had spoken them. He knew Raven's weak spot for sure.

What McLevy could not know was that they might not need the rope to finish Sarah, but certainly Raven could think of no greater horror than for her to survive only to be executed alongside him for a crime they did not commit.

He took some solace from knowing that someone capable was caring for her right now. To his shame, when Martha volunteered to stay with her while he went to Warnock's Close, it had crossed his mind that she was not as sought-after as her sister, and he had wondered if this reflected upon her abilities as a nurse. He could almost laugh. She was less sought-after than the sister who murdered her patients. Could there be a greater indictment of the value of reputation in this town?

Actually, yes. The word of a thief and forger could be beyond question because he had gone to Oxford and was ostensibly respectable. Quinton had sealed Raven's fate in order to protect himself and conceal the truth of his deeds from Simpson. And a man as caring as Simpson could be falsely accused of killing a patient, purely to satisfy the slighted honour of lesser men.

Raven now knew what had really happened to Mrs Johnstone, but Mary Dempster was dead, and he did not know what would become of her confession. Soutar could be using the pages as firelighters, for all he knew.

Still the snoring thundered from somewhere in the gloom. He wished for the same oblivion. Raven cradled his head in his hands, elbows on his thighs. He felt like all had been for naught. All was lost.

'When do we get something to drink in here?' someone shouted, though there did not appear to be a police officer present to answer.

'This piss pot is full,' a voice replied. 'You can drink that.'

As he heard this, it occurred to Raven how thirsty he was, and how long it had been since he last drank anything. This called to mind an image of the empty glasses and the gin bottle on the floor in Warnock's Close.

Two glasses.

His mind raced, suddenly alert. All in that room had not been as it appeared.

Raven began to reassess his memories of what he had seen, things that in his alarm and excitement might not have been apparent.

She had gone to the room to write her confession, and then to kill herself. In what vessel then had she brought the poison that she drank? Was it the gin bottle? If so, where was the bag or box in which she had brought it, along with the paper, the ink, the pen, the food, the glasses?

The *two* glasses.

Someone else had been in there and left again. Someone else had arranged the scene.

In chasing his new disease, Raven had seen only the evidence that suited him, only the evidence he had wanted to see. In that room, he had seen only the evidence *someone else* wanted him to see. It was a tableau, though not one intended to be presented to him, but to Martha.

Was it possible someone else sought to pin the blame for their deeds on Mary Dempster, leaving her poisoned body and her confession to be found by her sister? If so, how could the confession be in her words, her hand? Yet it had to be, he reasoned, for if it was not, Martha would have been able to tell instantly, and she was the one who had been summoned. So, if Mary had truly written her confession and killed herself, who had been in that room with her, sharing a bottle of gin?

He pictured the corpse, its face eaten away by rats, only her nurse's dress to identify her. Raven had once learned in the most painful manner not to make assumptions about who was inside a set of clothes.

He belatedly saw the truth of it. The other woman in that room had not been Mary Dempster's killer, but her latest victim: some prostitute of the West Port, lured there and poisoned, dressed in Mary's clothes and left alongside Mary's confession. A substitute left in her place so that Mary could abscond and those who had discovered her crimes would assume the author of them dead.

If that were so, he reasoned, she would have to move on, assume a new identity.

Then it dawned on him that she already had.

The Night Asylum fell silent, the noise of the other prisoners fading into the background until Raven was the only person in there, briefly alone with the most terrible discovery.

He knew the answer to the question of why Mary spared Martha.

She hadn't.

That nurse's dress: dark blue with braiding on the cuffs. He had seen it in Mary's bedroom at the cottage. Martha had been anxious when she found him looking in there, even though her sister was not home. Why, he had wondered, would Mary have the grand master bedroom, when it was Martha's inheritance that paid for them to stay there?

Because only one person lived in that house.

Martha's words echoed in his head: *It amused us down the years how often people would say we had a resemblance while they thought we were true sisters. Introduce an idea into someone's head and they will soon start to paint a picture around it.*

She knew Raven had seen her as Mary, albeit briefly, and had suggested a plausible explanation should he notice a similarity.

He was right: Martha had been useful to Mary. But only in death. After Mrs Dempster died, they had moved from Canonmills to Lochend: somewhere isolated, where nobody would know or recognise them. At some point after that, Mary had killed Martha, then assumed her identity; and with it not only her money, but the status and respectability her name conferred. But she separately retained the identity of Mary, having a professional reputation to trade upon: a means by which to gain access to patients.

She switched between accents and must have switched between appearances too. That was why Martha always seemed so insipid: she was a cypher, a mockery. That delay in answering the door, after Sarah spied someone in the window: she had seen unexpected visitors and needed a few moments to transform herself, then further time to ensure nothing was on display that shouldn't be.

Believing he was speaking to Martha, Raven had told Mary directly that she was under suspicion, and subsequently he had kept her informed of everything he had discovered about her. Then she had fed him evidence of her own guilt, intending to shed her compromised persona like a snake its skin.

Mary was Martha. Martha was Mary. And Raven had left Sarah with her, utterly defenceless.

SEVENTY

er memory was fractured. What used to be a path connecting moments had become a random series of discrete fragments. She remembered walking back from Stockbridge, the conversations she had that day jumbled and out of sequence. She remembered feeling weak, collapsing at her door. That was when what used to be linear had become splintered, the stained-glass windows of her mind shattered and transformed into a kaleidoscope.

She knew Raven had been there, but it felt like he was behind a gauze. Sometimes she was aware he was close by, but it was as though she could not break the surface to reach him. At other times, she felt his presence, but would open her eyes and find only Mrs Sullivan, or Martha.

She had heard him, but she was not always sure she had spoken in reply. She could not distinguish between words she had merely thought and what had issued from her mouth. Raven seldom answered her, merely told her to rest. Had she only dreamed her questions, or was there something he did not want to say?

She had been given chloroform, after that perhaps morphine, but she knew enough to understand that it was more likely infection that was addling her mind. She had felt the wound, touched the stitches. Raven had cut her open, and she knew why. She had been working for the Professor of Midwifery after all. That was how she knew she was dying. Raven had gone into her abdomen, an action of last resort. He had done whatever he could in order to save her, but she understood that it would not be enough.

Martha had been here too, off and on. She was here now, seated by the bed. Sarah had wondered why, until at one point the kaleidoscope turned and she remembered that Martha was a nurse. She felt grateful for her kindness, and from somewhere she summoned the strength to speak.

'I lost the child,' she said.

'It was in the wrong place,' Martha replied, matter-of-factly. 'In one of the tubes. Dr Raven had to act.'

'Does Archie know?' she asked.

Archie had been the blank in the frame, the missing fragment, his very absence like a presence in itself. Was he too weak to make the journey? Or were they keeping the news from him because he was so ill?

Martha wore a look of surprise, which Sarah could not read.

'Of course not,' she replied. 'Dr Banks is dead. He passed away the same night you fell ill.'

Though she lay on a bed, the bed she had shared with her husband, Sarah felt as though she had fallen from a great height, landing crumpled and broken on the ground. She had known it was inevitable, and yet as the truth of it enveloped her, she understood how little she had been prepared to accept it. The same was true of any fall: knowing the ground was rising to meet you did not lessen its impact.

In the agonising unknowing of the recent weeks, she had sometimes thought that when finally Archie died, she would feel a measure of relief. Instead, she belatedly discovered that uncertainty was so much better than resolution.

She wanted to see him again more than she had ever wanted anything, but not merely to say goodbye. She did not want one more day with him. She wanted a lifetime.

She wept, deeply. Though every shaking sob hurt where she was stitched, she wept. She wept for Archie. She wept for herself. She wept for the life together that they had lost and the life they would never have. The child they would not have.

Somewhere in the fog of grief, she found clarity in a question. Why was she only learning this now?

Part of the answer she knew instinctively: Raven was protecting her. He would not want her to know until she was strong enough, and if he feared she would not live, what would it profit her to learn such news on her own deathbed? But that being so, a more troubling question required an answer: why would Martha take it upon herself to break such news?

Then she saw the reason, through the mist of her tears.

Martha was intent upon her: not merely observing or even vigilant, but utterly rapt, so much so that she did not even appear to be aware that Sarah was looking back. Her face seemed transformed. She no longer wore the same benign, empty expression, as though apologising for herself. Instead there was a focus to her. An alacrity.

She was enjoying Sarah's grief.

SEVENTY-ONE

aven leapt to his feet and began banging on the bars.
'McLevy! Soutar!' he shouted. 'You need to act
– someone is in danger!'

'Aye, you if you don't pipe doon,' someone said.
Raven ignored him. 'McLevy! Soutar! This is urgent!'

A man on the floor to Raven's left looked up blearily from his
puddle of vomit.

'Haud your wheesht. There's folk trying to sleep in here.'

Raven became aware that the stentorian snoring had stopped.
He endured a moment's concern that he might have incurred the
wrath of whoever had been responsible for it, but it was far from
the greatest of his cares. He resumed his hammering and
shouting.

'Hey,' said another voice, to his right. He ignored that too.

'Hey! I'm *talking* to you.'

There was an aggression to the tone that his instinct told
him not to ignore. When Raven turned, he saw that he had
unwittingly attracted the wrong kind of attention. There before
him once again was the thief who had threatened him in Warnock's
Close. He had been apprehended too, perhaps having tried the
same thing with a policeman nearby.

'Aye. Me,' he said, acknowledging Raven's recognition. 'And I would wager that you don't have that fearful knife any more. But I wonder what remains in your pockets that you denied me before?'

Raven stood tall, bristling. For the second time that day, this cur had chosen the wrong time to cross him, for he was truly of a mind to beat a man with his fists.

'Why don't you come and take it from me then, you worthless wee skitter.'

His eyes locked on those of the thief, ready to read the signal that he was about to attack, whereupon Raven was felled by a blow from behind. Deliberately distracted by the man in front of him, an unseen confederate had caught him unawares from behind. There was a flash of light and pain as he took a blow to the back of the head, followed by a knee to the face as he fell. He was rolled onto his back and felt a heel to his ribs, then the thief was straddling him, rifling his pockets. He produced Raven's pocket watch, holding it up on its chain for a moment before slipping it into his trousers. Then he produced his grotty little knife.

Raven's eyes widened in horrified surprise.

'Aye,' the man said, raising it to strike. 'It's easier to hide a wee skelf.'

So this was it, then. Down an alley, or certainly off one. An asylum for the houseless, a place for vagrants, requisitioned for the police's overspill, making it the dregs of the dregs. Thrown in here as a murderer – and perhaps that was fair, for he was a murderer. He had killed three men, even if the last one had wished it so. He would die in disgrace, as he long feared he would. Also as he had long feared, it seemed a fitting end. But to crown it all, there would be no one to raise the alarm for Sarah.

Their eyes were locked again, Raven this time looking for the signal knowing he could not avert what followed. But before the thief could plunge his blade, a huge hand gripped his wrist.

'I would warn you not to deprive Dr Raven of his pocket watch,' spoke a deep, rumbling voice. 'It did not go well for the last fellow who did so.'

'What business is it of—'

The thief cut himself off as he turned and saw who was speaking to him.

Gargantua.

He dragged the thief off Raven and tossed the knife through the bars.

The one who had felled Raven from the back seemed undeterred. He looked a wiry and practised pugilist, adopting a fighting stance and demonstrating his fleetness of foot as he hopped back and forth.

'Let us discover whether size is a match for swiftness,' he said, a cocksure grin upon his chops.

The gathered throng discovered in roughly two seconds that size was more than a match for swiftness, particularly in such a confined space. Gargantua picked the man up and threw him like a rag doll. He did not get up to test his hypothesis a second time.

The giant's huge fist was then extended towards Raven on the floor, and when he opened it, it was to present the pocket watch. There felt something symbolic about his accepting it.

'Thank you,' he said.

'I owed you a debt,' the giant replied. 'You had reason only to hate Alec for what he did to you, and yet you showed him the greatest mercy.'

'Have you changed your mind about my profession?'

His voice was a low rumble, like the sound of a train heard beneath a bridge.

'Not about your profession, Dr Raven. Just about you.'

Gargantua beckoned him follow towards the back of the chamber, where a mere flaring of his nostrils was enough to disperse those who had taken the space he had vacated on the bench.

'It occurs to me that I do not know your name,' Raven ventured.

The giant looked deep into Raven's eyes, as though trying to read what he had chosen to call him, and for a moment Raven feared he was not going to be told.

'I am Gregor.'

'Will.'

Gregor nodded acknowledgement.

'I am sorry I woke you,' Raven said.

'On balance, I suspect that is not true. Don't worry yourself. It was time I roused. I thought sleep the best use of my time while I waited for McLevy to let me go.'

'Why would he let you go?'

Gregor let out a deep, booming laugh in response to the confused look on Raven's face.

'He has nothing to charge me with.'

'Then why are you here?'

'Half the men in here, and in the cells next door, McLevy has brought in because he thinks they might tell him something about the recent mail-coach robbery. Even if he suspects they know nothing about it, if he can make them think he is planning to charge them with it, they will be suddenly forthcoming on other matters in order to stay on the right side of him.'

It fleetingly crossed Raven's mind that he might inform McLevy of what he knew about the robbery, but it wouldn't count for much against a murder charge, and would most likely come at the cost of a death sentence from Flint.

'And are you planning to tell him something?' Raven asked, unable to mask his surprise at the notion he would betray his employer.

'I don't need to. McLevy is tenacious, he's wily and he knows how to play one man off against another, test their loyalties and probe for their weaknesses. But he's also clever enough to know his men made a mistake in even bringing me in. A robbery carried out by masked men? Put a mask on me and I'm still the most recognisable man in Edinburgh.'

Gregor laughed again, and Raven did too, despite himself.

'I only wish I had such a simple way of making McLevy see my innocence,' Raven said.

He told Gregor his situation. The giant listened intently, silently contemplating for a while after Raven had finished speaking. Then he nodded solemnly to himself, as though reaching some unspoken resolution.

'Dr Raven,' he said, 'there will come a time, perhaps not so long from now, when I must ask something of you.'

Raven met his gaze. 'I think I can guess what that might be.'

'Then I will endeavour to put myself in your good graces before that day should come.'

SEVENTY-TWO

hen Dr Raven had not returned by nightfall, I knew that providence was smiling upon me. I had feasted upon such exquisite anguish when I told her about her husband, but I had not thought I would be alone with her when Mrs Banks succumbed. It had been tantalising to know that her death was nearing and yet that I would most likely be sent from the house before it happened. If he had been detained elsewhere, then I had a precious opportunity.

Dr Raven had confessed the depth of his fears. He kept observing the wound, and told me that the paucity of pus concerned him. He would have expected far more. His deduction was that it had gathered somewhere inside her, from where there was no possibility of draining it. I knew from experience that, had infection taken hold, death would be a matter of course.

Earlier in the day, a policeman had come to the door enquiring as to Dr Raven's whereabouts. As the hours passed and still he did not reappear, I suspected something had befallen him, and I hoped it had not been before he discovered the confession that would liberate me. I had gone to great trouble and did not wish my efforts to be in vain.

I had long ago learned the importance of putting plans in place should I fear discovery, and how drastic such action might have to be. But what better way to deal with suspicion than to give the suspicious exactly what they were looking for? I would be sorry to lose my own name, but I had lost it once before, when I was taken into the Dempster household.

It was harder to give up all that came with my reputation. That said, I had already begun telling people Martha was a nurse too. I even had my first client, though I would not charge Dr Raven for my services. I did not intend for him to survive long enough to pay me. He had recognised my hand once, so I could not risk him doing so a second time, and I certainly had no intention of stopping. With him and Mrs Banks dead, I could indulge my appetites as freely as before.

Dr Raven would take his own life in despair at the loss of a woman he clearly loved. I would tell people that I believed he blamed himself for her death following the dangerous procedure he had carried out, against the wider wisdom of his peers.

And at a stroke I would be free of the only two people who had ever suspected me.

SEVENTY-THREE

aven felt a strangling helplessness as he watched darkness begin to fall through the small windows high on the wall on the other side of the bars. Sarah was out there in the night, at the mercy of a murderess who had wiped out whole families.

At least he no longer had to worry about his personal safety. As Gregor predicted, McLevy had called for him some time ago, and though Raven could not now draw upon his physical protection, no one dared molest him, for it was clear that he and the giant were in league.

He saw movement at the door and looked up, as he had done every time it opened, his automatic response an uncomfortable mixture of impatience and dread. At such time, it feels like the not knowing is the worst part, until certainty shows you otherwise.

Soutar approached the chamber and beckoned Raven forth, prompting him to spring to his feet.

'The fiscal is here,' he said. 'It's time for the charge against you to be made formal.'

The gate was opened and Raven stepped through.

'What then?' he asked, as his hands were bound once more.

'You will be taken to Calton Jail to await trial.'

Raven was led out of the asylum, down the alley and towards the police office. Up above, the sky was black with rain.

He was shoved roughly through a door, inside of which he found McLevy seated at a desk. He had a pen in one hand, the other resting upon a sheaf of hand-written documents. Next to him was a portly and bewhiskered gentleman in fine tailoring, reading over McLevy's shoulder.

McLevy looked up briefly then resumed writing. A long silence ensued. Raven interpreted its purpose as being to unsettle him, which seemed an unnecessary tactic. He thought of what Gregor had told him, and considered that McLevy was used to dealing with more hardened criminals.

Eventually McLevy stopped writing and looked up again.

'This is Mr Auberon Findlay, Procurator Fiscal,' he announced, with a gravity clearly intended to intimidate. 'Mr Findlay, this is William Raven.'

'Wilberforce Raven,' he corrected. 'Doctor.'

'Ah, yes, sorry,' said McLevy with a nasty twinkle. 'I forgot the significance of your profession with regard to the means by which Dr Banks was murdered.'

'There was no murder,' Raven countered.

'Silence,' McLevy commanded, holding up a palm. 'Save your words for the judge. There is nothing you need to say while the charge is being prepared. Mr Findlay has been apprised of all the relevant information.'

Then Raven heard a familiar and most welcome voice.

'I would contest that assertion most robustly, Mr McLevy.'

He turned around to see the front door being held open by Jarvis as the professor swept into the room in his hat and sealskin coat, water dripping off its tails.

'Dr Simpson,' Findlay said, his tone expressing surprise and, Raven was encouraged to note, an unmistakable degree of reverence. 'You have an interest in this matter?'

'I have just learned of Dr Raven's predicament and consider the accusation against him flawed to the point of absurdity.'

McLevy got to his feet.

'I understand your loyalty to your assistant, Dr Simpson, but I am acting upon information from a very reliable witness: a fellow of your acquaintance, in fact.'

'His witness is Quinton,' Raven said. 'The man has been stealing money from you, Dr Simpson. I discovered this and gave him an ultimatum to confess to you. Instead he went to McLevy, thinking if I ended up in jail, you would never be any the wiser.'

Simpson nodded sagely, as though this was no great revelation. 'Jarvis had guessed as much,' he said.

McLevy appeared unperturbed. 'That's as may be, but when I spoke to him earlier, Mr Jarvis himself corroborated certain details of Mr Quinton's testimony.'

'Indeed, and Jarvis told me all of this the moment I returned from Dunblane. However, Mr Jarvis and Dr Raven both withheld some important details in order to protect Dr Banks's honour. Dr Raven did so even when to reveal this might have assisted him in his plight. Bear that in mind when weighing his character and the credibility of his word against that of an employee who has been robbing me from under my own roof.'

Mr Findlay looked intrigued, McLevy wary, as though biding his time before he might pounce once again.

'Do elaborate,' said Findlay.

'Archie Banks was gravely ill. He had been suffering from carcinoma of the tongue and, as a medical man, he knew he was facing a painful and imminent death. Dr Raven suspected that Archie took his own life, to spare himself the worst. Dr Raven kept this conclusion from Mr McLevy for the same reason that he instructed Jarvis to dispose of the evidence of how Archie died: because he did not wish it to become a matter of public knowledge. He was concerned for the effect it would have on Dr Banks's widow, Sarah.'

Raven could have wept at the mention of her name from the lips of someone else who cared about her.

'To be clear,' said Findlay, 'you are saying you would concur with Dr Raven's conclusion that Dr Banks took his own life?'

Simpson paused a moment. The room fell perfectly still.

'No,' he said.

Raven gaped.

'Then who did kill him?' Findlay asked.

'I will show you. How is your circulation, Mr Findlay? Are your hands nice and warm?'

Findlay looked like he didn't understand the question, and certainly could be forgiven for not understanding the relevance of it, for neither did Raven.

Simpson signalled to Jarvis, who handed him his bag.

'This is a stock bottle of chloroform, filled to capacity, as was the one taken by Dr Banks from my store cupboard two nights ago. I know this for a documented fact, just as Mr Quinton knew it, because he wrote it down in his ledger. Hold it for me, please.'

Simpson placed the bottle in the palm of Findlay's hand, fixing his fingers around it.

'Typically, Archie would drop some chloroform onto a hand-kerchief and inhale it to aid sleep. Contrary to the nonsense you might have read in the newspapers, it would not immediately overwhelm him. He would put the stopper back on the bottle and then wait for the fumes to take effect. Normally he would place it on his bedside table, but he was very weak, and on this occasion it appears he fell asleep before he could do so. When Mr Jarvis found him, the bottle appeared to have rolled from his hand, minus its stopper, hence the fatal spillage.'

'Merely rolling on its side would not dislodge a glass stopper,' McLevy protested. 'I'll show you,' he added, moving towards Findlay, presumably intending to demonstrate the force necessary to dislodge it.

'Wait,' Simpson warned, stopping his hand before it could reach the bottle.

'For what?' McLevy asked.

Simpson merely held up a palm. The room fell silent, all eyes upon the vessel in Findlay's hand. They waited, Raven barely daring to breathe, the prospect of his freedom bound up in whatever might happen next.

Then the stopper dislodged itself from the neck with a pop and tumbled to the floor, landing with a piercing ring. Findlay dropped the bottle in his fright, Jarvis demonstrating remarkable reflexes in grabbing it before it could spill or even smash.

'The heat from Archie's hand caused the chloroform to expand,' said Simpson, 'and the build-up of volatile fumes forced the stopper from the bottle. His death was nobody's intention, but rather the result of an unfortunate accident.'

SEVENTY-FOUR

he hour was late when I chose my moment. The longer I waited, the less likely it seemed that Dr Raven would return that night; but equally, I knew that if I waited too long, she might die before I could take my chance.

It was one of the reasons I insisted on being resident with my patients. Night was when I was left as their sole carer, with nobody else awake. Where possible, I always ensured it was in the hours of darkness that they died.

You might assume this was in order to conceal my part in their deaths, with relatives waking to find their loved one had died in the night while they slept. In truth, that was barely the half of it, a mere practical consideration. The real reason was that I might taste the greatest conceivable pleasure.

On occasion, I have killed out of necessity, sometimes out of misadventure or curiosity, and sometimes out of vengeance. But mostly I have killed so that I might experience the voluptuous delight of holding someone as they die.

I recall hearing my mother's moans in that room in the Gorbals. Later in life, it comforted me to know that what I once thought was distress was in fact the throes of pleasure, but that pleasure could never compare to the delirious enjoyment I have known.

It is a commingling of the physical and spiritual, a transporting and transformative sensation. I wrap myself around them as I hear their breathing change, then there come waves of shuddering ecstasy, an exponentially compounding euphoria.

I hold them as I held Mrs Porteous, as I held Eleanor Eddlestone, as I held her mother, as I held so many before that.

And as I held Mrs Banks.

SEVENTY-FIVE

indlay gazed down at the stopper on the floor, then at Jarvis, then Simpson, then McLevy and finally Raven.

'On the basis of this evidence, there is clearly no charge to be brought here. Unless, that is, Dr Simpson wishes to take action against Mr Quinton over the thefts he has described.'

'No,' Simpson said. 'It is a matter I would rather deal with privately, and I would ask for the discretion of all parties here present.'

'As you wish,' said Findlay. 'Now, please have Dr Raven unbound.'

McLevy was clearly simmering. He looked like a dog that had just had a ham bone wrenched from its jaws and was thus an enemy in the making. Fortunately Raven felt able to pacify him by providing a juicier morsel to chew on.

'There *is* a murder charge to be brought. Several, in fact. Dr Simpson, my apologies again for going against your wishes with regard to the death of Mrs Johnstone, but were it not for the efforts of Sarah and myself in this regard, many more lives would surely be lost.'

Raven poured out all that he had discovered, as quickly and succinctly as he could.

'I will tell you more on the way,' he said, 'but we must get to Albany Street as soon as possible.'

'My brougham is outside,' said Simpson. 'I will instruct Angus to drive the horses as hard as he can.'

'My curricle will be faster,' said Findlay.

'Thank you,' Raven said, though as they all hurried to the street, he knew that no matter how fast the carriage, Sarah's fate was out of their hands.

SEVENTY-SIX

oo late, Sarah saw that Martha's previous face had been a mask and was disturbed by what had been lurking behind it. How much did she truly know about her sister's deeds? When she and Raven visited the cottage, had she been afraid of Mary, or of discovery?

Then in one simple act, Martha revealed all.

She pulled back the bedclothes and climbed in, wrapping herself around Sarah like bindweed.

'Sleep now,' she said. 'It will soon be over.'

Her voice was altered too: her accent no longer the gentle Edinburgh lilt, but a harsher register formed in the tenements of Glasgow.

Martha had not been wearing a mask. Martha *was* the mask.

'There, now. Sleep now.'

Sarah lay helpless, the light of a single candle casting twisted shadows upon the wall. She would have been paralysed with fear, had she not been too weak to move anyway.

Mary was coiled about her bodily, but Sarah had been in her clutches for longer than that. She had drunk from glasses Mary had given her, taking them gratefully in her thirst. The pages of Christison flashed in her memory, another fragment: a fierce thirst was symptomatic of atropine. She had been poisoned.

The candle flickered and the shadows danced as a wind blew through the house, a summoned spirit rushing closer. Death was coming for her. She could sense it. She could hear it.

The witnesses to Mary's other crimes had said the dying were assailed by phantoms, and there was one here now: a demon. A monster.

The last thing she saw was the creature's horrifying visage before blackness came upon her.

SEVENTY-SEVEN

aven leapt from the curricle even before it had stopped, his feet splashing through the puddles on the wet flagstones in the rain-lashed darkness. McLevy was scrambling at his back as he barged inside and tore through the house. It was strangely cold within, the chill air in the hallway indicative that there was a door open elsewhere.

They both stopped at the entrance to Sarah's bedroom, aghast at the scene which confronted them. The room was illuminated by a solitary candle, but it cast light enough to reveal that they were not the night's first visitors.

'God almighty,' McLevy said. 'Who did this to her?'

Raven turned on the gaslight and Sarah roused in the bed, responding to the intrusion. Before them Mary Dempster lay trussed on the floor, her hands and ankles bound behind her and tied together like she was an animal ready for the spit.

Her hair was black, as Raven remembered it, and a blonde wig was stuffed into her mouth. He recalled her grabbing at her head in the high wind, he had assumed to secure her hat. It had been to avoid revealing the true colour of her hair. He observed that the wig had been fixed in place by a length of ribbon, tied tightly around her head so that she couldn't shout for help. Raven approved. A neighbour or passing stranger responding to her cries might have freed her, providing her with the chance to escape.

'Raven,' said Sarah urgently, trying to sit up. 'She is . . . Martha is— '

'I know,' he told her, hurrying to her side.

McLevy knelt down next to Mary and pulled the gag from her mouth.

'Oh, thank heavens you came,' she said. 'I was attacked by a madman. My name is Martha Dempster. I am a nurse, working here for Dr Raven.'

'Martha Dempster is long since dead,' Raven retorted. 'You murdered her, along with her parents and her husband-to-be. You are discovered, Mary.'

He saw the briefest flicker of fear in her face at the use of her real name, before the mask came down again.

She was still insisting she was Martha Dempster as McLevy hauled her to her feet and bundled her towards the door.

Simpson appeared momentarily, and with him Findlay. The latter echoed McLevy's query.

'Who restrained her?'

'I thought him a demon, but he was my saviour,' said Sarah. 'He hauled her off me and tied her up.'

Simpson looked quizzically to Raven for an explanation.

Raven kept his voice low, mindful that McLevy might still be in earshot.

'I have friends in low places,' he said.

Raven put a hand to Sarah's forehead, feeling for fever and checking her pupils. All seemed normal, but that had been true of the other victims too.

'What did she give you? Did you drink it?'

'I don't know,' she said weakly. 'I drank but I thought it was water. It tasted of nothing.'

Sarah pointed to a bag sitting on the sideboard. 'That is hers,' she said.

Simpson opened it and began looking inside.

'I think that she combines atropine with morphine,' Sarah told them. 'That is how she disguised her hand. Each compensates for the signs and symptoms of the other.'

'How fiendishly clever,' said Simpson. 'Or cleverly fiendish. But it appears she has given you neither. There are vials here but they are mostly full.'

Raven knew Mary might have believed Sarah did not need her help in dying. He had confessed his fears to that effect to the professor on the ride here. Perhaps as a result of this she had been tentative in her dosing or had been interrupted before she could administer the lethal draught.

'Let me examine you,' Simpson said.

While the professor pulled away the bedclothes to look at the wound, Sarah gazed at Raven, her eyes filling. She said but one word.

'Archie.'

Raven nodded solemnly. 'He went peacefully, without pain.'

There remained an expectant look in her eyes. He understood what else she still wished to know.

'And without learning about his child.'

Sarah closed her eyes, the tears spilling down her cheeks, but Raven could tell she had found solace in what he had told her. She reached out her hand and fastened it about his.

'I owe you my life.'

'By my accounting that would make us even,' he told her, though he still feared she might have thanked him too soon.

Simpson looked carefully at the line of stitching, a frown upon his lips. As Raven had warned, there was no pus to be seen, and Simpson appeared perplexed by it, which Raven took to be a bad sign. He was wrong, though.

'Dr Raven, I believe there is no pus emerging not because it has accumulated elsewhere, but because there is no inflammation. I don't know whether it is down to luck or judgment, but I would aver that Sarah looks set fair to make a full recovery.'

Raven looked back and forth from Sarah's relieved expression to the wound, barely daring to believe the professor must be right.

'I used chlorinated water to ensure everything was scrupulously clean and I remembered what you had said about Lizars, how he had successfully carried out several ovariotomies.'

'Then presumably you also remembered that he incurred the lifelong disdain of his surgical peers.'

'There was something altogether more valuable at stake than mere reputation.'

Simpson nodded sagely. 'Yours was a courageous and skilful course of action,' he said, 'but one I would nonetheless advise we remain discreet about.'

'I understand,' said Raven.

Simpson turned his attention back to Sarah.

'And how are you feeling now? All this excitement is hardly conducive to recovery.'

'Better than I was,' she replied. 'And better than Mary believed, evidently. She seemed to think that I was dying.'

'I am pleased to say that she was wrong,' Simpson replied.

Sarah shook her head and endeavoured to sit up. Raven moved to intervene, but she warded him off.

'You miss my meaning, Doctor. I must elaborate. She climbed into bed with me. She wanted to hold me as I died. A nurse at the Infirmary gave me a similar account, though Mary was interrupted that night too, else her victim would not have lived to tell the tale.'

'She held you to comfort you?' Simpson asked doubtfully.

'Not to comfort me, but to gratify herself. She seemed . . . *excited*, in a particular way.'

Simpson's mouth fell open. There was no question but that he understood the way Sarah meant.

'I think that death pleasures her,' Sarah went on. 'As though death itself were her lover.'

Raven could not recall ever seeing Simpson truly shocked before, but there was a look of appalled bewilderment upon his face. He was scarcely less horrified himself.

'It is a manner of perversity the like of which I cannot comprehend,' Raven said.

'Nor I,' Sarah agreed, 'but I am certain that is what she was doing.'

Simpson shook his head gravely.

'We cannot comprehend it because we are not equipped to do so. She must be delivered into the hands of someone who is.'

'And by that,' said Raven, 'I trust you do not mean McLevy.'

SEVENTY-EIGHT

aven hammered at the door a second time, his thumps reverberating all the way across Castle Street and back again.

'I hope your treatment of that door is not a precursor to your intended treatment of Mr Quinton's face,' said Simpson. 'For if I fear you cannot contain yourself, I will be forced to send you back around the corner to Queen Street.'

'It is more of a proxy than a precursor,' Raven assured him. 'Every blow I deliver to his door is one fewer I will be inclined to visit upon his person.'

Raven had insisted on accompanying the professor because Quinton's ruthlessness in other matters meant he could not be sure what more the man might be capable of. He suspected Simpson had similar concerns, which was why he had acquiesced to Raven's suggestion.

They both stood back and waited, listening out for footsteps within. Still no such sound was forthcoming.

Raven raised his arm a third time. A look from Simpson stayed his hand. Then Simpson simply opened the door, which was not locked, and led Raven inside, unbidden. This act of impolite transgression was in its own way a sign of a greater rage on the part of the professor than Raven had thus far displayed.

They proceeded down the long hall and into the drawing room, where they found Mrs Quinton seated by the fire. The baby was on this occasion asleep in a cot, one of only two items of furniture in the room. Flint's big pay-day had evidently not yet arrived, or if it had, no dividend had been passed down. The place was still utterly denuded.

Mary Quinton got up in fright and alarm, standing with her arms folded.

'Dr Simpson.'

The professor gazed towards the cradle. 'Remarkable the bairn could sleep through all that hammering, is it not? Or perhaps the sound does not carry inside as I imagined it would, for surely your not hearing it could be the only explanation for why you would not respond.'

She stared guiltily at the floor.

'Where is your husband, Mrs Quinton?'

Mrs Quinton resembled a startled field mouse, her eyes gazing involuntarily upwards, as though seeking intercession from the Almighty.

'I do not know. He went out some time ago.'

'And when do you expect he will return?'

Again, the look of being cornered and afraid. Raven recalled she was neither a practised nor adept liar.

'I do not know.'

Once more her eyes flitted briefly up, this time towards the far corner of the room, where the door to the press was situated.

'It is imperative that we speak to him,' insisted Simpson.

'He is not here,' she repeated.

Raven had seen enough. He put a hand on the professor's arm.

'Let us away, Dr Simpson. I think I know where he might be. There is a place near Lady Lawson Wynd.'

Simpson gave him a sceptical look, which Raven answered with a subtle nod of assurance.

They exited forthwith, walking down the hall to the front

door, which Raven opened and closed again heavily, though they remained within. Raven put a finger to his lips and bade Simpson remain quietly where he was. Then, a few moments later, they heard Mrs Quinton speak.

'You can come out now, they've gone.'

Raven moved briskly and on light feet, covering the distance to the drawing room in a trice. He interrupted Quinton climbing down from a low shelf in the press where he had been hiding.

Quinton took fright at the sight of the intrusion and lost his footing. He half slid, half fell to the floor, where he cowered as Raven stood above him.

'Please do not strike me. I have injured my ankle.'

'You would have happily seen me hang, you supercilious turd. Sarah too, simply to protect yourself and hide your thievery.'

Simpson entered, wearing a look of concern at the scene confronting him, but there was no need for him to be afraid of Raven's intentions. What Raven had learned from Sarah was that the devil in him was an ally, and he was its master if he could decide for himself when to unleash it. That way, he controlled it, it did not control him. On this occasion the devil did not even come close to the surface. The sight of Mr Quinton cringing and snivelling was simply too pathetic to summon it.

'I am deeply sorry. I was in a state of desperation and was rendered insensible by my shame. I did not want Dr Simpson to learn of my predicament, and even less what I had done as a result.'

'You lied to the police and had them accuse Dr Raven of murder. Direct your apologies to him.'

'I did not lie. I merely raised my suspicions, as he and Mrs Banks seemed unseemly close.'

'You lied by omission,' Simpson reminded him. 'You knew Archie had taken a bottle of chloroform for himself.'

'I was confused. I am indeed truly sorry.'

He clasped his hands together and looked up at them in

supplication. There were tears in his eyes, though not of contrition, Raven suspected: merely self-pity.

'I could have you tossed in jail,' the professor told him.

Raven saw the instant change in Quinton's expression as the significance of Dr Simpson's words sunk in, the clockwork in motion behind his eyes. Simpson *could* have him thrown in jail, but by implication did not intend to.

Quinton ceased cowering and drew himself to his feet. His ankle injury seemed miraculously healed. He kept a wary eye on Raven, who despite his previous reflections couldn't help but wish Quinton would attack him and thus give him reason to retaliate.

'As Dr Raven might have explained, we were badly deceived when we came here,' Quinton said. 'My so-called friend left us more debts than prospects. And I would remind you that I declined other employment opportunities to come here and take up a post with you, Dr Simpson.'

His wife took her place beside him.

'Furthermore, we took on the added responsibility of Rochester here,' she added. 'As an obligation to yourself and Mrs Simpson.'

'Yes,' Quinton went on. 'If you wish the child to be raised properly, it would not do for him to grow up in a household empty of furniture and besieged by creditors.'

They both looked expectantly at Simpson, who nodded solemnly.

'Quite,' he said, a calm warmth to his face, met by relief on those of the Quintons.

'Dr Raven did say that you would be both generous and understanding,' Quinton simpered.

Undeservedly so in this case, Raven thought.

'Yes, yes, indeed,' said the professor. 'Under the circumstances, I feel it my duty to provide you with appropriate financial assistance in order to get yourselves out of this situation.'

Raven had to rein in his instincts. He had long since learned how boundless Simpson's compassion could be, but in this instance it seemed almost unseemly given what this man had done, and to both of them.

Simpson reached into his pocket and produced his wallet, Quinton drawing closer, eager and expectant.

The professor drew out a five-pound note and handed it over. 'I think this ought to be adequate.'

Quinton held up the note as though it were a filthy rag found upon a midden.

'Five pounds? How on earth do you propose we extricate ourselves from our debts with this?'

'It should be adequate to pay for travel back to Oxford, thereby ensuring that I never have to set eyes upon you again. It's that or Calton Jail. And on the basis of the evidence before me, only the latter deserves its reputation.'

SEVENTY-NINE

t was a source of pleasure for Sarah simply to walk so far, after being confined first to bed, then to home, and then only incrementally able to venture any distance. The dull weight in her legs was a mere precursor of how she would feel tomorrow, but she welcomed the coming ache amidst her profound gratitude for the restoration of something she had previously taken for granted.

This trip to Warriston Cemetery was not merely the occasion of a brisk stroll, but something of a pilgrimage, a worthwhile diversion on her way to another piece of business she wished to attend to that day.

She had visited Archie's grave first, and now she was standing over that of Mrs Glassford. She clutched a small bunch of daffodils she had picked on the walk here.

Sarah crouched to place them carefully against the marker. She had been concerned that they would look scruffy, but in the event, they appeared to be the first flowers laid upon this plot. It served as a reminder that Mrs Glassford had not only lost her husband but was also estranged from her family.

Was a lonely death the price a woman paid for not accepting the roles that men allocated her? For seeking autonomy, independence and a purpose beyond that of wife and mother? If so, then such women were unblessed martyrs. She deserved not a modest headstone but a mausoleum.

Sarah felt a slight twinge as she stood up again, her hand going involuntarily to the site of her scar. She recalled her introduction to Mrs Glassford, presenting at Queen Street with an apparent pregnancy that bore not new life but her own death.

Sarah's thoughts turned to her own doomed pregnancy, lodged in the wrong place. She should have died too, she knew. All those days she had spent wondering how long Archie had left, oblivious that inside her, the clock was ticking down to her own quite unexpected end. Though she had lost Archie and lost the child, she knew that every day from this one was time she was not supposed to have. She owed it to Mrs Glassford, to Archie, and to herself, that she should make of it everything that she possibly could.

Foremost in her mind of late had been the names of two other women: Charlotte Siebold and Elizabeth Blackwell.

It was a cold morning, with a blustery wind whipping off the river, but that also meant there was no fog, meaning she could see all the way across the Forth to Fife.

Sarah's view had never been clearer.

She had lived such a little life, its boundaries extending no further north than Perth, no further south than Musselburgh. Until speaking with Mrs Glassford, she had never even thought about those geographical boundaries, had fixed instead upon the other restraints that had been placed upon her. Sarah had been excluded from lessons on all but sewing and cooking since the age of eleven, even though she had outstripped the boys in every subject. Raven, by contrast, had been all over Europe, educating himself at the greatest institutions.

She had been like an incurious prisoner with no notion of the richness, breadth and wonder of the lands beyond the walls inside which she was confined. But now Mrs Glassford had shown her the gate, and Archie had given her the key.

EIGHTY

aven was sitting at his desk surrounded by piles of paper. He had not thought that Quinton would be missed, but since his departure the general disorganisation that plagued Dr Simpson's affairs had returned. Raven sighed, put his pen down and rubbed his eyes. He looked at the clock on the mantelpiece and then checked the time on his pocket watch, calculating how long Sarah had been gone.

He got up from behind his desk, stretched to ease the ache in his shoulders, and walked to the window. He looked out into the street hoping for some sign of her but there was none. He felt a now familiar creeping anxiety about where she might be and what might have happened to her. He was struggling to rid himself of a constant sense of foreboding. He knew it was irrational – she had recovered from her illness – but black thoughts persisted nonetheless.

He thought about grabbing his coat and hat and heading out in search of her. Nonsense, of course, as he had no idea of where she might be and had more than enough work to contend with without embarking on some fruitless pursuit. She insisted on walking every day when he thought she should be resting, but he knew better than to argue with her when she had set her mind on a course of action.

'There is no need to worry, Will. I'm quite well,' she had said when he questioned her intentions to venture out unaccompanied on a briskly cold day. 'But by way of a concession to your fussing, I promise to stop by on my way home.'

She was dressed head to toe in widow's black. Raven thought she had never been more beautiful. He could not look at her without thinking of how close he had come to losing her entirely.

She had looked around the room, taking in the general disorder.

'In any case, you are the one who appears to be in need of assistance.'

It was a fair comment, but Raven doubted Dr Simpson would be in any hurry to hire another secretary.

He heard the doorbell ring and looked hopefully out into the hallway, but it was Jarvis who came striding towards him clutching a rectangular package wrapped in brown paper.

'A parcel for you. All the way from Naples,' the butler said with an undisguised degree of curiosity and an utterly unfamiliar leavening of admiration. 'A book perhaps,' Jarvis suggested, 'though it seems a little light for that.'

Still wary of what any overseas mail might reveal, Raven accepted the package and retreated to the privacy of his room before opening it. He pulled carefully at the wrapping, mindful of damaging whatever might lie beneath, and upon exposing one side of the contents found himself greeted by the sight of his own face.

It was a painting, and the unexpected appearance of his own features was not the only aspect he recognised. The style and the brushwork were unmistakably those of Gabriela, which sent a thrill through him. The painting depicted him lying in repose, his eyes looking to the distance. She always said his thoughts were elsewhere, and now she had illustrated it.

He had not sat for her, and he deduced from the posture that she had sketched him while he was sleeping, then created the rest from memory. It was a flattering and affectionate portrait, one that made him yearn for her company, though not in the physical way he once had. He missed her wisdom, her unorthodox perspective. He thought he could smell her upon the canvas, but perhaps it was that she had often smelled of oil paint and he associated it with her.

Raven delicately pulled away the rest of the wrapping, whereupon a letter fluttered to the carpet. He rested the picture against the wall and bent to pick it up.

It bore no return address. He surmised that she could not afford to disclose her precise location for fear that the information might be intercepted, and when he read on, he understood just how well her fears were founded.

Dear Will,

I wanted to reassure you that I am alive and well, and to send this as a token of my gratitude for your actions.

Though I did not know it at the time, the men who set upon us were neither vagabonds nor strangers, their attack neither random nor robbery. They were led by my husband's brother. As you might already have learned, the police believe that he intended to abduct me, but they are wrong. If this were the case, Javier would not have been so ready with his pistol.

My husband wishes to marry again. As a prominently devout Catholic, his religion and position forbid him from divorce. However, his piety does not preclude plotting to murder his wife in order to rid himself of an impediment to future marriage the old-fashioned way.

I have no doubt Javier meant to kill me. He and his men posed as thieves in order to disguise their actions and their motives, that my intended death would have been attributed to common robbers.

I do not know what happened in that alley when you ran down there after them, but I know that had you not done whatever you did, Javier would have found a way to finish his mission. I would be dead by now.

This painting is a paltry offering, for I owe you my life.

I hope that all you missed and all you sought were awaiting you back in Edinburgh.

You once asked me if it is possible to become someone else. You were clearly fearful of your own nature, but your nature is the reason I am still here to write this.

I told you that you must first ask yourself who you wish to become. In truth, I believe that you are already who you need to be.

Yours,

Gabriela

Raven read it several times, hearing her voice clearly in his head. He was relieved that she was alive and at liberty, but this was tempered by the understanding that her self-imposed exile meant that they were unlikely to cross paths again.

It struck him that the two women he trusted most had now both told him not to fear his own nature. He would be a fool not to embrace such advice. He was not sure he shared Gabriela's confidence when she said that he was already the man he needed to be, but with Sarah by his side, perhaps such a thing was within his grasp.

He folded the letter and placed it in his breast pocket for now, not wanting to abandon something precious to the chaos of his desk. He thought of how the place missed Sarah. How he missed Sarah. And with a smile he saw what ought to have been obvious.

Soon enough he would be setting up his own practice here in Edinburgh, a challenge he could face with greater confidence if he might recruit Sarah to the cause. With Archie gone and with the prospect of motherhood lifted from her too, she would be in need of a new purpose.

He thought of her frustrations over the ambiguity of her

position at Queen Street and how her role was perceived, with some people still thinking her a housemaid and others a nurse. He had come up with the perfect solution for both of them. He would offer her the formal position of his assistant, a suitable vehicle for her burgeoning knowledge and experience.

Raven went to the window again, more impatient now than ever, aching to see her face when he made his proposal. Sarah would be delighted. He couldn't imagine her wanting anything more.

EIGHTY-ONE

he port of Leith was a teeming ferment, as always, but on this occasion Sarah saw something more than just the crowded foreshore. On past visits she had been afraid of its bustle: the aggressive profanity of the sailors, the burly stevedores hurling crates, the porters threatening to run you over with their handcarts. What she recognised today was that this was a portal through which she could already glimpse the wider world beyond. On the wharf she saw men of different races, saw unfamiliar and exotic styles of clothing, heard languages she did not understand.

She walked through the swinging double doors of the General Steam Navigation Company, finding herself in a busy lobby around which dozens of conversations loudly reverberated. She gazed up at the walls, adorned with notices, schedules, advertisements and route maps, and it was as she examined one of these last that she came to appreciate how small her own world truly was. This was not due to the sight of Scotland's tiny size in the greater scale of the globe, but of the more mundane deduction that she was on the wrong coast for her intended destination.

She would have to sail from Glasgow or Liverpool, which was not a problem, but she felt diminished that this hadn't even occurred to her, as her life had never given her reason to investigate such things before.

She approached one of the desks, where the smartly dressed clerk greeted her with a friendly smile.

'How can I help you, ma'am?'

'I am making a preliminary enquiry with regard to booking passage, though from a look at your maps, I realise I might be on the wrong side of the country.'

'I am sure we can point you in the right direction regardless. What would be your intended destination?'

Sarah swallowed, fearful her voice would dry.

'New York,' she replied.

'Yes, that indeed would depart from the west coast, but we can certainly assist with a booking. Can I have your name?'

'It's Sarah.'

He stared expectantly at her, the pause becoming awkward in its length until she understood he was awaiting more.

'Sorry. Sarah Fisher.'

'And would that be "Miss" or "Mrs"?'

It seemed a simple enough question, and yet it was far from it, and not something a man was ever forced to reckon with. She had reverted to her own surname, as Archie requested, but the thorny issue of her title persisted. She pondered briefly which appellation would provide the greatest protection to a woman travelling alone.

'It is "Mrs",' she said.

For now, at least.

One day, she vowed, it would be neither. One day, it would be 'Doctor'.

EPILOGUE

shaft of sunshine plunged through a single window into the otherwise stark-walled chamber as Dr David Skae took his seat. Glancing up, he could make out the national monument atop Calton Hill, a permanent sentinel overlooking the facility that shared its name. The room in which they had convened was abutting the outer wall of the jail; those confined to the cells would enjoy no such view.

Dr Skae sat at the centre of a long table, flanked on his right by Auberon Findlay, Procurator Fiscal, and on his immediate left by Dr Alasdair Drake, Skae's assistant. Next to him at the end of the table was Frederick Nicholson, a lawyer representing the subject.

Skae was Physician Superintendent of the Edinburgh Asylum and had been invited here by Nicholson to make an assessment of Mary Dempster's fitness to face the charges against her.

In the past, fiscals had resisted the likes of Skae's involvement in such matters, but the McNaughton Rule six years before had changed all that. McNaughton had been acquitted of attempting to murder Prime Minister Robert Peel, his pistol shot fatally injuring Peel's secretary Edward Drummond instead. McNaughton was ruled to have been guilty but insane, labouring under the delusion that Peel in fact intended to murder him. The case had established a precedent that Nicholson had invoked with regard to his client.

Bringing their sitting to order, Findlay read out the ruling verbatim: "'To establish a defence on the ground of insanity, it must be clearly proved that, at the time of the committing of the act, the party accused was labouring under such a defect of reason, from a disease of the mind, as not to know the nature and quality of the act she was doing; or, if she did know it, that she did not know she was doing what was wrong.'"

A thorough and exacting process was about to be undertaken, though there were those who had observed to Skae that it might be better if this case never came to trial. Society saw women as gentle creatures, given naturally to their appointed duties of tenderness and nurture, and it charged nurses with absolute trust in the care of the sick. Skae well understood the motivations of those who did not wish such comforting assumptions to be shattered by public exposure of Mary Dempster's deeds. And as for what was alleged to have motivated her, it would be a grave offence to most sensibilities to be forced to confront such notions.

Nonetheless, Skae would not let his verdict be subordinate to such considerations. His professional reputation, and thus the integrity of his other work – his detailed study and classification of mental disease – relied upon his clinical judgment.

'Before we commence,' Findlay stated, 'for what it is worth, I would like to remind Dr Skae that there is already a confession, of sorts.'

'It cannot be regarded as in any way reliable,' Nicholson objected. 'It was intended as a piece of misdirection, not as a sincere account of my client's conduct or motives.'

'It most certainly was not that,' Findlay scoffed. 'It pointedly did not include an explanation of her methods. We have Mrs Banks to thank for deducing that. The only thing it is reliable proof of is Mary's intention to effectively change her identity and resume her activities under a new guise, seeking her gratification elsewhere.

One might suggest that deploying such elaborate stratagems in order to avoid detection is proof that she well knew what she was doing was wrong.'

Nicholson opened his mouth to speak once more, but Skae interrupted.

'What I might infer from this feigned confession remains to be seen, and will only be considered once I have a fuller picture.'

'Indeed,' Nicholson acknowledged.

Dr Drake looked to Skae, who gave him a nod of assent. They were ready.

A short time later the prisoner was brought in, flanked by two guards. They were hardened and muscular types, used to dealing with violent men. Their brawn struck Skae as disproportionate and unnecessary. Mary looked all the more slight walking between them, and yet she did not appear cowed or intimidated. She seemed strangely care-free, which caused Skae to make the first of his notes.

She was released from her shackles and took her seat.

Skae instructed the guards to leave the room. They seemed reluctant, and he had to remind them that whatever danger she posed, it was not through her physical capabilities.

She looked curiously at Skae, sizing him up as though she were the one here to make an assessment of him.

'Good morning, Mary. I am Dr Skae. As your lawyer Mr Nicholson will have explained to you, I am here to listen to your account of your actions and to advise upon whether you might be regarded as fit to stand trial upon these charges. Do you understand?'

She nodded.

'I would advise you to be as forthcoming, honest and cooperative as possible, as we agreed,' Nicholson told her.

There had been some discussion two days before, regarding the extent to which the lawyer should brief her ahead of this session. The McNaughton Rule offering her only chance to avoid the rope, Findlay was concerned that she had incentive therefore to feign a degree of madness. Skae had assured the fiscal that he was adept at detecting pretence, and warned Nicholson that such behaviour was likely to be interpreted as proof that she was of sound mind.

'On my left here is Dr Drake,' Skae told her. 'He will be transcribing all that you say, so that we have a record of your account that can be reviewed later. But before we commence, might I enquire if you are healthy, and whether you have been treated well?'

'I have stayed in better accommodations, where I have been treated worse,' she replied.

'It is important that you feel comfortable and able to talk freely. That you do not feel intimidated.'

She smiled, as though grateful for his concern but eager to dismiss it.

He had encountered patients who did not experience human emotions the way others did. A sign that they had no empathy was often that they did not feel fear.

'You seem calm, despite what is at stake here. Do you know what it is to be afraid, Mary?' he asked.

She sat up straight and cleared her throat.

'There is not a woman in this realm who does not understand what it is to be afraid,' she began. 'No, not even she who reigns over us, for she was not born sovereign . . .'

HISTORICAL NOTE

ames Young Simpson was Professor of Midwifery at Edinburgh University and lived with his family and various pets at 52 Queen Street from 1845 until his death in 1870. The anaesthetic properties of chloroform were discovered in his dining room on 4 November 1847. His name became synonymous with this discovery, which became a point of contention for those who felt they had contributed to it but were denied the recognition that they were due.

In 1852, Simpson was accused by Professor William Henderson, Professor James Miller and Dr James Matthews Duncan of negligently contributing to the death of a patient by the name of Mrs Johnstone, wife of a doctor and fellow resident of Queen Street. A bloodstained mattress was cited as evidence. In response to this Simpson published a pamphlet comprising all the correspondence pertaining to the incident, including a letter from the patient's husband which exonerated him completely and finally laid the matter to rest.

James and Mary Quinton agreed to adopt a child, arranged and paid for by the Simpsons, and James Quinton was appointed as Simpson's secretary until it became apparent that he was misappropriating funds in an attempt to pay off his debts. According to one account, when his larceny was uncovered,

Simpson found him hiding from his creditors in an attic and paid him five pounds to leave Edinburgh.

The villain in the book is based on the mass-murderer Jane Toppan, whose exploits in the late nineteenth century scandalised New England. Toppan was a nurse who poisoned her patients and held them while they died for the sexual gratification that this produced. After her arrest she claimed to have killed thirty-one people using a variety of different poisons, often combining them to obscure their effects and evade detection. She was found to be insane and committed to an asylum for the rest of her life, where she became paranoid about being poisoned herself. Despite this, she lived a long life and died at the age of eighty-four.

Numerous nineteenth-century textbooks were consulted in an attempt to accurately reflect the medical thinking of the time. In trying to justify his decision to perform abdominal surgery on Sarah, Raven quotes from John Parry's *Extra-uterine Pregnancy* and from *Woman: Her Diseases and Remedies* by Charles Meigs.

ACKNOWLEDGEMENTS

nce again, thanks to Sophie Scard, Caroline Dawnay and Charles Walker at United Agents.

Thanks to all the wonderful people at Canongate for their belief in the series and for wanting to know more about Will, Sarah, Simpson, nineteenth-century Edinburgh and chloroform.

Thanks to the National Library of Scotland for digitising the town plans and Post Office directories which played such a crucial part in the research for this book.